HONEY'S FARM

IRIS GOWER

HONEY'S FARM

LONDON   NEW YORK   SYDNEY   TORONTO

This edition published 1993 by
BCA
by arrangement with Bantam Press
a division of Transworld Publishers Ltd

CN 3927

Printed and bound in Great Britain by
Biddles Ltd, Guildford and King's Lynn

To Zoe, Rachel, Joanne and
Charlotte, with love.

CHAPTER ONE

It was her wedding night. Irfonwy Parks stared around her at the bedroom that was both familiar and yet so strange, fitted out as it was for a newly wed couple. The covers were freshly laundered, the pillowcases sewn with ribbons and scented with herbs. Flowers stood in a tall vase on the washstand, and everything gleamed with polish, the work, Fon guessed, of Mrs Jones, Jamie's nearest neighbour.

Shivering a little, she stood at the window, moving aside the laundered curtains that smelled of sunlight. Outside, she saw the soft rise of the Welsh hills, green and pleasant during the daytime, but now dark and mysterious. Shadows hollowed the falling away of the land into the floor of the valley. The thin gleaming line was the brook that meandered through the farmlands, faint now in the moonlight, a silver thread lacing the cornfields.

Honey's Farm had been her home for some eighteen months now, sweet, happy months when she had learned the ways of farm life; studied herbal remedies that would cure fevers in cows as well as humans; months when she had become a farmer's wife, in all ways except one. How she had yearned to be Jamie O'Conner's wife. She had sat with him during the evenings, working on the books, watching him covertly over her sewing.

She had come from Oystermouth on the southerly tip of Swansea, from the oyster village where the fishing boats bobbed on the tide and where the sea was a demanding as well as beautiful master. She had been so young then, not only in years but in experience.

7

She had not known, not then, how carefully Katherine O'Conner had chosen her, the pure, innocent girl, to care for Jamie, handsome, loyal Jamie, and for little Patrick their son. Katherine, knowing she was dying, had deliberately planned for a substitute mother and wife for her loved ones. As she had faded away with an incurable lung sickness, she had begged Irfonwy to stay at Honey's Farm for as long as she was needed, realizing in her wisdom that Fon was already tied by bonds of love.

Fon felt tears come to her eyes. Today, in accordance with all Katherine had wished, Irfonwy Parks had married Jamie O'Conner, plighting her troth at the chapel in the fold of the hills. She had married him with love in her heart and hope for the future carrying her down the aisle in a cloud of happiness.

Now, standing alone in the bedroom, with its newly laundered patchwork quilt covering the double bed, and the vase of fresh summer roses brightening the deep sill of the window before her, Fon felt a pang of misgiving, of apprehension. Doubts assailed her. Jamie was a mature, experienced man; would he be disappointed in her?

She forced her mind away from such fearful thoughts, and her eyes became dreamy. She brought to mind again the beauty of the wedding ceremony, the loving words spoken between Jamie and her, the vows they so readily made, and she was reassured. She imagined herself standing at the doorway of the old chapel and twitching the folds of her full skirts into place, fascinated by the sheen of the soft satin fabric. Her head had been high and she had been proudly aware of the sighs of admiration from the crowds standing around her. She had savoured the moment, for this was her day.

And now came reality. The dream had been fine and wonderful, but it had encompassed Fon working in the kitchen, making her husband's dinner and bringing up

8

a brood of handsome children. It had not encompassed the intimacy of the bedroom.

The stairtreads creaked, and Fon tensed. She forced herself to think of Jamie, the fine handsome man she loved, had loved since the day she had set eyes on him – but it had been a loving of the mind, spiritual rather than physical. Soon, she would be his wife in fact as well as in name.

She heard the sounds of his footsteps with a feeling of panic; he was coming to bed already, and she still dressed in her wedding finery!

With shaking fingers she tried to undo the buttons at the back of her neck, but she was clumsy and the buttons eluded her.

If only Patrick was asleep in his room; she could have gone to him in the pretence that he had woken and needed her. Irfonwy sighed. Patrick was safe with her mother, tucked away under the eaves of the cottage facing the sea at Oystermouth.

Nina Parks had taken the small boy willingly into her empty arms.

'I hope you will give me my own grandchildren before too long, Fon,' she had said softly. 'I know I haven't been a perfect mam to you, but I do love you and want the best for you, my youngest.'

The stairs creaked and Fon sank on to the bed, defeated by the buttons and with butterflies cramping her stomach. She knew all about a man's lust for life; hadn't she seen it all before with her mam and Joe Harries?

She recalled even now the shame of it all, living in sin they'd been, Nina Parks and Joe Harries, who had a wife already. The scandal had been the talk of the village, Nina expecting Joe's child at an age when she should have known better. Gossip had raged for months until, at last, the villagers had accepted Joe and Nina's irregular union as just another fact of village life.

But as if to punish her, the fates had taken away from Nina both her child and her man, leaving her alone and lonely, a woman who evoked no pity because of her rebellious, independent spirit. Poor mam, Fon thought; she always was her own worst enemy.

But she had tried to do right by her youngest daughter. Knowing Fon was about to be married, she had taken her to one side and tried to prepare her for her wedding night.

'The thing between a man and a woman is beautiful, love.' Nina's voice had caused nothing but embarrassment.

The door opened. Startled, Fon felt rather than saw Jamie come closer. She looked up at him almost pleadingly.

'What's wrong, colleen?' he asked in concern. 'Are those tears I see?'

'I can't undo my buttons.' Her voice was small. Jamie sat beside her and turned her face to his.

'You're trembling, Fon. There's no need to be afraid of me, love.'

Fon stared into his beloved face. He was so handsome, his dark hair curling around his broad forehead, his eyes looking into hers with compassion. She loved him, there was no doubt about that, but this thing between men and women, she didn't know if she was ready for it.

Fon had always been reserved, keeping herself to herself. She supposed by the standards set by both her sisters, she was immature, naïve perhaps.

Sal, a full-bosomed, hearty woman, was ripe with the love of her man; and as for Gwyneth, she panted for the attentions of the boss of the boot-and-shoe shop where she worked, even though Will Davies was out of her reach.

'Look,' Jamie said softly, 'I'm not a bull pulling at the ring in my nose. I'm a man with feelings. I won't force myself on you. I know you are an untried girl, and I respect you for it. Come on, I'll undo your wretched buttons and then I'll sleep in the other room. I won't lay a hand on you, not until you are ready.'

When Jamie had gone, Fon stared up at the moonlight on the ceiling, wondering why she felt so empty. How Sal and Gwyneth would laugh if they could see her now, the bride, alone in her marriage bed. What a fool they would think her.

And Jamie, what of him? Where was the eager lover she had supposed him to be? Despairingly she turned over and faced the wall. He couldn't love her very much, not if he didn't want to lie with her on the instant they were alone. Perhaps he would never love her as he'd loved Katherine.

Suddenly, she forced herself upwards, pushing the bedclothes away angrily. She stepped out of bed and on to the cold boards and stood for a moment to still the panicky rush of blood to her head.

In the other room, the room that used to be hers, Fon stared down at the man in the bed. His eyes were closed; he was breathing easily, one bare, muscular arm flung out towards the empty pillow.

Fon slipped quickly into the sheets and took a deep breath as she felt his warm, naked flesh against her arm. She almost recoiled, but then, making a supreme effort, she leaned forward and pressed her lips to his cheek.

The scent of him was of freshness, of sweet grass and flowers. He turned and took her in his arms so easily that she wondered if he had been asleep at all.

His hands reached beneath the starched cotton nightgown and touched her, gently. He touched her breasts and she trembled; his fingers made a pathway over the flat of her stomach and towards her thighs. Fon sighed a little, fear warring with the desire that suddenly spread a languor throughout her limbs.

'There, my colleen, nothing to be afraid of, is there?'

he said softly. 'Loving is the most natural thing in the world.'

He touched her intimately, softly, teasingly, and Fon relaxed a little, wondering why she had been afraid; this was Jamie, her love – he would never do anything to hurt her.

His breathing became ragged, and she felt his flesh hard against hers. 'It will be beautiful, my love, you'll see,' he said, his mouth warm and sweet against hers.

She pressed close to him, not minding when he gently eased the nightgown from her shoulders, pushing it away impatiently.

'You have a little maid's body,' he said wonderingly, 'so beautiful, so sweet. I'll always treasure you, my love.'

She wrapped her arms around him, clinging to him, her face hot against his shoulder.

'Are you ready for me, colleen?' His voice was hoarse. 'I can wait no longer.'

She was suddenly trembling again. 'I'm feared of the unknown, Jamie,' she whispered.

He caressed her then as though gentling the animals in the field. He spoke softly to her, and she seemed to melt against him. She smiled wanly to herself in the darkness; the time had come when she must act like a woman, be a real wife to her strong, lusty husband.

He met resistance when he tried to make them one flesh. Fon winced as he patiently persisted, gently but firmly taking her to him, making her his own. She felt herself beginning to relax against him; fear departed and she was suddenly in tune with the old rhymes of nature. She cried out and clung to him.

'Jamie, my darling, my love! I want you so much.' Her voice was hoarse. His hands tangled in her hair, he kissed her mouth, her throat, her breasts. Together now they moved in harmony, and Fon was exultant. Now Jamie was truly hers, her dear, beloved husband, they were one at last.

12

Then he called out a name in his release, and the name tore into the silence like a blow, and that name was Katherine.

'So how is married life treating you, then?' Gwyneth Parks perched on the edge of the table, swinging her legs, oblivious of the fact that her slender ankles and shapely calves were exposed.

She spoke again without waiting for a reply. 'I must say I couldn't take to farm life, though it's nice enough up here, with the sun shining and the birds singing.'

Fon bent her head. 'Married life is wonderful,' she said lightly, and so it was. She loved the soft misty mornings when, head against the warm flanks of the animals, she drew the pure milk down into the bucket. Afterwards, with Patrick clinging to her skirts, she would collect the eggs, still warm, from beneath the hens.

She liked baking savoury, crusty pies and fruit tarts in the peace and tranquillity of the sunlit kitchen, bringing water from the spring – sweet water that tasted wonderful. She liked it in the evenings when Patrick was in bed and she and Jamie went over the books, working out the milk yield and deciding what stock to buy. These were comfortable times, close moments to treasure. It was only in the marriage bed that uncertainties seized her, and though he had never once, since that first time, called her by his first wife's name, the ghost of Katherine seemed to be between them.

She glanced at her sister. How would Gwyneth react if Fon were to confide in her? She would doubtless laugh, dismissing the incident as the way of men; but Fon still bore the hurt and the pain of feeling she was second-best.

'I must say you look every inch the blushing bride.' Gwyneth stared at Fon, head on one side. 'There's a bloom to the skin, a light in the eyes.'

She paused, an imp of mischief twisting her mouth

into a smile. 'Tell me, is he a stud in bed, your Jamie?'

Fon felt the rich colour suffuse her face. She turned away from her sister's eyes alight with mirth and tried to think of something to say.

'Oh, come on!' Gwyneth said derisively. 'Surely you are not still the prude you used to be?'

'Of course I'm not a prude,' Fon protested. 'Jamie and me, we do what every married couple does.' She lifted her head. 'There's no questioning my Jamie's vigour.'

'Well, I'm relieved to hear it,' Gwyneth said. 'For a minute there I thought my little sister had married a cissy.'

She poked her tongue between her teeth. 'Come on, then, tell me about it. What was your wedding night like?'

Fon stared at her hands. 'It hurt at first, but then it was wonderful.' And so it had been until the moment when Jamie had called out Katherine's name; and now the knowledge of his mistake hung like a stone between them.

'Well, of course it did!' Gwyneth said. 'It always hurts the first time, and it pleases the men, they know then they have taken a virgin.'

Gwyneth gave a sigh of exasperation. 'How can you be so ignorant? It's bound to be difficult at first, and a real man gets carried away with his own feelings, but it's worth it, isn't it?'

'Yes, I suppose it is,' Fon said, wondering just how much her sister really knew about love. She had dallied with the fishermen at Oystermouth, it was true, but her words now lacked conviction. Still, Fon was feeling better than she'd done since the first night with Jamie; men had to be excused their strange ways. She smiled. 'Anyway that's enough talk about me, what about you?'

'I'm still hoping that Will Davies gets over his infatuation with the do-gooding Eline Harries. How he can fall for a dull widow woman, I don't know,' Gwyneth said acidly. 'He was turning to me before *she* put in her oar, her and her damned soup kitchens – who does she think she is?'

'Well, she did save our lives,' Fon said mildly. 'You were hungry that time in the village too, mind.'

'Aye, but she was only giving back money she'd made on the backs of the workers, her running her posh art gallery while we starved through lack of oysters.'

Fon shook her head. She didn't like arguing with her sister, but sometimes Gwyneth was totally unjust.

'What difference did running an art gallery really make to the village?' Fon asked, rubbing her hands on her apron. 'The art gallery didn't make the oysters disappear; over-fishing did that.'

'Whose side are you on, anyway?' Gwyneth said petulantly. 'Eline Harries was always an outsider in Oystermouth; she left her man when he was injured at sea, didn't she? Oh, yes, our mam could take over and nurse Joe when he was sick, and *she* was free to clear off to Swansea.'

Fon sighed. 'Joe wasn't faithful to Eline, was he?' she said patiently. 'He went with our mam of his own free choice, gave her a baby, even. What was Eline supposed to do?'

Jamie entered the kitchen, his eyes bright, his face fresh from the soft breeze that swept over the sunlit fields.

'Hello, Gwyneth, love,' he said. 'Having a day off from work, then, are you?'

'Aye.' Gwyneth made no attempt to cover her legs, but Jamie appeared not to notice as he put his arm casually around his wife's shoulder. ' 'Bout time, too,' she continued. 'Like a bailiff I am these days, trudging round the houses trying to collect money that's been owing for boots and shoes since last year.'

'Things improving in the village now, though, aren't

15

they?' Jamie asked. Gwyneth nodded. 'Getting better, slowly, but it'll take a time, mind. They oysters are coming back, but it'll be a long job before things get back to normal.'

'What's for dinner, love?' Jamie turned to Fon. 'I'm starving.'

Fon, turning to cut into the freshly baked loaf, heard her sister's low, throaty chuckle.

'Need to keep up your strength, Jamie boy, from what I've heard of your prowess between the sheets,' she teased.

Fon felt her colour rise, and she concentrated on liberally spreading the butter, watching it liquefy as it ran into the crevices in the hot bread.

'Give me plenty of cheese, love' – Jamie good-naturedly ignored Gwyneth's remark – 'and some pickle. I've got a lot of work up on the top end field; some fences down again, with the cattle walking all over them.'

Gwyneth subsided into a chair and leaned forward, elbows on the table. 'Where Pat?' she asked, looking round the kitchen as if expecting him to come out of a corner somewhere.

Fon smiled. 'He's having a nap. Up early he was, helping me with the hens. Leave him be in peace until we've eaten, is it?'

'Right enough,' Jamie said. 'I'll take him off up the top end with me later on, give you two girls some time alone to gossip to your hearts' content.'

Fon poured tea, weak but hot, and then handed round the plates of cheese and pickle before sitting down. She was aware of Gwyneth smiling wickedly.

'How's my little sister shaping up as a wife, then?' she said, leaning towards Jamie, her broad mouth revealing perfect teeth. 'I *know* how well *you* are doing, but our Fon – pleasing as a wife, is she?'

Fon shook her head in despair at her sister's wickedness, and she glanced at Jamie anxiously. He rested his hand on her shoulder.

'She all right,' he said, his expression quite sober. 'She's a good mammy to the boy, and as for me, I couldn't ask for better.'

Fon glanced away. Jamie hadn't said he loved her, had never said he loved her, not since their wedding. Doubts assailed her afresh; was she just a substitute for Katherine?

'That's men for you, Sis; only get excited when it's bed-time, they do.'

Fon looked quickly at Jamie, but he didn't seem to mind Gwyneth's teasing.

'Not given to romance, our men – not the men I've met, anyway,' Gwyneth continued mercilessly. 'It's food in their belly and pretty quick about it, and clean shirts to put on their backs, or there's hell to pay. It's only when the sun goes down do they like a bit of kissing and cuddling.'

She laughed out loud. 'Oh, I bet you get really full of vigour then, don't you, Jamie? A real stud you are, come on, admit it now.'

Jamie buttered a crust without turning a hair, but a smile played around his mouth, and with a dart of surprise, Fon realized he was not at all embarrassed by her sister's remarks; rather he was pleased by the praise to his manliness.

'Been talking about me, have you, love?' he said softly to Fon, and she bit her lip, hoping that Gwyneth would keep quiet for once. It was too much to hope.

'She's been talking all right.' Gwyneth tossed back the thick hair that had escaped from the flash of red ribbon. 'I think my little sister has picked a real man in you, Jamie boy.'

He was smiling broadly now, and Fon sat back, realizing she was learning a great deal about her husband; he loved a bit of flattery, loved to have his

17

prowess praised. Were all men like that, she wondered, so easily pleased by a few nice words?

'How's Mammy managing?' Fon asked, determined to change the embarrassing turn the conversation had taken.

Gwyneth shrugged. 'With her usual crabbiness, I suppose. You know what our mother is like as well as I do, a right misery when there's no man around to distract her.'

'That's not fair!' Fon said, and then realized she had done just as Gwyneth wanted, provoked an argument.

'You know it's fair,' Gwyneth said placidly. 'Nina is only happy when there's a man in her bed.' She looked coyly at Jamie. 'I can quite understand it, mind; I like a man's company myself.'

Jamie rose from his chair and picked up his coat, swinging it over his shoulder. Fon saw him suddenly as Gwyneth must see him, sun-browned and muscular, his shirt sleeves rolled up above strong elbows, his face handsome, with the curling black hair clinging to his brow. He was, without doubt, a desirable, fulfilled man. Why then was she, his wife, having doubts about his love for her?

'I'm going down to the fields,' he said. 'I'll call in a bit later for the boy.' He left the kitchen, and for a moment there was silence, except for the droning of a bee trapped inside the window seeing freedom but unable to get out.

'He's no womanizer,' Gwyneth said, with a hint of disappointment in her voice, 'I'll give him that. You got a good man there, Fon. Look after him in bed, I'm warning you, for if you don't someone else will do it for you.'

'Meaning you, I suppose.' Fon was suddenly angry – though with herself, Jamie or Gwyneth she wasn't quite sure.

Gwyneth shrugged. 'Could be, Sis.' She relented then

18

and put her hand on Fon's shoulder. 'Look, love, I'll flirt with any man, you know me, but I wouldn't take your husband from you even if I could.' She sighed. 'And to be truthful, I don't think he'd bite. No, your Jamie is a rare being, a one-woman man. Make the most of it, and don't be a fool.'

'One-woman man,' Fon repeated. 'Perhaps you're right.'

Gwyneth didn't seem to hear her; she stared round the kitchen for a moment, her face thoughtful. 'You've got what you want, Fon; you are a very lucky girl. It don't look like I'll ever have the man I want. I'll never find happiness.'

Suddenly, Gwyneth, happy-go-lucky Gwyneth, was sitting at the kitchen table with her head buried in her arms, her shoulders heaving.

'Love!' Fon put her arm around her sister and hugged her. 'You are so beautiful, much prettier than me. Of course you'll be happy, you wait and see.'

Gwyneth looked up, her cheeks stained with tears, the light gone from her eyes.

'Will I?' she said softly. 'I know I talk big, but all I want is the love of a fine man. I'm afraid that Eline Harries will win, as she always seems to do, damn her!'

She thumped her fist on the table, and the cups leapt in the saucers. 'I hate Eline Harries! I wish she'd never set foot in Oystermouth. Since she came there, she's been nothing but trouble.'

Fon was silent; what could she say? Eline Harries had not always found life easy. She'd had her share of tragedy, and who knows if she even *wanted* Will Davies? But Gwyneth was in no mood to listen to reason.

'Come on,' Fon said, forcing a cheerful note into her voice, 'I'll make us a nice, fresh cup of tea.' She patted Gwyneth's shoulder, wondering at the strangeness of life. Her sister had always got everything she'd ever wanted, or so it had seemed to Fon. She was pretty, with a fine figure that would attract any man, while Fon had been a mouse, quiet and withdrawn, with curling tawny hair but unremarkable features, a girl no-one would lose his heart over, unsure of herself, diffident in the extreme.

But now the roles were reversed; Fon had a husband, a home and a family. She had blossomed; even she could see that. Her body was filling out, her face more mature, its lines fined, so that her eyes appeared larger. In the eyes of the world, she was a success, a woman with a fine husband.

She squared her shoulders with new resolution, knowing that whatever she had to do, whatever compromises she would have to make, she would ensure that nothing spoiled the almost perfect life she was leading.

CHAPTER TWO

Eline Harries sat back on her heels, disregarding the hammer and nails and lengths of wood that were spread around the bare floorboards of the room. Disregarding even the painting that lay beside pieces of wooden frame, the painting she had been so pleased with earlier but that now seemed mundane, ill-conceived.

The room, a high attic with a southward-facing aspect, was sunlit and mellow, the newly whitened walls reflected the light. For a moment, Eline paused, imagining the pictures she would paint hanging in the deep shadows of an alcove. It was a perfect studio for an artist, and though Eline would have hesitated to call herself that, she was nevertheless excited by the prospect of actually working in the room.

It was already her workshop, where she had spent hours designing shoes, working on drawings for practical boots; but now it would house a high, sloped bench which would make her designing work so much easier and in addition, at the far end, she would install an easel where she could paint to her heart's delight.

She had come a long way, she mused, a very long way. Her life as a farmer's daughter on Honey's Farm had once filled her childhood with light and happiness; then she had married Joe Harries, a man twenty years older than her.

Eline sighed. She had tried so hard to do her duty by Joe, but she had failed miserably. How could she blame him for taking a mistress when she did not welcome him into her own bed? And now he was dead she felt nothing but sadness that she had never made him happy.

21

Outside, the Sunday bells of All Saints were ringing out into the soft air, echoing across the village. Eline felt the sad memories fade away, and suddenly she was at peace with the world.

'So here you are.' The voice was low, melodic. 'I might have known.'

'Will!' Happiness flowed through her, as it always did at the sight of her beloved husband-to-be. Eline rose to her feet and dusted her fingers against her skirts.

'I was just trying to fit one of my pictures into a frame. I'm not very good at it really.'

'Hmm.' He encircled her waist from behind, chin resting on her shoulder as he looked down at the picture. 'That's a lovely watercolour of the Mumbles,' he said. 'I like the feeling of the rocks rising out of the morning mist. You are a talented girl, Eline.'

He turned her to face him and kissed her mouth. 'I'm a very lucky man, though I don't know if I relish the prospect of marrying a lady who has more money than me.'

'Ha!' Eline's voice was sceptical. 'Don't fool yourself that you are getting a rich woman, my love. I have only debts and the good-will of the people who have invested in me.'

'And I have only debts,' Will said ruefully, releasing Eline, 'though I must admit the villagers are doing their best to repay me for the shoes they bought on credit last year, when times were hard.'

Eline sighed. 'The hard times are far from over, Will.' She shrugged. 'I know the oyster fishing is better now, but only a little. The villagers are still finding things difficult.'

'I know,' Will said soberly, 'and that doesn't make it any easier for me to make a living, either. If it wasn't for the customers Hari Grenfell sends me from Swansea I'd have been finished long ago.'

Eline put her arms around his neck. 'You are a fine

man, William Davies, and you will be rich one day, I know it.'

Will sighed heavily. 'I can't wait, Eline.' He kissed her throat, and his voice became hoarse. 'For one thing I can't wait to get you into my bed.'

Eline clung to him, feeling the usual sweet longing for him, and though she knew she was being unfair, playing with fire, she pressed herself against him.

'Let's get married anyway, Will,' she urged softly. 'We'll be all right, you'll see.' She kissed his mouth. 'Between us, we'll make a reasonable living.'

Will moved away as though putting as much distance between Eline and himself as he could. 'We'll marry when I think I can support a wife,' he said sternly. 'I don't want to have to take handouts from you, Eline, surely you can see that?'

'Don't be so pig-headed!' Eline replied, and then bit back the angry rush of words. This was an argument she'd had with Will many times, and she recognized it was an argument she would not win.

'Look, I've come to a decision,' Will said, and there was something in his tone that alerted her, heightened her senses, bringing a tingling feeling of anxiety.

Eline glanced at him, deliberately keeping her voice even. 'What decision?' she asked quietly.

'I'm returning to Swansea,' he said. 'I'll give up the shop in Mumbles, cut my losses. Hari Grenfell is willing to take me on to manage part of her shoemaking empire.'

Eline felt a pang of fear. Will could not move away, not now, just as she was establishing herself as a successful businesswoman in the area.

'Don't look like that.' Will smiled. 'Swansea is only five miles away, you know, and Hari is a dear friend. She virtually brought me up.' Will paused for a moment. 'Come on, Eline, Hari would not be happy if I made a wrong choice. She is a fine, intelligent woman; I trust her judgement, and she feels as I do over this, the best thing is to pack up the business now.'

'I know you love and trust Hari Grenfell, and I respect her too, but, Will, you can't give up your shop and move away.' Eline caught his arm. 'Please, Will, I can't bear it if you are not here with me.'

'My mind is made up, Eline,' he said firmly. 'The business is not viable any longer. I'm not making a profit, I'm simply increasing my debts. I can't go on like that, it's simply not responsible.'

Eline stared around her at the bright, sunlit room, at the large windows overlooking the sea, and suddenly she felt as though she was standing on shifting sands.

'I'll hold a sale of my stock of boots and shoes,' Will continued, 'let the villagers have the benefit of it before I leave.'

He took her hand and, turning it, kissed the palm lightly. Eline tried to suppress her anger; was it directed at Will, at herself, or at the fates that seemed intent on dragging them apart?

'Don't you understand, Eline?' Will said softly. 'I can no longer afford even the small rent I'm paying Mrs Parks. Things are that bad.'

'Oh, Will, why don't you let me help?' Eline protested. 'You could come here, live in these rooms above the gallery.' She gestured around her. 'You can see how pleasant they would be.'

Will shook his head and, squaring his shoulders, moved to the door.

'That's impracticable and you know it.' He spoke softly but there was an edge of anger beneath his words.

'How is it impracticable?' Eline demanded. She went to him, resting her head on his shoulder. 'Let's not quarrel about it, Will.'

'We won't quarrel, not if you don't insist on trying to run my life, you little bossy boots.' Will rested his cheek against her hair. 'You see, Eline, I couldn't live here

24

under the same roof as you. There would be talk. In any case, these are your rooms, your workshop; you need them.'

'There wouldn't be talk, not if we were married,' Eline said, knowing she was persisting in a line that would only anger Will; and yet she couldn't help herself. She wanted to be with him, to have him all the time; she loved him so much that it almost hurt.

Will eased her arms from round his neck. 'Eline!' he said in exasperation, 'I will not be a kept man.'

'That's absurd!' Eline was growing exasperated too. 'Does Emily Miller's husband look on himself as a kept man?'

'That's different,' he said. 'Emily Miller took John in marriage when he was a successful cobbler. I admit he was poor by her standards, but at least he wasn't a failed businessman like me. Anyway, I'm not going to argue with you any more.' Will moved towards the door. 'I'll speak to you later, when you're in a more reasonable frame of mind.'

Then Eline was alone in the sunfilled room, the room that suddenly seemed to have lost its charm for her. She tried to return to the job in hand of getting the place ready to work in, but her concentration was gone.

She left the studio and wandered down the stairs. Aimlessly she went from room to room, not seeing the paintings hanging on the wall, not even seeing the red dots alongside some of the works that indicated they were sold to some eager customer. Business was good, very good, and yet suddenly Eline was full of doubts about her future. Perhaps she would be better off if she had no business; perhaps then Will would not be too stiff-necked with pride to marry her.

The building was silent. Penny, the girl who did the cooking, had gone home to her parents for the weekend, and Carys Morgan, who kept the place spotless, was with her husband in the little house further along the

25

village street. Everyone, it seemed, except Eline had a family, someone to spend Sunday with.

Eline moved out into the street. The sun spilled over the pavements, washing the buildings with light. Along the shore the beached boats lay, idle now in the summer months, waiting for the start of the oyster season in September.

On the edge of the sweeping bay Eline paused, feeling the sand fall away beneath her feet, soft and golden, with a rim of deeper colour where the tide had retreated, leaving a trail of seaweed.

She picked up a group of oystershells that had fused together. It was almost a work of art. She dusted it free of sand and decided to put it in the gallery, a good luck charm, an omen, perhaps.

Across the bay, she could see the pilot ship skimming, it seemed, over the calm waters. Overhead, gulls wheeled and cried, echoing her own loneliness. Tears filled her eyes, and she brushed them away impatiently; self-pity did no-one any good.

Eline returned to the roadway. As she passed the row of small fishermen's cottages, Carys Morgan called a greeting to her.

'*Bore da*, Eline.' She was sitting on the step of her house, knitting needles flying between deft fingers, her face wreathed in smiles. 'Having a quiet time, are you?'

Eline paused, glad of someone to talk to. 'It's such a lovely day, I felt I had to get out for a while.'

'A bit lonely, like, are you?' Carys said, with such perception that Eline stifled the instinct to deny any such thing.

She sighed. 'I am a bit sorry for myself today. I'll be glad when Will and I are married, I must say.'

'Come and have a nice cup of dandelion and burdock with me,' Carys said. 'I could do with a bit of company too.' She rose from the step and retreated into the darkness of the kitchen. Eline followed her.

'My Sam's gone drinking beer with his pals in one of the cottages,' she said, raising her eyebrows. 'Always does on a Sunday, the heathen.'

Eline sat at the scrubbed table and looked around the spotless kitchen. Carys in her home, as well as in the gallery, made a virtue of cleanliness and order.

During the awful months of hunger and famine that had gripped Oystermouth in the oyster famine, Carys had lost her baby son, a loss doubly tragic because Carys had despaired of ever becoming a mother.

'I miss him, mind,' Carys said softly, and it was as though she had picked up on Eline's thoughts. 'Some days my poor old arms ache for my baby. I'll never get over it, for all the old women tell me time heals all wounds.'

'I know,' Eline said. 'I've never had a baby, but when I lost my father I felt the world had come to an end for me too. In a way, I've been alone ever since.'

Carys looked at her curiously. 'Even when you was married to Joe you felt like that?'

Eline nodded. 'Because Joe was so much older than me and was Dad's friend, I thought he could fill the gap in some way. I was sadly mistaken.'

'He was a good man, though,' Carys said, 'and he loved you. Mind, I'll never understand why he took up with that hussy Nina Parks.'

Eline was silent. She blamed herself for Joe's infidelity. Had she been a better, warmer wife, Joe wouldn't have strayed to another woman's bed.

'Funny how he gave her children and yet you . . .' Cary's words trailed away and Eline smiled.

'I know, I often wondered at that myself. Perhaps I can't have children. I worry about that sometimes.'

'Probably you are all right,' Carys said confidently. 'It just wasn't meant, not between you and Joe. I spects him and Nina were . . . were – fitting for each other. Any rate, poor man's gone now, God rest his soul.'

Eline sat quiet, still, wondering why she was exploring past wounds and present doubts with Carys. Probably because she instinctively trusted her; Carys was so down-to-earth and sensible when it came to dealing with her own life.

Eline drank the mug of dandelion and burdock and smiled at Carys, determined to switch the conversation back to more mundane topics.

'Sam be glad to get back to sea?' she asked lightly.

Carys poured more cordial and shrugged. 'I suppose so. He don't talk much about his feelings; but then men never do, do they?' She sighed. 'Let's hope the oysters are more abundant than they were last season. I wouldn't like to face a winter of going hungry, not again.'

'Will you still be able to work at the gallery?' Eline asked. 'I know the oyster beds need a lot of time and attention, but I need you too, Carys.'

'I'll be cleaning for you, don't you worry,' Carys said firmly. 'It's my bit of security in case the oysters fail again.' She leaned her elbows on the table that gleamed white in the splash of sunlight, the wood pale with much scrubbing.

'The oyster beds are hard, mind; you know that, to your cost!' Cary's eyes were suddenly full of merriment. 'Stubborn, you are, mind, I'll never forget you struggling with the sack of oysters and the tide coming up round your belly, ready to suck you down.'

'I won't forget either!' Eline grimaced. 'I thought I was going to die, but I wasn't going to let the oysters fall back into the sea.'

'If it wasn't for William Davies coming like a hero and bringing you out, you would have been a goner.' Carys sighed. 'So romantic, it was.'

Eline glanced down into her mug, watching the swirling brown liquid as she raised it to her lips.

'When you getting married, soon is it?' Carys asked innocently.

Eline shook back a stray curl of hair. 'He's so stub-born,' she found herself saying. 'He wants to be rich before he makes me his wife – as if I care about that.'

Carys looked at her with clear eyes. 'Let him have his way,' she said softly. 'Otherwise he might blame you for the rest of his life; that's the way men are.'

She might be right, Eline thought. If Will failed to make himself the rich man he so wanted to be, would he feel Eline had held him back?

'You're very wise, Carys,' she said softly. She placed her mug on the table, noticing it had made a brown ring on the white surface.

'*Duw*, not wise, at all, just lived a bit longer than you have, that's all.'

There was silence in the small kitchen save for the droning of a bee in the fragrant roses growing around the cottage doorway. Eline realized quite suddenly that Carys might sometimes feel just as alone as she did. Carys had only her cleaning job at the gallery to occupy her during the summer months. And now, with no baby to fill her time, she must find the hours long and tedious.

As if reading her thoughts, Carys spoke. '*Duw*, I'll be glad when the oyster fishing starts,' she said quietly, her eyes moist with tears. 'The devil finds work for idle hands, or at least wicked thoughts to fill the mind.' Carys swallowed hard. 'I sometimes find myself blaming the Good Lord for letting my son die, forgetting that He who gives sometimes sees fit to take away.'

She looked appealingly at Eline. 'But I *was* a good mother, wasn't I?'

'Of course you were!' Eline said at once. 'It was the poor conditions, the lack of food and medicine, that was to blame, not you.' She reached out and touched Carys' hand, feeling the roughness of her skin with a sense of shock. How quickly, Eline thought, she had become used to the niceties of life. Living in comfort as she did, doing little hard labour, she had become soft and perhaps more

29

vulnerable. If hard times came again, would she be able to survive them? She shuddered a little.

'There now, I've depressed you,' Carys reproached herself. She picked up the mugs, took them to the big stone sink and dropped them in with a clatter.

'What do you think of little Irfonwy Parks then?' she said, changing the subject with a forced brightness of tone. 'Nina Parks' youngest, married to that handsome man from up at Honey's Farm? Lucky girl, mind.'

'I heard,' Eline said, trying to shake off the feeling of gloom that had settled over her. 'She's got her hands full, with a young child to look after as well as a husband and a fully working farm.'

'Aye, from there, weren't you?' Carys said, turning to look at Eline. 'Hard work farming, mind, I spects.'

'Hard indeed,' Eline agreed. 'Picking potatoes in spring and summer, and gathering the harvest in the autumn, and then the fodder for the creatures to be baled and kept in the barn until winter as well as a hundred and one other chores. It's hard, all right.'

'I spects they got help,' Carys said. 'Labourers to work the fields and that sort of thing.'

'Perhaps one or two at the busiest times,' Eline said, 'though most of the year a small farmer can't afford help.'

She rose to her feet, suddenly overcome with memories of Honey's Farm, of her childhood spent in the meadows, where poppies grew brightly and where her days had seemed filled with sunshine. Days before her father died. Days before she had married Joe Harries.

'I'd better get back,' she said. 'Thank you for the cordial and for the chat; it's been good to have company.'

'*Duw*' – Carys smiled – 'I spects you'll get enough company when the gallery is open and all the customers are coming in thick and fast. Good thing you got a Sunday to yourself, really.'

30

'You'd think so,' Eline said, moving to the door. 'See you tomorrow bright and early, then, Carys.'

She walked briskly back along the street towards the gallery, thinking of the empty hours stretching ahead. Usually she spent the evenings with Will, but perhaps tonight he wouldn't come, not after the argument they'd had earlier. And soon, when he was in Swansea, she would scarcely see him at all. She couldn't bear it.

When she arrived home, the door of the gallery was open, and she knew, with a lifting of her heart, that Will was inside waiting for her. She straightened her shoulders, resolving never to argue with him again, just to be thankful that he loved her enough to want to do what he thought was the best for her.

But, a small voice inside her said, why couldn't he accept that the best, the *very* best for her, for them both, was to be together as man and wife?

CHAPTER THREE

The sun was warm on Fon's back as she toiled up the hill to the top field with Patrick clinging to her skirts. The little boy was sun-kissed, his chubby arms golden, his round face brown beneath his curling hair. Fon smiled. He was so like his father, so handsome, so dear. In that moment she wished that he was her own, that she had given birth to him. She shivered suddenly and pushed away the thoughts of childbirth; it was something she did not wish – did not dare – think about.

The basket on her arm was draped with a pristine white cloth, and absently Fon adjusted it, rearranging the already careful folds. Beneath the cloth was concealed a crusty loaf, a small round cheese and a bottle of home-made beer, enough to feed six men if need be. Fon smiled. Jamie did the work of six men, and in the marriage bed he had the strength of six men.

'Your daddy will be glad to see us, Patrick, my boy.' Fon smiled down at the small child struggling manfully over the uneven pathway. 'I bet he'll be dying of thirst by now.'

Jamie had been up at first light, wanting to start cutting down the field of red clover while the weather was fine, for the clover, when dried out, would make fine fodder for the ewes.

As Fon moved slowly over the rise, she caught sight of Jamie, bending and cutting, his muscles gleaming with sweat as he laboured on the land, the land he loved.

Much of the field had been cut, looking like an over-large cottage garden through which the winds had wreaked havoc. Red clover flowers lay brightly against the cut stalks of grass, and the air was sweet with the smell.

Fon waved to Jamie, and he waved back, throwing down the scythe and pressing his big hands into the small of his back to ease the ache.

Fon looked round for Tommy Jones, who usually helped Jamie on the farm, but there was no sign of him.

She spread the checked cloth over the cut grass and brought out the bread and cheese. Patrick sat obediently, mouth half open like a small bird waiting to be fed.

Jamie came towards her, rubbing the sweat from his eyes with the back of his hand, and Fon marvelled at the strength of him and the rugged handsomeness of his face.

'Where Tommy?' she asked, kneeling in the grass and opening the bottle of beer before handing it to her husband.

'Dunno, must be sick.' Jamie hunkered down, his strong thighs straining against the seams of his breeches. Fon glanced away, remembering the feel of his hard, masculine body against hers as they lay side by side in bed. The sun was hot above her; the birds were singing so sweetly, it was a perfect day, and suddenly Fon desired her husband desperately.

She handed Patrick a crust from the loaf, and the small boy chewed on it contentedly. 'There's a good boy. Fon will give you a drink of milk when we get home.'

After a time, the silence and the heat told on the boy, and Patrick abandoned his crust and snuggled down in the grass, his eyes heavy with sleep.

'Why don't you teach Patrick to call you his mammy?' Jamie said quietly. 'After all, you are the only mother he will ever know.'

Fon looked into her husband's eyes questioningly. 'But you wouldn't want him to forget Katherine,' she answered quickly, saying the name with difficulty.

He chewed in silence for a full minute, his brow furrowed, his eyes turned away from her. He seemed to be weighing his words before answering. 'No, not altogether, but when we have other children we don't want Pat feeling the odd man out, do we?'

'I suppose not.' Fon felt the hot colour rush into her cheeks, but when Jamie turned to her and searched her face for any clue to her feelings, she held his gaze. He smiled slowly, and, leaning over, kissed her lips. His mouth became urgent, and he drew her closer; she fitted into his arms as though she had always been there.

Why hadn't she been the first woman in his life, his first love, Fon thought, with a dipping of her heart. She resented what Katherine had with Jamie, even though she knew it was wrong and wicked of her. But if there had been no first wife, if Katherine had not existed, then there would be no ghosts between them.

'Patrick has fallen asleep, look,' Jamie whispered. The boy was spread out on the sweet grass, his chubby fists above his head; his lashes, brushing the plump cheeks, were gleaming in the sunlight. For a long moment Fon watched the little boy, the soft rise and fall of his breathing, the way his hair hung back from his face. She loved him fiercely; no-one could have loved Patrick more, not even Katherine.

Jamie's hands were upon her then, gently pushing Fon backwards so that she was lying in the sweet grass. A blade tickled her cheek and Fon smiled, all gloomy thoughts dispelled. She was here now, with Jamie. She looked up into his face and knew the haze of passion that etched lines into his features.

He looked down at her for a long moment, at the relaxed abandonment of her body, and then he stretched himself alongside her, his face close to her own.

His hand traced the outline of her breasts with featherlight touch, and she felt her nipples harden with desire. Her breathing became ragged, and she knew she must possess Jamie here, under the hot sun, with the scent of clover in his hair, and sweet grasses as their bed.

She wound her arms around him and felt the heat of his skin through his thin shirt. 'I love you,' she said shyly as, slowly and deliberately, she began to unbutton her bodice. He bent and kissed her breasts and she felt herself respond, lifting herself towards him, wanting to feel him within her.

She closed her eyes, and hot, orange particles of light dazzled her senses. She was aware of Jamie's fingers, as though in a dream, as he teased her to screaming point, his mouth hot on her breasts, her stomach, her thighs.

'I want you, Jamie,' she said thickly, and she heard his words sighing through the air like a soft prayer.

'And *I* want *you*, colleen.' He took her roughly, with abandon that she had not known before. He plundered her, and she welcomed it, she clung to him, her fingers digging into his back, the skin silk and sun-hot beneath her fingers. They seemed to battle to possess each other as if neither of them could get close enough. Fon closed her eyes and felt the hot sun against her lids, her bare breasts, her thighs, and the world seemed full of light and sensation. This was what she had been born for, to love and be loved by the man who had possessed all of her, even her very soul.

She wanted to cry out to the blue arc of the sky, to the soft breezes that caressed her, to the gods, never to take this away from her. She was weak with love, and desire was only part of the magic of the moment.

Later she lay in the shade of the hedge and watched Jamie back at work cutting the field, and marvelled at his apparent feeling of renewed vigour. The gleam in his eyes was because of her, she told herself; one day, slowly perhaps, she would replace Katherine in his life, and then Jamie would be all hers.

When Patrick woke, Fon wiped the crumbs from his face and hair, and packed the remains of the food into the basket. She waved farewell to Jamie, who was too far away to hear her voice, and led Patrick back across the fields.

35

Fon decided she had better call at the small cottage where Tommy lived; she was anxious about the young farm-hand. It wasn't like him to miss a day's work. But if he had to, today was as good a time as any, she thought, smiling.

'Come in, Mrs O'Conner, 'tis good of you to call.' Tommy's mother was a plump woman, looking every inch a farm wife with her apple cheeks and sun-kissed hair. But now there were lines of anxiety around Mrs Jones's mouth.

'Come about my Tommy, have you?' she said, without preliminary, as she pushed the blackened kettle on to the fire. Fon nodded, watching as Mrs Jones put out the thick, earthenware cups and poured in the milk, drawn fresh from the cows by Jamie that very morning.

'Right sick, he is,' Mrs Jones said. 'Something the matter with his belly; complains of cramps, he does, and him normally a strong healthy boy. Perhaps you'll go through to the back room and take a look at him later,' she said beseechingly. 'I put him in there so I could hear if he called.'

Fon drank the tea as quickly as the hot liquid would allow, for Patrick was sitting on the floor pulling the ears of the patient collie dog which crouched beside him.

'Don't tease the poor animal, Patrick,' Fon said reprovingly. 'He might bite you.'

'Bless you, our Sheeba wouldn't hurt a fly,' Mrs Jones said, rising to her feet and putting down her cup. Clearly she was too anxious about her son to pay much attention to anything else.

Fon followed her to the back room, where the curtains were drawn against the sun, and the smell of sickness hung like a pall in the air.

Fon aproached the couch and looked down at the sleeping boy. He was browned by the weather, but now his face had an unhealthy tinge, as though, somehow, he was an apple turning bad.

'Perhaps you'd better fetch the doctor to Tommy,' Fon said slowly. 'He does look very poorly.'

When Mrs Jones didn't reply, Fon looked up at her. 'I'll stay with Tommy until you come back, if that's what you're worried about.'

'Lordy me!' Mrs Jones said softly, 'I can't afford no doctor, my love. Can't you do something for him? I've heard my boy praise you to the skies many times what with those herb things you use on the sick animals.'

'Me?' Fon said in surprise. 'But I don't know anything about sickness in men; animals are different, you must see that.'

Mrs Jones frowned. 'You know enough to suit me,' she said reasonably, 'and folks is same as animals, get the same sickness they do, mind.'

Fon moved closer to where Tommy lay and rested the back of her hand against his skin. It was burning hot to the touch. It was clear he had some sort of fever. She opened his shirt and saw an area of reddened flesh spreading to his waist. The problem was in the region of the abdomen, and reluctantly Fon lifted the shirt and exposed Tommy's thin shanks.

She stifled a gasp at the angry flesh just above his pubis and compressed her lips for a moment, trying to think calmly, trying to dredge up the memory of the remedies she used for fevers when dealing with the farm animals.

'I think,' she said at last, 'it might be a fistula.' She glanced at Mrs Jones and saw with dismay that the woman was hanging on her every word.

Patrick tugged at her skirt and began to cry. Almost gratefully, Fon looked down at him.

'I'll take the boy home,' she said quickly, 'but I'll pick up some remedies and be back in the morning to do whatever I can, I promise. Until then, try bathing his head with fresh water from the spring; it sometimes helps.'

'Bless you, Mrs O'Conner,' Mrs Jones said gratefully. 'There's good of you, I can't tell you how relieved I am. I've been that worried about my boy.'

'I can't promise to cure him,' Fon said quickly. 'All I can do is try to bring down the fever and ease the pain. It's not much, I'm afraid.'

By the time Fon left the Joneses' house, the sky had become streaked with evening light. The sun was dying in a blaze of colour, promising another fine day, and suddenly Fon realized that Jamie would be home from the fields wanting his supper.

She thought quickly and decided that cold chicken pie and pickle would suffice for this evening's meal. Jamie had a hearty appetite and never complained about the food she put before him.

He was at the pump in the yard, stripped to the waist, cold water running over his broad shoulders and down his wide muscled body to his narrow hips. His dark hair was plastered around his head, and droplets of water still lay like diamonds of light among the dark curls.

Love for him surged through Fon's veins, and she realized with a heat in her cheeks that she was every bit as hot-blooded as her mother. How often had Fon blamed Nina for her lack of caution where men were concerned, and now here she was, Nina's youngest, supposedly prim daughter, feeling the hot blood pound in her veins after only a few hours had passed since she had made love with her husband in the sweet grass of the fields.

She hurriedly set the table, putting out the cutlery with precise movements, trying to think calmly about her remedies, for she knew Mrs Jones would not rest until Fon returned to see to her son.

Jamie came into the kitchen, a big man, swinging through the low door, his frame filling it, blocking out the light from the rising moon.

'Tommy's sick.' Fon placed the food on the table,

thick slices of fresh crusty bread and a pat of salt butter standing alongside the plate of pie and the dish of pickle. She knew she was excusing her failure to make her husband a proper meal.

'I said I'd go back over there tomorrow and see what I could do for him.' She sank into a chair and stared across the table at Jamie, waiting for him to speak. He forked some pie into his mouth and stared at her, waiting for her to continue.

'I don't know enough to be any real help, Jamie, but Mrs Jones seems to have such faith in me.'

'Then you must not let her down' – he smiled warmly – 'and I'm sure you won't. What is it?' Jamie leaned across the table to help his son by slicing the chicken pie, cutting it into smaller, more manageable pieces.

'Some kind of inflamed fistula,' Fon said slowly. 'At least I think that's what it is.'

Jamie frowned. 'What makes you think that?' He wiped his son's mouth and helped him down from the chair, patting the boy's plump rear with a large, tender hand. 'Go play for a minute, give your father a chance to fill his belly.'

'The skin is red and angry,' Fon said. 'Swollen too. Tommy looks real bad.'

'Bit of thistle might do the trick,' Jamie said. 'Why don't you look it up in that book you're always reading?'

Fon nodded. 'That's what I thought I'd do.' She poured some hot fragrant tea and placed the cup beside Jamie's plate. She was worried, unsure of her ability to deal with Tommy's illness; and the knowledge that she was the only one Mrs Jones could turn to for help weighed heavily upon her.

Fon pushed away her uneaten food and moved to the table, turning up the lamp so that she could read. She looked up 'fistula' in her book of herbal remedies and saw that Jamie's advice about using thistle had been sound.

' "Star thistle",' she read aloud. 'That's just what you told me to use, Jamie. You are clever.'

He shrugged. 'No, just experienced,' he said, smiling. 'Go on, then, let's hear what more this wonderful book of yours tells you.'

' "Government and virtues of thistle",' Fon read out. ' "Almost all thistles are under the government of Mars".' She looked at Jamie. 'Mars, that's good.'

'Is it?' Jamie asked, with raised eyebrows, and Fon glanced up at him.

'It flowers early, so there should be some in the fields right now,' she explained. 'I haven't any dried thistle around the kitchen, but I'll remember to put some ready for the winter, just in case.'

'Plenty of thistles up where I've been working; if you'd said, I'd have brought some down with me.' Jamie bit into a crusty piece of bread, enjoying the food she had prepared. For a moment, Fon was distracted from her book, watching his strong face with renewed sense of wonder, seeing how the brows arched darkly over his eyes, seeing how firm was his jawline.

She forced herself to return to her book and read once more. ' "The root, powdered and distilled in wine, is good against plague and pestilence" . . .' She glanced at Jamie, who seemed engrossed in cutting another doorstep of bread. ' ". . . And drunk in the morning while fasting is profitable for ulcers and fistulas in any part of the body." '

She sighed heavily. 'I can't see young Tommy wanting to eat anything at all, so the fasting will be no problem.' She rose to her feet. 'I'll go and pick some thistle now. It can be distilling while I put Patrick to bed.'

It was cooler in the fields now, but the warmth of the day still seemed to be captured in the cornfields that were turning from green to golden. Here and there a tall standing poppy waved translucent red petals towards the sky that seemed to reflect their redness. Fon sighed, drinking in the peace and tranquillity of the land.

Her back ached as she gathered the green, woolly-leaved star thistles, careful to pull the plants up at the root. Once or twice she caught her fingers on the prickly whitish-green heads and paused, rubbing at her apron with stained fingers.

She thought of Jamie and the way he had worked the clover field tirelessly, bending and dipping over the land, and was awed at the strength of his muscles.

Her apron full of thistles, she turned to walk back towards the farmhouse, climbing easily over the stile and making her way around the field where the big Welsh black bull, Jamie's pride and joy, stared balefully at her, as though challenging her to invade his domain.

'It's all right, *tarw fawr*,' she said softly. 'I'll keep well away from you, big bull, don't you worry about that.'

When she entered the cool, whitewashed kitchen, there was no sign of Jamie or Patrick, and Fon smiled as she heard soft footsteps on the stairs.

'Put him to bed, have you?' Fon dropped the green thistles on the table. 'I hope you washed his face first.'

'Don't worry, girl.' Jamie caught her from the back and cupped her breasts in his hands. 'I know how to look after a little boy, well enough.'

He kissed the warmth of her neck. 'I know how to look after my wife too.'

Fon felt him harden against her buttocks and drew away from him smiling. '*Duw*, there's a man!' she said, bringing a large pan from beneath the sink. 'Like that big black bull up in the field, you are, mind. I sometimes think that's all you married me for.'

He watched as she began to cut the leaves from the long, thin roots and put them in the pan. 'What you going to do with those?' he asked, and Fon glanced over her shoulder as she opened the oven door and placed the pan inside.

'I'll dry the roots and then crush them in a little of my

elderberry wine,' she said, rubbing her hands on her apron. 'The leaves I'll soak in water and then boil them up. I shan't waste any of it, don't worry.'

'Turning into a real little physic, aren't you, my love?' The banter had gone from Jamie's voice and, turning, Fon saw a shadow fall across his face. She knew instinctively that he was thinking of Katherine, of how nothing, no remedies, no amount of loving attention, had saved her. The knowledge that his thoughts were with his dead wife was like the pain of a knife cutting through Fon's flesh.

'I'll go to bed when I've finished making the cordial,' she said briskly, and suddenly wanting to punish him for his thoughts, which she knew was foolish of her, she put down her book and let herself outside, without another word.

She stalked along the pathway and seated herself on the bench below the apple trees at the edge of the garden, her heart pounding. So he still thought of her, his first wife; even all their love-making had not eradicated Katherine from his mind.

He did not follow her, and Fon's lips tightened. What had happened to the moment of intimacy when he held her against him, his desire for her evident in the hard lines of his body? A rush of pain filled her; was it just a solace to him, did he just enjoy the animal pleasure of taking her and owning her? Would she never reach that inner core of him, be truly one with him except in the flesh? If so, that was what she must accept, because she loved Jamie beyond all reasoning, and she would take whatever he offered her and be glad of it.

Suddenly, she wanted his closeness, she wanted to know that he was hers, at least in some measure. She rose and returned to the house and saw that Jamie was pouring over the books, his pen in his hand.

She had never been the one to approach him before. He always took the initiative, making her feel desired and desirable. It was difficult for her to go to him, to put her hands on his shoulders, but she forced herself to do it. He was her husband, they were bound together for mutual comfort and joy.

He did not look up when she touched him, and Fon knew that he had been aware of her moodiness and was not to be easily won over.

She slipped her hands downward over the broad, muscled chest, feeling the beating of his heart beneath her fingers. She loved him so much that it was like an agony within her. She touched the buckle of his leather belt and felt him tense, his back was solidly against her, and for a moment she expected him to shake her away.

'Jamie,' she said softly in his ear, 'I want you to make love to me, please.'

He hesitated for a moment, and then he rose, knocking over the chair in his haste. He took her in his arms, pushing her suddenly against the hard wood of the cottage door.

She wanted to beg him to say he loved her, but his mouth crushed down on hers, and in any case she would have been afraid to speak the words out loud.

He pushed up her skirts. 'You smell of the fields, of the corn, of the grass, and I want you so badly, my little colleen.' He breathed the words in her ear and then he thrust against her so that she gasped and flung her head back, while her body arched towards him.

It was a silent struggle of wills as well as flesh, punctuated by sighs and moans, though who was trying to punish who, Fon didn't know. But she revelled in his hunger for her, she pressed his strong thighs against her, as though she couldn't have enough of him, and his lips were hard, forcing her mouth open so that he seemed to be within her, capturing her like a butterfly on a pin. And she did not want to break away, did not want the joy to end.

Now, in this moment, he was hers. This was her

43

triumph, that she and Jamie were bound together at least in this. A searing heat filled her, rising like the flames of a fire to engulf and consume her. She seemed to lose consciousness of anything but sensation, and in that moment Fon knew she had surrendered every last part of herself to her husband.

Fon was up before daylight, ready to make her way across the fields to the farmhouse on the narrow strip of land bordering Honey's Farm, where she knew Mrs Jones was depending on her with touching faith.

Tommy did not at first respond to the effects of the cordial of thistle roots; his fever seemed unabated, and the unnatural colour still pervaded his body. Not knowing what else to do, Fon bathed him continuously in the water from the bowl beside the bed, and finding it seemed to ease him, bade his mother bring more cold water to soak the flannel she pressed to his head and chest.

Though surprised, Mrs Jones did as she was told and even helped to spread the icy flannel on her son's skin. Gradually, as the sunlight began to poke inquisitive fingers through the window of the little bedroom, Tommy's breathing became easier.

'Time for hot poultices, now, I think.' Fon seemed possessed of an uncanny knowledge of what was needed next. She spread the poultice on a piece of dry flannel and, while it was still hot, placed it on the inflammation on Tommy's groin.

The boy winced but did not open his eyes. Wearily, Fon moved away from the bed. 'There's nothing more I can do for now,' she said softly. 'I'd better go home and fetch Patrick in from the fields' – she smiled wryly – 'and I'd better make Jamie a good hot breakfast. He'll be starving by now.'

'I'll send my little girl over, later, to help with the milking,' Mrs Jones said. 'Come back from staying with her auntie she has, and restless as a leaf in the wind.'

44

She spoke cheerfully, but her eyes were shining with tears. 'It was good of you to stay with me so long and help me with our Tommy, the way you did. I'll never forget it.'

'It's not much,' Fon said. 'I only hope I've done some good.' Fon was doubtful. She glanced at Tommy and was relieved to see that he seemed easier and the unhealthy tinge to his skin was giving way to the more normal colour of the outdoors.

At the door, she paused. 'The fistula should break some time today,' she said. 'But whether it does or not, put on some more of the poultice to draw out all the badness.'

She ached from bending over the bed, and she felt weary as she walked back home; but in spite of her tiredness she was content. She knew she had done her best for Tommy, untutored though she was. She had worked by instinct more than knowledge, and now she could only pray.

In spite of all her reading of the herbal book, she had never been given reason to put any of the remedies into practice on human beings. Even now she wasn't sure if it was purely luck that Tommy Jones had begun to recover.

She thought of Jamie, waiting for her at home, and she felt warmed by the thought. She touched her breasts where her soft skin was marked by Jamie's passion, a passion that was well matched by her own.

Fon marvelled at the change in herself, from a wide-eyed romantic to a sensual woman, and all because of the love of a fine man. Or was it lust on Jamie's part, a small voice within her asked with soft insistence.

She shrugged as she moved forward with renewed vigour. Whatever Jamie was offering her, she would accept humbly. She had his passion, and on her finger was the ring of the man she loved, and that was more than many women achieved in a lifetime.

CHAPTER FOUR

'But are you sure it's what you want, Will?' Hari Grenfell's voice was soft with concern, and Will felt a warmth run through him. She was on his side, always; he could rely on it.

'Of course I have a job for you, a job you would do very well, no-one better; but if you would like to keep the shop on, then I'll help you in any way possible.'

Will touched her hand, smiling down at her. He loved Hari as a brother loved a sister, more perhaps, because he owed her so much. Hari had taken him in when he was barely nine years old, had given him an apprentice-ship, given him hope, given him love.

Will remembered with vivid horror the hovel where he'd been born and where he had seen his family die, one by one from the Yellow Jack. The pestilence had come suddenly to Swansea and had brought tragedy to many families, not only his own. When it was too late to remedy the matter, the cause had been found: the fever had been brought into Swansea docks by a sick seaman who had passed it on to the pilot who had guided the stricken ship into the arms of Swansea pier.

Will pushed the unpleasant thoughts aside. 'I must give up the shop. I wouldn't want to fall even deeper into debt, Hari,' he said reasonably. 'Better that I cut my losses now, get out while I can salvage something from the business.'

'But surely the worst is over, Will?' Hari poured tea from a fine china pot, and Will watched as the sun shone through the bone china cups, illuminating the finely painted flowers that adorned the service, as bright as any real flowers growing in the garden. He paused for a moment, thinking of the skill that had gone into the painting, the patience as individual pieces were decorated. Then he sighed; he could not avoid the consequences to his business brought about by the oyster famine, could not keep the unpleasant thoughts at bay for ever. They had to be faced; problems needed to be solved, and it was up to him to take the initiative.

'I don't think the worst *is* over, Hari,' he said softly. 'People with wealth like yours, established businessmen' – he smiled – 'and women, will be all right, but it's the folk owning small businesses that have suffered. At least those in the village of Oystermouth.'

'Well, my dear Will, take that job with me. I would be overjoyed to have you on my payroll once again. I couldn't ask for a better manager.'

She paused. 'It would mean travelling a little. I want the ties I've forged in Cardiff strengthened.' She grimaced ruefully. 'Mrs Bell, who owns the emporium, can be a right dragon. She needs to be charmed into renting me a larger, more suitable spot in her premises. You, with your charm, would be an ideal person for that.'

'Thank you,' Will said. 'Do I detect a compliment there?'

'Maybe,' Hari said. Then she became serious. 'But, Will, while you are in Swansea you are more than welcome to share our house for as long as you like, you know that.'

'Your offer of a job I accept with no hesitation,' Will said firmly, making a mental note that the solution would only be a temporary one. He could not remain tied to Hari's apron strings for ever, fond as he was of her. But now was not the time for pride; he needed to earn a living, to take stock of his situation.

'But as to living accommodation, I'm a big boy now, Hari, used to living on my own.' He took her hand and

47

kissed it. 'I'll find somewhere suitable, don't you worry.'

Hari smiled broadly. 'A big boy is right!' Her Welsh accent became more marked, purposely so, to express her amusement. 'And a real charmer into the bargain. I see the girls swooning over you, and there's proud I am.'

Will leaned back in his chair. Hari of course was exaggerating, influenced by her love for him.

Amused by his silence, she continued. '*Duw*, Eline better snap you up quick before some pretty new face comes along to take your fancy.' She paused. 'Why are you taking your time getting married, Will? I'd have thought you'd have got Eline to the altar long before now.'

Will's humour vanished. 'How can I marry her?' he asked in a hard voice. 'I've nothing to offer, not even a roof to put over her head.'

'Proud you always were, Will Davies, too proud for your own good, man.' Hari sounded cross. 'Do you think Eline cares so much for material things, then?'

Will shook his head. 'Maybe not, but I won't marry her until I can offer her a secure future.'

'William.' Hari put her hand over his. 'Who can assume security for anything? The entire world is insecure; the only thing that keeps us sane is love. Don't waste it.'

Will looked round the sumptuous sitting-room, the plush hangings on the windows, the rich carpeting on the floor. It was easy for Hari to talk when her world was cushioned with money, her own and her husband's not inconsiderable wealth.

'I wasn't always rich.' Hari as always read his thoughts. 'You know that better than most, Will.'

'I know.' He leaned towards her. 'But you made something of yourself. Before you were married to Craig, you had already begun to make a name. You took risks and they paid off; I'm not so clever as you, obviously.'

The words were not spoken with bitterness, only with

a deep regret on Will's part that he had failed to make his business the success that he and Hari had hoped it would be.

'It was the loss of the oysters that made the business fail, Will,' Hari said softly, 'and not any lack on your part. You shod the villagers when they could not pay for shoes, helped them when they were in dire straits. You have nothing to reproach yourself with.'

'I know.' Will rose to his feet, stretching his arms above his head, easing his cramped muscles. 'None the less, I must accept defeat. I'll go home now, make the necessary arrangements to wind everything up.' He smiled ruefully at Hari. 'I'll be back.'

He kissed her cheek, and for a moment she clung to him. 'You'll work things out, Will,' she said firmly. 'I just feel it in my bones.'

As the Mumbles train careered its way along the narrow tracks, past the large expanse of calm sea towards Oystermouth, Will sat on the top deck, staring back in the direction of Swansea.

His home town, the mean streets and the broad, the hovels and the big houses, all were familiar to him now, courtesy of Hari Grenfell. She had taken him with her on her rise to riches and fortune, had lifted him from his deprivation and poverty to enjoy a world that he now adopted as his own, the world of fine living and of good manners, of good bed and board, and mostly of the respect of those who thought of themselves as his peers. His background was forgotten or never known; he was now William Davies, beloved protégé of the rich and successful Hari Grenfell.

His gaze was drawn towards Oystermouth. It was here his heart lay. It was here that the woman he loved lived and breathed and made for herself a fine living, and the fact of it only served to highlight his own failure.

Why was it, Will asked himself in exasperation, that the women in his life were destined to be rich and successful, and he who loved them was doomed to failure?

But he would triumph again, he told himself, in time. For now he must give up his shop and work for Hari instead of for himself. But he was young and strong and determined; he would make his way in the world, and next time there would be no failing.

Eline stood in the slant of late sunshine pouring through one of the large south-facing windows of the gallery, watching the surge of first-night viewers as they moved elegantly from room to room.

It was a good exhibition, and Eline knew a moment of triumph as she looked around. Paintings by the late Alexander K. Brander and one by Joseph Walter of Bristol adorned the room, while upstairs was an entire room dedicated to the paintings of James Harris, whose stormy colours and rich seascapes intrigued Eline and filled her with a longing to be able to paint with such accuracy and skill the moods of the sea.

There was only one thing troubling her. Will had promised to attend the opening of the exhibition, and so far there was no sign of him.

'Good show, Mrs Harries.' Gerald Greyfield stood before her, a portly gentleman come all the way from England for the early viewing, his round, good-humoured face wreathed in smiles. 'There are a few of the pictures I shall want for myself. Will you mark them off for me, my dear lady?'

He paused. 'Oh, and may I introduce a colleague of mine, Calvin Temple? He's been just itching to meet you.'

Eline was aware, as Lord Greyfield made the formal introductions, of the tall stranger staring down at her with open admiration. It was something that amused, rather than pleased her; but all the same, the flattering attention was a salve to her feelings of pique at Will for being late on such an important occasion.

50

Then she forgot Calvin Temple and became occupied with the business of selling the pictures. And yet a worry niggled at the back of her mind; the thought of Will's absence would not be pushed aside. She was worried about him. Had he perhaps stayed in Swansea for the night? But surely he wouldn't do that without telling her? Questions flew through her mind even as she mentally worked out the payment she must make to the artists of the pictures and the commission she would claim on the sales.

She was delighted when one of her own paintings, modest in comparison with the artistry around her, sold to Lord Greyfield. She was realistic enough to know that he bought it because he liked the look of her, rather than for any store he set by the painting itself. His blue eyes, crinkled in a bronzed, weathered face, twinkled down at her.

'You must promise to visit my home in Worcester, my dear,' he said, standing tall above her. 'I would like you to see my modest collection of contemporary paintings, as well as my one or two treasured old masters.'

'I'd be delighted,' Eline murmured, her eyes glancing beyond Lord Grayfield to where Will had just appeared in the doorway. Joy filled her, suffusing her face with warmth, so that Lord Grayfield blinked rapidly.

'Excuse me.' She was barely aware that she had left Lord Grayfield's presence rather more abruptly than was polite and that he was looking after her with bushy eyebrows raised.

'Will!' She stood looking up at him. Her heart was beating swiftly as he smiled at her, and all she longed to do was lean against him and have his arms hold her safely.

Instead, she frowned. 'Where have you been – you're late.' It was an accusation; her voice was slightly raised. Eline knew that she had made Will angry, by the almost imperceptible tightening of his mouth.

'I apologize for not being here to listen to your opening speech,' he said, in even tones that should have warned Eline to tread carefully. 'I'm sure it was a triumph, but I did have rather important things to do, such as arranging my future.' He glanced around him almost scornfully. 'Yours, obviously, is well taken care of.'

'The implication being,' Eline said shortly, 'that I'm a selfish person who considers only myself.'

'Perhaps.' William made to turn away; his eyes were narrowed and in his jaw a muscle tightened.

'Well, I'm sorry for wanting this show to be a success,' Eline said icily. 'It seems one of us has to make an effort to run a business successfully.'

Will looked directly at her then, and the colour drained from Eline's face. She couldn't believe that she'd uttered the hurtful words that had widened, with shocking suddenness, the rift between them into a chasm.

Will turned and, without another word, left the gallery. As though it were thundering within her, Eline could almost feel the heaviness of his footsteps moving ever further from her.

'What is it? You seem upset.'

Eline became aware that Calvin Temple was standing beside her, looking down at her in concern. She suppressed the desire to rush into the street and, if need be, chase Will to the ends of the earth.

'Nothing, it's quite all right – please, enjoy the exhibition, Mr Temple.' To her own ears, Eline's words seemed garbled. Calvin took her arm and led her outside to where the sweet, salt air drifted in from the incoming tide.

'I think it best you have time to compose yourself, Mrs Harries,' Calvin said calmly. 'It's clear that . . . that person – I won't call him a gentleman – has upset you. Is there anything I can do?'

'No!' Eline said abruptly, and then added a lame

'Thank you.' She was aware that she was making a conscious effort to smile. 'I'm sorry for my rudeness, but today, it seems, I have the knack of doing and saying the wrong thing to everyone, including my fiancé.'

'Your fiancé, I see.' Calvin Temple smiled ruefully. 'I am destined to be pipped at the post in the matters of the heart. My loss, I'm afraid. Still, is there anything I can do?'

Not at all annoyed by the question, Eline felt it would be a relief to confide in him. Calvin Temple seemed wise beyond his years.

She sighed. 'Will's business must close; it's a touchy time for him, and I'm afraid I'm only making things worse for him by being downright hurtful.'

'By being successful, perhaps,' Calvin said smoothly. 'That can be hard for any man to take.'

'Well, no, he doesn't begrudge my success, not really,' Eline said softly. 'I was angry with him and so I was cruel, rubbing salt into his wounds. I'm not surprised he walked away from me.'

'We all say things we don't mean, sometimes. I'm sure your fiancé has far too much sense to take any notice of words spoken in anger.'

Eline only wished she felt as confident, but the pain in Will's eyes told her she wouldn't be forgiven so easily.

'Come back inside,' Eline said, smiling up at Calvin, grateful for his sympathy. 'I might have made some more sales by now, who knows?'

She cast one long last look down the street, her eyes aching to see the tall upright figure of the man she loved; but the roadway was empty. Sighing, Eline went into the noise and laughter of the gallery.

A week had passed, a long, endless week of long days and even longer nights with no word from Will. Eline stared round the gallery. It was almost empty now of paintings, but then the exhibition had gone well since that very first night, the night she had inflicted such a wound on the man she loved that he obviously found it difficult to forgive her.

She had gone over her words a thousand times, and each time they seemed more harsh and cruel than when she'd spoken them; and though her heart seemed to be breaking in two, and she longed to speak to him, to apologize abjectly for her words, she was too proud to go into Swansea looking for him.

And yet, she reasoned, wasn't it up to her to make the first move? It was she who had uttered the awful words that had driven him away, wounding words telling him that he was a failure. She hadn't meant to sound like that, a woman crowing at her own success; but anger had tipped her tongue with barbs, and they had struck home.

Eline forced herself to concentrate on the task before her. She took one of the few paintings left and moved it from its place on the wall. With her head on one side, she stood it on the easel in the window.

The painting was one of her own, a seascape that captured Mumbles Head rising like a mythical island from the mists. It was a good picture, and she knew it. Perhaps not technically faultless, but the mood evoked by the sky and sea blending in shades of grey and violet gave it the atmosphere of a fairy-tale world, a place of mystery, but also a place of peace. But Eline knew no peace, had known none since the day Will had walked away from her.

She made up her mind quite suddenly. Damn her pride! She would close the gallery and go up to Swansea and face him, apologize on bended knee if need be, beg his forgiveness. She would find him easily enough; he would have gone to Hari Grenfell's house, where else?

Eline took off her apron and wiped her hands on the starched linen almost absent-mindedly. What would she say to Will? Would he even see her? For a moment, her courage failed. What if he'd left instructions that he was not to be bothered?

She must try. It was no good sitting still allowing the bitterness between them to go unresolved. So Eline brushed back her hair, tucking the stray curls into the confining pins, and, after a moment's hesitation, she let herself out of the gallery into the warm sunshine of the day.

The Mumbles train was crowded. Men in tall hats and women in wide-skirted frocks laughed and chattered together as though life was one long holiday. And so it was for some, Eline mused. The rich of Swansea could spend the day at the seaside in Mumbles eating oysters, drinking dandelion cordial, without a care as to where the next penny was coming from. For people like her and like Will, life was a struggle to survive.

For a moment, anger bit at her with sharp teeth. Will thought he was so hard done by; losing his business was a blow, of course it was, but he was young and strong, he had advantages that she'd never had – the backing of people like Hari Grenfell, for example.

Eline had made a success of things by her own talent and ingenuity. She alone had found backing for the gallery in Lord Greyfield, a fine English gentleman who had been so impressed with Eline's portrait of his bride-to-be that he had decided there was a profit to be made from her talent, profit that would benefit both of them.

Shame washed over her then. She was doing it again, comparing her own success with Will's failure. How could she even think like that? Look what Will had given to the stricken village. He had given the people boots and shoes they would never pay for, had lost his own living in the process; he was a fine, good man, a compassionate man. And what had she done to ease the anguish of Oystermouth? Set up a soup kitchen that was paid for mainly out of the pockets of others.

Eline glanced out of the train and saw the soft sea gently lapping the golden sands of Swansea Bay. Out on the horizon, she could just make out the lines of a paddle steamer, making, no doubt, for the busy docklands to the east of the town.

Eline knew that she wasn't really concerned about the sea or the ships upon it; she was trying her utmost not to think about her meeting with Will, or what words she would find to say to him.

When she alighted at Rutland Street, Eline looked around her and wondered at the size of the town. Swansea had grown very big over the last years; copper and tinplate works dominated the east bank of the river, pouring smoke and grime into the once tranquil air above the houses.

The sun was hot as Eline made her way into Wind Street, pausing to look into the hatter's window as if to admire a fancy creation of crisp feathers and straw. She was trembling in spite of the heat, and she wondered if she could bear to face Hari, to admit to the cruel words she'd used to wound Will.

The Grenfell emporium was impressive in its size and scope, and once within the portals, Eline was overcome with the familiar scent of new leather. It reminded her so much of Will's shop that she felt tears come to her eyes.

She became aware that a young gentleman assistant was bowing politely before her. 'Anything I can show you, madam?' he asked obsequiously.

'I'd like to speak to Mrs Grenfell, please.' Eline spoke with as much authority as she could muster, but the young man's gaze barely flickered.

'My apologies, madam, but Mrs Grenfell is out of town, just for today.' He smiled, and Eline felt a

56

momentary sense of relief. She took a deep breath and tried to muster all her courage.

'Well, then, I must speak with Mr Davies,' she said, as though Will was nothing more than an acquaintance. But how could she tell this young man that she and Will were betrothed, that they had quarrelled and now she had come to make amends?

'Didn't you know, madam?' He smiled again. 'Mr Davies is not with the Swansea branch any longer.'

'Not with you? I don't understand.' Eline felt the words leave lips that were suddenly numb.

'I understand that Mr Davies is working out of town, madam. I've no idea when or even if he intends to return.' The words fell like stones into the silence, and Eline heard her own inane question as though from a distance.

'Gone away?'

'Yes, madam, gone away, and I'm afraid I don't have his address.'

He had forestalled her next question, and hopelessly Eline turned towards the door. How she got outside the shop she didn't know, but she felt the hard, hot stone of the building against her fingers as she struggled for composure.

Then there was nothing in her but a great emptiness. Will had gone away, and he hadn't cared enough even to leave her a message. She drew herself upright and slowly, very slowly, she made her way back to the train terminus.

CHAPTER FIVE

Within two weeks, Tommy Jones had recovered from his fevers enough to help on the farm again and Fon was free to return to her usual tasks of milking the dairy cows and caring for the chickens. Along with her household chores and looking after young Pat, she had quite enough to do. Often she was needed to work the fields with her husband, and then she tumbled into bed at nights aching in every limb. And yet, she smiled at the thought, Jamie, in spite of working like a dog, was never too weary to turn and take her in his arms and make love to her as though every time was the first.

Ruefully, she looked down now at her fingers. They were calloused and sore, stained from the clover she'd been helping Jamie gather, a backbreaking job at the best of times; but at last, the fodder to feed the sheep and the ewes was secure and dry in one of the big barns.

Fon never ceased to be amazed at the amount of work Jamie and young Tommy got through in a day. It seemed there were never enough hours. The summer crop of potatoes had to be lifted soon, and then Fon would be needed to help in the fields once more. She groaned at the thought.

Last year Jamie had taken on two casuals, but they had proved to be townies, with little or no interest in the country, and in the end Jamie had given them both their marching orders.

Fon sighed inwardly. Used as she was now to farm work, she hated the early mornings on the dew-wet land, bent double over the rows of stubborn vegetables that refused to part company with the rich soil. But it had to be done. On a farm, every hand was necessary. Even the faltering baby fingers of young Patrick would contribute to the picking this year.

She sank down on the milking stool and, cheek against the warm flank of one of the dairy cows, began to squeeze the full teats. Having recently calved, the animal was rich with milk, which spurted readily into the ridge-bottomed bucket. In the byre on the other side of the fence, the cows in calf were kept aloof and segregated from the rest of the herd. Big and cumbersome and with no milk to yield, these animals were in a favoured position, cherished until the precious calves were born.

Patrick leaned against Fon's knee, chewing at his thumb, his eyes still glazed with sleep.

'Fon will put you down for a nap in a minute – right, boy?' she said softly, troubled at the necessity for rousing the child so early in the mornings. Perhaps she should leave him in bed while she milked the cows; after all, she would be only a stone's throw away from the farmhouse, Patrick could come to no harm.

And yet, the thought of her duty to Katherine hung heavily on her shoulders. Fon was always conscious that she must live up to the faith Jamie's first wife had placed in her. There were dangers in a farm kitchen, where the fire was kept stoked to facilitate the cooking of huge meals. Water boiled constantly on the hob, and a small boy could find no end of mischief to occupy his time should he wake and find himself alone.

The milking over, she led Patrick across the dusty yard to the farmhouse and tucked him back into the warmth of his bed. He closed his eyes, lashes brushing plump sun-kissed cheeks, and was immediately asleep. Fon smiled down at him; he was a fine boy, his skin shining with health. Katherine would have been so proud of him.

Sometimes, Fon found herself resenting her memories of Katherine. She was always there, a persistent ghost of the past, and Fon felt it was as though she was constantly measuring herself by Katherine's stringent rules and finding herself wanting.

She heard voices in the kitchen below and hurriedly made her way downstairs. The men would be hungry; having worked for hours already, they would want good food to fill their empty bellies.

Jamie smelt of earth and grass and the fresh sunfilled air, and Fon resisted the temptation to put her arms around him and hold him close, reasserting her possession of him. Instead, she brought out of the deep pantry some crusty fresh bread and a plate filled high with cold ham and pickles.

'How are you feeling, Tommy?' Fon asked, pushing a thick mug towards him. He grinned lopsidedly.

'My belly is all healed now, missis,' he said, breaking off a chunk of bread and chewing on it with gusto.

'Good little doctor is my wife,' Jamie said, his eyes meeting hers, holding her gaze with a hint of laughter.

She looked away, not knowing if he was making fun of her. 'I did only what I could.' Her voice sounded prim, cold even, and Fon quickly lifted the heavy pot and poured more of the fragrant, steaming tea into the waiting mugs.

The silence in the kitchen lengthened. The sound of a bird singing in the trees outside the window gave the day a feeling of laziness, which was quickly belied by the briskness in Jamie's voice when he spoke.

'I want you to make a proper meal later on,' he said, leaning big arms on the table. Fon was stung, wanting to ask him what he meant by a proper meal: wasn't ham and fresh bread and butter good enough for him? The people of Oystermouth would be glad of such fare, even now, when the worst of the hardship caused by the lack of oysters was over.

He must have caught something of her mood because, lazily, he leaned across and touched her cheek. 'I mean a meal fit for hearty farmers, my love,' he enlarged. 'Hot

60

spuds, a roast joint, plenty of vegetables and rich gravy.'
He pulled at a small curl that hung down from the pins
that held her hair. 'And perhaps an apple pie to follow?'

'I'll see to it,' Fon said, hating herself for her timidity.
Why didn't she demand to know what was going on?
She was part of this farm now, wasn't she?

It was young Tommy who supplied the answer. 'Mr
Ian Evans is coming to see if the bull is suitable,' he
explained.

'Suitable?' Jamie echoed scathingly. 'My bull is the
best old Evans will find in these parts. Near a ton-weight
of beef in that one. Fed the best hay and the best
mangolds, treated like a prince, him.'

Jamie looked at Fon, his eyes shining with laughter.
'And always eager to serve is that one.'

Fon felt the colour come into her cheeks as she looked
away from her husband's playfulness. Jamie left the table
with a suddenness that startled Fon.

'Come on, Tommy, boy, there's enough to be done
before Evans brings his cows over. Let's try to get the
work finished early, because it will be all talk and
beer-drinking later on.'

When Fon was alone in the kitchen she stood for a
moment looking around her, a feeling of anger stirring
within her. What did Jamie think she was, a machine?
Why hadn't he warned her there would be company?
Then she could have planned the meal in advance. Now
she would have to rush about like a scalded hen to get
things done in time. She rolled up her sleeves with a
sense of purpose; the more she did before Patrick woke,
the better she would fare.

Later, as she set out the table with a snowy cloth kept
especially for visitors, Fon brushed back her hair wearily
and congratulated herself on her achievements. The beef
was falling apart, so succulent was it, and the hot spicy
aroma of apple pie had begun to permeate the kitchen.

'There, Jamie O'Conner,' she said, folding her

61

arms across her thin body, 'see if you can find fault in that!'

Tommy came panting up to the door. 'The master's asking will you bring a jug of beer out to the stalls, missis,' he said breathlessly. 'Old Evans' thirst is well known in these parts – drink any man under the table, him.'

'But . . . the meal is ready,' Fon called, but Tommy was already retreating across the yard, his thin legs covering the ground in huge strides, his shoulders hunched in a way that told of his anxiety to please. This man Evans must be a demanding customer indeed, Fon mused, a well-paying one too.

Fon glanced at Patrick. He was playing happily with his wooden animals on the floor, but she dare not leave him in the kitchen with the fire stoked up to heat the oven and the hot food standing ready on the large hob. With a sigh, she fetched the beer from the cold pantry and placed in on a tray with the heavy mugs.

'Come on, Patrick,' she said. 'Let's go and see Daddy.' The little boy rose eagerly enough and followed her outside into the sunshine, chasing the ducks from his path with swooping kicks of his small feet.

Fon heard the bellow of the bull and shuddered, glad that the huge creature was penned behind one of the stalls. As though in reply there came the mournful bawling of a cow, sounding as though she was in pain.

She carried the tray to the side of the stall just in time to see Jamie releasing the black bull from the shining steel ring that held him.

The bull pawed the ground, nostrils flaring in and out, as though the creature was in the grip of a terrible anger; the evil eyes gleamed, and then, in a sudden movement, the huge bull mounted the cow, which was standing patiently waiting.

Fon felt the colour rush to her cheeks. She was being silly, and she knew it; to farmers this mating of the animals was a business transaction and nothing more. She had come to the farm as a shy, untried young girl, but since then she had become used to the ways of the farm, and the bull was just another animal, she reminded herself.

Just then old Mr Evans, who had his back to Fon, called out joyously, 'Go on, you devil, give my Bessie a good rogering! Let me get my money's worth!'

Jamie had seen Fon, noticed her high colour, but did not seek to ease her embarrassment. Instead, to her chagrin, he appeared amused by her discomfort.

'Ah, look, some refreshments,' he said loudly. The men surrounding the pen turned and took the mugs from the tray, waiting stoically as Fon poured out the strong beer.

Mr Evans tipped his hat to her. 'Sorry if I was a bit coarse, missis,' he said. 'Didn't see you there, mind.'

Fon muttered something, wanting to make her escape, but Jamie was smiling, leaning against the fence, allowing her to hand out the beer.

The bull had stood down, breathing heavily, his task seemingly completed. The evil eyes seemed half-closed, but Fon shuddered, knowing she was afraid of the black beast.

'Refill, missis.' Farmer Evans held out his mug, and Fon bit her lip at his abrupt tone.

She heard the harsh rasping of the bull behind her and turned to look over her shoulder. She had thought the mating over, but now the huge black creature was pawing the ground once more, eyes glinting, his readiness to repeat his performance alarmingly plain for all to see.

Fon placed the tray on the ground, determined to remain no longer, and, catching Patrick's hand, she led him back to the kitchen.

She was angry with Jamie for embarrassing her and more for enjoying her discomfiture. But by the time the men came indoors for their meal, everything was under control. including Fon's emotions.

'Where's Pat?' Jamie asked, seating himself at the head of the table.

'Gone to bed. He's worn out,' Fon said coldly, 'and, incidentally, so am I.'

The last words were spoken quietly, so that Jamie alone heard them.

'A bit of cooking too much for you, is it, then?' Jamie asked, his eyes meeting hers in a level gaze.

It was on the tip of her tongue to tell him that trying to keep the food hot after spending hours cooking it was no joke, but farmer Evans was helping himself to a liberal plateful of meat and a burst of laughter from his companion reminded her that they had company.

'Good job done there, all right.' The farmer's companion, who was so like Ian Evans that he could only have been his brother, slapped a big hand against his thigh. 'Get a good calf out of that cow in due course, I shouldn't wonder.'

'Aye,' Ian Evans agreed, helping himself to more beef. 'Got a fine randy animal there, Jamie, lad! A bit like his master, is he?' He winked suggestively, and Jamie smiled without replying.

'Got another cow coming into season any day now,' farmer Evans said more soberly. 'Bring her up here will I?'

'Please yourself,' Jamie said reasonably, 'though I don't think you'll get finer stock from any other animal in a twenty-mile radius.'

Fon wished they'd stop talking about the animals, at least for the duration of the meal. She told herself it was something she must get used to; it was Jamie's living, after all, and the bull had to pay somehow for its keep.

As though sensing her thoughts, Ian Evans took some shillings out of his pocket and spread them on the white cloth like a conjuror demonstrating his sleight of hand.

64

'That do you, Jamie, man?' he asked, and before any reply was made he turned to Fon. 'Bit of apple pie now, missis, if you please.'

At last the farmer, along with his more jocular brother, took his leave. Tommy stayed to help Fon wash the dishes, and he glanced at her shyly.

'They mean no harm, missis,' he said apologetically, 'though I suppose to a town girl farm ways seem rude and coarse-like.'

'It's all right, Tommy,' Fon said, but even as she smiled at the boy and saw him to the door, she was thinking it should have been her husband apologizing, not the farm-hand.

The late sun was waning, streaking the sky with redness, and suddenly Fon felt lonely for her life in Oystermouth. How simple it had been then; she had worked the oysters in the daytime, gone to chapel, sung in the choir in the evenings, and come home to her bed. Her empty bed, a voice in her ear said, with insidious suggestion.

Was that what she wanted for herself, a lonely bed, empty of Jamie and all that his presence entailed? She put away the dishes and returned to the kitchen, where Jamie was already writing in the account book.

Fon stared at his back, at the dark curls lying against the collar of his shirt, and suppressed the urge to run her fingers through his hair. She straightened her shoulders and took a deep breath.

'I would be obliged if you would warn me in good time when I'm to expect company,' she said, and the tone of her voice was more icy than she'd intended it to be.

Jamie looked up and slowly closed the book. 'Are you giving me orders, then, Irfonwy?' he said, his voice matching her for coldness.

'No.' She felt less certain of her ground. 'I would just like some consideration from you. It takes a long time to cook a dinner, mind.'

65

'It takes *you* a long time, that much is obvious,' Jamie said, his eyes unreadable.

Anger poured like wine through Fon's blood. There he was, silently comparing her with Katherine again.

'No doubt your first wife cooked a fine dinner at the drop of a hat!' she said hotly.

Jamie rose in a swift movement and caught her arms, shaking her a little. 'Don't talk like that, I don't like it.'

Suddenly, all the pent-up frustrations and uncertainties she had felt since her marriage flooded to the surface. Fon put her hands against Jamie's chest and pushed him away from her.

'Leave me alone, don't touch me!' she said fiercely. 'I'm no farm animal, I'm a human being, and I do have some finer feelings even if you do not.'

'Finer feelings, is it?' Jamie said, his eyes narrowing. 'Putting yourself above the likes of me, is that what you mean?'

Fon looked at him stunned. Is that what he thought, that she was looking down on him and all he stood for?

'Go to bed,' he said, suddenly sounding weary, and when she paused uncertainly, not knowing how to heal the rift that had suddenly appeared between them, he raised his voice.

'Go to bed, do you hear me?' He seemed like a stranger to her then, a man with a hard look in his eyes and with a strong set to his mouth, the mouth that had so often kissed her with such passion. Passion, yes, but not with love, Fon thought in despair.

She turned without another word and hurried to her bedroom, undressing quickly, as though her nakedness made her vulnerable. Shivering a little in spite of the warmth of the night, she crawled beneath the sheets and closed her eyes tightly, forcing back the tears. She was still awake when later, much later, Jamie came to bed and, instead of taking her in his arms, instead of holding her against him until sleep overcame them, cupping her breasts, he turned his back deliberately against her.

She felt the broadness of his shoulders and the slimness of his hips before he moved away as though the very feel of her was too much to bear.

Fon lay rigid for a long time and then, slowly, she moved closer to him and put her arms around his waist. 'Jamie.' She whispered his name as though they might be overheard. 'Jamie, I love you.'

He did not reply, and he did not turn towards her, and after a long bitter moment, Fon realized that he was asleep, his breathing even and regular, as untroubled as a babe's. She lay sleepless in the darkness, feeling bereft as, for the first time in her married life, she lay without the joy of her husband's arms holding her safe in their bed before sleep claimed them.

In the morning, after milking, Fon took Patrick to the wood to check on the cows that were in calf. It was a fine day, with a haze of heat mist hanging over the fields. Except for the sound of the birds in the trees, the world seemed a silent place.

Jamie had been awake and out to the fields before she'd risen from bed, and Fon ached to talk to him, to reassure herself that everything was all right between them.

'Moo-moo,' Patrick said softly, and Fon looked in the direction he was pointing.

One of the cows was leaning into the hedge, head down, and somehow Fon knew that something was wrong. She moved closer and saw that the animal's flanks were thinner than they should be for six months in calf. She put her hand to her mouth.

'*Duw!*' she said softly, realizing with a feeling of chill that the cow had aborted of her calf. She looked around the soft fields, under the hedgerows near where the sick animal stood, and eventually found the corpse of the tiny premature calf.

She trembled. Something was wrong, very wrong; healthy cows did not slip their young so easily.

'Moo-moo sleeping.' Patrick pointed to the calf, and Fon took his hand, leading him away. She made her way towards the open fields where Jamie was working, knowing that the news she must give him would cause dismay. To lose animals was always a tragedy, but to lose calves meant something was seriously wrong with the stock.

Jamie was bent over the furrows where the summer potatoes protruded through the soil. His shirt sleeves were rolled up above big muscles, his thick neck standing strongly free of his collar.

Fon stared for a moment, watching him, wanting to go into his arms and make him tell her he loved her. Instead she spoke to him calmly, her voice even, her eyes refusing to meet his.

'There's trouble,' she said quietly. 'One of the cows has aborted. It looks like the cow sickness.'

Jamie straightened and stared at her frowning. 'Go back to the farmhouse. Stay right away from the cows in calf, do you understand?'

Fon was taken aback. Anyone would think she had caused the animal to fall sick. 'But, Jamie, perhaps I can help,' she said, and Jamie brushed the earth from his hands without looking at her.

'Do what I say. Take my son back to the house. Keep him indoors until I come.'

Without a word, Fon led Patrick back to the farmhouse, and as soon as he was occupied with his toys she began to build up the fire, ready to heat the oven for the dough she had proving in the hearth.

What had gone wrong with her marriage, she wondered. It seemed that Jamie couldn't even trust her with the animals now. She sank down at the table and stared at her hands. They were grimed with dust from the udders of the milk cows as well as streaked with coal.

She rose and went to the pump in the yard and washed diligently before dealing with the bread-making.

Later, Jamie and Tommy came back to the farmhouse, and Fon heard them talking outside at the pump. She could not hear the words but she sensed from his tone that Jamie was very troubled.

They ate in silence, and Fon, still smarting from the tone of Jamie's voice, didn't attempt to make conversation. Tommy glanced at her worriedly and Fon stared back at him until the boy looked away in embarrassment.

It wasn't until she and Jamie were working at the books that she managed to get the words out that had been irking her all day.

'Is it my fault the cow is sick?' she asked quietly. Jamie looked at her in surprise. 'Is it something I did wrong in the feeding, or what?'

'Of course not. What in God's sweet earth gave you that idea?'

She wanted to tell him that he did, his tone of voice intimating that she had mishandled the situation, but she kept quiet, waiting for him to go on.

'The cow sickness will surely spread,' he said evenly. 'It can be transferred somehow to humans, so I don't want you going near the animals at all, do you see? And you must keep Patrick away too. I don't want anything happening to either of you.'

A warmth spread through Fon. He cared, he really cared about her as well as his son. Then she realized the utter seriousness behind his words and suddenly she felt chilled. 'Do you think the other animals will get it?'

'Maybe,' Jamie said. 'For sure the cows in calf will abort, but I'm going to do my damnest to try to save the herd and put them to the bull again once they are dry.'

'Dry? You mean we won't even have any milk from them?' Fon asked incredulously.

'The milk, it will be full of the sickness,' Jamie said sternly. 'I will see to the disposing of it, me and Tommy.'

69

'How will you do that?' Fon asked, feeling fear creep over her. If the sickness was serious, what were Jamie's chances of catching it?

'I'll buy in a healthy calf,' Jamie said. 'It will take the milk from the cows until they run dry. It'll have to suckle day and night – it won't be easy.'

He smiled at her suddenly.

'Don't look so worried, I've survived worse things in my time. We'll be all right, trust me, my colleen.'

Her face softened. He had not called her colleen for what seemed a very long time. She reached out and took his hand and the look he gave her healed the breach between them in an instant.

One by one, the cows cast their calves at six months, and Fon knew that for each calf aborted Jamie was losing money. Not only would there be no calves to sell at spring market next year, but the herd of mature cows might have to be slaughtered if they became barren through the sickness.

It was Fon who turned to Jamie now, took him into her arms and kissed and caressed him until she felt him harden in desire. They made love almost desperately; Jamie thrust into her with almost painful intensity, as though at any moment she might be snatched away from him.

Afterwards, as they lay in each other's arms, Fon knew a cold fear that Jamie might contract the sickness and die. She turned her face into his warm shoulder and realized that he too was lying awake, staring the uncertain future in the face with courage, which was more than she could do; for, without her husband, her life would be over. She was bound to Jamie O'Conner with the strongest bonds of all, the bonds of love.

CHAPTER SIX

At the edge of the O'Conner farmland, on a rise of a softly sloping hill, stood the big barn where in the lambing season the ewes were kept. This was Gary the shepherd boy's domain, and here he ruled supreme.

It had always amused Fon that Gary was still referred to as a 'boy', because he was fifty if he was a day, with grizzled white hair that protruded from under a worn cap, and a thin face, as craggy as the hills that sheltered his sheep. But, for all that, Gary was still upright and strong enough to handle the herd at all seasons, from the lambing to the shearing.

His method of shearing was one that fascinated Fon. Gary would manhandle the animal and hold it close to him, almost tenderly, like a lover, and swiftly cut away the thick winter fleece, scarcely ever nicking the vulnerable flesh beneath the wool.

But the sheep, for now, must take second place, because with the cow sickness causing a crisis on the farm, even Gary was needed to help. In just a few short days, all of the breeding cows had become infected.

Gary grumbled constantly and bitterly, but he took his turn bringing the bought, healthy calf to the milk-laden cows morning and night in an effort to save the animals. Everyone on the farm knew the consequences of losing an entire herd of beasts; it would be little short of a catastrophe.

The milk, Jamie insisted, was infected with the sickness, and, in contrast to what other farmers in his situation would do, he ordered that the milk not taken by the calf was to be poured away. It ran, in a white river, into the ditch, much to the disgust of old Gary and the wide-eyed disbelief evinced by Tom.

As a precaution, the big black bull was taken from the vicinity of the farmyard, and tethered high on the hill, away from the infected cows, for to lose his prize bull would be a more bitter blow to Jamie than losing the herd.

Fon was allowed to take no part in any handling of the sick animals; Jamie was set against it. He had his reasons, and Fon understood them well enough. Jamie had lost one wife, he didn't want to lose another.

So Fon's days were easier, but with no animals to milk in the mornings, the first early daylight hours seemed to drag. Fon tried to fill her time with baking good meals for the menfolk and looking after Patrick, but her mind was obsessed with worries about Jamie, fearing that he would wear himself out on what seemed to be a battle he could not win. The only sign of progress so far was that at least one of the cows had dried up, the bad milk having ceased to flow.

These quiet mornings, Patrick could sleep in for as long as he liked, and this gave Fon the opportunity to gather in the eggs from under the hens without the small boy's probing fingers frightening the birds, sending them flying to the ceiling of the hut with raucous cries.

'Good girl, Celia.' Fon's voice hung softly in the quietness of the hen-house. The contented clucking of the birds was soothing as she extracted the still warm egg from under an obedient hen and placed it carefully with the others in the basket.

She straightened, thinking she heard a noise in the yard. Surely Patrick hadn't come down from bed and wandered outside?

She hurried out of the hen-house, fastening the door behind her almost absent-mindedly. Head bent, she was half-way across the stretch of dried earth flanking the farmhouse when she became aware of the black bull standing only a few feet away from her. She took a sharp, indrawn breath; the beast was a solid, dangerous barrier between herself and the farmhouse.

Fon froze in her tracks, not knowing whether to back into the hen-house or try to skirt the huge animal and make for the safety of the house.

She measured the distance with her eyes and saw that there was little chance of outrunning the beast; her only alternative was the hen-house, a frail enough structure which would surely collapse should the bull decide to charge.

The creature lowered his great head and began pawing the ground. As if in a nightmare, Fon saw the dust spurt up in small clouds beneath the angry hooves; the beast was not called the Black Devil for nothing. She swallowed hard, knowing she must think clearly. Any sudden movement on her part would only anger the bull.

Slowly, she began to back up, inch by inch, watching the bull every second. The animal sniffed the air, as if scenting her fear, and moved a few paces towards her, seemingly still uncertain whether to charge or not.

Fon took another step back, caught her heel in her skirt and to her horror found herself falling in a flurry of petticoats. She hit the ground so hard that the breath was knocked from her body, the basket fell from her hand, scattering eggs across the dry ground. Fon stifled a scream and edged away from the towering creature.

There was an evil look in the animal's eye as the bull continued to paw the ground. At any moment now, the creature would charge, and she would be at the mercy of those cruel horns.

Quickly, Fon slipped her skirt over her hips. As she tried to clamber to her feet, she waved the skirt threateningly at the bull.

'Get away!' she shouted, climbing to her knees. 'Go on, shoo!' The act served only to enrage the animal, and with a snort of seeming contempt the bull began to

73

rumble towards her. Fon thought she screamed, but the thunder of hooves against the hard ground filled her head.

She closed her eyes, waiting for the impact, waiting for those pointed horns to pierce her flesh. She imagined in that brief instant what it would be like to be flung like a piece of rag, tossed to and fro, helpless at the mercy of the black bull.

Then she heard Jamie's voice and her eyes flew open. He had a stick through the ring in the bull's nose and was leaning back on it with all his might.

'Fetch the dry cow, Tommy!' he shouted. 'She must be bulling.'

Fon backed up against the hen-house, watching, mouth dry, as Tommy began to run towards the pastures. She knew then what Jamie was about; he would put the cow to the bull, knowing that was the only way to distract and quieten the animal.

Jamie was having difficulty controlling the bull. He cursed and shouted at the beast, which at any moment threatened to toss his great head and dislodge the offending stick and Jamie with it. Jamie was well-built and muscular, but no man's strength was equal to that of an animal like the Black Devil.

Fon saw the sweat on Jamie's muscled arms as he strained to hold the creature still. She had begun to shake; she feared for Jamie more than she had ever feared for herself. It seemed an eternity before Tommy re-appeared, bringing a thin, scrawny-looking cow with him.

He led the creature into the yard and looked un-certainly at Jamie as though waiting for directions. Jamie jerked his head in a fierce gesture of dismissal. 'Let the cow loose and get to hell out of here!' he called.

The bull suddenly scented the nearness of the cow and his huge nostrils opened and closed like door-flaps. Slowly, Jamie removed the stick and stood back, and

74

Fon held her breath as the bull swung his great head to and fro as though to clear it. Then, nostrils flaring, the bull turned towards the cow.

'Thanks be to the good Lord!' Fon said softly.

Jamie was at her side in seconds. 'Come on,' he said quickly. 'Into the farmhouse, and stay there until I tell you it's safe.'

Fon wanted to hold him to her, to feel his heart beat against hers; she feared for him, for his task was far from over.

He seemed to sense her feeling, for his features softened. 'I'll be all right now,' he said. 'The bull will be well pleased with his day's work, and he'll go peaceably when he's had what he came for.'

From the safety of the window, Fon watched as Jamie stood aside waiting for the bull to approach the cow. The animal still seemed angry and uncertain, turning his great head as though sensing a trap.

Patrick came into the room, rubbing his eyes sleepily, and in that moment the bull charged. Fon heard Tommy cry out; she felt her heart lurch, and then before her startled gaze the bull was retreating across the yard.

She saw that Jamie was wielding a thick branch; he had apparently struck the animal a hefty blow with it, and the bull had thought better of attempting to charge such a formidable opponent again. Instead, the animal moved purposefully towards the waiting cow.

It was some time later that Tommy led the now docile bull away from the farmyard and back to his field, and Fon knew that the danger was over. She sighed with relief and moved away from the window, sinking down on to a kitchen chair, realizing that she was trembling.

Now the full import of what Jamie had done washed over her. He had risked the magnificent animal, his pride and joy, putting the beast with the sickly cow. Tears sprung to her eyes; Jamie had risked everything, even his life, to save her. How could she doubt his love? But if only he would say the words out loud, how happy she would be.

She covered her face with her hands. The tears burned against her lids, but she swallowed hard, telling herself not to be so weak and foolish. She was a farmer's wife, she must not break down and cry whenever there were difficulties. But it was a long time before Fon stopped trembling.

Eline closed the door on the gallery with a sigh of relief. It had been a long day, a busy day. She moved tiredly towards the kitchen, where Penny was cooking supper, and sank down into one of the kitchen chairs.

'Tired out, are you?' Penny's soft Welsh lilt was more in evidence than usual: a sign, Eline thought, of her concern.

She smiled at Penny and pushed back a piece of stray curl. 'I am a bit tired, I suppose.' She made an effort to smile; how could she explain to the young girl that it was weariness of spirit that made her tired, that it was the longing to see William, and to tell him she was sorry for her cruel words, that drained her energy, not the honest day's work in the gallery?

Penny was a sweet girl, entirely lacking the usual subservient attitudes of the run-of-the-mill serving maid. But then Penny was from an unusual family. Her parents did not care a fig for convention; they were happy in their unity and left their daughter free to pursue her own ambitions. They did not, as many parents did, insist on her making an early marriage.

Penny's family had been as glad of handouts of food during the hardships of the oyster troubles as everyone else in the vicinity, but now that finances had improved there was every opportunity for Penny to give up her job if she so wished.

'What's for supper?' Eline asked. She enjoyed Penny's

bright company and, in spite of the girl's youth, her almost motherly attitude towards herself.

'A nice bit of rabbit pie,' Penny said proudly. 'The crust is as light and tasty as you'll find anywhere.'

Penny served the meal straight from the stove to the table and sat down to eat. Eline smiled. She had long since abandoned any attempt to act the lady; with Penny there was no need for pretence.

'I'm going up to Swansea, tomorrow,' Eline said softly. She knew she *must* swallow her pride, make a determined effort to see Hari and ask her where Will had gone.

'*Duw*, that heathen place, you want to watch out you don't get your purse robbed while you're there, mind,' Penny said, issuing the dour warning without the least realizing that she knew very little of Swansea except what she'd heard from her parents.

'I'll be careful,' Eline said, suppressing a grimace. Oh, she would be careful all right, careful to ask discreetly about Will's whereabouts, though she had no doubt that Hari Grenfell would see right through her; Hari was nothing if not perceptive.

Eline sighed heavily. Why had she allowed such a situation to develop? She would marry Will tomorrow, give up everything she had worked for if only she could be his wife. But Will was proud and stubborn; he wanted to make his own way in the world, to become a success in his own right, and she couldn't in all honesty blame him for that. The thing she most regretted was her angry, unjust words to him, underlining his own sense of failure.

Eline found it difficult to sleep again that night; indeed, she scarcely seemed to have had any sleep at all since the separation from Will. She lay awake now, eyes wide and dry, looking up at the ceiling, dappled with moonlight, burning to be in Will's arms, to feel his lips on hers. Well, she would not let him go so easily.

Tomorrow she would learn where this shop in Cardiff was situated; she would travel the fifty or so miles to see him, if need be.

She sighed and turned her face into the pillow. Who was she trying to fool? She knew that her courage would fail her when it came to actually making the journey. What if he would not see her, had really finished with her for good and all? She pressed her face into the pillow, and the hard, painful tears came at last.

Hari Grenfell welcomed Eline in her fine suite of rooms above the emporium. 'Please sit down,' she said softly. 'I'm very pleased to see you, Eline, it seems such a long time since you used to come here and discuss patterns with me.'

Eline sank into an upholstered chair and looked down at her hands. She could not make small talk, not even to be polite, because she felt sick and ill and fear seemed to rob her of words.

'It's about Will, isn't it?' Hari urged gently. Eline looked up at her and swallowed hard. She seemed to have suddenly become bereft of pride; nothing mattered save learning of Will's whereabouts.

She nodded her head miserably, wondering if Will would have left instructions that his address should be kept secret, but Hari had drawn a sheet of paper towards her and was busy writing on it.

'Here's the address of the shop in Cardiff,' she said softly. 'I hope you and Will can make up your differences, whatever they are.' She smiled and her lovely face was illuminated. 'You are so obviously in love with each other, it seems foolish to be apart.'

Eline suddenly found her voice. 'I said things, unforgivable things.' She spoke quietly. 'I wouldn't blame Will if he never wanted to see me again.'

'When we're angry, we all say things we regret,' Hari said. 'I'm sure Will knows you didn't mean any of it.'

Had he told Hari about their quarrel, Eline wondered.

She felt the urge to confide in Hari; she had always been fair-minded in the past and she undoubtedly cared very much about Will.

'He won't marry me, not until he's made his way, as he puts it,' Eline said, her voice trembling in spite of her efforts at control. 'I would live in poverty with him, I wouldn't care about anything so long as we were together.'

'Will would care,' Hari said gently. 'He knows what real poverty is.'

Eline looked at her, trying to search beneath the calm expression in Hari's eyes. Hari smiled wanly. 'William will never forget the time when his family fell sick of the yellow fever, all of them dying in poverty and pain,' she sighed softly. 'He would not risk putting you through the humiliation of living and possibly dying in such straits.'

Eline thought about Hari's words, digesting in silence what she had said. Will rarely talked about his childhood; as far as he was concerned, his life seemed to have begun when he became apprenticed to Hari Grenfell.

'Write to him.' Hari's soft words broke the silence. 'Tell him how much you love him; he needs to know that.'

Eline looked at the composed, beautiful woman sitting opposite her, Hari Grenfell, successful, rich and so very kind. She rose to her feet, clutching Will's address like a talisman.

'Thank you for your help,' she said humbly. 'I'll write to him at once.'

'No need to thank me,' Hari said. 'I care very much about Will, and I know you do too.'

Eline let herself out into the street, leaving the plush richness of the emporium behind her with a feeling of reluctance. She glanced back, seeing the fine window display with a feeling of loss. She realized quite suddenly that she missed the world of shoe-making very much.

Why had she left it? Given it all up for a gallery in Oystermouth where she felt loneliness pressing in on her, more and more every day.

Just at the entrance to the emporium, she almost bumped into a slight figure and had apologized in quick embarrassment before she recognized that the young lady standing before her, hugging the hand of a small boy, was Irfonwy Parks.

'Mrs Harries, sorry to bump into you like that!' Fon said in a rush, the colour flooding into her cheeks.

Eline realized that Fon still felt unhappy at the way her mother had laid claim to Eline's husband.

'Fon, don't worry, it was as much my fault as yours. What are you doing in Swansea?' Eline spoke warmly; she had always liked the quiet, shy, youngest daughter of Nina Parks.

'I brought Patrick here for some new boots,' Fon said, drawing the child close to her skirts. 'He's growing so fast that nothing lasts him very long.'

Eline remembered then that Fon was now a married woman, wife of Jamie O'Conner, the handsome Irishman who had bought Honey's Farm, the very farm where Eline was born.

Fon looked well; her skin held the bloom of a life led in the open air, her eyes were bright, her smile ready, and Eline felt herself envying the girl.

'How are you enjoying farm life?' she asked, and Fon's smile widened.

'It's hard work but it's where I belong, with my husband,' she said simply.

Eline wondered that a girl brought up to live at the edge of the sea could adapt so easily to a life of hardship in the fields, of long days, sometimes of sleepless nights when the lambing season came. But then, Fon loved her husband and a woman would do anything for love.

'No problems, then?' Eline asked, and she saw a frown crease the fine skin of Fon's forehead.

'There's been some trouble with the cows,' Fon said. 'Some sickness that made the beasts throw their young too soon, but I think the worst is over now.'

Eline knew the sickness well; it was something most farmers dreaded. 'You didn't have to slaughter the animals, then?' she asked in concern, knowing what such a loss could mean.

Fon shook her head. 'Jamie cared for the poor creatures, looked after them as if they were babbies,' she explained. 'And now they seem to be better. At any rate he's putting them to the bull again, and the first one to recover is in calf already.' She spoke proudly, as though the achievement was shared with her; and so it probably was, Eline thought.

Suddenly, her strivings at the gallery seemed so trivial. Here was Fon facing real problems day by day, alongside the man she loved, and Eline was stuck with selling pictures that merely mirrored life when life was to be lived to the dregs, even though they might be bitter.

Her mind, in that instant, was made up. She would sell the gallery, or at least bring in a manager. She would rearrange her life, give herself something to strive for. She was tired of the blandness of her day-to-day activities, for the gallery practically ran itself; there was no longer any excitement, any challenge left to stimulate her in mind.

'I'd better be going,' Fon was saying. 'I've got plenty of work to do when I get back home.' Her face softened. 'And Jamie, my husband, will be getting anxious.'

Eline watched as Fon led the small boy along the street. She who was going home to where she was needed, to where her presence mattered.

A great loneliness swept over Eline; she was not needed by anyone, she had no-one who would know or even care if she stayed out all day and all night too. Her shoulders were slumped in an attitude of despair as she walked unseeing along the hot pavements to the town.

People – there were people in her life, of course, there were her customers, her neighbours in Oystermouth. There was Penny, who cared for her needs and was concerned with her well-being; but she wanted more than that, she wanted to belong somewhere, to someone, to Will Davies.

'Will,' she whispered, 'why did you go away and leave me?'

But there was no answer to her question. There were only the everyday noises of a busy street, a street on which Eline was totally alone.

CHAPTER SEVEN

It did not take Eline long to put her plans into action. Her first task was to find a suitable person to take over the gallery, and this turned out to be much easier than she'd anticipated. She had for some time been aware of the admiration of Calvin Temple, who patronized her gallery frequently, not always buying, but on occasion taking a few of her paintings up to London to sell there.

Calvin Temple was tall and personable, not shy of showing his admiration for Eline as well as for her gallery. When he next came into the gallery, Eline approached him with a warm smile and invited him to take some tea in her private rooms.

Calvin bowed over her hand, and the light in his eyes showed his pleasure. When she had made the tea, Eline outlined her idea, and Calvin's handsome face broke into a smile.

'You mean you want me to run the gallery for you?' he asked, with such surprise that Eline wondered if she'd overstepped the bounds of propriety. She had believed that, given the opportunity to run the business, in any way he saw fit, Calvin would jump at the prospect.

'It's only a suggestion,' she said quickly. 'If the idea doesn't appeal to you, then of course you are not obligated in any way.'

He sat in the sunny workroom of the gallery, the china cup appearing ridiculously small in his large hands, looking at her with unmistakable warmth in his dark eyes.

'Mrs Harries,' he said with enthusiasm, 'I should be delighted to work with you.'

Eline shook her head. 'You will be working for yourself, Mr Temple. I shall be nothing more than a sleeping partner.'

By his smile, Eline knew that she had used an unfortunate phrase. To his credit, he said nothing, but she couldn't mistake the twinkle of merriment in his eye. At any other time, Eline might have been flattered by his obvious admiration, but now she felt she just wanted the whole business of the gallery over and done with, so that she could get on with making the best of the shambles her life had become.

'You will be here to let me down gently, should I make mistakes?' Calvin asked easily.

Eline's level gaze didn't falter, but she felt suddenly needed for the first time in a long time. 'Do you think you will – make mistakes, I mean?' Eline asked, uncertain of her ground in the light of his apparent amusement.

'I don't think so,' Calvin said thoughtfully. 'But I confess myself ignorant of running a gallery.'

'But the important thing is, surely, that you know how to sell paintings?' Eline asked, moving from her chair to stand at the window. She gazed out at the sea, at the plethora of boats bobbing at the moorings. Everything here at Oystermouth looked so peaceful, so enchanting, and yet now, with Will gone away, it was a place of emptiness for her. But she would go to him, beg him to forgive her; she was determined on it.

'I have no doubts on that score,' Calvin said firmly. 'I have studied paintings all my life; I grew up as the son of one of the best, most famous artists in England.'

'You did?' Suddenly Eline saw Calvin Temple with fresh eyes. She took in his immaculate linen, his fine-cut coat and the hand-made shoes; and the colour came to her cheeks. Calvin was clearly not, as she'd supposed, a gentleman fallen on hard times. Instead, she realized, he was comfortable, to say the least.

'I'm sorry,' she said quickly. 'I hope I haven't insulted you by offering you work, work that I see now is far beneath your station in life.'

'On the contrary,' Calvin said, 'I'm honoured at the trust you put in me. I need something to fill my time, and this gallery is just the thing. Apart from which, I love looking at paintings.'

Eline turned to him and smiled. 'I know. That's why I thought of you when I began to look for someone to run the gallery. I'm afraid I didn't realize that you were a well-to-do gentleman.'

Calvin's smile was disarming. 'That was part of your charm, my dear Mrs Harries. Yes,' he continued, 'running the gallery will be right up my street. I might not be able to paint like my father, which is my great misfortune, but I can recognize talent, even when it is only in the bud. That, I think, is my strength.'

'You'll do it, then?' Eline asked. 'You will take over the gallery, as from, let us say, a week tomorrow?'

'So soon?' Calvin asked. 'And what will you do?' His question might have sounded impertinent, prying even, but he spoke with such gentleness and such a real need to know that Eline unbent enough to tell him the truth.

'I don't feel fulfilled here,' she said softly. 'Oystermouth has many unhappy associations for me. I think it's time I moved away, found something completely different to do with my life.'

He came towards her, standing very close, his eyes searching hers. 'I would very much like to be part of that life,' he said softly.

Eline looked up at him. He was a fine handsome man. Calvin would never have to worry about making a success of anything, for, apart from his illustrious background, as the son of a greatly talented painter, he had a flair all his own for saying and doing the right thing; Calvin was a gentleman in every sense of the word.

There would be no barriers to divide them, Eline

85

realized with surprise, no stiff-necked pride to stand in the way of their happiness. But there would be no love, not on her part; she had given all her love to Will, but Calvin's friendship, that she would treasure.

She sighed heavily. 'I am grateful,' she said, 'but I have a great deal to think about just now.' She added apologetically, 'I must be alone for a time, I feel so confused.'

'I can wait,' Calvin said, smiling down at her. 'I'm a very patient man, and I usually get what I want in the end, you'll see.'

It would be wonderful to have someone strong to take care of her, to make her decisions for her, to hold her and comfort her. Eline smiled up at Calvin, resting her hand for a moment on his arm. 'What will be, will be,' she said softly, and then she moved away from him, remembering that those self-same reasons had made her marry Joe Harries. She'd wanted his support and his strength, but the marriage had been far from a success.

Her tone became brisk. 'I'll leave everything to you, then?' she said, without looking at him. 'You'll see to the legalities concerning the gallery?'

'You can trust me on that,' Calvin said easily. 'I will make sure that our partnership works, don't doubt it.' If there was a double meaning in his words, Eline chose to ignore it.

Later, she walked alone along the edge of the sea, staring out at the distant horizon, where the coast of Devon was just faintly visible like a mysterious land rising up out of the sea. She sighed. Was she doomed to be alone for the rest of her life? It certainly seemed that way. Perhaps she should enjoy Calvin's overtures? Begin to live life to the full, instead of being for ever on the periphery of it, an empty shell of a woman without love or family?

'Rubbish!' She said the word out loud, and a startled seagull flew screaming up into the sky. Eline sank down on to the sand, and it felt soft and hot beneath her fingers. She plunged them deeper into the warmth, catching a shell between her fingers and drawing it free. It was luminous, pearl-like and delicately shaped, and so thin that the edges were razor-sharp. She stared at it. It wasn't an oystershell: she had handled enough oysters to know the craggy, hard feel of an oyster. Perhaps this was a mussel shell; it certainly looked like it, but it was fragmented and broken, and it cracked as her fingers pressed it. Fragile, just as she was at this moment.

Impatient with herself, Eline rose to her feet and moved away from the beach. She was becoming introspective, self-pitying, and it would not do, not at all. She must think rationally now, plan her future, a future that would have some meaning, even if she was to live it out alone.

As she left the beach, she became aware of the shapely figure of Gwyneth Parks, outlined against the pale sand. The girl was standing at the roadside watching her; she was smiling in a way that warned Eline to beware. There was a crisp piece of paper held between her fingers.

'*Bore da*, Eline,' Gwyneth said, and Eline stared at her suspiciously. There was no love lost between them, and it was unlike Gwyneth to make the first move to speak. Her reasons quickly became apparent as she held out what appeared to be a letter.

'Heard from William, I have, see.' She spoke triumphantly, her eyes alight. 'Bet you haven't had a letter from him, have you?'

Eline felt sick; she wanted to run and hide from the pain and the almost violent feelings of jealousy that gripped her. Her mouth was dry. She couldn't speak, but in any case there was no need to; Gwyneth had read her silence well.

'I thought not. I mean, you was probably the reason he wanted to get away from Swansea in the first place.' She hugged the letter to her full breasts. 'Be

87

joining him, I will. In Cardiff.' Her head was high, her chin thrust forward, as though she expected her words to be challenged. They were, at once.

'I don't believe you,' Eline said, but of course she did. Gwyneth must be speaking the truth, otherwise how would she even know that Will was in Cardiff? She could hardly have asked Hari Grenfell; it was doubtful that Gwyneth even knew her.

'Believe what you like,' Gwyneth said, 'but I'm going to see him tomorrow. He wants me, see, not you.'

Slowly, Eline walked away, unable to bear the girl's bright, triumphant look a moment longer. Why did the Parks family always dog her heels, making unhappiness for her on all sides? What had she ever done to them that they hated her so much?

There had been one moment of softening, during the days of the sharp depression that had hit Oystermouth. Gwyneth and her mother had come to the soup kitchen organized by Eline; they had eaten the food she had provided and the two women had been almost approving of her. It had lasted only as long as the soup kitchen, and thereafter the friendliness vanished, to be replaced by the old hostility.

It seemed that where once Nina had taken Eline's man away from her, now it was the turn of Gwyneth, her daughter, to interfere in Eline's life, to destroy any last hope of a reconciliation between her and the man she loved.

Eline longed to cry, but the tears would not fall; instead they lay hard and hot and bitter like a stone deep inside her.

Gwyneth returned to the kitchen and sank into a chair. She smoothed out the letter and read it yet again, even though she knew every word by heart.

It told her that William was sorry he had needed to terminate her employment so abruptly, and that he hoped that she would accept two weeks' wages instead of proper notice. The wages he would give her when he next came down to Swansea.

She sighed over William's flourishing signature, and, holding the sheet of paper to her lips, kissed it longingly. If only it was true, if only Will had asked her to come to Cardiff to work with him. He probably hadn't even thought of it; he didn't know that she would fly to the ends of the earth to be at his side.

She smiled more cheerfully. He was coming down to Swansea; she would see him, talk to him, perhaps persuade him to find her a job in the shop in Cardiff. There, if it was a large store, they would both be living in; she would have every opportunity to be with him.

She began to plan. Tomorrow Mam would be gone to market most of the day; she always did on Wednesdays. The house would be empty. Gwyneth smiled to herself; she would look her best, she would be her most beguiling. She moved to the speckled mirror over the mantelpiece and looked at herself critically. She was quite presentable; there was something of her mam about her, not a bad thing when you remembered that Nina had a way with the men – at least they always seemed to want all they could get from her.

Gwyneth knew she had fine breasts, perhaps a bit too big. They strained at the bodice of her calico frock as though trying to break free. But men liked that, didn't they?

Gwyneth didn't really know, she'd never had a man, not properly. She'd kicked up her heels with the village boys more than once, allowing them just enough familiarity to be exciting, but balking at what her mam called 'going too far'. That way babies were made, and her mam knew that better than most.

Babies, according to Mam, were the ruination of a woman's figure; their coming made the breasts and belly slack and put grey hairs on a woman before her time.

Well, Gwyneth wanted none of that. She was proud of her firm body and she would keep it that way, at least until she had a wedding band safely on her finger. Then it might be a fine thing to have a son, a boy who looked just like William Davies. Hope filled Gwyneth's blood like fine wine running in her veins. Tomorrow, she would see William; that was enough happiness to be going on with.

It was later that day that a bit of good news came Gwyneth's way. She was at the butcher's, buying some fresh pork to make a meal for Will, when she heard the gossip.

'*Duw*, that posh gallery of Eline Harries's is being passed on to a new owner, then?' Mr Bockford in his blood-stained apron was leaning on his cutting slab, talking to the girl who worked for Eline. Penny lifted her head as though to deny such loose-tongued gossip, but Mr Bockford was a handsome devil, and when he smiled it was enough to melt any girl's heart, especially, Gwyneth saw with glee, that of a young girl like Penny.

'Well, yes I suppose there's no harm in you knowing,' Penny agreed. 'A Mr Calvin Temple is taking over, but not buying outright, mind; him and Eline will be partners, sleeping partners, they call it.'

'Do they now.' Mr Bockford took the liberty of pinching Penny's cheek. 'I could do with one of those myself.'

Penny dimpled at him. 'We all know what *you* are like with the ladies.' Penny giggled. 'Need copper drawers they do when you are around.'

Gwyneth listened impatiently, longing for Penny to say more about this Mr Temple who had suddenly come on the scene. As though picking up her thoughts, Penny did just that.

'He's a lovely man, mind, young and handsome, nearly as handsome as you, Mr Bockford.' Penny smiled up at him, and he put an extra rasher of bacon on the snow-white cloth she was holding towards him.

'Soft on Eline, he is, mind. Anyone can see that,' Penny continued. 'If I was her, I'd marry him straight off, no trouble. Worth a fortune he is, so they say, and him such a gentleman.'

'But Eline Harries was walking out with William Davies, wasn't she?' the butcher said, and, noticing Gwyneth, he nodded affably towards her. 'Serve you now, Gwyneth, girl.' His grin widened. 'Always willing to serve the ladies, me.'

Penny, becoming aware of Gwyneth's presence, quickly paid the butcher and wrapped up her purchases. 'I'd better be off then, if I'm to get any work done.' She was wary of Gwyneth and loyal to Eline, and it was clear that she was annoyed with herself for having said so much.

'Day to you, Mr Bockford,' she said quickly and hurried past Gwyneth without looking in her direction. Gwyneth didn't care. She felt elated. What a bit of luck; she had some juicy gossip that would surely drive the wedge between William and Eline deeper than it was already. She had no compunction about it; all was fair when it came to catching a man, and she would be more suitable for Will than Eline, who, when all was said and done, was a widow – used goods, so to speak.

Gwyneth smiled to herself as she walked out into the sunshine, a good piece of roasting meat nestling in the dish in her arms, a nice bit of dripping surrounding it. She would add some fresh-cut carrots and potatoes and pop the lot into the oven to cook slowly. She would show Will what a good wife she could be to him.

'Will is coming back tomorrow.' Hari Grenfell looked elegant in a blue coat and matching skirt, but Eline scarcely noticed, so intent was she on what Hari was saying.

91

'William has some business he wants to discuss with me,' Hari continued, casually. 'Would you like some iced coffee?' she invited. Eline found herself agreeing, thankful that she had unexpectedly met Hari Grenfell in the street.

Eline's mind was racing. Had Gwyneth lied? But then, she *had* known about Will's visit, even if she'd made it sound as if he was coming solely to see her.

As she sat in Hari's luxurious office watching her pour coffee for the both of them, Eline bit her lip, wishing for the niceties to be over and for Hari to talk some more about Will's plans.

As if reading Eline's mind, Hari looked levelly at her for a moment before speaking. 'I think it's about time you two sorted things out,' she said. 'I know you'll think I'm interfering in what doesn't concern me, but I love Will dearly and I happen to think you two are meant for each other.'

Eline forced a polite smile. 'Will is so stubborn, he has such pride.' She paused and sipped the coffee without tasting it. 'I know the gallery was a barrier between us and I've brought in a partner to run the place.'

'I see.' Hari spoke slowly. 'But what do you intend doing now?'

Eline had thought very long and hard about just that question, and through the long, sleepless nights she had come to a decision.

'I'm going to work at new designs for those children with defects of the feet and legs,' she said. 'We've both done work on those lines in the past, and I found it most rewarding.' She smiled apologetically. 'If that sounds pompous, I'm sorry.'

Hari shook her head but didn't comment, and after a moment Eline spoke again. 'My life seems to have been taken up with trivialities, and I've got to do something about it before it's too late.'

'Do you need any help?' Hari asked quietly. 'I'd be glad to inject some funds into the project; it's one dear to my heart, as you know.'

'Thank you, but no. I want to do this alone. I'll work with the less fortunate who can only afford one pair of boots, boots that have to last until they are outgrown. I'll be renting the cheapest premises I can find and buying the most inexpensive leather. The boots and shoes will be functional, not fashionable.'

'Sounds like a very good idea.' Hari sounded doubtful. 'But are you sure you could survive financially, like that?'

'I must try,' Eline said, and Hari nodded as though she realized there was no going back for Eline; she must go forward to a future she had mapped out for herself, a future that might or might not include William Davies. Hari's smile was a little sad.

'Don't worry about me,' Eline said. 'I'll survive. I always do, somehow.'

If both women knew that the words carried more bravado than conviction, none of them spoke of it.

It was a fine sunny day and Gwyneth had the door of the cottage standing open. She had bathed and washed her hair in sweet-scented herbs and put on her best frock. It was one she had worn to work at Will's shop, but she had deliberately left the top buttons of the bodice undone. If she had the charms, she might just as well show them, she reasoned.

The beef was cooked and sliced, ready to serve, and on the table stood a bottle of Nina's home-made wine. It was not a feast such as Will was accustomed to, but the food was good and well cooked, and the wine which Nina had laid down last year was fine and potent. Her mother would not be best pleased that Gwyneth had opened one of her precious bottles, but it was all in a good cause.

Impatiently, Gwyneth waited in the doorway, staring

longingly down the empty street. A dog lazed in the sun, spreading across the cobblestones like a fur carpet, paws outstretched as the animal luxuriated in the warmth of the day.

Then, at last, the tall figure came into view. The springy step was unmistakable, and Gwyneth drew a sharp breath as she watched the man she loved coming towards her. She could scarcely breathe; he was here, William Davies was actually here.

Common sense told her that his visit was simply business. He was paying her money he owed her, nothing more, but surely she *must* be able to make an occasion of it, make it a day he would never forget.

She welcomed him into Mam's parlour with bated breath, trying her best to seem at ease. 'Please sit down by the window,' she said. 'I've got some nice wine for you and a plate of meat and oysters. I hope you'll stay and eat with me.'

He sank easily into the depths of the old, sagging sofa, his long legs spread out before him. 'That's very kind, Gwyneth, but I'll be having a meal with Hari – Mrs Grenfell – she'll be expecting me.'

'That's all right.' Gwyneth hid her disappointment. 'But you'll have a glass of wine, though, won't you?'

'Yes, of course I will.' He sat up straighter, and Gwyneth knew her bodice had fallen open to reveal the curve of her breast as she bent forward over the glasses.

She knew Will was watching her; he was a man after all, a young, strong red-blooded man. As far as Gwyneth knew, he hadn't had a woman, not in the time she'd worked for him, anyway.

He took the glass and smiled up at her. 'I owe you an apology,' he said. 'I know it was wrong of me to go off so suddenly the way I did. I tried to contact you, but when I called round there was no-one in.'

'It was a bit of a shock, mind, I won't deny it,'

Gwyneth said. 'You closing the shop so sudden, like, gave me a real turn.'

'I can only apologize once again.' Will lifted the glass in a salute.

Gwyneth, encouraged, spoke softly. 'I've missed you – I mean missed working for you.' She sighed and topped up his glass. 'I'll have to look for something else, though what I don't know, there's nothing around here.'

Will drank in silence, and Gwyneth knew, with a feeling of triumph, that he was feeling guilty. 'I was going to ask Eline for a job,' she said casually, 'but I don't know if that would be the wise thing to do.'

She looked at Will from under her lashes, but his expression hadn't changed. 'But of course now she's got a partner, she won't want anyone else working for her.'

'A partner?' Will's voice was equally casual, and Gwyneth knew with a dart of excitement that he hadn't heard about this man, Calvin Temple, going into the gallery with Eline.

'He's so handsome,' she enthused, 'a fine gentleman and rich too, from what they say. A Mr Calvin Temple. I suppose you'll have heard of him?'

Will's nod was non-committal. 'I'll have some more of that wine, if I may,' he said. 'It's really quite good.'

Willingly, Gwyneth refilled his cup; he didn't realize, she felt sure, just how potent home-made wine could be.

'Here.' He reached in his pocket. 'I'd better give you your wages before I forget.' He fished about unsuccessfully for a moment, and Gwyneth sat down beside him, pouring wine neatly into his glass. The anger he felt against Eline Harries was making him careless, and he was drinking much too quickly.

'Here, let me,' she said breathlessly and leant across him, pressing herself close as though by accident. She heard his harsh in-drawn breath with a glow of exultation; he might think himself in love with the bloodless Eline but he needed a real woman to take care of him.

95

He must have sensed her feelings, because he put his arm around her in what she believed was a protective gesture which quickly turned into an embrace. She turned her face up, so that his mouth was very close to hers, and closed her eyes, waiting for the kiss that must surely come.

When his lips touched hers, such a fire of joy flared through her that she knew that she could not resist this man. She loved him so much that anything he desired, he could have.

His kisses became more demanding, his lips parting hers. She took his hand and placed it against her breast, and after a moment, he reached inside her bodice, his fingers gentle and caressing.

Her breathing became ragged and she clung to him, knowing that she must have him. If it was only to be this once, if he never came to her again, then so be it; but this moment would be hers.

'Come upstairs, *cariad*,' she whispered softly, and drew him towards the bedroom. 'You need me, Will, come on, it will do no harm, let us enjoy the moment, shall we?'

She was in bed then, in his arms, and he was undressing her slowly and deliberately. He was heady with the wine, but he was far from drunk, and Gwyneth was glad of it, for when he took her, he would remember it and want her again and again, she felt sure of it.

He was a skilled lover, and she knew that she could not be the first with him. Gwyneth felt jealous of the unknown woman. Was it Eline? Had she been Will's mistress all this time, and her pretending to be the good and upright wife of Joe Harries?

Then, when he took her, all thoughts of anything else but his love-making faded. It was so wonderful, so all-consuming, that Gwyneth felt she was drowning in a sea of emotion and sensations.

At last, it was over and they lay curled together side

by side, she against his naked shoulder. How she loved this man, how she wanted him for all time.

'Will,' she said softly, 'you're not sorry, are you?' He leant up on one elbow and looked down at her, his face sober.

'No,' he said, 'I'm not sorry.'

But as he covered her body with his own, desire urging him to take her once again, Gwyneth knew with a sinking of her heart that, well enough intended though his words were, they were lies.

CHAPTER EIGHT

'I intend to buy the fourteen acres belonging to Tommy's mother.' Jamie was seated at the kitchen table opposite Fon, his sleeves rolled up above his elbows, his strong arms browned by the sun. 'Mrs Jones is not too well these days; she's set on moving away to the town to be with her sister.' He paused. 'They'll find the money from the land very useful.'

Fon waited for him to go on.

'We'd keep young Tommy with us, sure enough; perhaps he'd even want to cultivate a few acres for himself. Anyway, we could work all that out.'

Fon looked at her husband doubtfully. 'But, love, there's the few head of cattle that graze those lands; we'd have to take them on as well.' She sighed heavily. 'Anyway, I can't see why those few acres should be important to you.'

Jamie shook his head at her as though he was exasperated by her lack of comprehension. He was frowning, but Fon felt compelled to air her reservations.

'Our own herd is still recovering from the sickness, mind, and prices for cattle are falling; is this a good time to expand, do you think?'

'Got to take the opportunity while it's there, Fon,' Jamie said shortly. 'It could be crucial to us to own the ground rather than allow God knows what to go on alongside our fields.'

He didn't explain further, and Fon watched him as he flicked a page of the account book to look at the previous figures. 'Anyway, one bad quarter doesn't mean all that much,' he said thoughtfully. 'Looking at last year's profit, we should be well away come next spring.'

'We've got the winter to see out first, though,' Fon said, 'and with more beasts to feed we'll be hard put to find the fodder.'

'You may be right,' Jamie agreed, 'but it's buy now or lose the land.' There was a note of determination in his voice.

He looked directly at her then. 'Bob Smale is keen to put in a bid. The land divides their farm from ours, and I don't want that man as a close neighbour. Never did get on with him. A townie, he is, at heart.' There was a wealth of scorn in Jamie's voice. 'Dabbles in newspapers while he neglects his land, letting it run wild. He only wants the Joneses' land because I want it.'

'He's got a lovely daughter,' Fon said. 'I've seen her riding about the place, her silver hair streaming behind her.'

'Aye,' Jamie said, 'she's neglected too, from what I can see of it. A bad lot, is Bob Smale.'

He paused and rubbed at his chin. 'Anyway, Mrs Jones said she'd give me first chance of the land, her Tommy having worked here so long and me prepared to make a deal with him. I'd never have a better opportunity, you must see that.'

Fon sighed. 'Yes, I can see it's tempting. All right, Jamie, but I'm worried. It don't seem right to go spending out money at a time like this, that's all.'

Jamie caught her hand. 'Don't worry, I know what I'm about. I've not farmed all my life for nothing. Look, I've got more tatties than I need, haven't I? We'll sell some of them and some of the root crop too. I've got to clear the fields soon in any case, and that means putting down the surplus crops and covering them over with grass until I can get shot of them. The sooner the better as far as I'm concerned.'

'Tatties and carrots won't bring in much, though,' Fon said gently.

Jamie rubbed back his fall of dark hair. 'They will if I cart the stuff to the market in Swansea. Always wanting good clean vegetables down there, aren't they?'

'I suppose so,' Fon conceded doubtfully, 'though there's plenty of competition from the Gower farms, mind.'

Jamie closed the book with a snap of finality, and though he said no more, Fon knew that he meant to go his own way, whatever objections she raised.

'How's the black bull?' Fon changed the subject. 'Not taken sick since you started him with the cows, has he?' She warmed to the smile that lit Jamie's face.

'The devil couldn't be better! That bull is good and docile, now he's serviced the herd. Looks as if we'll have a fine new bunch of calves out of that prize bull of mine.'

'You think the beasts are over the sickness, then?' Fon asked anxiously. She had been worried that the cows would abort again, and, worse, that Jamie's expensive bull would catch the sickness and die. That would be disaster indeed.

'I told you, my little worrymonger, everything is going to be all right.' Jamie stretched his arms above his head. 'I think it's time we went to bed, don't you, wife o' mine?'

Later, as Fon lay curled in Jamie's arms, her head against his chest, hearing the pounding of his mighty heart against her cheek, her worries seemed to disappear.

Jamie knew what he was doing, she told herself. He had farmed in Ireland when he was a child. And once in Wales, he had taken over Honey's Farm, building up a good stock of cattle for beef and for dairy products.

Fon smiled to herself in the darkness; eventually, if Jamie added to his acreage, he would doubtless work hard and long to make a success of things. The fourteen acres Mrs Jones intended to sell was valuable; he was right, it was too good an offer to pass up.

She snuggled into the warmth of his body and closed

her eyes, and when she fell asleep, she dreamed that she and Jamie owned the whole of the land spreading above the town of Swansea and that she had given her husband fine sons to till the soil. And in her dream, giving birth was beautiful and painless, the way Fon would have liked it to be.

It was a good dream, and in the morning she woke Jamie, kissing his mouth, rousing him to hardening awareness of her as his arms encircled her. 'I dreamed we had sons, Jamie,' she said softly.

He held her close, his hands caressing her with skill, even though he was scarcely awake. 'I'll do my best to make that dream come true, colleen,' he whispered against her neck. 'It will be my pleasure.'

She sighed in apprehension; not yet, her mind cried, she didn't want children yet, not until she was ready for them.

But as he kissed and caressed her, she closed her eyes, surrendering herself to him with a feeling of joy. Everything was going to be all right, of course it was; nothing could hurt them, now or ever.

Will stared at the busy Cardiff street, aware of the strangeness of the place, of the rapid progress of carriages that jostled between the crowds of people, scarcely giving them time to jump clear of the striding hooves and spinning wheels. The noise was incredible; voices were raised of necessity, and everywhere people seemed to be making wide gestures with parasols, walking sticks, or even their arms, as though to emphasize what their voices were failing to express.

He came to the huge shop where Hari Grenfell had a boot-and-shoe counter and pushed open the door of Bell's Emporium with a sigh of relief. At least indoors it was moderately quieter than the street outside.

The shop was something of a bazaar, crowded with ladies in large gowns picking with inquisitive fingers at

101

displays of headless dummies draped in elegant clothes set in an alcove bearing the legend 'Costume Room'.

Further into the long room, almost right at the end, Will could see a small desk at which an elderly lady sat writing painstakingly in an open ledger. This must be the owner. He had not yet met her; she was strangely elusive, and most of his time in Cardiff had been spent in finding himself suitable accommodation.

'Good morning,' he said politely, and after a moment the lady looked up at him, spectacles perched on the end of her aquiline nose, grey hair hidden under a scrap of lace.

'Yes?' she enquired, a trifle coldly. Will's smile froze; it wasn't going to be much fun working with such a dragon, he decided.

'William Davies – I'm Mrs Grenfell's manager,' he explained patiently.

Her frosty gaze didn't waver, though she rose to her feet and stared at him more closely. 'And I am Mrs Bell,' she said, as though he should fall back in amazement at the revelation.

Seeing that her words had very little effect on him, she waved her hand in dismissal. 'You'd better run along downstairs, then, hadn't you?'

She watched him as he looked about him for the stairwell.

'Over there, behind the curtain,' she said impatiently.

Will bowed and, with a sigh of relief, left her and made his way down the stairs.

He gazed round him with a feeling of dismay. If Hari thought that her stock would sell here, then she was sadly mistaken. This place was dark and silent, with no windows and very little lighting. To tempt a customer into such a dismal place would be the work of a genius.

Will made a quick inventory of the stock and saw that virtually nothing had sold in the few weeks since Hari had placed it here. She was wasting her money by renting

102

the premises in Bell's Emporium, and he would have to tell her so as soon as possible.

He returned to the main salon and confronted Mrs Bell. 'I'm not pleased,' he said evenly, and almost smiled as her greying eyebrows shot up in surprise.

'I beg your pardon!' she said in annoyance. 'Let me tell you, young man, that your Mrs Grenfell is privileged to have part of my *very* successful store. I could have let that spot many times over, don't you realize that?'

'I doubt if you could have let the space as anything other than a storage area,' Will said firmly, 'and once I apprise Mrs Grenfell of the facts, then I'm sure she'll wish to make other arrangements.'

Mrs Bell fanned herself with her hand. 'Such audacity!' she said, her coolness vanishing. 'Come with me to my private rooms. I have something to say to you.'

Will followed her upstairs, determined to hold his ground. Hari would be better off cancelling the deal altogether than continuing to throw money away on such a useless venture as this had turned out to be.

Mrs Bell's quarters were light and airy, handsomely furnished and smelling of beeswax polish. 'Sit,' she said commandingly, and Will good-naturedly seated himself in the chair she'd indicated.

'What would please you, then, young man?' she asked, leaning back in a deep, plushly upholstered chair. 'I mean, would you like the front window, perhaps, for a display?' She was being sarcastic, but Will smiled at her, realizing that she was not quite the dragon she'd first appeared.

'That would be a good start,' he said, quietly. 'Mrs Grenfell's window displays are a feature that would attract a great deal of attention.' He paused. 'But then I'm sure you know that.'

'Ah, but would Mrs Grenfell travel here personally?' she said quickly. 'I hear she has a husband and a child

103

to care for. She'd scarcely wish to move about the country, would she?'

'You're right,' Will conceded. 'But she has a protégée, a lady so talented that you must have heard of her.'

'Must I?' Mrs Bell sounded dubious. 'Who is this protégée?'

Will's throat was dry. 'Her name is Mrs Eline Harries. She designed the ladies' boots and shoes with a wide removable cuff – I believe the line was called the cloak boots and shoes?'

'Ah.' Mrs Bell's attention was caught. 'Tell me a little more about this Mrs Harries. Has she got any ties that would keep her at home?'

'She's a young widow,' Will said. 'She has no children, and I think I could persuade her to come to Cardiff, at least for long enough to set up a window display.'

Will was by no means sure he could do any such thing, but matters could not be allowed to rest as they were – Hari would never sell her stock. In any case, he was looking for an excuse to see Eline, to talk to her; he had missed her more than he'd ever thought possible.

'Very well.' Mrs Bell capitulated so suddenly that Will was thrown off guard.

'You mean you want to have Eline, here, to actually do a window display in one of the big windows?' he asked, and a small smile etched the edges of Mrs Bell's mouth.

'That's what I mean. Now go away, young man, and don't come back until you have something more than criticism to offer me.'

Will found himself out in the street, walking aimlessly along through the crowds. His mind was racing: return to Swansea again, try to see Eline and persuade her that this would be a fine opportunity for her – but would she listen?

He was afraid she might be involved with this man Temple; at least that's what Gwyneth's words had implied. Gwyneth. Will took a deep breath. He had been foolish to take the girl to bed. It had all happened on a whim; he was feeling angry at Eline, and the wine had made his blood race. Gwyneth was a very attractive girl, after all. Still, excuses were no good. God knows what she would expect of him now; total dedication and fidelity, no doubt.

What had made matters worse was that Gwyneth had not been the well-practised woman of the world he'd anticipated. He'd lain with her thinking her experienced and ready for an hour's dalliance as he was. It had come as a shock to find that she was a virgin and he was the man who had taken that away from her.

He had been weak, he admitted it. The feeling of having conquered the world that lying with a woman invariably brought him was too much to resist. He was human, a full-blooded man, and when Gwyneth had been so warm, so loving, he had taken her eagerly. The knowledge that she wanted him so badly had been a balm to his pride and release from the emotions so long contained. But at what cost, he wondered ruefully.

Later, when Will had made his way back to his small suite of rooms in one of the narrow back-street boarding houses, he quickly packed a small bag. He would spend a few days in Swansea this time, explain to Hari the problems of the shop in Cardiff and tell her how he intended to remedy them. Then he must see Gwyneth, make his apologies, beg her to forget that the incident ever took place. Then, only then, could he feel free to approach Eline with his proposition.

If Mrs Rees, his landlady, was surprised at his sudden departure, the coins he pushed into her hand quickly mollified her. She agreed that she would keep his rooms aired and ready for his return, and, no, she would allow no-one else the use of them in his absence. This last promise he took leave to doubt, but there was no pinning down a lady the like of the redoubtable Mrs Rees, who

105

was more used to whores and their casual amours than she was to respectable businessmen.

Glancing behind him at the tall grim building, Will knew that he must find more suitable rooms once he was settled; and of course somewhere must be found for Eline, if she agreed to come to Cardiff.

He felt in a light-hearted mood as he strode along the street. He was going home to Swansea, if only for a short time, and soon, very soon, he would be seeing Eline.

'There, that's the last of the tatties picked.' Tommy's voice was hoarse with weariness, and behind him, Fon picked up a small potato that Tommy had missed.

'Here,' she said, smiling, 'pop this into your sack. There's nothing going to waste on this farm.'

'*Duw*, missis, you got sharp eyes,' Tommy said, thrusting the potato into the mouth of the sack. He lifted it up on to his thin shoulder and carried it towards the waiting cart.

Fon watched him move towards Jamie, who was up on the cart, with his son at his side, rearranging the sacks of vegetables in order to make more room. Jamie rubbed his arm across his forehead, and his thick dark hair stood up on end, accentuating his broad forehead and fine-boned jawline.

Her heart ached with love for him. She couldn't wait for the quiet times in the evening when they were alone together in the farmhouse. Soon all that would end; Tommy would be moving in with them, taking the small bedroom next to Patrick's. Then the only times they would have alone would be when they were in their bed.

Tommy's mother had moved out of her cottage earlier that day, taking her small daughter with her. Once Tommy had cleaned up the little place, it would be occupied by the labourer Jamie had taken on to help with the extra land.

Fon's spirits sank. How could they afford the extra

expense? The labourer had a wife and a young family; they would all expect to live on what Jamie could pay. It was a bad time to be taking on extra responsibilities, just when farming seemed to be meeting with hard times.

'Let's get these tatties put down,' Jamie called to Tommy. 'We'll get them in the old shed and cover them with grass, and next week we'll be down the market with them.'

Fon sighed; of course they needed an extra hand. There would be more work with the sheep, for a start. The animals would have to be sheared before long, and Gary could not manage it all alone.

The cows in calf still needed close watching, and now Jamie was proposing to spend some time in the market, he would be worn out with it all.

She followed the slowly moving cart to the hollow of land to the rear of the farmhouse, where Jamie was resting the potatoes. Patrick, sitting at the back of the cart, clung to her hand, and Fon saw that he was chewing on an earth-covered potato.

'*Uch a fi*,' she said, scoldingly, 'Fon's got to wash that before you can eat it, and cook it in the pot on the fire too, otherwise it'll make your tummy bad.'

Patrick gave up his prize without resistance and toddled after the horse and cart, his plump legs working like pistons as he tried to keep up.

Fon left Patrick with Jamie while she saw to the stew and cut up huge chunks of freshly baked bread for the evening meal. She sang as she worked, determined to stop worrying about the future of the farm. Jamie was a man grown; he was more experienced at farm matters than she could ever be, and perhaps he was right, risks sometimes needed to be taken. And yet she couldn't help but see the figures in the accounts book and how alarmingly the costs were rising above the profits.

Later, she took advantage of what might be one of her last evenings of privacy before Tommy came to live with them and stripped to the waist, washing out her long hair in the tin bath in the kitchen.

She sensed rather than heard Jamie come up behind her. He cupped her breasts in his hands and kissed the nape of her neck.

'You are so beautiful, colleen,' he said softly.

'Don't!' she reacted instinctively. 'Patrick will see.'

Jamie kissed her again. 'No, he won't, I've put him to bed, where he obligingly fell fast asleep almost at once. I've got you in my power now, Fon, my colleen, and I am your husband, and you will remember that you promised to obey me in all things?'

'I promised,' Fon said smiling. 'But let me dry my hair, Jamie, it's dripping all over the place.'

He turned her over on her back and set her gently against the softness of the blanket he'd put ready on the floor.

'Ah, got all this planned, have you?' Fon pushed the wet hair out of her eyes and saw Jamie poised above her. He smelt of fresh soap and water, and his hair, too, was hanging in wet strands across his forehead.

'You fool!' she said tenderly, and then he lowered himself towards her, and she gasped with the suddenness of it, and then she was no longer laughing but clinging to him as though she would never let him go.

It was dark when Fon opened her eyes. She sat up in bed wondering what had woken her. Then she heard the sound of banging coming from somewhere at the back of the house.

'Jamie!' she said urgently. 'Wake up, something's wrong!'

He was out of bed in an instant, pulling on his trews. 'Jesus, Mary and Joseph! It sounds as if the bull is loose again, and in a fearful temper, by the noise of him.'

Quickly Fon pulled on her skirts. A cold fear gripped her as she remembered the way the bull had of looking at her with evil eyes.

108

It was difficult to see in the darkness, and she heard Jamie's voice calling urgently for her to stay back, out of harm's way. She held her shawl around her shoulders, and as her eyes grew accustomed to the gloom, she saw that Jamie was making for the shed where he'd stored the spare tatties.

She heard his voice shouting at the enraged animal, which had somehow become trapped inside the shed. Already some of the wooden sides were splintered into fragments, and, as Fon watched, the bull broke out of the shed and careered off across the fields.

'Jamie!' she called, running frantically across the ground, 'are you all right?'

He was standing where the door of the shed had once been. In one hand was a piece of wood with which, she guessed, he had fended off the bull; in the other was the lantern, which Jamie was holding high above his head.

Before him, the ground was stamped into nothing but a bed of turned-up soil; the potatoes were gone, crushed into nothingness.

She flung herself into his arms and held him fast. 'Jamie, thank God you are all right,' she said breathlessly.

'Aye.' His tone was dull. '*I'm* all right, but the tatties have gone, and, worse, so has the Black Devil.'

He led her away from the ruined shed. 'This was purposely done,' he said. 'There is no way the bull could shut himself inside the shack and close the door.'

'But who?' Fon asked in bewilderment. 'Who would do this to us?'

'I don't know for sure,' Jamie said, 'but I intend to find out.'

Fon felt a chill of apprehension. Someone, it seemed, hated Jamie enough to wish him harm. She shivered as he led her back to the farmhouse, glancing behind her at the darkness. Somewhere out there was an enemy; but what face did that unknown enemy wear?

CHAPTER NINE

Eline stared at the trees surrounding her, at the great lake where the swans glided elegantly along the surface of the water, at the soft clouds above her head, anywhere but along the pathway where, at any moment now, Will would come walking towards her.

He had asked to see her, and Eline, opening his letter, had felt hope surge through her. Her hands had been trembling as she'd read his signature, and in that moment, she realized how very much she had missed him.

Common sense told her not to see him again, but she had been unable to resist the opportunity of being with him, seeing his handsome face, watching the way his mouth curved into a smile as he looked down at her; then she could pretend, if only for a few moments, that everything was all right between them.

Her hopes were false, because his letter had been formal enough; he needed, it said, to talk to her about business. Eline told herself she was foolish to feel such disappointment at the lack of any warmth and personal communication in his words, but she had agreed to speak with him.

Perhaps, she thought hopefully, the business proposition was simply a ploy, an excuse for them to be together again. She loved Will; she wanted to live out her life with him; why not tell him so and test his reaction? If he turned her down, then at least she would know where she stood.

Something caught her eye, and looking along the path she saw the tall, familiar figure striding towards her. She

110

would know those broad shoulders and that easy stride anywhere. Now that she had set eyes on him, her gaze seemed fixed on him; she couldn't look away and she didn't want to. She drank in the sight of him, the square jaw and strong mouth. How she longed to feel that mouth capture hers.

Then he was there, beside her, seating himself, not too close and yet not leaving too much distance between them. His eyes were unfathomable, and suddenly Eline found that she was frightened; how could she ask him a direct question about his feelings for her? She simply was not brave enough.

'I've missed you, Eline.' The quietly spoken words brought hope flaring within her, and Eline smiled up at him tentatively.

'I've missed you too, Will.' She held out her hand, and he enveloped it in his; and suddenly the whole world seemed to be full of sunshine and happiness.

'I've been so stupid,' Will said, looking away from her and across the lake.

She trembled, forcing herself to speak evenly. 'Haven't we both been acting like children?' She rushed on before he could speak again. 'I'm to blame, I said cruel words to you, words I didn't mean. I'm sorry, Will.'

'*You* are sorry!' He sounded angry, but not with her. 'Then you don't really know the meaning of the word.'

He seemed to make a great effort to smile then. 'I've something I must tell you; you might hate me for it, but I must speak the truth. Will you listen to what I have to say, Eline?'

She put her finger on his lips. 'Don't, Will. Let's just forget we ever quarrelled.' She felt frightened, knowing, intuitively, he was about to say something she wouldn't wish to hear.

'Please, Will, let's put the past behind us and look to the future. Tell me about the business proposition you wrote about in your letter.'

He sighed heavily. He was silent for a long moment, as though trying to make up his mind about what to say to her, then he smiled.

'It's Hari Grenfell's business, really,' he said. 'She's taken a place in Mrs Bell's Emporium in Cardiff. She's put me in to manage it.' He shrugged and leant a little closer to her. Eline felt her heart begin to beat more swiftly as she breathed in the fresh, clean scent of him.

'But it's not doing well, not at all. What we need is a good showcase, a well-dressed window, and that's where you come in, Eline.'

Eline was surprised and not a little disappointed at Will's words. She'd imagined that Will was going to suggest they went into partnership, or at least ask her advice about a business of his own.

'You want me to come to Cardiff?' she asked, wanting to go into his arms and kiss away the line between his brows, not talk about business. But he was frowning, as though this issue was the most important thing in the world to him.

'Yes, I want you to come up to Cardiff,' he said, and his tone held much more meaning than the mere words expressed. Or was that just wishful thinking on her part?

'No-one else could do the window justice as you could,' he continued enthusiastically. 'It will save the enterprise, that's how I feel about it. Something must be done, or otherwise Hari might just as well pack it all up and leave the premises. She'll never sell anything from the black hole where Mrs Bell has put her stock.'

'I see,' Eline said thoughtfully. She had no objection to working for Hari Grenfell, none at all, and if she could promote her own ideas for remedial footwear along the way, then it might be worth going to work in Cardiff.

In any case, the urge to be with Will, to work with him, have a chance of repairing their relationship, meant that she couldn't think of turning the opportunity down. She and Will seemed to be edging tentatively towards a renewed understanding, and she didn't want to do anything to spoil it.

'Your gallery,' Will said. 'I don't want you to neglect your painting, but on the other hand . . .'

Eline waved her hand. 'That's no problem,' she said. 'I've brought in a manager; he'll take care of everything. I wanted to get out of that and do something different anyway.'

A strange look crossed Will's face. 'A manager?' he asked, and for some reason Eline felt she was on the defensive. It was clear from Will's tone that he had already heard about her move.

'Calvin Temple,' she said quietly, 'a very capable, personable man. I'd trust him implicitly; he is more than capable of running the business alone, if that's what you're worried about.'

Will seemed to relax. 'You'll come then, to Cardiff?' he said, a smile turning up the corners of his mouth. The frown had gone from his forehead, and it was as though an important point had been cleared up to his satisfaction. It couldn't be that he had been just a little jealous of Calvin Temple, could it?

'Will.' She put her hand on his arm; she felt brave suddenly, able to conquer the world. 'This man, Calvin, he means nothing to me. I don't know if you've been told anything to the contrary, but if we are to begin again, there must be complete trust between us.'

Will looked away from her. His eyes seemed to be anguished, and a cold finger of fear touched her as she stared at him, waiting for him to speak.

'You're right,' he said. 'And now I know there is a matter I *must* talk to you about, Eline.'

She felt her stomach lurch. She had prevented him from speaking about what was troubling him once, and now by her own words, she had forced him into what she knew was a confession she would not want to hear. She longed to put her hand over his mouth, to stop him

113

from uttering the words that she knew were going to spoil things for them. But instead she clasped her hands in her lap and forced herself to remain still and silent.

'It's Gwyneth Parks,' he said, and the words seemed forced from him.

'I somehow thought this would have something to do with *her*,' Eline said bitterly.

William looked at her appealingly. He tried to speak, but it was as if he couldn't utter the words.

'You've slept with her,' Eline said flatly, making it easy for him.

'I can't explain what I did, Eline' – he sounded defensive now – 'except that I'm a man, with a man's needs.'

'And that excuses everything,' Eline said harshly, unable to bear the pain of his betrayal. The picture of him in bed, holding Gwyneth close, kissing her, making love to her, sprang into Eline's mind, and the thought was like a knife tearing into her heart.

'I know it excuses nothing,' William said, his voice hardening, 'but I'm only human and Gwyneth was there, warm and wanting me. Do you know what a balm that was, to actually be wanted instead of being turned away all the time?'

His words turned the knife deeper, more painfully. Jealousy seared through Eline, hot, blind jealousy.

'Oh, I can count on the Parks women to be always there to take my man from me. This isn't the first time it's happened, after all.'

Eline's voice rose in anger. 'Gwyneth's mother, Nina, was the first – she took my husband from me, remember?'

Eline wanted to hurt Will, to pay him back for the deep pain she was feeling. 'I suppose I should be used to it by now. I should know the shallowness of men well enough. A pretty face, a willing whore, and they fall, just like a child.'

'Eline,' William said forcefully, 'you are reacting like a child yourself. I was carried away by the moment; it meant nothing to me, believe me.'

'Tell that to Gwyneth Parks,' Eline said, anger burning at her. 'I'm sure she'll be delighted and flattered to hear it.'

Will turned away in exasperation. 'I can't say anything right now, can I?' he said, his voice low.

'No.' Eline rose to her feet feeling as though her world had crumbled around her. 'You've destroyed everything between us, Will, you know you have.'

He stood up, towering over her, his face dark. 'So that's how little I mean to you! That one act could ruin everything between us.'

He stared down at her, as angry as she was now. 'You are a cold woman, Eline, and do you know what I think?' He rushed on without waiting for a reply. 'I think you are glad this has happened, glad of an excuse not to commit yourself to a relationship with me. Are you afraid of giving, Eline, is that what it is?'

'Just like a man,' Eline said, wanting to strike him. 'Turn the tables, make everything my fault, then you can feel better.'

She lifted her hands in the air and resisted the urge to beat at him with her fists. 'Oh, just leave me alone, can't you? Leave me alone!'

She strode away down the path, not seeing where she was going for the blind rage that consumed her. She hated William Davies, she wished she'd never set eyes on him.

Gwyneth Parks stared around at the unfamiliar streets of Cardiff, feeling a sense of unreasoning panic. She was used to the quiet village streets of Oystermouth. She visited Swansea, of course, and there the busy streets were cluttered with carriages and thronged with people; but somehow none of it seemed as foreign as the pavements she walked now, seeking the emporium where Will worked.

It was only her driving need to see him again that had forced her to make the journey at all. She had lain in his arms, they had become lovers, and yet since then she had seen nothing of him.

She had waited for him to come to her, but she had waited in vain. Common sense told her she meant nothing to him, but her heart and her body longed for him. She knew that, whatever the cost to her in pain, she must see him again and talk to him.

It had taken her a long time and a lot of questions to find out where Will had gone, but at last she had found him and now her hands trembled in anticipation as she thought about being close to him once more.

She stood outside Bell's Emporium, looking up at the shabby but elegant façade, and her heart was beating so swiftly that she thought she would be ill. What would he say when he saw her? Would he be angry, reject her, or would he smile and welcome her?

Well, she would never know if she just stood here in the street like one of the stuffed dummies in the shop window, she told herself fiercely.

Inside the emporium, it was like nothing Gwyneth had ever seen before. It was not an orderly place like the emporia of Mrs Miller or Hari Grenfell, but a hotch-potch of clothing and bales of material and dusty shelves that stared emptily across the shop.

An elderly woman came towards her, her long black gown and jet beads reminiscent of the queen in mourning for Prince Albert. She looked frostily ahead of her, and it took all Gwyneth's courage to ask about William.

'Mr Davies has his boots and shoes downstairs,' she said coolly, as though begrudging him the room he occupied. 'I do hope you are a customer and not some – some *follower*?'

She said the word as though it implied that Gwyneth

was a harlot, and, resisting the urge to retort rudely, Gwyneth put on her 'posh' voice, one she'd used when serving customers in Will's own shop at Oystermouth. Those had been happy days; she'd had Will all to herself then.

'Of course I'm a customer,' she said, glad that she had worn her best frock and her good boots.

The woman walked away, head high, as though anyone low enough to visit the boot-and-shoe counter was beneath her notice.

Gwyneth made her way down the curving stairs to what seemed a long, dark cellar. How Will expected to sell shoes in this place, she couldn't imagine.

He was placing boots on a shelf, his long frame reaching upward, his face turned slightly away from her. She ached for him. She longed to go to him and put her arms around him and beg him to love her.

'Hello, Will,' she said softly, feeling suddenly shy of him. The thought of being in his arms, of becoming his lover, burned in her mind, and she felt the heat come to her cheeks.

'Gwyneth.' He came towards her and took her hands, and relief and joy flooded over her. 'What brings you up to Cardiff, then?'

'I wanted to see you, of course,' Gwyneth said quickly, nerves making her trip over her own words. 'I missed you so much, I didn't know what to do, so in the end I decided to come and see you.'

'Well' – he looked at the clock on the wall – 'it's time I stopped for a break. How about coming to the tearooms with me?'

She swallowed hard; it was as if he was offering her a pearl beyond price. 'That would be lovely,' she said, the words coming out in a rush.

The Cambridge Hotel was only a few doors away from Bell's Emporium, and Gwyneth felt that she floated rather than walked into the sunlit room decorated with

117

potted palms and scattered tables covered with gleaming white cloths. At the back of the room, a trio of musicians were playing softly. It was so romantic, so unlike anything Gwyneth had ever seen, that she stared around her, wanting to savour every detail of the wonderful moments she was sharing with Will.

Gwyneth was nonplussed when an elegant waiter held her chair for her. She looked uncertainly at William.

'Please' – he gestured with his hand – 'take a seat, Gwyneth, and then we'll see what we can order for luncheon, shall we?'

She was grateful to him for putting her at ease, and when the waiter glided away she relaxed a little, glancing around at the other people in the tearooms. There were elegant ladies wearing sweeping skirts with enormous bustles, and suddenly she felt shabby and ill at ease.

William seemed to understand her feelings, because he smiled at her encouragingly. 'You are the envy of the other ladies,' he said. 'You look so fresh and charming and so much younger than most of them.'

She warmed to his words; she'd not known what to expect from him. He might well have been angry with her for chasing after him in what was a most unseemly, unladylike manner. But they were lovers, after all, she reminded herself with a feeling of warmth; she had the right to some consideration, didn't she?

'Now, how about some fresh salmon to start and then some lamb with a side dish of creamed potatoes?' Will said, reading the page before him with what appeared to be intense interest.

'They *cream* new-picked potatoes here?' Gwyneth asked in disbelief. 'What a waste of a good spud!'

She saw that William was trying not to smile. 'Aye, it *is* rather wasteful, isn't it?' he agreed, 'but very, very tasty, spiced with pepper.'

'All right, then,' Gwyneth said, and added, as an after-thought, 'That would be lovely, thanks.'

The meal was, as Will had promised, a delicious treat, and the salmon was followed by lean lamb chops in mint jelly and baby carrots and a small portion of creamed potatoes.

Even though Gwyneth protested that she needed nothing else to eat, Will insisted on ordering a dish of fresh fruit soaked in brandy.

'I've never tasted such food,' Gwyneth said in wonder.

Will smiled rather wryly. 'I must admit that it's not my usual fare, but today is rather special, isn't it, Gwyneth?' he said.

She looked at him, trying to read his expression, wondering what exactly he meant. Was he, could he be, proposing marriage?

When they had finished eating, Will led her through to a huge room that was furnished with soft leather sofas and enormous leather chairs. Above her head were chandeliers with what looked like diamonds suspended from them, droplets of light and colour.

'*Duw*, will you look at this, then?' she said in awe. 'I've never seen anything so wonderful in all my life.'

She looked at William and made up her mind to ask him a direct question. She took a deep breath, but before she could speak, he'd leant forward, his expression earnest.

'Gwyneth,' he said softly, 'the other day, I shouldn't have – have taken advantage of you. I'm very, very sorry.'

Gwyneth felt her elation fading, along with the belief that he was going to ask her to marry him.

'Well, I'm not sorry,' she said quickly, 'not a bit sorry. I wanted you then and I want you now.'

She had nothing to lose, she might as well put her cards on the table, she decided. 'I'm not going to go away and forget you, if that's what you're going to ask me to do.' She stared at him defiantly. 'I love you, Will, I can't help it, I . . . just love you.'

He frowned, and she saw that he didn't know what to

say, so she rushed into speech again. 'I know I'm far beneath you, I'm not a lady as some of your fine friends are.' She lifted her head high. 'But I'm as good as Eline Harries, mind, *and* you are the first, the only man in my life.'

Will looked away, and Gwyneth felt tears burn her eyes. 'Look,' she said, 'just let me be with you sometimes, *please*, Will. I can't live without you, you must know that. Why else did I follow you all the way to Cardiff?'

She saw a mixture of feelings cross his face; he didn't know what to say. 'Let me stay with you tonight,' she said softly, 'and I promise I won't ask you for things, I won't ask to sleep with you or anything like that.'

'Gwyneth!' he said beseechingly. 'I can't offer you anything. I'm just a working man with no private means. This' – he waved his hand to encompass the grandeur of the room – 'this is as much a treat for me as it is for you. I don't live like this all the time. I have a room, a small suite of rooms, in a cheap boarding house. I'm *poor*, Gwyneth, just like you.'

'Let me come home with you for tonight,' Gwyneth begged again, only hearing what she wanted to hear, that he had a suite of rooms. 'I will go home tomorrow. Just let me have this one night with you; can't you even give me that much?'

William sighed. 'All right.' He took a key from his pocket. 'Here, I have to get back to work. The boarding house is a few streets away, in Compton Court. The landlady is not the type to ask questions; she minds her own business.'

Gwyneth took the key and held it as though it was a good-luck charm. She clutched it between her fingers, feeling as though Will had given her the whole world.

When he'd returned to work, she wandered around for a while looking at the fine array of shops. The streets did not seem so alien now. For tonight she would be in

Will's arms; for tonight he would be hers, she was determined on it.

Later, when he came in from the emporium, Gwyneth greeted Will with a pot of tea and some fine lardy cake that she had bought in the shop on the way to his lodgings.

'This is nice,' he said as he shrugged off his coat. 'I am grateful, Gwyneth, but you shouldn't have gone to any trouble.'

'It was no trouble,' she said, and she meant it, shopping for Will's tea had given her the illusion that she was married to him, a respectable housewife going home to her man.

'I'm not very hungry after that huge luncheon,' Will said, sitting at the table. 'A bit of cake and a cup of tea is just right.'

'I know what you mean.' Gwyneth smiled. 'I don't want much myself.'

Will seemed almost ill at ease, and after he had eaten, he got up and paced through to the bedroom. Gwyneth cleared the table and took the dishes into the tiny kitchen.

She had soon made herself at home there; the place was so small there was hardly room to stand at the strange-looking stove to boil the kettle. Will must be very hard up indeed. This was a far cry from his rooms in Oystermouth, where he was waited on like a lord, his meals cooked, his rooms cleaned daily. But Gwyneth didn't mind that he was hard up; in a way, it drew them closer. He did not seem so unobtainable any longer.

The evening passed in desultory conversation. Will was working on some figures, something to do with the stock in the boot-and-shoe shop, and now and again he would look up at Gwyneth and smile apologetically.

After a while, she searched out some of his shirts, looking for missing buttons, and spent a happy hour repairing his linen.

121

She glanced covertly around her. In the light from the fire, the room looked more intimate, more comfortably furnished, than it had seemed at first. From outside came the sound of children playing, voices raised in shouts of laughter as the dying sun faded behind the buildings.

Then, at last, Will closed his books and stretched his arms above his head. 'I think I'd better get to bed,' he said. 'I've got to be up early in the morning. I'm no man of leisure, just a hard-working shop manager, and it's not much of a shop at that.'

He glanced uncertainly at Gwyneth, and she smiled up at him. 'Don't you mind me; I'm going to finish this bit of sewing and then I'll get my head down on this lovely big sofa by here.' She looked away from the relief in his eyes. 'Don't you worry, now, you just get to bed, right?'

When she heard the door close behind him, Gwyneth hugged the shirt she'd been mending to her and breathed in the faint scent of William that clung to it. She closed her eyes in anguish. She loved him; it wasn't right that he should be shut in there, away from her, she wanted him, and she knew he was a hot-blooded man; so how could he turn her away if she went to his bed?

She slipped off her best dress and put it carefully over the arm of a chair; she would have to wear it tomorrow to go home. The thought tore at her painfully, and with renewed determination she took off the rest of her clothes.

Quietly, she opened the door to his bedroom, and on bare feet made her way between the shadows cast by the curtains, to his bed.

She lifted the covers and slid in beside him, and after a moment she put her arms around his waist, her cheek against his back.

'I'm sorry, Will, I can't keep away, I love you so much,' she whispered. 'Just give me tonight, just tonight, and tomorrow I'll go home like a good girl.'

He hesitated, his shoulders tense, and then, with a sigh, he turned and took her in his arms.

Gwyneth drew in a sharp breath as his flesh touched hers. She knew in a moment of triumph that he was roused, he wanted her as she wanted him.

'Will, *cariad*,' she breathed, 'my fine handsome man, I'd die for love of you.'

She clung to him, and as his mouth came down on hers she felt humble and grateful; for at this moment, for this moment at least, Will Davies was her man, and no-one could ever change that.

CHAPTER TEN

It seemed to Fon that their bad luck, hers and Jamie's, had begun on the night the spare crop of potatoes was ravaged by the angry bull. It had been bad enough losing the revenue from the surplus potatoes, which they had hoped to sell at the market in Swansea; but since then matters had become decidedly worse.

Tom had decided to go with his mother when she moved, instead of coming to live at Honey's Farm, which left Jamie short of a farm-hand at a time when he most needed help.

Facing him was the enormous task of lifting the later variety of potatoes and liming the fields ready for the transplanting of the cabbage and cauliflower. There was the grass to cut for hay, and the cows still needed to be carefully watched in case the sickness returned. With only one labourer, times were going to be very difficult indeed.

'We can't go on like this, Jamie, love.' Fon threw down her pen, the list she was making swimming before her tired eyes.

'I know, colleen,' Jamie said. 'I think perhaps you should go into Swansea and place an advertisement in the *Cambrian* for more help. Even casual labourers would be better than nothing.' He shrugged. 'I don't like going to Smale for anything, but as he owns the paper, I've no choice. Anyway, I shouldn't think he'd actually work in the office himself, and to advertise is the only thing we can do, now I must have help.'

Fon picked up the list and studied it again. 'You're right, the grey cow should be coming into season any day now,' she said, 'and shortly after that, it'll be Bessie's turn. Thank God the Black Devil came back. You want to use him again, don't you?'

'Aye, sure I do, if I can spare the time.' He leant back in his chair, and Fon saw with a feeling of pain that he had dark shadows beneath his eyes and a new furrow between his brows.

'Can't we sell off some of the herd?' she said quickly. 'That would cut down the work a little bit.'

'Well, love' – Jamie rubbed at his eyes – 'we could sell off the finished beasts, the few bullocks we've been growing for beef, I mean. I could do with the money, to tell you the truth.'

He sighed. 'But it's help in the fields I really need, or all my hard work will be lost. If the greens are not transplanted soon, it will be too late and we'll lose the whole crop.'

'I know, and then there's the grass,' Fon added. 'You must have help to cut it, Jamie, or you'll lose more than the crop; your health and strength will suffer.'

He smiled suddenly, his white teeth gleaming against the tan of his skin. 'Don't fret, girl, I won't lose my health and strength for *some* things.'

Fon felt the colour run into her cheeks even as she laughed with him, for Jamie was indefatigable in bed; however tired he was, he always found the energy to make love to her.

'If only Patrick was older,' Jamie said thoughtfully, 'he would be a great help to me. A farmer needs sons to survive in these difficult times.'

Fon looked down at her hands. 'We will have babies, Jamie,' she said wistfully, 'but now is not the right time.'

Jamie shrugged his big shoulders. 'Now is not the right time, Fon.' His reply was a little curt, and Fon knew why, well enough. It was becoming something of a bone of contention between them that she wasn't anxious to have children.

125

'I'll go into town, later,' she said, changing the subject, 'put an advertisement in the *Cambrian*, as you suggested. It might help.'

Jamie worked the potatoes all the morning, and Fon, with Patrick at her side, did her best to help him. It was a backbreaking task, bending and lifting the earth-bound vegetables, and Fon stopped and eased herself upright, pressing her fingers against her spine. Perspiration gleamed on her forehead, and her entire being felt as though she had been on a rack.

Patrick did his best, his chubby fingers digging into the soil. Smiling encouragingly, Fon looked down at him.

'Good boy,' she said. 'Look how quickly the sacks are getting full.' But when she looked ahead at the field stretching out before her, with only a quarter of the crop lifted, her heart sank.

'Can't we get the other labourer in to help us?' she asked, but Jamie shook his head.

'Dewi's working on the grass. His wife is helping him for the present, though even *he* is going to leave when the new baby is born; going to the town to get work, so he says.' Jamie sighed. 'No good standing here talking. It's all got to get done and quickly. We don't know how long the fine weather will last.' He moved closer and kissed her mouth, and he smelled of earth and grass and sun, and love poured through Fon's veins, bringing a sense of renewed energy.

Later, she left Patrick in the fields with Jamie and made her way down the hill, glad to be walking instead of constantly bending over the furrows of potatoes. The air was fresh coming in off the sea, and Swansea, as always, was a busy bustle of people, all intent on following their own pursuits.

Fon was glad of a change of scene and of a rest from the seemingly endless work on the farm. The town was thronged with traffic, with colour and excitement, then

Fon became aware of the shadows falling from racing, stormy clouds on to the cobbled streets. One or two of the grander ladies sported bright parasols, clearly anticipating rain. Fon sincerely hoped they would be proved wrong; rain, right now, would delay work on the farm for some time, especially the cutting of grass.

At the *Cambrian* offices, the man at the desk, with his collar askew and ink on his fingers, looked somewhat familiar to her. She smiled, attempting to be friendly, as he took the slip of paper from her.

'Work on Honey's Farm, do you, missis?' he asked, his eyes falling to her bodice, his open gaze making Fon feel vulnerable and threatened. 'There's a lovely colour on your skin; comes of being in the open air so much, I suppose.'

His attempt at flattery was embarrassing, and Fon spoke quickly. 'I'm the farmer's wife,' she said quickly. 'Mrs Jamie O'Conner.'

'Wife?' he echoed, and somehow his attitude altered a little. '*Duw*, you look too young to be married.' He smiled, but somehow there was little warmth in it.

'I'm Bob Smale,' he said. 'I own the property adjoining Honey's Farm – at least it does now that your husband has bought the strip between us. You have a small son, don't you?' he asked.

Fon's first instinct was to tell him to mind his own business. Instead she replied as politely as she could. 'No, he's my stepson,' Fon said, pointing to the slip of paper and wishing Bob Smale would get on with the business in hand and stop asking her personal questions.

He ignored her gesture and leaned closer over the counter, looking at her closely. 'You're a real lovely girl, mind, pretty as a picture and smelling of the sunshine. Experienced too, being a farmer's wife.'

Fon was disconcerted. She didn't know how to deal with the man's almost leering interest.

'I own this paper,' Bobby Smale said softly. His hand lightly rested on hers. She drew away quickly.

'Yes, I know,' Fon stuttered. 'I've heard about you, of course, you being a neighbour and all that.' She didn't wish to appear rude but she moved impatiently, wanting nothing more than to be out of the office and back in the safety of the street.

'Could I take you out for a pot of tea, and we can talk about this advertisement?' he asked, and, not wishing to hurt his feelings, Fon thought carefully about her reply.

'It's very kind of you but I don't think my husband would like it,' she said at last.

'But, lovely, I'm not asking your husband, am I?' he persisted.

Fon looked down at her hands, before putting them behind her back. She felt stupid and inept. She should know how to repulse unwanted attention at her age. She was sure Gwyneth wouldn't be at a loss in such a situation; but then Gwyneth was used to men.

'Right, then.' Bob Smale's voice was suddenly brisk as the door opened and a group of ladies came into the room. 'Let's see to the wording of this advertisement, then, shall we?'

Fon watched, grateful for the interruption, as Bob Smale took down the details in a surprisingly neat hand.

'I'll see to it,' he said, smiling, and yet there was something menacing behind his expression.

Fon was glad to be back out into the street. The smell of the ink had given her a headache, and keeping Bob Smale at arm's length had been something of an ordeal.

The prospect of the long walk home was not a pleasing one, but Fon knew she was needed at the farm. Patrick would be ready for his sleep about now, and there was the evening meal to prepare. Still, a few minutes looking round the shops would do no harm, she decided.

It was growing colder as Fon set off for the hill leading upwards from the town in the direction of Honey's

Farm. Her legs ached, her back ached, and a feeling of weariness was creeping over her. She sank down on the grass, feeling she would like to rest, if only for a few minutes.

A pleasant breeze was drifting in from the sea. Up here on the hill, the air was clear and bright, and above her was the vast arc of the sky, with the clouds more settled now; hopefully the rain would keep away for a while.

Fon sighed and stretched herself out in a hollow in the grassy slope. A bee lazily hovered near by, doubtless seeking some late flowers, and faintly the sounds from the town drifted upward, a background to the chirping of crickets in the grass.

Fon closed her eyes, comfortable in her little nest of grass, and eventually she must have slept, for she was dreaming of being in Jamie's arms; he was holding her, caressing her breasts with his fingertips, but his hands were unusually rough.

She woke suddenly, frightened to see a strange face looking down at her and to feel unfamiliar hands inside her bodice.

She reacted instinctively, pushing the man away from her with such force that he fell back into the grass, an expression of surprise on his face. She recognized him then, and her heart was suddenly in her throat.

'Bob Smale, what do you think you are doing?' she demanded with more ferocity than she'd intended.

'What's wrong?' he asked in an innocent voice. 'Were you *really* sleeping, then? I thought you were putting it on.'

'Keep away from me.' Fon attempted to rebutton her bodice, but Bob Smale had recovered his composure and was forcing her fingers away from the buttons.

'Oh, come on, now don't play the little Miss Innocent with me,' he said grasping at her breast with one hand and pushing at her skirts with the other. 'I know what

129

you married women are like – love a bit of a change, don't you? At any rate you led me on enough back there in the office, simpering and blushing and all that nonsense.'

'*You* are talking nonsense,' Fon said, pushing herself upright, but he put all his weight upon her and she was forced back into the hollow of the grass.

His fingers yanked her skirts aside and began probing, painfully and intimately, and a sense of disbelief and outrage filled Fon's senses.

'Come *on*,' he said. 'You farmers' wives see it happening all the time, don't you? A little bit of playing around won't do anyone any harm. I want you! You are a lovely girl. Why are you resisting? You know you want me, I can hear it in the way that you breathe,' he laughed.

Fon felt horror and fear overwhelm her as he fumbled at his buttons. His mouth came down on her breast, catching her nipple, and at the same time he was pressing himself against her.

'Don't be silly, now,' he said. 'Let me do what I want. 'You'll like it, you'll see. Just relax now, don't keep fighting me. I know you mean yes even when you are saying no – women are like that.'

Fon relaxed suddenly, as though submitting, although the touch of his cruel hands made her feel physically sick. Bob Smale looked down at her and grinned. 'That's better! I knew you wouldn't say no when it came down to it. Come on now, let's have a bit of fun, is it?'

Fon took her chance while he was off guard. She instinctively brought up her knee, catching him between the legs. Before he could utter a sound, she had scratched at his face and was tugging his hair even as she twisted away from him.

'Bitch!' he gasped as he rolled away from her. 'I'll have you for that, you'll see if I don't.'

Fon was on her feet, trying to run uphill, her feet

slipping as the ground grew steeper. The farmhouse was in sight but still some distance away. Smoke rose from the chimney, and Fon wished with all her heart that she was in the kitchen, away from harm.

She heard footsteps pounding behind her, and the sound of Bob Smale's rasping breath brought goose pimples out on her skin. She cried out in pain as she felt her hair caught in a cruel grip and she was dragged backwards. She was pushed down on to the ground, and his knee was across her stomach, so that she felt she couldn't breathe.

'Keep still!' He slapped her hard across the face. 'I mean to have my way with you, and the more you cry out, the more I'll enjoy it.'

Fon felt her skirts being lifted above her waist, her underwear torn away, and shame burned in her cheeks. She screamed out loud, her voice ringing on the quiet air. She screamed again and again, as she felt him force her legs apart; at any moment now she would be violated, and she knew then she would rather be dead.

She tried to lash out with her feet, but he hit her again, so that her head reeled, and coloured lights flashed before her eyes.

'Jamie!' The cry of anguish was wrenched from her, and for a moment she almost welcomed the blessed darkness that seemed to be descending over her.

With a suddenness that made her gasp, the cruel grasp upon her body eased. She heard a pounding and didn't know if it was the sound of her own heart.

The pounding came nearer, and she struggled to raise her head. She saw Bob Smale standing over her, and past him, like an avenging angel, she saw the big grey, with Jamie riding bare-backed, clutching the animal's mane as he rode towards where Fon lay, hunched over now, her hands desperately trying to rearrange her torn clothing.

'Bloody hell!' There was no fear in Bob Smale's voice,

even though Jamie had a murderous look on his face as he bore down upon the man.

Bob Smale stood his ground as Jamie jumped down from the back of the horse and ran towards him. Fon saw Jamie's clenched fist connect with the man's jaw. Smale snapped back and immediately a swelling began to rise around his eye. Jamie shook him to his feet as though he was a rag doll and punched him again and again.

As Fon rose shakily to her feet, she saw that Bob Smale was sagging at the knees now, his eyes turning black, his mouth bleeding.

'I'll teach you to molest my wife,' Jamie growled and hit the hapless man again.

'Stop!' Fon said. 'For God's sake, stop before you kill him.'

'Kill him?' Jamie echoed. 'Sure and shouldn't I be castrating him, for what he's tried to do to you today?'

But Jamie stood back and looked down at the man, who was on his knees, swaying from the beating he'd received.

'Get out of here,' Jamie said, 'and don't let me see you on my land again, or I'll take a gun to you, do you understand?'

Bob Smale lurched to his feet, glowering through the eye that remained open. The venom in his face made Fon shudder.

Jamie watched for a time making sure the man was well out of sight before turning to Fon and folding her in his arms.

'The bastard!' he said, 'daring to lay hands on you. He's lucky he can still walk.'

Fon clung to him. She was trembling, but she made an effort to smile. 'I tried to beat him off,' she said, 'but I couldn't run very fast up the hill.'

Jamie's shoulders were tense with anger. 'Come on home, colleen,' he said. 'You're safe now. I can only thank God I heard you calling my name.'

In the kitchen later, Jamie washed her gently and helped her put on fresh clothes.

'The bastard has bruised you,' he said, 'and from now on I'll make sure he won't touch you again.' He fetched a gun and stood it near the door. 'I'll put the ammunition on the shelf,' he said. 'With Patrick around we can't keep the thing loaded. But don't answer the door to anyone, do you understand? No strangers must cross this threshold.'

When Jamie had returned to the fields, Fon brought in the tin bath and washed again, soaping herself liberally, closing her eyes as she saw the blackening bruising on her breast and thighs. She felt so tainted, so unclean, and she hoped that washing would make her feel better.

She could still feel hands upon her breasts, on her waist, gripping her, preparing to violate her, and she shuddered. It would be some time before she would be able to forget what had happened today. Never again, she told herself, would she venture into Swansea alone.

How awful it would have been if Jamie had not come to her aid when he did! Imagine being taken by force by a man who was nothing more than a violent stranger. It didn't bear thinking about.

She stayed in the hot water until it cooled, and only then did Fon step out on to the flag floor and rub herself dry.

Her torn clothes she pushed on to the fire; she never wished to see them again, not ever. Quickly she dressed in fresh clean underwear and a good serviceable skirt Jamie had found for her. She felt refreshed and almost normal again as she brushed out her long hair; soon, she promised herself, the incident would fade in her memory.

When Jamie came in for his supper, he took her in his arms and held her close, kissing her face and neck, his hands tender as he held her.

She cupped his face in her hands. 'I'm all right, love, really I am,' she said softly.

He buried his face in her neck, and she felt him tremble. 'If anything happened to you, Fon, my little colleen, I think I'd want to die.'

'Nothing is going to happen to me, my love,' she said softly, 'except that I'm going to be the best wife in the world to you.'

'Let's forget about supper,' he said, kissing her mouth so tenderly that tears came to Fon's eyes.

'That's the best idea I've heard for a long time,' she whispered, and together, arms entwined, they climbed the stairs to their bedroom.

Over the next few days, there was a response to the advertisement in the *Cambrian*. A labourer by the name of Mike the Spud came to work on the farm, and as the potatoes were lifted and the fields limed sooner than expected, Jamie was ready to start the replanting of the greens.

Fon had seen him go out to the fields looking fitter than he'd done for some days, and she was happy that a great deal of pressure had been lifted from his shoulders. So she was surprised when she saw the men come back to dinner early.

'Hello, love.' She looked anxiously into Jamie's drawn face. 'What's wrong?'

'Clubroot,' he said as he flung himself down into a chair. 'The whole field of caulis diseased – what a waste!'

Fon felt chilled. Bad luck seemed to be dogging their footsteps; just as one problem was solved, another came to take its place.

In silence, she served the dinner to the new labourer, keeping herself distant from him – a little afraid, if the truth was told. She could have sworn that Mike, who kept giving her covert glances from the corner of his eye, was no stranger to these parts, as he had claimed.

Mike the Spud, as he called himself, made Fon uneasy, and something about him seemed to be vaguely familiar; but she couldn't place him anywhere in her mind. Still, she reasoned, once the hay was cut the men wouldn't be needed until September, when Jamie would be busy again, lifting late potatoes, reseeding the grass as well as cutting the corn.

As Fon served the potatoes from the huge black pot, Mike moved his chair deferentially, and Fon forced a smile, telling herself she was being ridiculously suspicious; not all men were like Bob Smale.

It was later, when the men had gone out to the barn to bed down, and Jamie had brought out the books, that the crash came. Fon leaped out of her chair at the sound of breaking glass, and Jamie pushed her to one side, making his way through to the kitchen.

There on the floor lay a large stone with a piece of paper wrapped around it. Jamie picked it up and smoothed out the creases while Fon stood watching him, her heart in her mouth.

'What is it?' she asked shakily, catching Jamie's arm.

Grimly he turned to her. 'Here,' he said. 'Read it for yourself.' He handed her the note.

The words wavered beneath Fon's eyes:

IF YOU THINK YOU'RE SAFE, THEN YOU ARE VERY MUCH MISTAKEN. NOTHING IS FORGIVEN OR FORGOTTEN.

'What does it mean?' Fon asked, crushing it between her fingers. Jamie took the note from her and ripped it into tiny shreds.

'Stay here and lock the door behind me,' he ordered. He moved outside, as silent and stealthy as a cat, and Fon closed the door and bolted it as he'd ordered. Her heart was beating so swiftly that it sounded loud to her own ears, and her breathing was ragged in the silence.

It seemed an eternity before Jamie returned. He

tapped on the door and spoke her name quietly. She let him in and clung to him in relief.

'Nothing,' he said. 'But what worries me is that we have a complete stranger in our barn. I should have vetted Mike the Spud more closely before I took him on.'

Fon suddenly felt chilled. She had realized in that instant who Mike reminded her of. It was the man who had tried to rape her, the man whom Jamie had beaten within an inch of his life; Mike bore more than a passing resemblance to none other than the hated Bob Smale.

CHAPTER ELEVEN

'Well, everything seems to be in order.' Jamie spread the handwritten letters on the table before him. 'Mike the Spud has worked on most of the farms around here; good references he's got too.'

In the cold light of day, Fon realized that her fears of the previous night had been groundless. Why should the casual labourer harbour any grudge against her and Jamie? Mike and the older hand Dewi were glad of the work, and even more glad of the food and shelter and the generous remuneration Jamie gave them. The resemblance of Mike the Spud to Bob Smale must have been a figment of her imagination.

'I suppose all we can do is trust people a little,' Fon said, though her doubts persisted, in spite of all her reasoning.

'I'll keep an eye on Mike,' Jamie said. 'And as for trusting, I don't trust anyone as far as I can see them, not unless I've vetted them personally.'

Jamie folded the letters away. 'I've asked Gary the shepherd boy to keep an eye on things for today, because you, me and our boy are going to have the day off. I think we all deserve it.'

Fon looked at him questioningly. She was hot from having cooked a hot breakfast for the men and was glad to sit down for a moment and drink her tea.

'Can we afford to take a day off?' she asked weakly, knowing that nothing would be more wonderful than to spend the whole day with Jamie.

'Whether we can or not, we're going to,' Jamie said firmly. 'The potatoes are all raised, and while we're out

137

the men can lime the odd field that hasn't been done already. We'll start cutting the grass tomorrow up on the top field. That's the last then, the rest has been done.'

'What will we do, and where shall we go?' Fon felt as excited as a child. She looked at Jamie in his crisp clean shirt, open at the neck to reveal the strong column of his throat, and felt the ache of love within her. She was so lucky to have found him, and, more, to have become his wife, protected and cared for by him.

'There's a fair in Swansea,' Jamie said. 'Perhaps I'll buy you some lovely green ribbons for your hair. It's high time you had a treat, colleen.' He smiled at her warmly, and Fon sighed, a feeling of happiness enveloping her like a blanket.

It was only occasionally that the ghost of Katherine, his first wife, rose like a spectre between them now, like the times when Jamie had talked of having more children. But mostly she felt secure now, sure of his love, and it was a wonderful feeling.

Patrick wandered into the kitchen, his hair tousled, his eyes still full of sleep. Fon lifted him on to her knee.

'We're going tatters,' she said to him. 'Daddy is taking us out. What do you think of that, my fine boy?'

'Tatters,' Patrick repeated. 'Daddy taking us tatters.' He snuggled against Fon's breast, still half asleep, and she smiled over his head at Jamie.

'I'd better get him some breakfast. We'll be ready in about an hour – is that all right?'

'That will be just fine.' Jamie rose from his chair and scooped the letters of recommendation up in his large hands, thrusting them into a drawer.

'I'll just give the men their orders for the day and see to one or two things, then I'll bring the cart around the front. We'll ride to Swansea today.'

Fon kissed Patrick's hair. 'Fonny'll get you some breakfast, and then you must have a nice wash. We're going to the fair, Patrick, what do you think of that?'

It was later, when she sat with Patrick on the narrow planking of the cart, that Fon felt a dart of apprehension. What if they should come across Bob Smale while they were in Swansea? Jamie would surely set about him again.

She smiled then at her own foolishness. Swansea was a big town; the fairground would be swarming with copper workers and Romany gypsies and all sorts of people; why should they come across Bob Smale? She supposed it was the events last night. The stone through the window and the threatening note that had put her on edge.

She glanced up at the cloudless sky. The threatened rain had not come after all, and she sighed, exasperated with herself. She must stop worrying about every little thing and enjoy the day; it was what Jamie wanted for her.

She looked up at him as he guided the big grey down the hillside towards the town. Jamie's hair gleamed darkly, with red lights shining through the curls, and his broad shoulders were straight and strong. He was a fine man, this husband of hers.

On the way, Patrick curled up beside her and closed his eyes. He was very sleepy, and Fon smiled down at the plump cheeks and sweet mouth. For a second she frowned; he was inclined to sleep a lot these days. Perhaps the work in the fields was too much for him; he was only a small boy, after all.

It didn't take long to reach Swansea, where the streets gleamed in the sunlight and the tall buildings threw deep shadows on to the roadways.

Jamie had chosen to take the route through the village of Sketty, and the crossroads were comparatively quiet, an indication that many of the inhabitants were, like them, taking the day off to go to the fair.

Past the church of St Paul's and down the leafy lane in the direction of the beach, the cart jogged and jolted, and still Patrick slept on. Fon put the back of her hand against his forehead. It was a little hot – but then the day was hot, the sun now rising overhead.

Patrick stirred and opened his eyes and smiled so sweetly at Fon that she hugged him impulsively. 'Want a nice drink of dandelion and burdock?' she asked him quietly.

'*I* do.' Jamie turned to look at her. 'I'm that thirsty I could drink the sea dry.'

Jamie reined in the grey and Fon handed him a drink. He smiled at her and then drank it in one long swallow.

'That went down well,' Fon said, refilling his cup.

He took it and nodded his head. 'Would have gone down better if it had been a mug of ale, though,' he said, with mock seriousness. 'I could have got drunk and forgot all about my nagging wife, if I had some ale inside me.'

Fon pretended to throw the empty bottle of cordial at him, and the dregs flew through the air and landed against the side of his face, trickling along his cheek and into the collar of his shirt.

He moved like lightning, gripping her hands in his and drawing her close. The cart swayed precariously and Patrick laughed out loud in glee.

'Sure I deserve a forfeit for such an attack,' Jamie said, holding Fon tightly. 'You must give me a kiss, I insist on it.'

'Silly fool!' Fon twisted away from him. 'Why should I kiss such a nasty, insulting husband?'

'And why should I tolerate a scold?' Jamie caught her chin between his fingers and, holding her, kissed her lightly on her mouth.

'Take that for now,' he said, 'but you will prove yourself an amenable wife when I have the time to teach you a proper lesson.' His eyes were filled with laughter.

'And I shall do my best to obey you in all things, lord and master,' Fon said, with a pretence of meekness.

140

Jamie's hand lingered for a moment on the back of her neck. 'You are very precious to me, colleen, do you know that?' he said softly.

She could have wished he'd spoken of love, but his words were enough for now. 'And I love you, very much, Jamie O'Conner,' Fon said, a catch of tears in her voice.

'I want to go on the horses.' Patrick's voice broke into the silence. 'I want toffee apples and goodies.'

'Right, my son,' Jamie said, 'let's get on, we'll soon be at the fairground.'

The fair was held on a large field, with the lovely trees of a valley on one side and the long stretch of the bay on the other. Music blared out in a distortion of a tune from the barrel organ at the entrance to the ground, and further into the field a group of musicians dressed as clowns played their own kind of music.

At her side, Patrick jumped about in glee, and Fon felt just as excited as her stepson. It was rarely she'd gone to fairs, for before her marriage there was the hard business of oyster fishing and the backbreaking work on the perches to occupy most of her time. In any case, there had been little money to waste on frivolities.

Fon glanced at Jamie, knowing that if she was to be realistic, she shouldn't be allowing him to waste money on such pleasures as fairgrounds, for times were difficult. But the look of relaxed pleasure on her husband's face told her that it was money well spent.

Patrick insisted on riding on one of the small donkeys that did nothing more than plod sedately around the perimeter of the ground.

'The boy has got horses on the farm to ride whenever he wants,' Jamie said, shrugging, 'so what can be the attraction of these little beasts?'

Fon shook her head. 'It's just that it's something different,' she said. 'It's a day out, a bit of fun, that's all.'

Jamie stopped before an old man in a battered hat

who was dressed in a long dark coat in spite of the sunshine. Ribbons spilled from the man's hand, ribbons in many colours, but, as he promised, Jamie bought her one in green shiny satin.

'Here, colleen,' he said, 'to do up your pretty red hair.'

'My hair isn't red!' Fon said, pretending to be indignant, 'it's a lovely shade of chestnut.'

'Whatever you say,' Jamie agreed, 'but, whatever it is, I like it when I lie beside you in bed and bury my face in it.'

'Hush!' Fon felt the colour rise to her cheeks. 'You are a wicked man, Jamie, talking about such things in public.'

'And you are a funny little girl,' he said. 'I'm married to you, remember?'

'How could I not remember?' There was the hint of a smile curving Fon's lips. 'You give me enough reminders.'

'Well, if it isn't my very own daughter!' A voice broke into Fon's thoughts, taking her attention away from the look in Jamie's eyes. 'Irfonwy, why didn't you let me know you were coming to Swansea?'

'Mammy!' Fon embraced her mother and stood back a little. 'I didn't know you'd be coming in from Oystermouth. *Duw*, aren't you looking well?'

'Oh, aye,' Nina Parks smiled. 'Well enough. Gwyneth's here somewhere, with Mr William Davies, would you believe?'

Before Fon could speak, Nina carried on. 'Brought me with them, they did – chaperone, like.' She smiled. 'Being a gent, he don't want any gossip about our Gwyneth, see?'

Fon concealed her surprise. It wasn't like the gentry to be seen in public with one from what they thought of as the 'lower orders'. But then, to be fair to Mr Davies, he wasn't like that, and perhaps the rumours about him were true and he himself had come from a humble background.

'There she is now.' Nina waved her arms in the air. 'Gwyneth!' she called. 'Come and see who's here! It's your little sister.'

Gwyneth looked well and happy; her hair was glossy, her eyes gleamed, and even her skin seemed to glow with good health.

'Fon!' Gwyneth hugged her. 'So you've managed to get that fine man of yours out of bed for long enough to come to the fair, then, have you?'

Fon concealed her embarrassment and glanced up at Jamie, who as always seemed amused by Gwyneth's openness.

'Will, have you met Fon's husband?' Gwyneth stepped back to introduce the two men, and Fon measured them both with her eyes. She was biased, of course, but wasn't Jamie just a fraction taller than Will Davies? A little broader in the shoulder, and, of course, much more handsome?

Where Jamie had the look of the outdoors about him, Will Davies was paler of countenance, a fact due, no doubt, to the hours he spent indoors selling boots and shoes.

'Will is working in Cardiff now,' Gwyneth said when the two men had shaken hands in greeting. There was a proprietary tone in her voice that Fon didn't fail to notice. 'Came all the way down to Swansea specially to see me, and so I persuaded him to come to the fair.'

'Bamboozled the poor man into it, more like,' Nina said, smiling. 'Only came down on business, that's the truth of it, and you dragging him out for the day, shameless hussy.'

'Do you good, won't it, Will?' Gwyneth protested, laughing up at the man at her side.

'I suppose I was glad of a day off myself,' he agreed. 'It's good to be out of doors in weather like this.'

'Aye, and that shop Mrs Bell runs in Cardiff is as dark

143

as a grave,' Gwyneth said, displaying her knowledge of Will's working conditions.

'Let's go and get a mug of ale.' Jamie spoke to Will, but he winked at Fon. 'Give these ladies a chance to talk among themselves.'

'Give you men a chance to get away from us for a while and fill your bellies with beer, more like,' Nina said good-naturedly. 'I could do with a little drop of something myself, but we won't keep you men cornered, we'll drink ours alone.'

The women followed the men to the large tent erected at the edge of the fairground and sat in a huddle around a table covered with a cloth which bore the imprint of more than one mug of cordial, judging by the circular stains on it.

The women talked together good-humouredly. Though Fon was listening, her eye was on Jamie, who stood with Will Davies near the entrance to the tent.

She and Jamie were never far apart, she thought, with a small dart of surprise; even when he was in the fields, she saw him at regular intervals and much of the time worked side by side with him.

'Oh, blast!' Gwyneth said sharply. 'Trust that Eline Harries to poke her nose in where she's not wanted.'

Fon saw Eline pause uncertainly in the doorway of the tent and look round as though searching for someone. Will too was looking at Eline and, after a moment's hesitation, approached her, a worried look on his face. Fon, glancing at Gwyneth, saw her bite her lip.

Eline only glanced briefly at Will, though she did appear to be saying something to him. She seemed uneasy, almost embarrassed, Fon thought. Then she saw Eline smile in recognition as a man who had his back to Fon moved to Eline's side, taking her arm in a proprietary manner and drawing her away from Will.

Gwyneth, seated beside Fon, gave a small sigh of relief. 'Good! She's meeting that Calvin Temple,' she said. 'He's the man who's running the gallery for her.'

Gwyneth rose and moved swiftly across the tent, dodging between the crowds until she reached Will's side. Casually, she slipped her arm through his, and he looked down at her with a somewhat strained smile.

Fon knew then that Will was not in love with her sister; they had something between them but on his part at least it was not love.

'I hope that girl is keeping herself respectable,' Nina said, as though picking up Fon's thoughts. 'It does no good to give a man your all unless there's a gold band around your finger.'

She rested her hand on Fon's shoulder in a rare moment of tenderness. 'I'm happy for you, my girl,' she said, 'happy that you've got a good husband, a man who will look after you properly. You of all my girls deserve that.'

'I love him, Mammy,' Fon said. 'But Gwyneth is in love too, and it's not easy when you're second choice.'

'What are you talking about, Fon?' Nina asked. 'I know your Jamie was married before, but that makes no difference; you are his wife now and mammy to his son. Don't look a gift horse in the mouth, my girl.'

She hardly paused for breath. 'As for William Davies choosing our Gwyneth for second best, at least he's single and a free man and that uppity Eline Harries doesn't own him. It's fair enough for your sister to set her cap at him, mind.'

'I know.' Fon was relieved to see Jamie coming back across the tent towards her.

At the entrance, Gwyneth was waving her arm in a gesture of farewell. 'Come on, Mam,' she called, 'we're going home.'

She disappeared outside and Nina rose to her feet. 'Right then, it looks as if I've got my marching orders; better be off before they go without me. Take care of my little girl,' she said to Jamie, who had come to stand behind Fon with his hand resting on her shoulder.

Fon smiled up at her husband. 'My family are a bit much, I know,' she said. 'They talk loud, but they mean well.'

'Come on,' Jamie said, 'let's enjoy the fair before Patrick gets too tired and wants to go home to bed.'

'Do you have to go back to Cardiff tomorrow?' Gwyneth's voice intruded into Will's thoughts. He looked down and saw that her lip was trembling. 'I wish you could stay for a little while. I do miss you when you're away.'

'I've got work to do,' Will said patiently. He felt such a heel; here he was with Gwyneth, and his thoughts were occupied by Eline Harries.

He took a deep breath, fighting the burning feeling of jealousy that the sight of her with Calvin Temple had evoked. He had wanted to smash the man in the face, take Eline's arm and drag her away from the fairground by force. But what had he to offer her? Not marriage – he was no better off now than he'd been when he closed his shop – and certainly not fidelity – for he had been unfaithful more than once with Gwyneth Parks.

It was true that with the wages Hari Grenfell was so generously paying him, his debts were lessening month by month, but he was in no position to take a wife, any wife. He glanced guiltily down at Gwyneth. To be truthful, there was only one wife he wanted, and that was Eline, who was far out of his reach.

He sighed. He knew he was not being fair to Gwyneth; he was in effect stringing her along, lacking the moral courage to tell her that he did not want her. It wasn't that he was cowardly; he would square up to any man; but deliberately to destroy Gwyneth's hopes and dreams took a great deal of courage. Yet things could not be allowed to drift on as they were. He must end the silly,

146

foolish affair with Gwyneth; he had not wanted it to happen in the first place.

Gwyneth, as though sensing that he was far away, reached up suddenly and kissed him. 'I love you so much, Will,' she said, the contours of her face softened. 'I didn't know it would be like this, this tearing at me whenever you look at another woman. Jealousy is an awful thing, isn't it, Will?'

He knew exactly what she meant. Hadn't he felt ready to kill at the sight of Eline even talking to another man? He wished now that he had not agreed to Gwyneth accompanying him to the train stop. If only he had left her at her mother's door. And yet he'd wanted an opportunity to talk to her, to be honest with her. But that opportunity had not come.

To his relief, the train came into sight, the horses dragging at the carriage, which appeared to rock, precariously, along the metal lines.

'I'll see you soon, won't I?' Gwyneth said pleadingly, 'and you'll write to me some time in the week? Let me know when you're coming home, please, Will.'

He squeezed her hand; perhaps writing to her, trying to explain his position, would be less hurtful than rejecting her face to face.

'I'll write, if I can,' he said, and climbed aboard the Mumbles train with a feeling of relief, glad to be heading back towards Swansea.

As he sat staring out at the placid sea, he knew that he must try to see Eline; he had to talk to her about the shop in Cardiff. There, with them working side by side, perhaps he could re-establish the warmth there had once been between them.

He remembered with an ache how cool Eline had been when she'd seen him at the fairground. She'd barely been civil, had refused to meet his eyes. Instead, her own eyes had been searching the crowd for a glimpse of Calvin Temple. How Will would have loved to take the

147

supercilious smile from the face of the man whose proprietary manner towards Eline set his teeth on edge.

Well, he was on his way back to Swansea now. He would stay the night with Hari and Craig, talk about business and have a meal with them; and tomorrow he would be back in Cardiff, not knowing what Eline's future plans might be. The thought caught him by the throat and almost choked him. He stared out at the moving landscape beyond the train window and knew that he had never felt so miserable in all his life.

'Something's wrong.' Jamie's voice roused Fon from the half-sleep into which she had fallen. In her arms, Patrick was a heavy weight; sweat beaded his brow as he slept, and as Fon struggled to sit up he curled into a ball on the floor of the cart.

'What do you mean?' Fon pushed herself to her knees and stared towards the farmhouse, unable to see anything amiss.

'I don't know, but I don't like the look of things.' He pointed. 'See, there's no smoke coming from the chimneys.'

'But where are the labourers?' she said quietly, and Jamie stared across the grass towards the house, straining to see in the growing gloom of evening.

'That's what I'd like to know,' he said quietly. He rode the horse into the yard and Fon looked around with a feeling of dismay. Everywhere there was chaos. Dead hens were strewn across the dry earth, and feathers drifted about in the breeze.

'Stay here,' Jamie ordered and as he disappeared into the farmhouse, Fon shuddered, wondering if someone was there, lying in wait for him.

He returned a few minutes later, his face strained. 'It's a mess,' he said. 'You'd think there'd been a hurricane in there.'

He lifted Fon from the cart and took Patrick in his

148

arms. 'Come on inside,' he ordered, and walked ahead of her with rapid strides.

Although she had been warned, Fon couldn't have anticipated the scene of destruction that met her eyes. Furnitute was overturned and crockery smashed. Cushions lay about the place oozing feathers, and the big pot of soup that had been hanging over the fire was tipped all over the floor.

'What's happened, has the bull got loose and come in here?' Fon asked. Jamie didn't answer. He righted one of the chairs and put Patrick gently down in it before fetching the shotgun from near the door and placing it in Fon's hands.

He hurried upstairs and Fon could hear him searching the rooms.

When he returned he shook his head. 'Nothing's been touched up there,' he said. 'Now, Fon, I want you to lock the door after me, and if anyone other than me tries to come in, shoot, do you hear?'

Fon nodded, her mouth dry. 'Where are you going, Jamie? What's happening here?'

'I don't know,' he said grimly. 'But I mean to find out.'

When she was alone, Fon looked around her at the mess, and a terrible anger filled her. She placed the gun at the ready and began to clean up her kitchen.

Fon moved swiftly, fetching the broom from the lean-to. She had no intention of sitting still and whimpering. If anyone thought she could be frightened away from her home, then they could just forget it. Jamie was her life; if Jamie could act with courage, then so could she.

She stood for a moment looking down at the broken pieces of a pretty flowerpot strewn, with the broken plants, over the grey flagged floor; and then, with a sigh, she set to work.

CHAPTER TWELVE

'This is Mrs Harries.' Mrs Bell spoke officiously. 'She's been sent up from Swansea to help you get things organized up here.'

Will felt as though the breath had been knocked out of him. He spun round and looked at Eline, drinking in the unexpected sight of her. He almost stepped forward to take her in his arms and then stopped in his tracks, realizing that Mrs Bell was watching him suspiciously.

'Good morning.' Will's pulse slowed as he saw that Eline was acting as though they had never met.

'Glad to see you took the job, after all,' he said, forcing himself to speak calmly. 'What made you change your mind? Was it something Hari Grenfell said to you?'

'I had my reasons.' Eline did not meet his eye. 'Very private reasons.'

'I see.' William felt that he was rebuffed and knew that was just what Eline had intended. 'Well, I'm sure you'll soon get the hang of things here.' He looked at her, trying to make her meet his gaze, but she would not.

'I understand I will be dressing just one of the windows?' she said, directing her question to Mrs Bell.

'Aye. Not that I approve, you understand.' Mrs Bell spoke almost truculently. 'New-fangled windows are not my cup of tea. Give me plain displays every time. Folk don't want to see a pantomime when they come to my emporium; all they want is to buy clothes and such.'

Eline smiled warmly, her gaze sweeping over Mrs Bell's no-nonsense dress and plain accessories, and Will could almost see her mind working as she planned a

150

wardrobe that would do justice to the elegant posture of the older woman.

'I'm sure you are very experienced and knowledge-able,' Eline said quietly, and the icy expression on Mrs Bell's face thawed visibly.

'Perhaps you will give me the benefit of your advice once I begin work,' Eline added.

Will concealed a smile. Mrs Bell's gratification was apparent in the upward tilt of her mouth. He felt sure that, had she any feathers, she would have fluffed them out with pride by now.

'Well, perhaps I could spare you a little time,' she said grudgingly.

Eline's smile would have melted an iceberg. 'Thank you so much,' she said, drawing off her gloves. 'Perhaps I'd better start looking round for some materials right away.'

Mrs Bell took her long skirt between stout fingers and moved to the stairs. 'You just wait here until I have a word with my staff, and then I'll come and help you,' she said, and her tone could almost be described as amiable.

'You certainly have a way with people,' William said, breaking the awkward silence that had fallen after Mrs Bell had departed.

'I feel that being tactful helps.' Eline was on the defensive, and Will knew that she hadn't changed in her feelings for him at all. She was still angry and bitter at his betrayal, and could he honestly blame her? Still, they must work together now, and at least she could offer the olive branch during business hours.

'Unforgiving sort, aren't you?' he said, with sudden anger, and Eline's fine eyebrows arched in assumed surprise.

'Have I anything to forgive Mrs Bell for, then?' she said, with some sarcasm.

Will caught her arm. He could see the gentle swell of

her breasts at the vee of her neckline, and he longed to touch her intimately, to make her yield to the passion that burned in him. He had never possessed Eline; he felt that no-one had possessed her, not really reached her inner core – not even the husband she had been married to since she was little more than a child.

He drew her close and pressed his mouth fiercely on hers, trying to force a response from her. She didn't protest, she didn't push him away, she simply remained passive and unresponsive.

He released her angrily. 'You *are* a cold woman, Eline,' he said. 'I think you should have become a nun, remained chaste; you weren't cut out for anything as human as passion.'

She didn't rise to the bait. She simply moved away and picked up a lady's boot from one of the the shelves. After a moment, she looked over her shoulder at him, and Will thought he saw a flicker of something like sadness in her eyes.

'Can't we make a new start?' Will said humbly. 'I don't want us to quarrel, it achieves nothing.'

'You're right,' Eline said. 'We should try to develop a reasonable working relationship at least. Life would be much easier then.'

'That's a start anyway, now,' Will said, feeling exultant. It was just the start he'd been hoping for, but he kept his voice deliberately businesslike.

'Let's see what we shall put in the window, shall we?' he said, and his gaze lingered on her mouth as he suppressed the desire to kiss her.

Will scarcely saw Eline for the rest of the day. She worked hard, he had to admit that; she asked no quarter but carried stock upstairs on her own and left him free to serve the few customers who did venture down to the basement.

Later, they sat together in the modest tearooms at the top of the emporium building and talked in a desultory manner about work. But at least, Will thought, they were no longer at each other's throats. It was possible, he reasoned, that, given time, Eline's hostility would fade.

'Where are you going to stay in Cardiff?' Will ventured a personal question, and Eline looked up at him coolly.

'I have a room in an hotel,' she said, 'just for a few days, then I will be returning to Swansea.'

Will felt disappointment grip him. 'You wouldn't like to live in Cardiff, then?' he asked, and she shook her head.

'Oh, no.' She fiddled with a bracelet on her arm. 'I'll just be coming up for a few days each week to see how things are going, but I'll be based at home.'

She met his gaze squarely for the first time. 'I'm going to begin to make a new life for myself. I think it's high time I cut away from the past and started again.'

'I see.' Will felt as though the bottom had dropped out of his world.

'You know that I want to design and make shoes for children and adults who have difficulty walking properly. Well, at last I'm putting that wish into practice.'

'And Calvin Temple, is he helping you?' Will regretted the words as soon as they were spoken, for the shutters came down on Eline's face and she retreated into her shell once more.

She picked up her bag. 'I'd better be getting back to work,' she said, not looking at him. 'There's plenty to do if I'm to modernize the display area; it doesn't look as if anything's been changed for years.'

As Eline's window display began to take shape, Will found that the number of customers patronizing his basement area of the emporium grew steadily. Some came to buy, but most came out of open curiosity and appeared disappointed with the dark and dour shelves and old-fashioned fixtures.

When the emporium closed for the night, Will went

out into the street to study Eline's finished window. He stood back amazed; she had excelled herself.

In the background was a hazy backdrop, the outlines depicting accurately the sturdy lines of Cardiff Castle. The foreground appeared to be a grassy area, with a cricket pitch to one side of the display and a croquet lawn behind a hedge of shrubs on the the other. Sporty shoes danced across the lawn; ladies' pumps and men's fancy shoes rested on the lawn, while along the cricket ground, like an edging of spectators, was a plethora of boots and shoes, men's, ladies', and children's, in a carefully arranged scene of disorder.

Will felt a flood of admiration. Eline was a remarkable woman, not even Hari Grenfell herself could have created a finer display.

'Like it?' Eline spoke from behind his shoulder, and Will spun round, his face alight.

'Eline!' he said. 'It's a masterpiece!' He wanted to hug her, but he contained himself and simply took her hand in his. 'Congratulations on a fine piece of work,' he said warmly.

Eline smiled up at him, and for a moment it was as if they were back on the old footing.

'Is it really all right?' she asked with the modesty that Will found so appealing.

'All right?' he echoed. He put his earlier feelings into words. 'Even Hari couldn't have done better.'

Eline sighed. 'It's taken a few days' hard work, but I think now it's finished.' She shrugged, sounding almost regretful. 'I can't do any more to it. Tomorrow, I'd better make arrangements to return to Swansea.'

'Eline,' Will said quietly, 'would you please stay another day – help me make the shop area more appealing, if that's at all possible? It's like a dungeon down there.'

Eline searched his face, as though suspecting a trap. 'I don't know if I can spare the time,' she said, uncertainly.

154

'Please, Eline,' he urged. 'I assure you that it's a request that's based on business, simply that.' He paused and gestured towards her display. 'However good your window might be, the customers are put off once they enter the shop and see how dreary it is.'

Eline inclined her head; obviously she saw the truth of his words. 'All right,' she said. 'I'll stay for another day, see what I can do.'

In the event, Eline did a great deal. She somehow persuaded Mrs Bell to move the stocks of boots and shoes to a much better location on the first floor of the emporium, so that, as customers mounted the ornate staircase, the first thing they would see was the Grenfell boot-and-shoe mart.

'It will take a little time to set out the shelves and counters,' Will said, feeling desperate to keep Eline near him for as long as possible.

Mrs Bell was fussing around, ordering her staff to rearrange the china displays to accommodate the Grenfell stock. She looked up curiously at Eline, and Will turned his shoulder, not wanting Mrs Bell to witness his discomfiture should Eline turn him down.

'I don't know if I can keep on my room at the hotel,' Eline said doubtfully. 'It must be costing Mrs Grenfell a fortune.'

'Stay here, my dear Mrs Harries,' Mrs Bell said quickly. 'I have a spare room in the staff quarters, if you'd like it.'

'That's very kind of you,' Eline said. 'I'll stay a little while, then.'

Will gave a sigh of relief. 'I am grateful, Eline,' he said quietly. 'And I'm sure Hari will be too.' He looked round him in satisfaction. 'We should do well here. It's so much better than I thought it could be.'

And, he thought joyously, he would have Eline close to him for just a little longer. Smiling, he began to move the stock towards the counters and fixtures, ready for

Eline to choose some boots and shoes for display purposes. Things were not turning out too badly after all.

In Oystermouth, Gwyneth was just leaving the house of Mary Preece, midwife. She stared up at the cloud-filled sky without seeing the signs of the gathering storm. Neither did she hear the wash of the sea against the dull gold of the wet seashore. Gwyneth was locked into her own thoughts and fears; her emotions were mixed, she didn't know if she should laugh or cry.

She put her hands up to her hot cheeks and tried to think clearly. She, Gwyneth Parks, was going to have a baby, Will Davies's baby.

She walked across the road to the beach and sank on to a wooden bench, clutching at the slatted wood for support. For a moment, she didn't want to think about the consequences of her passionate nights with Will; all she wanted to do was marvel in the knowledge that she was going to bear his child.

She didn't know how long she sat, dreaming in the wash of the sea and the dullness of the day, and she didn't care that, back in the small house flanking the beach, Mary Preece was probably standing in her window, watching the harlot who was with child and no gold band on her finger.

The midwife's attitude had been clear. She disapproved. Even as she'd questioned Gwyneth about her courses and conducted a thorough examination, her mouth had been pursed together like a squeezed lemon.

'Nina Parks know about this yet?' she had said, and her tone implied that it was a case of like mother, like daughter.

Gwyneth had dressed without making a reply, and, as she'd handed over the money due, the midwife had sniffed her disapproval.

Gwyneth wrapped her arms around her body as if to

156

protect her child. The midwife had suggested that she slip the baby, now, while it was still in the early stages. Gwyneth had looked around the bare clinical room and shuddered, shaking her head vigorously.

Mrs Preece had shrugged. 'Well, then, bring your bastard into the world if that's what you want.' She'd issued a word of warning. 'Don't expect the father to marry you, mind. They hardly ever give a fig for you once you give them what they want.'

Gwyneth stopped dreaming and faced reality. What would Will do? He was an honourable man, no doubt about that. He was a real gentleman, but marriage to the daughter of an oyster fisherman was something he might not even wish to consider; and who could blame him? His future was set fair. He was cared for by the rich and powerful Grenfells. His life was destined to go along different, better paths than her own. In one thing the midwife was right; Gwyneth had just been a moment's pleasure to Will. He had never promised her anything.

She rose and shook the drifting particles of sand from her skirt. She had better get on home; she was hungry now, thirsty too. She smiled; she had better look after herself, she had another life to think about now.

Nina Parks was in the kitchen, pushing a bowl of cowl on to the table. 'There you are, girl, just in time for some dinner. Where you been then?'

'Sitting by the beach,' Gwyneth said evasively. The soup looked appetizing, filled with mutton, carrots and swede, and beside the bowl was a plate of chunky bread slices.

'*Duw*, I'll be glad when you can work on the oyster beds again, girl,' Nina said, placing another bowl on the table and sitting down with a loud scrape of her chair legs against the flagstones. 'Money's getting a bit short now.'

'I won't be working on the beds for much longer, Mam,' Gwyneth said softly.

Her mother looked up at her, eyebrows raised. 'Oh, planning on going back into shop work, are you, then, girl? The beds not good enough for you now, is it?'

'I'm going to have a baby, Mam.' Gwyneth's heart was beating fast. She dipped a chunk of bread into the stew, her hand trembling.

'You are being funny, aren't you?' Nina said uncertainly, and Gwyneth shook her head.

'I'm being serious. I'm sorry, it's definite, I've been to see Mary Preece.'

Nina sank back into her chair, her soup forgotten. 'Dear lord, what's wrong with you, girl? Haven't you learned by my mistakes?'

'No, Mam, sorry.' Gwyneth smiled. 'Don't give me a row, Mam. I love him, I couldn't help it, see.'

'It's William Davies's child, of course,' Nina said, shaking her head helplessly. 'I suppose I saw it coming, if I was honest. Well, he'll have to help pay for the baby's keep, won't he?'

'I haven't thought that far ahead,' Gwyneth said. 'I suppose the best thing is to go up to Cardiff and see him, tell him the good news.'

Nina gave a hollow laugh. 'I doubt he'll think it good news, my girl. Men never do, not even when there's a gold ring on your finger.'

'Well, you should know, Mam,' Gwyneth said good-naturedly. 'You've had enough experience, haven't you?'

'Don't get lippy, now, girl,' Nina said, but without rancour. 'I am telling you the truth; men don't like babbies – not much, anyway.'

She sighed. 'Kevin used to deny that he'd slipped up; used to tell me I was all right, he'd been careful.' She grimaced. 'I don't think he knew what careful meant.'

'What about Joe, what did he say?' Gwyneth was curious, because Joe had fathered bastard children on

158

her mother, same as Will had done to her. The only difference being that Will was a free man and Joe had been married to Eline.

'Oh, Joe was a real man,' Nina said, her features softening. 'There was no compromising with him; he admitted straight off he was the father, and they don't all do that, mind.' She made a rueful face. 'Some try to blame the woman, call her a whore, all sorts of things – but not Joe, not him.'

Her voice trembled. 'That Eline was no match for him, not her, with milk and water in her veins instead of red blood.'

She looked at Gwyneth sharply then. 'So you've taken Will Davies away from Eline, have you? Funny we should both have pinched her man from under her nose, isn't it?' But Nina wasn't laughing.

Gwyneth sighed. 'I don't know if I've got him or not yet, Mam. I'm not counting any chickens, mind.'

'He'll marry you,' Nina said positively. 'He's a man with a conscience, you'll see. When are you going to tell him?'

'I'll go up to Cardiff in a few days' time, if you can lend me some money,' Gwyneth said. 'I think he should know as soon as possible, don't you, Mam?'

'Aye, best get it over, girl.' Nina paused. 'I hope he does right by you and makes the wedding before the baby begins to show. You can always tell folks it's a premature birth.' She smiled. 'Not that they'll believe you, mind, but it saves face a bit, see?'

Gwyneth shook her head, half in apprehension and half in anticipation. 'Imagine me, Gwyneth Parks, strutting about the streets of Cardiff with a wedding band on my finger. Wouldn't it be wonderful?'

'Aye, if it comes to pass, it will be wonderful – a damn miracle,' Nina said dourly.

'Mrs William Davies.' Gwyneth spoke the name softly. 'It has a fine ring to it, doesn't it?'

'Aye, it does that, girl, but don't go making plans that might not come to anything. He could always walk away, mind.'

'But you said he had a conscience, that he'd marry me,' Gwyneth protested.

'I know I did, and I think he will, too, but it don't do to believe in good things happening to folk like us. Remember that, girl. These menfolk are strange creatures; there's no way of telling how they'll turn, and shouldn't I know that better than most?'

Nina looked thoughtful. 'I know when he had a second chance, Joe stood by me, like; but not the first time he didn't. I might as well tell you now, I'd have staked my life on it that Joe would marry me when I fell pregnant for our Tom, all those years ago, when Joe and me were both free as air. I thought he loved me, see. And so he did, in his way, but he ran a mile.'

She paused as if the memory was painful. 'Once he knew about the baby coming, I didn't see him for dust.'

Nina looked at her daughter and her face softened. 'But I think you got a good one in Mr Davies, don't think he's the sort to run, but then he's a mite older than Joe was and more educated, like. You'll be all right.'

'I hope so, Mam,' Gwyneth said, and she drew her shawl around her shoulders, feeling suddenly chilly. 'I do hope so, because if he lets me down, I don't know what I'm going to do.'

'We'd manage. Come on, don't be down in the mouth,' Nina said cheerfully. 'Haven't we Parks women always got by?'

'But how, Mam?' Gwyneth asked, feeling suddenly lost and alone in a strange and alien world. What if she had a baby, and no father to help support it?

'I'd mind the babbie and you'd take a job, work the oysters like always,' Nina said practically.

The prospect was a daunting one, and Gwyneth thought with horror of the long months waiting for the child to arrive, months when she would be talked about, an outcast in the village – a true Parks, people would say.

More practically, how would she and Mam survive those months, months when there would be little money coming in? She squared her shoulders and forced herself to look on the bright side. Will was too good a man to leave her to face her problems alone. He knew he was the first with her; he had taken her virginity, he would stand by her.

Nina seemed to sense her feelings, and with a rare show of emotion, she leaned forward and touched her daughter's hand. 'It will be all right, *merchi*,' she said softly. 'You'll see, it will be all right.'

'Will it, Mam?' Gwyneth wanted reassurance; she wanted Mam to make things right as she'd done when Gwyneth was a child. But this was the world of grown-up emotions and grown-up repercussions. Not even Nina, with her redoubtable strength of character, could help her now. It would take the good intentions of Will Davies to do that.

She loved Will so much; she had given him her trust as well as her passion. Surely he must feel something for her too, otherwise he wouldn't have taken her to his bed.

But as Gwyneth lay awake that night, staring up at the ceiling, hands resting lightly on her still flat stomach, she realized that she had led Will on, *she* had seduced him. Her body had cried out for him; she had thirsted for his love.

In return, he had given her his manhood; his urgent needs had been assuaged by her love. He was a man, a red-blooded man, and who could blame him for not turning such a willing slave away?

Gwyneth stared up at the ceiling and thought with trepidation of the journey she must make to Cardiff to face Will. She tried to think of the words that would break the news to him gently, for, in all fairness to him, he hadn't meant to put her in this position.

The moon spread a soft light across the room, washing everything in silver; even the quilted bedcover seemed to lack colour. It was a strange, unreal world, a world where Gwyneth Parks suddenly felt very much alone.

CHAPTER THIRTEEN

Fon sat in the kitchen and stared around her. It was clean now, the cushions mended and floors swept, the chaos she and Jamie had found on their return from the fair restored to order. But the memory of that night remained with Fon in the days that had followed, and often she lay awake at night, thinking she heard sounds from downstairs.

Of Mike the Spud nothing had been seen or heard; it was as though he had disappeared from the face of the earth. Dewi, in his cottage with his wife and children, had heard nothing of the intruder, and Fon could not in all conscience blame him; the cottage was quite a distance from the farmhouse.

Apart from which, Fon felt it in her bones that somehow Mike the Spud and Bob Smale were connected, and between them they had thought up this act of revenge against her and Jamie.

She said nothing of her fears. Jamie was so toweringly angry at the violation of his home that she hesitated to raise the subject, for fear of upsetting him even more.

At the time, Jamie had questioned both Dewi and Gary closely, his longing to find the men he believed were responsible for the outrage burning within him; but the shepherd, like Dewi, had heard nothing. Indeed, he had slept soundly until woken by Jamie.

When he'd entered the devastated kitchen on the night of the damage, Gary had shaken his grey head and narrowed his eyes, and though he grumbled continuously as he helped Jamie and Fon clear up the chaos in the farmhouse, he nevertheless worked well.

'You got an enemy, boss,' he'd said to Jamie. 'Thought at first the Black Devil might have got out, but no beast made this mess, not even a bull scenting a heifer.'

Gary coughed noisily. 'I never trusted that Mike, mind. I didn't like the look of 'im, from the start; not our sort, he weren't.'

After he had passed on his opinions, Gary remained silent, his supply of conversation seemingly used up for the time being.

Fon sighed, staring round at the now neat room, trying to shake off the memory of that awful night. She moved across the kitchen and stared down at Patrick, who was asleep on the sofa, and frowned in concern as she realized the boy had been asleep for longer than was usual.

The small boy was flushed; his cheeks, once so plump, were now thinner than they should be. It was clear he was not well.

Fon glanced out of the window. She should be helping the men in the fields. It was harvest-time; the corn, ripening late, was being gathered in, and Jamie had been able to employ only one casual to help him. And yet he had insisted that Patrick must remain indoors and Fon with him.

There had been talk of the scarlet fever over at Greenhill in Swansea, and Fon feared that Patrick might have caught the sickness one day when she and Jamie had taken him into Swansea to do some shopping. He'd not been himself since then: nothing she could put her finger on, but the normally placid Patrick had been fretful. He'd refused to eat and had fallen asleep at odd moments of the day. Now he had developed a red, angry rash, and Fon was certain he had the fever.

According to her herbal recipe book, the fever should be treated with the roots of bugloss, made into a syrup, but so far she'd used the remedy on Patrick without success.

At dinner-time the men came in from the fields, and Fon, glancing anxiously at Jamie, saw that he was bone tired. She knew he would work twice as hard as any help he hired; that was his way.

The labourer was little more than a youth, thin, with fair hair flopping over his forehead; he looked more suited to poring over books than working the fields. In this assessment Fon turned out to be right.

'Sit down, Eddie,' she said politely. 'I'll put your dinner out in a minute.'

She liked Eddie; from the minute she'd set eyes on him, Fon had instinctively trusted him, but he was no farmer. Still, in these busy days, any help was better than none at all.

She served Jamie with a huge plate of meat pie, hot from the oven, and pushed the dish of vegetables towards him.

'Eat up, love,' she said softly. 'You look as though you need it.'

He met her gaze, and even though he was tired, he had a light in his eyes that stirred her senses. A wash of warmth filled her, she loved him so much. Since her marriage, Jamie had filled her whole world; she couldn't imagine now ever being without him.

She concentrated on serving the meal, and Eddie thanked her nicely as she handed him his plate of pie.

'How's Patrick this morning?' Jamie asked, glancing towards the front room.

'He's sleeping,' Fon said. 'I'm hoping the remedy I've given him will start to work soon.'

Jamie pushed aside his plate and left the table, disappearing into the other room.

Eddie looked up from his plate. 'What's wrong?' he asked, and it was the first time he'd spoken two words together.

165

'I'm afraid he's caught the scarlet fever,' Fon said quietly. 'I should have the doctor to him, but money's so tight, just now.' She shrugged. 'I don't know what to do for the best.'

'Will you allow me to have a look at him?' Eddie said.

Fon stared at him in surprise. 'Do you know anything about the sickness, then?' she asked.

Eddie shook back his lock of fair hair. 'My father was a doctor,' he said. 'I began my training, supposedly to follow in his footsteps, but' – he shrugged – 'it wasn't to be.'

'What do you mean?' Fon asked, and immediately apologized. 'Oh, excuse me, it's none of my business, is it?'

Eddie smiled. 'I don't mind telling you what happened,' he said, rising to his feet. 'My father died, quite suddenly. His heart gave out, I fear. I found then that we were heavily in debt; the house had to be sold, and there was no money for me to continue with my training.'

He smiled, and his thin face looked quite handsome. 'So I took to the hills, literally.'

He pointed in the direction of the parlour. 'May I?'

Fon nodded, eager for another opinion, and followed him from the kitchen into the other room. She drew Jamie back from the bed, holding on to his hand, watching as Eddie gently lifted the blanket and exposed Patrick's small frame.

'What the . . . ?' Jamie began.

Fon looked up at him, shaking her head. 'It's all right. Eddie was going for a doctor,' she explained quickly, 'but when his dad died there was no money for it. Let him look at Patrick. It can do no harm.'

'His chest,' Eddie said, with a sudden, unexpected air of authority. 'It's congested. We need a poultice and some hot flannels, and perhaps we could have a kettle boiling on the fire. The steam will help him a little.'

166

'Well, I'll be damned,' Jamie said softly, but he brought the kettle and poked up the flames beneath it.

'Can you make a poultice?' Eddie looked at Fon, and she nodded willingly.

'I'll do it straightaway.' She moved quickly, knowing that what Eddie wanted would do nothing but good. She was only sorry she hadn't thought of it herself.

Afterwards, when Patrick was sleeping more easily, Fon returned to the kitchen. 'Eat your dinner,' she said to the menfolk, and at once Eddie was the quiescent labourer again, meekly obeying her commands. She smiled. How strange it was, the way a man would obey a woman when it came to childhood habits, like eating up his dinner or changing wet clothes, and yet could be so assertive out there in the harsh world.

That night Fon was seated at the table with the books spread open before her. The figures swam before her tired eyes, but she saw with alarming clarity that the stock of fodder for the animals was much lower than it should be; and that wasn't the only problem. New seed was needed, and the money was fast running out. If Jamie didn't get the corn cut and most of it sold in the next few weeks, the farm would be in real trouble.

The egg yield from her hens was still good, but the money from that enterprise brought in scarcely enough to put food on the table. In addition, the cows were a liability; with some of them in calf, and the rest still dry, they were a drain on resources rather than an asset.

The rams had been sold weeks ago, but the money from the sale had dwindled away alarmingly. Fon shivered; it seemed that ruin was facing them, in spite of all Jamie's efforts to make the farm a success.

But no, she would not let that happen, she told herself. Matters would improve when the beasts were productive once again. The milk was always a good source of revenue. And when the corn was cut and sold, the farm would be in funds once more. In the meantime she

167

would have to see to it that they cut back on everything except bare necessities.

Even so, she wondered uneasily, would the little money that was left last long enough to sustain the farm until things improved?

Jamie came into the kitchen and kicked off his boots. Fon closed the books with an air of finality; her husband had quite enough to worry him without knowing how bad things really were.

'How's Patrick?' He slumped wearily into a chair and rubbed his hand across his eyes.

'Much better,' Fon said truthfully. 'His breathing is easier, and he's sleeping soundly in his bed.' She knelt down before Jamie and put her head against his chest, listening to the strong beat of his heart.

'I think our boy is over the worst, thanks to Eddie.' She was grateful that she had one piece of good news to impart. 'Hungry, love?'

Jamie shook his head. 'I'm too tired to be hungry,' he said, with a hint of anger in his voice. 'I know Eddie tries, but he's useless with the sickle. I don't think we'll ever get that field cut.'

'Come on to bed then, love,' Fon said softly. 'Try to forget all about the farm for now.'

He touched her hair lightly. 'I'm not giving you much of a life, colleen,' he said. 'It's nothing but work from dawn to dusk.'

'And isn't that what I'm used to?' Fon said fiercely. 'I've always worked, mind, and worked hard. If you think the farm is any worse than the oyster beds, you're mistaken.'

Jamie cupped her face in his hands and, bending, kissed her mouth. 'But then you didn't have a husband making demands on you during the night-time, did you?'

He drew her on to his knee and rubbed his hand against the nape of her neck, caressing the skin beneath her hair. 'I don't think I'll ever stop wanting you, colleen.'

'Come to bed and prove it,' Fon said, her eyes alight, her pulse beating rapidly. 'Talk is cheap, mind.'

Later, as they lay entwined, with Jamie's head in the crook of her arm, Fon looked down at his face, the lines of weariness eased away by sleep, and tears came to her eyes. She loved him so much that it dragged at her heart to see him tired and worried. If only she could do something to help him, something constructive – but what?

She curled up beside him and tried to relax, but it was a long time before she could forget her problems and fall into a restless sleep.

A few mornings later, Fon was hanging the washing on the line when she saw a figure coming towards the farmhouse. She hurried indoors and took up the gun that stood, these days, near the door. But as the tall figure drew nearer, she recognized him and put the gun away.

'Tommy!' she said joyfully. 'You've come back to us?'

She hugged the boy and drew him into the kitchen. 'I'm that glad to see you! But what made you come?' She pushed him into a chair and put a cup of cordial before him. 'Didn't you like living with your auntie?'

Tommy shook his head. He seemed older and somehow more mature than the boy who had left with his mother some months ago.

'I couldn't stand the town,' Tommy said bluntly, 'and I couldn't stand working indoors, never breathing the fresh air or seeing much of the sun, come to that.' He sipped the cordial. 'Can I have my job back, do you think?'

Fon thought of the lack of money and hesitated, and then she imagined the fields of corn waiting to be harvested. She nodded briskly.

'You can have your job back and welcome,' she said.

169

'But you'll have to wait a bit for your pay.' She smiled at him. 'You can have bed and board as always, and I'll keep tally of what's owing you. As soon as things pick up, I'll settle with you. How's that?'

Tommy smiled. 'Shall I start now?'

Fon watched as Tommy made his way along the perimeter of the hedge and towards the field where Jamie and Eddie were working. She knew that Tommy, thin as he was, would do more than his fair share of the work; he was a farmer by birth, and his heart was in it. She sighed happily. Things would be easier now for Jamie, and if she asked Eddie too to wait for his wages, the money would be easier.

With Tommy's return, it was as if fortune was smiling on them for the first time in months, Fon thought happily as she dressed Patrick ready for the fields. The corn was in stooks and drying in the sun, and the seed that Fon had bought in Swansea market, with no money and on the strength of Jamie's good name, was safely sown. It was true they owed a debt for the first time ever, but at least they had been given time to pay.

Money was still short, but now there was the prospect of selling off the corn, and soon the late potatoes would be lifted, some of which Fon would take into the market and use to pay off the debt for the seed.

She picked up her basket, covered with a pristine cloth, and, taking Patrick's hand, led him out into the September sunshine. The air was rich with the scents of the drying corn, and as Fon stared across the fields she saw in the distance the figures of her husband and his labourers like dark dots on the horizon.

'Your daddy will be waiting for his dinner, Patrick, my boy,' Fon said. 'And so will Eddie and Tommy; they both eat enough to feed a bull!'

'*My* Eddie,' Patrick repeated. His small face was filling out again now, and the red rash had quite disappeared. He had taken a liking to Eddie, who spent a great deal of time with him, telling him stories and playing games.

Eddie was wasted on the land; Fon realized that he was cut out to be a doctor, with his keen interest in people and his clever mind, as well as his clever hands.

Fon smiled. Eddie's hands were calloused now, like those of any farm labourer, but they were still gentle as they cut out paper shapes to amuse Patrick.

As Fon drew nearer to the field where the men were working, she realized that Jamie had seen her approaching. The men had stopped working and retreated to the shade of the hedge, drinking from the big brown jug Fon had provided that morning.

Patrick let go of Fon's hand and ran towards Eddie, flopping down beside him on the ridge of ground and looking adoringly up at him.

'You would almost think the boy understood what Eddie'd done for him,' Jamie said, rising and taking the heavy basket away from Fon. 'Eddie would have made a good doctor, no doubt about that.'

He removed the white cloth. 'Ah, pasties still warm from the oven,' he said, turning to the men, 'and cheese and crusty bread. That'll fill a corner or two, boys.'

Fon sank on to the ground and leaned against the gate-post, pleased to be resting in the late, unexpected sunshine, if only for a short time. During the afternoon, she would help the men in the fields, and later she would return home with Patrick and make the main meal of the day for all of them. It was a hard life, but, as she'd pointed out to Jamie, it was no harder than working the oysters.

She glanced covertly at her husband; his eyes met hers, and the look he gave her sent shivers of desire flowing through her. She smiled. It was good to be married to the handsomest man in the whole world.

By the time she returned to the farmhouse later that afternoon, with Patrick hanging on to her skirts, Fon

171

ached in every limb. But as she neared the doorway, the hairs on the back of her neck seemed to rise.

'Stay by here a minute, Patrick,' she said and moved quietly into the kitchen, glancing around her uneasily. Ever since the night when the place was wrecked, she had been half afraid to walk into the empty house. Her eyes went to the gun placed near the door. It was still there.

From round the back, she heard the dogs barking, and, though everything appeared to be normal, she had the strangest feeling someone had been in the house.

She searched the rooms. All of them were empty, and yet her strange feelings persisted. She shrugged. 'Fon, you're getting like an old hen!' she said out loud, but the sound of her own voice in the silence was not reassuring.

'Come on, Patrick, my boy, better come inside out of the chilly breeze,' she said. The boy came obediently and climbed into the old rocking chair, his eyes closing wearily.

Fon smiled, relaxing a little. It was time she put the potatoes on to boil, or the men would be coming in and no meal ready.

She built up the fire and lifted the heavy pot into place on the hob. She'd spent much of the morning peeling potatoes and cutting up swede; they would be boiled together to make the 'potch' that was a favourite of Jamie's.

It was only when she went to set the table that she saw the note. It was pinned against the table by a pebble to which the dirt of the yard still clung. With trembling hands, Fon picked it up and tried to decipher the scrawled words.

YOU THINK I'M FINISHED WITH YOU, BUT I'M WATCHING YOUR EVERY MOVE AND I'LL HAVE YOU ONE DAY, MISS HIGH

AND MIGHTY. BUT FIRST I'LL RUIN THAT PRECIOUS HUSBAND OF YOURS.

Fon burnt the letter and then went out to the yard and threw the pebble as far away from her as she could. She washed her hands and dried them carefully, as if to rid herself of any trace of the note.

She would not tell Jamie about it, she decided; he had enough to think about as it was. In any case, it would only anger him, and he would be constantly worrying about going out into the fields and leaving her alone in the house.

Fon picked up the gun from near the door and felt its reassuring weight against her. Woe betide any man who tried to do harm to her or hers.

It was several days later when Fon awoke to the smell of burning. During the moments of half-sleep, she thought Jamie must be burning the stubble from the empty fields prior to sowing the winter barley. But when she turned Jamie was asleep at her side.

She scrambled out of bed, flinging off her nightgown and pulling on her clothes. 'Jamie!' she panted, 'wake up! Something is burning.'

He was awake in an instant; there seemed to be no transition between sleep and full alertness. He stood there on the opposite side of the bed, his strong back bent as he drew on his trews.

'Christ!' he said. 'It must be the corn.' He ran down the stairs and out of the door. Fon could hear raised voices in the yard and knew that Eddie and Tommy must have been alerted to the fire at the same time as she was.

She moved to the window, and her worst fears were confirmed. Smoke billowed upwards in dark clouds; some of the stooks were flaring like torches in the early morning light, whilst others smouldered darkly.

Fon sank on to the bed. 'All that work!' she whispered. 'All of it for nothing.'

They would be ruined. There would be no money

173

coming in, not from the corn now. And the potatoes would take time to lift; it was sheer hard backbreaking work, with only Jamie and herself and two lads to do the work of half a dozen strong men.

Rage filled her. If only she had her enemies in her sights, the men who wanted to harm her and Jamie, she would shoot without compunction.

She roused herself. She must run for help; all the neighbouring farmers would join in to fight the fire, for it might spread to other fields, ruin other crops.

She wrapped Patrick, still asleep, in a blanket and carried him outside to where the grey horse was nuzzling grass. Without stopping to saddle the animal, Fon climbed up on the broad back, clutching, with one hand, at the grey's flowing mane, Patrick held tightly before her.

'Come on, girl,' she urged the horse, 'don't gallop too hard, mind, or you'll have us off.'

The acrid smell of scorched corn and earth brought tears to her eyes, and she began to cough as she skirted the perimeter of the burning field. The stooks were well alight, and in her heart Fon knew that her journey was futile. By the time help came, it would be too late. Much too late.

CHAPTER FOURTEEN

'We'll work for nothing for as long as needs be, boss.'
Tommy's young face was grimed with smoke, his eyes
red-rimmed, and Fon felt her heart contract with pain.

'We'll soon catch up, you'll see. Once the potatoes
are picked, there'll be a bit of money coming in,' he
added earnestly.

'I'll second that,' Eddie said, his young face grim. 'I
don't hold with hooligans trying to drive honest farmers
out of their living.'

'Aye, you're all right, sure you are. I've got myself two
fine young men,' Jamie said, rubbing a weary hand over
his eyes, 'and I'll accept your offer most gratefully,
though the Lord knows when I'll catch up with all the
wages I'll owe you.'

'The fire was set on purpose then?' Fon said, pushing
the kettle on to the newly mended fire. As Jamie nodded,
the last faint hope that somehow this was an accident,
not the work of a vengeful enemy, vanished.

'Aye, colleen.' Jamie's hand rested on her shoulder.
'It was set deliberately, the work of evil men all right,
and I've got a good idea who those men were.' He
rubbed at his tousled hair and it sprung in curls around
his face. 'Bob Smale was behind it all, no doubt; and
somehow Mike the Spud is in it with him, up to his
neck.'

Fon shivered. She knew that Jamie would not let
matters rest there; it was a matter of honour for him to
settle the score between him and the men who had done
their best to take away his livelihood.

'Look, love,' Fon said, 'let's just think about getting

175

on our feet for now, is it?' She was frightened for her husband. These men that threatened them were not ordinary human beings; it seemed they had no compunction in destroying anything that stood in their way. That they were a very real threat she did not doubt; and they would try again, for sure.

She knew suddenly that she had to tell Jamie about the note. But not yet, not until he'd calmed down a little and sorted out what to do next.

It was as though he'd read her thoughts. 'The only thing we can do now is to sell the bull,' he said. 'The Black Devil will bring a good price at market.'

Fon knew what it cost Jamie to come to such a decision. The bull was a prized possession; it put him in a position of respect, as well as bringing in business from the other farmers who came to Honey's Farm to have their cows served.

But facts needed to be faced; the bull cost a great deal to keep. The huge animal seemed to have a boundless appetite, and most of the time the Black Devil led a sheltered, indolent life.

'We'll all have some tea and then get ourselves cleaned up,' Jamie said decisively. 'We've rescued enough corn to serve our own needs throughout the winter, and later on we'll carry what's left into the barn nearest the house.'

Jamie forced a smile. 'What if when we're cleaned up we'll have one of my wife's fine breakfasts? A platter of bacon and eggs will set us up for the day, boys.'

While the men were gone to the pump in the yard, Fon put more coals on to the fire, rubbing at her tired eyes, impatient with herself for the tears that threatened to spill over. And yet fear raged within her, fear that somehow this vendetta would go too far, that she or Jamie or even Patrick might be hurt.

And there was always the spectre of failure, the fear that Jamie might lose the farm if something wasn't sorted out soon.

Perhaps, she thought, she should go to see Bob Smale, talk to him, try to reason with him; it might help. But instinctively she knew she mustn't even mention such an idea to Jamie. The last thing he would want was his wife lowering herself to ask help from a villain like Bob Smale.

By the time the men came in for their breakfast, her mind was made up. She would go into Swansea, call at the *Cambrian* offices, see what could be done.

She smiled as she ladled crispy-edged eggs on to the large plates she was warming on the hob. The bacon still sizzled in the pan, sending out a tempting aroma. The menfolk settled themselves expectantly around the table, looking clean and fresh washed, hair still damp from the cold water of the pump. It seemed that nothing, not hard work or near disaster, could rob them of their appetite.

It was chilly in the streets of Swansea, and the roads seemed busier than ever. Fon was glad she had left Patrick with Jamie on the farm. He grew tired easily since his bout of fever, and a cough still lingered, sometimes keeping him awake at nights. Fon worried about him, thinking of the way Katherine had died, a victim of the lung disease.

She pushed the thoughts away and glanced up at the sky between the buildings. The late September sun seemed to hang with a dull glow, obscured now and then with scudding clouds.

Fon walked towards the offices of the newspaper with footsteps that dragged. She felt a heavy sense of apprehension, remembering the way Bob Smale had attacked her. Perhaps she was simply being foolish, coming to Swansea to talk to the man; perhaps he had no better nature to appeal to.

It was suddenly dark in the offices after the light outside, and Fon blinked a little, trying to adjust her eyes to the gloom. She closed the door quietly behind her and moved towards the desk.

As she became accustomed to the change of light, she saw with a feeling that veered between relief and despair that Bob Smale was not there. Instead, a pimply youth with thick spectacles stared across the room, a pen poised in his hand and an impatient look on his face.

'Yes?' He spoke abruptly, his look indicating that she was disturbing him. Fon felt a sudden rush of anger; just because she was dressed in the simple clothes of the countrywoman he was daring to look down on her.

'I want to speak to Mr Smale,' she said, forcing down her anger and smiling as pleasantly as she could.

The man looked more closely at her as she drew nearer to the desk, and when he saw that she was young and personable, his attitude changed.

'Bobby? He's left the office this couple of weeks since,' he said more kindly. 'Can I help?'

Fon smiled at him and leaned closer, as though confiding in him. 'I *hope* you can help me; I have to see Mr Smale on a personal matter.'

'Right.' The man opened a small drawer and withdrew a card. He winked at Fon and touched the side of his nose with his forefinger. 'I shouldn't be telling you this but our Bobby's gone and joined the landed gentry.' He handed her the card. 'See, his place is somewhere up on Townhill.'

Fon felt herself grow cold. The only land not already being farmed was the acres adjoining the piece of land Jamie had bought from Tommy's mother. She'd known it was owned by Bob Smale, but she didn't know he was actually living up there. She'd imagined the old farmhouse was deserted.

'But I didn't know Mr Smale was interested in farming the place,' Fon said. 'I thought his work kept him in the town most of the time.'

'Used to,' the young man said knowledgeably. 'But

our Bobby has taken to the bottle again; a right little boozer he is when the mood takes him.' He laughed. 'That's when I step in and take over the *Cambrian*. Couldn't do without me, could our Bobby.

'I don't know what he means to you, miss, but I'd keep out of his way if I were you. He's evil when he's in drink.' He paused and looked Fon over speculatively.

'Bobby will never *farm* that piece of land; oh, no, that's too much like hard work. No, he'll just hole up there until his binge passes again and he comes back to the land of the living. God help that daughter of his, that's all I can say.'

'You're very kind,' Fon said. 'I'm very grateful to you for your help.'

She made her way back into the street, and the sudden warmth of the sunshine bursting through the gloom brought her confidence rushing back.

She *must* see Bob Smale, challenge him to tell the truth, ask him what exactly it was he wanted. Perhaps matters could be settled in a reasonable way, without any more violence and destruction. And if he had a daughter living with him, surely Fon would be safe enough.

It was no wonder, she thought angrily, that Smale was able to strike at the farm with such good timing; he was probably watching them night and day from the safety of his own land. Why it hadn't occurred to her before that his work in the town kept him busy for only a part of the time, she couldn't think. It was all so obvious now; Bob Smale had wanted the land between the two farms for some crooked scheme of his own, and Jamie had thwarted him.

As she climbed back up the hill, she knew what she would do; she would try to reason with the man, but not without the security of a gun in her hand.

When she reached the farmhouse, Fon stood for a moment in the dreaming silence of the autumn day.

179

There was no-one about; all the men, along with Patrick, were in the fields, it was so peaceful here on Honey's Farm, so tranquil. But if she didn't do something, it might not remain that way.

With an air of resolution, Fon picked up the gun and moved outside once again into the brightness of the day.

Gwyneth looked around her, glad to be away from the bucking and clattering and the horrid, gushing steam of the train. She was becoming familiar now with the Cardiff streets, and it was with ease that she made her way towards Bell's Emporium. Once there, however, her task would not be so easy.

Fear gripped Gwyneth, and she took a deep ragged breath, trying to think of a palatable way to tell Will that she was carrying his child. But she knew in her heart there was no way to gloss over such news; it had to be said straight out in simple phrases.

Mrs Bell was moving about the huge entrance with a watering can in her hand, bending over lush palms and pinching at them with arthritic fingers as though testing them for dust.

She looked up at Gwyneth, took in her workaday clothes, and approached her with the watering can held before her like a weapon.

'What can we do for you?' Her voice would freeze the sea to ice even on a summer's day, Gwyneth thought ruefully.

'I must speak with Mr Davies,' she said, mustering all her confidence. 'It's business.' She wondered if Mrs Bell recognized her; there was no way of telling, not from the woman's stern expression.

'I see. Well, he's out to lunch, so I'm afraid you'll need to call back some other time.' Mrs Bell was about to turn dismissively away when Gwyneth spoke again.

'But it's important,' she said. 'I've travelled all the way from Swansea.'

Mrs Bell took in a deep breath through her nose. 'Very well, he's gone to lunch in the little restaurant next door.' She looked disapproving. 'But don't keep him; he's due back in just a few minutes and I don't approve of unpunctuality.'

Gwyneth hurried outside and took a deep breath. For one awful moment she'd thought the old bat wasn't going to tell her where Will had gone.

Gwyneth looked in through the window of the restaurant and hesitated. The tables were laid with gleaming silver resting on pristine cloths; the room was full of well-dressed people, and, try as she might, she could not pick out Will's big frame.

Gwyneth's stomach knotted and she gripped her hands to her sides as she suddenly spotted him. 'Hell and damnation!' She breathed the words, her whole being aflame with jealousy, for Will was with Eline Harries and his head was bent towards hers as though they were talking secrets, like lovers.

Gwyneth's first instinct was to run, to put as much distance between herself and Will and the smiling face of Eline Harries as she could. Then common sense reasserted itself; nothing would be gained by running away.

She glanced into the window again and saw that Will was rising to his feet. He was moving Eline's chair for her, and as Gwyneth watched, Will smiled down at her with such love in his face that Gwyneth despaired. How could she make him marry her, knowing he didn't love her but was in love with Eline? Could she bear to make him unhappy for the rest of his life? Perhaps she should simply catch the train back to Swansea, leave Will to live his own life.

Gwyneth turned and hurried away from the restaurant, and she could see nothing ahead of her but a long tunnel from where there would never come even a glimmer of light.

As Fon was making her way across the fields, she saw Eddie waving to her. She stopped walking and waited for him to catch up with her. He looked at the gun in her hand and seemed, instinctively, to know what she intended.

'I'll come with you,' he said firmly.

After a moment's hesitation, Fon nodded. 'I'm not going to use this' – she indicated the gun – 'but I thought I should take it with me, just in case of trouble.'

'You know who's been doing the damage and you are going to confront him,' Eddie said, and it was a statement, not a question.

Fon nodded. 'I have to try to talk to Bob Smale. He has a grudge against Jamie.' She smiled ruefully. 'Well, it's a bit more than a grudge, I suppose.'

'He *must* have!' Eddie said. 'To go to the lengths this idiot has, he must hate Jamie's guts.' He moderated his long stride to match Fon's shorter steps, and she looked up at him.

'What are you going to do?' Eddie asked, and Fon found herself talking to him like a trusted friend. And that was what Eddie had become, she realized suddenly, a man she could rely on.

'Bob Smale not only hates Jamie for the hiding he gave him,' she concluded, 'but he's furious at him for buying the land from under his nose as well.'

'I'm not surprised Jamie gave him a thrashing,' Eddie said fiercely. 'Anyone messing with another man's wife deserves all he gets.'

Fon didn't reply. She thought ruefully about her mother taking Eline Harries's husband, not once but twice, and wondered what Eddie would have to say about such carryings on. Eddie was a gentleman, a real gentleman, Fon thought, and it was a great pity that he'd been unable to continue with his profession. He would have made a fine, compassionate doctor.

It took a good hour's walking to bring Fon to the perimeter of the land Bob Smale owned. The acres spreading out before her were a morass of wild grasses and shrubs, good soil gone to waste.

'Not a working farmer, this man,' Eddie said. 'He must have something else in mind for the land.'

'What, though?' Fon asked, puzzled. 'What other use could he have?'

Eddie frowned and scratched at his head. 'There could be minerals here, coal even. This is hilly terrain, might be good seams lying beneath the surface.'

'Coal!' Fon said in horror. She tried to imagine the land desecrated, scarred with slag heaps, dust flying across what was now sweet grass.

'Might even be a prime place to build new houses on,' Eddie said reasonably. 'We won't know unless . . .'

'Unless what?' Fon asked, looking up at Eddie in bewilderment.

'Unless the old copies of the *Cambrian* might give us a clue,' Eddie said. 'What if we abandon our plan to talk to this man? I can't see it doing much good anyway. Let's just try to find out exactly why he wants to buy up as much of the hill as he can.'

Fon leaned against the warmth of a wooden stile and stared around her, as though seeking inspiration from the landscape.

After a moment, she nodded. 'I think that's sensible, Eddie,' she said, 'much more sensible than trying to shoot in the dark.'

'Hey!' A high feminine voice rang out. 'What are you doing here? This is private property, mind.'

Fon spun round and saw a young girl riding towards them on a bay mare. Her hair, streaking behind her in the breeze, was a beautiful silver, rippling in waves like a moon-kissed sea.

'Sorry.' It was Eddie who spoke. 'We were just out walking, didn't mean to trespass.' He was

183

smiling, and Fon could see he was stricken by the girl's beauty.

'Why the gun, then?' the girl persisted. Her brown eyes, huge and fringed with thick lashes, watched them both with suspicion.

'Oh, just in case I saw a rabbit or two,' Eddie said easily. 'Live here, do you?'

'That's my business.' The girl spoke abruptly. 'Now, if you know what's good for you, you'll go right away from this piece of land.'

'Why are you being so nasty?' Fon asked. 'What have you got to hide? We mean you no harm, mind.'

For a moment, the girl seemed nonplussed by Fon's gentle tone. She rubbed her hand down over her bodice, not realizing that the act emphasized the young curve of her breasts.

'It's for your own good,' she said at last. 'My father isn't here at the moment, but I know he'd object to anyone nosing about his property.'

'Your father is Bob Smale, isn't he?' Fon asked, and it was as though a shutter had come down over the young girl's face. Her large eyes suddenly wore a guarded expression.

'Just go away,' she said, at last. 'Don't you know a bit of good advice when it's offered to you?'

With a quick movement, she wheeled the horse around and was riding away in the direction from which she'd come.

'Well, what do you make of that?' Fon asked, and then smiled as she saw Eddie's pole-axed expression. 'I know what *you* make of it all right,' she said in amusement, 'you're in love.'

'You know,' Eddie said, as they set off back across the fields, 'I do believe you are right.'

The next day, Eddie took time off to go to the newspaper offices and search out what was contained in the files. He dressed in his best suit, and as he stood

184

before Fon at the kitchen door he looked to her for approval.

'You'll do all right,' Fon said. 'What with your fine appearance and that posh voice of yours, they'll let you see anything you want to see.'

'This will help too.' Eddie tossed the coins that Fon had given him the previous night. 'I feel quite wealthy.'

'I suppose you were used to having money before . . .' She broke off in embarrassment, but Eddie simply smiled.

'I took money for granted. That's something I'll never do again, believe me.'

When he had gone, Fon stood at the window, staring out into the fields. Tomorrow, Jamie would take the Black Devil to market, and with the money buy some winter barley and, more importantly, buy in some cattle for finishing.

With farming it was always a waiting game, she mused; you planned, you planted and, hopefully, you reaped. And you could do without enemies who burnt your crop.

Jamie came into the kitchen, his hair tangled by the breeze blowing uphill from the sea, his cheeks wind-burned. He smiled and took her in his arms, his hand caressing the small of her back in a way that sent shivers running through her.

'What are you up to, colleen?' he asked, his mouth pressed against the warmth of her neck. She put her arms around him, holding him close, her eyes closed as she listened to the beat of his heart.

'Never you mind, Mr O'Conner,' she teased. 'You'll know it all in good time. Just be patient.'

Jamie tipped her face up to his and kissed her mouth. Fon longed to cling to him, to tear off her clothes and make him love her; amazed at her reaction, she drew away from him.

'*Duw*, you're turning me into a real hussy! For shame on you, Jamie, kissing me that way, and it's still daylight.'

He sat at the table and put his elbows on the scrubbed boards. 'If you don't like it, why are you smiling so happily, then?' he challenged, his eyes bright.

'Who said I didn't like it?' Fon placed her hands on her hips and stared at her husband provocatively.

'Where's Patrick?' he asked.

Fon pointed in the direction of the parlour. 'Having a nap in there,' she said. 'Why . . . ?'

She broke off as Jamie rose suddenly and swept her up into his arms. 'In that case, I might just as well have my wicked way with you, colleen,' he said.

In the bedroom, he dropped her lightly on the bed, and then he was beside her, his hands caressing, his eyes alight. The scent of him was of the sun and the grass and the open air, and Fon was as desperate as he was as her fingers opened the buttons of his shirt.

He took her quickly, and she moaned in surrender, feeling the fire in her that he always roused. The second time, calmer now, he was tender, teasing and tantalizing her until she could have screamed out for release.

Afterwards, they lay in each other's arms, bathed in late September sunlight from the open window. Fon pushed herself up on one elbow and looked down at her husband.

'You are a fine man, Jamie,' she said softly. 'I don't know what I would have done with my life if I hadn't met you.'

'You'd have turned into a dried-up spinster, no doubt,' he said, kissing the breast nearest to his face, 'and I would have found myself a rich widow who would have died in gratitude for a kiss and would not be wearing me to a shadow with constant demands.'

Fon leaned over him. 'Wearing you to a shadow, am I?' she said softly and put her mouth against his throat. Gently, her hands stroked him and she felt him become aroused to her touch.

186

'What are you doing, colleen?' he asked. 'Don't you know I've got work to do?'

'The work can wait,' she whispered, 'but first I want to wear you to a shadow.'

It was almost dark by the time Eddie returned from Swansea. He joined the others at the supper table and looked at Fon questioningly.

'It's all right, Eddie,' she said. 'Let us all know what you've found out.'

'It's quite staggering,' Eddie said, accepting the plate of meat and potatoes that Fon handed him. 'There's going to be a new road, a big road running all the way through the hill and down into the town.'

Jamie was ahead of him. 'And the road will go through the piece of land I bought from Tommy's mother.'

'That's right,' Eddie said. 'You made a good investment when you bought that, Jamie, for now you're all set to make a quick profit.'

Jamie sat back in his chair, a satisfied expression on his face. 'You can fill me in on the details later of what you and my little wife have been hatching between you,' he said. 'For now, eat your supper; you've earned it.'

Jamie's eyes met Fon's and she read admiration in his gaze; desire she was used to, but the way he appraised her now, as though seeing her as an adult woman for the first time, gave her a heady sensation of triumph.

Slowly, meaningfully, she smiled at him. 'You see,' she said softly, 'you're better off without your rich widow, after all.'

CHAPTER FIFTEEN

'But, love, you've *got* to see him, tell him about the baby. He's the *father*, and he's got the right to know.'

Gwyneth listened to her mother's words, but they seemed to be washing over her like the waves of the sea outside.

Gwyneth looked through the window, wishing herself any place but here, in Oystermouth, bearing this terrible feeling of hopelessness.

'I can't ruin his life,' Gwyneth said slowly, her lips almost failing to form the words. She felt weighed down with misery. She couldn't forget the picture of William and Eline Harries, so close, so *right* together.

'Well, *I* won't sit down and watch my daughter go through the hell that I did,' Nina said fiercely. 'I know what it's like to be looked down on, mind. I know the feeling of being an outcast, a fallen woman, and I don't want any daughter of mine experiencing that sort of treatment.'

'Just let me think things out, Mam,' Gwyneth begged. 'Give me a few days and then I'll decide what's the best thing to do.'

Nina moved to the window and stared along the street. Her mouth was a tight line in her pale face. Gwyneth realized that Nina was suffering more heartache for her daughter's plight than she ever had for her own.

Had Nina yearned to be with Joe Harries as she yearned to be with William, Gwyneth wondered? Had Nina felt the tearing, destructive force of jealousy that wanted to kill the obstacle between her and her love?

'I know it hurts,' Nina said softly, as though reading

her daughter's inner thoughts. 'It hurts like nothing on God's earth to see your man with another woman. And it *had* to be that Eline Harries standing in your way, didn't it? I wish she'd never come to Oystermouth.'

Gwyneth felt suddenly very tired. She longed for silence, for rest from the feelings that warred within her, and for respite from her mother's indignation.

She moved towards Nina and rested her arm around her mother's shoulders. 'Thank you, Mam,' she said softly. 'Thank you for not judging me or blaming me.'

Nina looked into her daughter's face. 'How could I judge you, when you got your nature from me?'

In an unexpected show of affection, Nina hugged her. After a moment, Gwyneth disentangled herself from her mother's arms and moved away slowly towards the stairs. 'I'm going to lie down, Mam,' she said softly. 'I've got a bit of a headache.'

'A bit of a heartache more like,' Nina murmured, but Gwyneth didn't answer. She made her way wearily upstairs and sank on to her bed, staring around at the room as if she'd never seen it before.

It was as neat as it had ever been, but the curtains were growing shabby; the patchwork quilt on the bed was faded with washing; even the enamel washbasin on the table was chipped and discoloured.

Mam was getting older, Gwyneth thought, with a dart of pity. Nina could no longer go out and work on the oyster beds as she'd done when Joe Harries was alive. It was as though, with his death, Nina had given up her youth, allowed herself to become older, a woman in a shawl content to work in the house, cooking and cleaning and sometimes even spending the evenings near the fire knitting or sewing.

Nina had always provided for her family, and now, it seemed, it was Gwyneth's duty to repay her mother for all her years of toil.

Sal was married, and so was Fon, the youngest of the

189

sisters; they both had their own lives to lead. It was left to Gwyneth to take care of Mam.

Gwyneth sighed. Perhaps the solution to her problem was a visit to Mrs Kenny. She was known only by word of mouth, but she was reputed to be adept at helping young girls to slip an unwanted baby. And she charged much less than the proper midwife.

Gwyneth hugged her stomach. She was carrying Will's child; it was growing here within her. How could she even think of getting rid of it? And yet – her mind went round like a trapped fly in a web – what was the alternative? She couldn't work on the beds with the other women, not once her condition began to show; she just couldn't face it.

Mrs Kenny, it seemed, was the only way out. Tomorrow, Gwyneth would go to see her. There was nothing else for her to do.

She curled up on the bed and pulled the quilt over her head, trying to burrow down into the darkness. She didn't want to think any more, or to feel any more pain. She just wanted to go to sleep and never wake up again.

'You've done an excellent job, Mrs Harries, I congratulate you.' Mrs Bell positively beamed, and Eline smiled warmly in return.

'Thank you, Mrs Bell. It's very kind of you; but, even though I've worked very hard, I've enjoyed every minute I've spent at your emporium.'

And Eline meant it. She had felt the creative juices flow as she'd decorated first the window for Will and then, at Mrs Bell's insistence, the other windows in the store.

'I confess myself wrong.' Mrs Bell eased herself into one of the chairs strategically placed around the store for the comfort of her customers. 'It was old-fashioned of me to think that people don't change. They do; at least my customers seem to have changed.' She smiled.

'There's more of them, for a start, since you had a hand in things, young lady.'

Eline was pleased and warmed. It wasn't like Mrs Bell to make congratulatory statements, and she usually meant every word she said.

'Well, I suppose you'd better be on your way, then. I mustn't keep you.' Mrs Bell smiled to soften the edge to her words. 'But you'll be back in two weeks? That's definite, I trust, for I shall want my new stock shown off. It will have arrived by then.'

'I will be back in two weeks, I assure you,' Eline said, holding out her hand.

Gravely, Mrs Bell shook it. 'That's a promise, then?' she insisted, and Eline smiled warmly.

'That's a promise.'

Eline felt strange walking out of the store into the pale sunlight. She looked up at the trees, bare now, stripped of the last of the red and gold leaves. The last of the warm weather had gone; the streets would grow cold, and in the country the earth would seem to be quietly drifting off to sleep.

Eline thought suddenly of autumn on Honey's Farm, the days spent among the ripe corn, the backbreaking work of cutting and drying it, and the threshing and winnowing. It had been hard, but she had loved it. And then in winter, the ground hard, appearing as though nothing would ever grow on it again. And yet spring always came, bringing green shoots thrusting strongly through the ground, looking for sunshine. In a way, this was the winter of her life. The old ways were over and done with; she must face the future with courage.

She walked more briskly now. She was meeting Will to say goodbye before she returned to Swansea. Good-bye – it was such a sad word. And yet, in spite of herself, Eline felt warmed by the thought of seeing Will again, even for a few minutes. At least they were friends now, and, though she could never forget his infidelity with

Gwyneth Parks, she *could* believe now that it had happened in one weak moment when he felt as lost and alone as she sometimes did.

And for men it was different; she knew that from her marriage to Joe. Men had greater urges, urges they found it hard to control. She didn't condone it, because love wasn't to be given carelessly – that way led to pain and suffering – it was a thing to be cherished, encouraged to grow.

But, to be realistic, how many times had she surrendered to her husband, not out of love at all, but out of duty? Joe had wanted her so much; he had earned the right to take her to his bed, he had married her.

Will had simply used Gwyneth Parks as a momentary assuaging of his loneliness and passion: not a kind act, certainly, but one she could understand.

Eline felt suddenly sorry for Gwyneth. She loved Will just as surely as Eline loved him, and now her feelings of rejection must be terrible.

For a moment, anger with Will filled Eline. How could he be so thoughtless, so careless with his passion? He had no doubt aroused hopes in Gwyneth that could never be fulfilled. It was cruel of him to have shown her happiness only to have taken it away from her again.

The ornate doorway of the Cardiff tearooms was only a few steps away now. Eline paused and took a deep breath. She must not meet Will with the tumult of anger and jealousy and love – yes, love – warring within her; she was simply saying farewell to a friend.

Don't fool yourself! The inner voice was insistent. *You want him as much as you ever did*, the voice said.

The inner voice was right; she wanted to forgive Will, but some perverse sense of anger wanted to make him suffer first.

He rose when she entered the room, and she saw no-one but him. Across the white-covered tables, the chatter of people and the clinking of china, she saw only Will, and her heart seemed to stop beating.

But she appeared serene as she moved towards him and sat with superb composure in the elegant chair that he held for her.

'I was beginning to think you weren't coming after all,' Will said softly.

Eline looked at him with deliberate coolness. The anger was still with her at her thoughts of his betrayal with Gwyneth Parks; she just couldn't help it.

'We could have said our goodbyes at the emporium,' she said. 'Mrs Bell was very reluctant to see me go.'

'Damn Mrs Bell!' Will leant towards her. 'I wanted to say goodbye to you properly, in private.' He glanced round him ruefully. 'Or as private as you would allow.'

Eline made no comment, but there was a happy glow within her that she couldn't deny. She looked up as Will poured her a cup of tea; his manner was proprietary and she smiled a little to herself.

'I promised Mrs Bell I'd come back in two weeks' time,' she said. Her eyes met Will's, and the light in them made her colour rise.

'I love you, Eline,' he said. 'And I know you love me. We must be able to find our way back together.'

'Perhaps,' Eline conceded, 'but don't try to rush things, Will, please.'

He put a small velvet box on the table. 'No ties, but I want you to have this small gift,' he said. 'I wish I could say it was my mother's, but my mother had nothing but poverty all her life.'

Eline touched his hand impulsively. She knew how his whole family had died from 'Yellow Jack', the fever that had swept Swansea some years ago, and the thought of Will as a child left alone tugged at her heart-strings.

She opened the box slowly. Inside was a gold ring set with a single pearl. 'It's beautiful, Will,' she said, 'but you can't afford to be buying such gifts, not the way things are at the moment.'

193

'I know,' Will said, 'but I wanted so much to give you something to make you think of me once in a while.' He laughed. 'I'll probably spend the next few months working for nothing to pay for it, but that's my problem.'

Eline was touched. Her heart felt heavy with love and compassion. She was spiteful and jealous and unforgiving – but how could she change that? He had hurt her; there was no getting away from it, and the hurt went deep.

She closed the box and placed it in her bag. 'I'll treasure it, Will,' she said softly.

'But not wear it?' Will's voice was harsh with pain, and Eline felt a stab of satisfaction. He should be hurting; he had hurt her, hadn't he?

'Eline, are you never going to soften your attitude?' he asked impatiently. 'I didn't murder anyone, you know, I simply slept with a woman. Your husband had a mistress and you accepted it as part of man's nature. I did nothing of that sort; we weren't even married, Eline, so why are you passing such harsh judgement on me?'

She was silent for a long moment. 'You are right,' she said at last. 'I could forgive Joe because I didn't love him.'

His face softened; the tenseness went from his shoulders. 'You do love me, then?' he asked, and his hand reached out, rested warm on hers.

'Yes, I love you, God help me,' Eline said in a whisper. She rose to her feet. 'I have to go, I've got to catch a train. I'll see you in two weeks?'

'Before that,' Will said. 'I'm coming to Swansea to talk business with Hari the day after tomorrow. Will I see you then?'

Eline smiled. 'Yes, I'd like that, Will. I'd like it very much.'

He rose and accompanied her to the door, and

194

she looked at him in surprise. 'Where are you going?' she asked, and he looked down at her, a smile in his eyes.

'You don't think I'm going to let you walk to the station alone, do you? Some discerning man might snap you up on the way.'

Eline laughed. It was good to laugh with Will again, and good to walk along with him at her side. It was time, after all, for forgiveness; she'd carried on the feeling of hurt pride for far too long.

She looked up at Will and then deliberately tucked her arm in his. He smiled and drew her close, and together they walked in the sunlight beneath the falling leaves.

'The gallery is doing well.' Calvin Temple smiled down at Eline as she stood in the largest room, staring round at the paintings.

Eline returned his smile; she felt good, somehow refreshed. She had spent a good night dreaming about Will, and the ring he'd given her was hung safely on a gold chain around her neck. She had relished the closeness of their last meeting, and now she felt ready to face the world.

She hugged the thought to her that he was coming home tomorrow; she would see him, be with him, and that, she realized, was very important to her. The days they had spent together in Cardiff had made her understand how much she loved and needed him. Will was part of her life's blood, and whatever he had done, it was past and over with. And what had he done, except make one mistake?

'Did you hear me, Eline?' Calvin's voice held amusement. 'I've been accused of many things, but never of being boring.'

'I'm sorry.' Eline put her hand on his arm. Calvin was a personable, pleasant man; not handsome, as Will was, of course, but he had charm and Eline liked him enormously.

'You've done well here,' she said, looking round her. 'You have some fine paintings in, and it's clear from the books that they are turning over very nicely.'

'We never have anything for too long,' Calvin agreed, 'which is very fortunate for us.'

'More due to your efforts than to good fortune, I think,' Eline said quickly.

'You know something, Eline?' Calvin said. 'You and I make a very good pair; we should be partners in more ways than one, don't you think?' He was smiling, and Eline pretended to slap his hand.

'Don't tease,' she said amiably. 'It's not kind to trifle with a lady's affections.'

'Who said I'm teasing or trifling, come to that?' Calvin had trapped her hand, and now he raised it to his lips.

'I would be more than honoured if you would accept me as a suitor.' He was serious now, and Eline was at a loss for words.

'If you had a father, I would ask him most humbly for his daughter's hand in marriage,' Calvin continued. 'As it is, I can only ask the lady herself.'

'I'll consider it,' Eline said, in a spirit of lightness, doing her best to distract him, 'but for now, let's get on with the business in hand. I thought you wanted me to arrange the window for you.'

Calvin sighed. 'It's my burden never to be taken seriously,' he said, but the mocking gleam was back in his eye.

'And serve you right,' Eline said. 'You are far too charming for your own good.'

It was later, when Eline was leaving the gallery, that she came face to face with Nina Parks. Eline smiled in greeting; old scores were long forgotten. Or at least she'd thought they were, but Nina was looking at her with hostility in every line of her face.

196

'What's wrong?' Eline said quickly.

Nina moved closer, keeping her voice low. 'You don't know that you are coming between my daughter and the man she loves?' she asked.

Eline stepped back as though she'd been slapped. 'I know they . . . went together once,' she said hesitantly, 'and I'm sorry for Gwyneth, I am; but there's nothing I can do about it, is there?'

'You can keep out of his life,' Nina said, 'give my girl a chance. She loves him; and, with you out of the way, he'd love her too, especially when he knows.'

Eline's mouth was suddenly dry. 'What do you mean?' Her voice was scarcely more than a whisper, and suddenly Nina's hostility vanished.

'You poor, foolish girl,' she said. 'He's deceived you just as he's deceived my Gwyneth.'

Eline took her arm and drew her away from the gallery. 'Tell me, Nina,' she said humbly, 'tell me, what it is you are trying to say?'

'It wasn't only the once that Will Davies slept with Gwyneth,' Nina said. 'Oh, damn these men!'

'How can I believe you?' Eline felt as though the ground was moving beneath her feet, that a gaping chasm was opening before her.

'My girl is expecting Will Davies's child,' Nina said baldly. 'Sorry, but there's no other way of saying it.'

'No!' Eline said, the word dragged from dry lips. 'I don't believe you, it can't be true.'

'It's true, all right,' Nina said, 'and what's more, Gwyneth came up to that awful place where you and him were working. Going to tell him she was, then she saw you together in some posh tearooms.'

Nina's face softened. 'I'm sorry for you, girl, just as my Gwyneth was sorry for you. She saw how Will loved you, and how besotted you were with him, and she just came away without saying anything about the baby – going to face it all alone, she was, and I can't allow that.'

Eline felt physically ill. She felt as though she was going to faint, and she put her hand on the wall to steady herself.

'Come in by here with me,' Nina was saying. 'You need a cup of sweet tea; it'll make you feel better.'

'No, I'm all right,' Eline protested. 'I don't need a cup of tea, I just want . . .' What did she want? She wanted Nina to vanish, for her words to be unspoken; she wanted it to be yesterday, when she was with Will, happy in the belief that he loved her.

Nina drew her the few yards along the road to her house, and then Eline was seated in the kitchen, the familiar kitchen where once she had lived in matrimony with Joe Harries, the house that now belonged to Nina Parks, Joe's mistress.

'Why do you Parks women always want to wreck my life?' Eline asked as Nina made the tea, swirling the water round the brown china pot.

'I don't know what the answer to that one is,' Nina said, 'but whoever is to blame, our paths keep crossing, that's for sure, and it never brings any good, I'll say that.'

She handed Eline the tea, laced with honey, and then poured herself a cup of the fragrant weak brew.

Eline looked round the kitchen. Little had changed; the same curtains hung at the windows and the same china stood on the dresser against the wall. She had left all this behind, moved on, made a new life for herself. But it was all emptiness, and Eline wished she had stayed on Honey's Farm and never come to Oystermouth in the first place.

There was the sound of footsteps overhead, and with a sense of dread, Eline realized that Gwyneth was at home. 'I've got to go,' she said, but then Gwyneth was in the kitchen. If Eline had doubted the truth of Nina's words, there were no doubts now: Gwyneth was pale and drawn, and there were lines of fatigue around her eyes. Gwyneth was with child all right.

'What are you doing here?' she said to Eline, and then without waiting for a reply turned to her mother. 'Give us a cup of tea, Mam.'

Gwyneth sank down at the table, her elbows on the scrubbed surface, supporting her chin. She seemed to be sapped of all her fight, all her spirit. Strangely, Eline felt sorry for her.

'You've told her, then, Mam?' Gwyneth said. 'There was no need. I've decided to go to Mrs Kenny.'

'No!' The word exploded from Nina's lips. 'I'll have no murdering of innocent babies under my roof.'

'What else can I do?' Gwyneth said, and the hopelessness in her voice cut into Eline like a knife.

'Tell him,' Eline said softly. 'You must talk to Will; your mother's right.'

Eline had heard of Mrs Kenny, and it horrified her to think what a desperate way out of her problem Gwyneth was considering.

'Let Will face up to his responsibilities. It's the least he can do.' She heard the bitterness in her own voice, but she couldn't hide it.

Eline swallowed hard. She couldn't yet come to terms with the shock of the situation. Gwyneth Parks, expecting Will's child – it just wasn't bearable.

She rose to her feet, and it was as though she was someone else, as though she was an outsider looking in on a tragedy happening to other people.

'He'll be coming to Swansea tomorrow to see Mrs Grenfell.' She heard her own voice as though from far away. 'Let him know about the . . . the baby.'

Gwyneth looked at her with a dawning of hope in her eyes. 'But I thought you and him – I thought . . .'

'We are nothing to each other,' Eline said, 'though I did think that at least we were friends. It seems even in that I was wrong.'

She moved to the door as though in a dream, and she didn't hear Nina's voice calling anxiously behind her.

199

She left the house and walked across the road to where the bay curved inwards. A gentle sea was running, and Eline thought distractedly that it would have been more appropriate if there had been a storm, with thunder and lightning and huge waves crashing against the rocks.

She put up her hand and yanked the fragile chain from around her neck. It broke in two pieces, as weak as the promises Will had made her, thought Eline numbly.

She looked at the ring for a long moment. 'Pearls for tears,' she said softly, and then she raised her arm and threw the ring as far into the water as she could. It disappeared into the waves, scarcely rippling the surface.

It was an ending, Eline thought, an ending of all her hopes and all her dreams. She felt lost, like a child without its parents for the first time. She was filled with doubts and uncertainties about her ability to go on. She stared at the sea longingly; it would be good to surrender to the pain within her and sink beneath the waters into dark oblivion.

She turned and, almost stumblingly, made her way back to the gallery. Calvin was talking to a customer, but when he saw her face, he quietly and courteously ushered the man out and closed the door, putting the bolt into place.

Without speaking, he took her in his arms, and gratefully she was wrapping her arms around him. It felt strange; he was not Will, it was not Will's heart beating against her cheek, but at least it was a loving heart, an honest heart. Eline looked up at him.

'Calvin, did you mean it when you said you wanted me as your wife?'

'I meant it,' he said tenderly. 'And I don't know what devils have driven you into my arms, but I swear I'll look after you. I'll be worthy of you, and most of all I'll love you until the day I die.'

Eline sighed heavily and closed her eyes; she was so

tired, so drained of emotion, and Calvin's arms were a haven.

'You know I don't love you,' she said softly. 'I'm not sure I know what love is any more, but I do think you are wonderful and, what's more important, I trust you.'

'I'll settle for that, at the moment,' Calvin said. 'Love will come; and until it does, I have enough love for both of us.'

CHAPTER SIXTEEN

'Fetch me my dinner, girl, and hurry up about it.' Bob Smale's voice held a harsh, imperious note, and his words were more than a little slurred.

'And if there are any more strangers trespassing on our land, let me know at once, do you hear?'

Arian Smale moved quickly to the kitchen and served up her father's meal of boiled potatoes and rabbit stew, trying to control the trembling of her hands. Her bruised face ached, and she knew that she would have a black eye by morning.

She sighed heavily. Her father didn't set out to be cruel. Most times he was reasonable and treated her well enough. It was when the drink was in him and the dark shadows of the past came down on him that he lashed out in a frenzy at whoever stood in his way.

For some years the *Cambrian* newspaper had kept her father occupied; he had spent most of the time in town, living with his mistress. But once that affair had ended, Bob Smale had turned to the drink again. Now it seemed he was set on becoming involved with the land once more, and Arian sighed wearily. When her father talked about being involved, he usually meant he was obsessed with something.

Uncle Mike only helped encourage Bob Smale's fantasy of being a rich land developer. Mike was there, egging him on; Mike must have been born under an evil cloud, he liked to hurt and wound. He did not hit out, as her father did, in frustration and anger; he was coldly calculating.

Arian had once seen him stare down at a rabbit in a

trap, a gloating look in his narrowed eyes. She shuddered. It was wicked to hate anyone, but Uncle Mike made it difficult for her to feel anything but hatred and fear of him.

She took her father his dinner and set it before him. His eyes were clearer now; the drink was wearing off, and it would be late evening before he started on the bottle again. She let out a small sigh of relief.

He caught her arm and looked up at her. 'I'm sorry, *cariad*,' he said. 'I don't mean to lose my temper, but you know how I feel about the land.'

She knew all right, for didn't her father go on about it all the time since the idea of making a fast profit had been put into his head? She rested her hand on his shoulder.

'It's all right, Dad, I understand.' And she did. Her grandparents had been well-to-do people; they had farmed wisely, selling off parts of the estate at just the right moment. They had left their eldest son an inheritance to be proud of, an inheritance Bob Smale had slowly frittered away on madcap schemes.

'We had servants once, girl.' It was as though her father had picked up on her thoughts, and, with a sigh of resignation, barely suppressed, Arian seated herself opposite him and waited for the inevitable diatribe to begin. He would play her the same old tune of how he could have been a rich man except for the vagaries of wicked fortune. But at least now her father was bordering on being sober; he would not strike out blindly as he sometimes did at anyone near him.

He waved his hand around the large dining-room, which had grown shabby now, the paint peeling from the wall, the wood of the windows rotting with lack of attention.

'Wealthy, we were, respected round here, gentleman farmers, until that Irish itinerant O'Conner came here and set himself against me. Could have had that piece of land between the farms right here' – he curled his big fingers – 'right here in the palm of my hand. Trying to buy up all the land in sight, that bastard is, and it belongs to me.'

Though it was true that Jamie O'Conner had bought Honey's Farm some time ago and now the piece of land adjoining it, it was hardly fair to say he was buying up all the land in sight. Arian looked at her father; it was useless to try to reason with him.

'That upstart O'Conner raised his hand to me, and that I will not put up with from any man. Come from Irish tinker stock, him; why doesn't he go back to the bogs where the man belongs?'

Arian felt pity for her father war with her impatience; he was so abusive, and to a man he hardly knew. In any case, her father had doubtless been given far more privileges than ever Jamie O'Conner had; he'd had a good education, his family had been respected members of the community. He still owned a good parcel of fertile land and a house that could with a little effort be restored to its former grandeur. Bob Smale would have had a brilliant future if it hadn't been for the drink.

'Haven't you done enough to him now, Dad?' she asked, her voice light and breathless; she didn't think he'd be angry with her now that he was a little more sober, but you never knew, not with her father.

'I won't have done enough until I've driven him out of Swansea altogether,' Bob said dourly. 'I hate the man's guts, don't you realize that, girl?'

He paused to eat some of his dinner, then he looked up at his daughter again. 'If there's a road going through this land, the profits from it should be mine by right; we should be rich again, girl, the Smale family should be lords of the manor once again and that trash driven out from here.'

'But his wife looks sweet enough,' Arian said, in an

effort to calm her father. 'She's very young, not much older than me.'

'From peasant stock,' Bob said flatly, 'but pretty enough, I'll grant you.' A strange look came into his eyes. 'She will be part of my revenge.'

Arian felt suddenly sorry for the young woman who had come to the perimeter of the Smale land, a determined look on her face and a gun clutched in her hand. She dreaded to think what fate her father had in store for Mrs O'Conner.

Arian thought too of the man who had been in company with Mrs O'Conner, a young, tall, handsome man. She had read the interest in his eyes, but she had turned away from it. Her place was with her father; he needed her, he would always need her, otherwise the drink would take him over completely.

She looked at him now, a man in his prime, some would say; his hair was still dark and waving, his eyes, when he was not filled with drink, were blue and clear. But there were heavy pouches beneath them and deep creases from nose to mouth. He had thrown away his youth, and it was so sad.

'You are a good girl, Arian.' Her father smiled and touched her silver hair. 'Arian. You were given the Welsh name for silver, did you know that, girl?'

He didn't wait for a reply. 'Your mother was a lovely, fine woman. She gave birth to you in the moonlight, and when she looked down on you, lying there in her arms, she saw that your hair was silver like the moon.'

Arian almost flinched away from his touch. She was more used to abuse from her father rather than affection.

'Bring me some brandy, girl.' Bob Smale's mood switched abruptly. He pushed away his empty plate with some irritation. 'I've got a thirst on me that even the sea wouldn't quench.'

Arian's heart sank. 'But, Dad . . .' She got no further. He banged his fist on the table.

'No buts, I want a drink and I'll have one!' His anger subsided, and he half-smiled. 'I need it, girl; it takes away the ghosts.'

Arian left the room without further comment. She would bring him his drink and then she would quietly slip out into the fields. When her father was in this awful mood of self-pity, there was no reasoning with him.

Arian touched the tender skin around her eye and it felt puffy beneath her fingers. She didn't want another black eye, she decided wryly.

Eddie saw her before she saw him. Her hair looked silver in the moonlight, lifting away from her face as she walked. The slimness of her body was accentuated by the soft swell of her breasts. She leant against a tree, her head back, her eyes closed, and Eddie caught his breath, feeling as though he was intruding on a private moment. He moved slightly; a twig snapped beneath his feet, and she must have heard the sound, because suddenly she was alert, looking round her like a startled fawn.

'I'm sorry if I frightened you,' Eddie called softly. 'I didn't mean to trespass.'

He came out into the open, half-expecting her to run away; but she stood her ground, her small chin defiantly lifted.

'Trespassing again?' she asked, and when Eddie heard the note of something like sadness in her voice, a feeling of pain dragged at him. He wanted to sweep her into his arms, to hold her against him to protect her.

'I wanted to see you,' he said simply. Even in the moonlight, he could see the look of surprise on her face.

'Why?' she asked, folding her hands across her body as if for protection, though he still kept his distance from her.

'I find you attractive,' he said, half-amused. 'Is that so strange?'

'You are not a farmer,' she said, and it was a

statement. 'What are you doing here up on the hill, meddling in what doesn't concern you?'

'I work for Jamie O'Conner,' Eddie replied, 'and I don't consider that trying to find out why one man wishes to ruin another is meddling.'

She began to walk away. 'You and I have nothing to talk about, then,' she said.

On an impulse, Eddie reached out and caught her hand. 'Please, I want to know more about you; I can't get you out of my mind. Give friendship a chance, can't you?'

'Look . . . ?' She hesitated, and he stared down at her, seeing with concern the bruising to her face. He resisted the urge to take her into his arms, knowing he must tread carefully; he must do nothing to startle her into flight.

'Edward is the name,' he said softly, 'though most people call me Eddie.'

'Look, Edward,' she said, 'there's no future in any friendship between us, my father wouldn't allow it.'

'Your father needn't know,' Eddie said. 'I realize he has some grudge against Jamie, but that has nothing to do with you and me.'

'While you work for Jamie O'Conner and take his side, it has everything to do with you and me.' She shook his hand away. 'Just go, Eddie, before you get hurt.'

He touched her eye lightly. 'As you've been hurt?' he asked, feeling his gut contract with anger at the barbarian who could put his hand on such a delicate creature.

Her eyes were shuttered by thick lashes, her expression hard to read. 'Put some leeches on it,' he said. 'It will work, believe me; the swelling will go down almost immediately.'

'How do you know that?' she asked. He could see that she was intrigued in spite of herself.

'I was training to be a doctor,' he said, 'and before that I took a great interest in what the village women

207

advocated for treating ills. A good deal of what they practise makes sense.'

'They would have been burned as witches at one time,' she replied, and Eddie thought she was actually relaxing a little with him.

'What's your name?' he asked.

She withdrew into herself like a snail into a shell, but she gave him an answer. 'Arian.' She half-smiled. 'It means silver.' She moved away from him, and he felt a momentary panic; she was slipping away.

'Please stay and talk, Arian,' he said. 'I'm perfectly harmless, I assure you.'

After a moment, she nodded. 'Right, I'll believe you. Let's walk down to Mare's Pool, shall we?'

At her side, he felt ten feet tall. She was so small, so beautiful and so vulnerable, he felt she could be crushed like a petal. And to think she was at the mercy of that brute Bob Smale!

'He's not so bad, you know.' It was as though Arian had read his thoughts, and he looked down at her in surprise.

'Are you sure *you* are not a witch?' he asked, and she glanced up at him, shaking back her shining hair.

He touched it lightly. 'If you are, you're the most beautiful witch I've ever come across.'

'Don't change the subject,' she said. 'My father, he's driven by a sense of injustice, he wanted that strip of land. It should have been his – or so he thinks.'

Eddie was silent, choosing his words. The land had been there for anyone to buy, and it was Jamie who had got there first.

'Jamie is a good man,' Eddie said with conviction. 'I know he bought that land fair and square from Mrs Jones.'

'I know,' Arian agreed. 'The land belongs to Mr O'Conner and his wife, but Dad set such store by it, for some reason.'

208

'To profit from the new road that will run through it,' Eddie said, and then he could have bitten out his tongue, because Arian turned to him, a sad look in her eyes.

'I'm sorry,' he said at once. 'You didn't know. Come on, sit down by the pond. I have no right to judge you or yours.' He took off his coat, rolled up his shirt sleeve and dipped his hand in the water.

'What are you doing?' Arian sat beside him and stared at him as he stretched out along the bank. 'Oh no!' she said, as he brought out his hand with a leech clinging to the pad of his thumb.

'Come on, it won't hurt – don't be a baby, now.' His voice was teasing.

'It's not the hurt I'm afraid of; it's the thought of having that creature stuck to my face I don't like. Anyway, how are you going to get it off your hand? It'll stay until it's gorged.'

'No, I have the knack,' Eddie said. He began to stroke the back of the leech, and after a few moments it curled away from his thumb as though dead.

Quickly, before Arian could protest, he put it against her eye. He smiled as she squealed but remained still.

He held her hand and she didn't resist. 'It'll fall off soon,' he said reassuringly, 'and in the morning your eye won't look half bad.'

'What a pity you didn't go on with your career,' she said. He knew she was talking in an effort to ignore the leech that was fastened to her eye.

'Yes, a great pity,' he agreed. 'But sometimes fate takes a hand, and here I am sitting by a pond silvered with moonlight with a lovely girl at my side with a leech on her face.'

'You're laughing at me,' she said. 'I don't think I can stand this much longer. Can you get it off me?'

Eddie cupped his hand and held it near her cheek, feeling the softness of her skin with a sense of great tenderness.

The leech fell into his hand as though on cue, and deftly he placed it back in the water. Then he took out his handkerchief and dipped it in the pond and gently wiped her eye.

'There, all over,' he said, and looked down at her soft mouth, so invitingly close to his. Her eyes met his and then she leant slightly closer. Emboldened, he kissed her.

He knew he was trembling. He'd kissed girls before – not too many, but some – and he had enjoyed the experience; but never had he felt so moved, so earth-shatteringly aware of a woman as he was of Arian Smale.

He groaned and moved away from her, his body betraying his arousal so that he was embarrassed.

She touched his shoulder lightly. 'I can't commit myself to anyone, Eddie,' she said, 'but I don't want to go through life becoming a dried-up spinster either. If you can accept that, then I'll be whatever it is you want me to be.'

He touched her face gently. 'I'm in love with you, Arian,' he said. 'I think I would die for you; but I couldn't take advantage of you.'

She moved closer and put her arms around him. 'I'm ignorant of love and of men, Eddie,' she said simply, 'but I know that with you I think I would be content to learn. Will you be patient with me, Eddie?'

He groaned. 'How could I be anything else?' he said. 'We will learn together.'

He kissed her throat and, with a skill he didn't know he possessed, he undid her buttons, releasing her full sweet breasts. She drew away, startled, her eyes wide.

It was then he felt the shock of leather lashing against his back. The first impact was just like a blow, and then the leather bit deep and he was suddenly on his knees, facing the aggressor.

Bob Smale was white-faced in the moonlight. He must have crept up through the undergrowth and been watch-

210

ing them for several minutes. The thought made Eddie burn with anger.

The whip crashed down again, this time across his chest, and wound around him like a streak of fire. Eddie became aware of Arian calling out in anguish.

'Stop it, Daddy!' Her voice was shrill, and it made no difference to the man standing glowering at Eddie, whip raised to strike again.

The whip wound a line of pain around Eddie's body, and this time he clutched at it, hauling the handle towards him.

'You bastard!' Eddie said, enraged. His fist lashed out, catching the man squarely on the jaw.

'No!' Arian was in front of him, her breasts full and upright, her nipples hard in the chill of the night air. He wanted her with a fierce desire, and he'd so nearly possessed her.

'Don't hurt him, Eddie,' she said, 'or all will be over between us before it's begun.'

She took the whip from him and turned to her father, catching at his arm and helping him to rise.

'Come on home, Dad, let me put you to bed,' she said softly. For a moment, it looked as though Bob Smale would push her aside.

'Come *on*,' she insisted. 'If you don't come home now, I'll leave you for good and go away with Eddie. You'll never see me again.'

'Arian,' Eddie said softly, 'please . . .' He watched as she moved away over the uneven ground, her hand clutching her father's arm.

After a moment, Bob Smale turned and held his ground, his face hard. 'You come near my daughter again and I'll kill you.' He spoke coldly,. without anger, and Eddie clenched his teeth, wanting to hit out at the man again and again, until he closed his foul mouth.

Arian shook her head and dragged at her father's arm. Eddie watched until they were out of sight. Then he turned and with slumped shoulders made his way back to Honey's Farm.

'Now don't start, Dad.' Arian closed the large front door and turned to face her father. He was more angry than she'd ever seen him in his life, but he was sober.

'You and that *scoundrel*!' he said. 'Together in the fields like beasts, you lying there like a wanton waiting for him to get between your legs! Have you no shame, girl?'

'You forget, Dad,' Arian said quietly. 'I'm not a girl, I'm a woman, and I have feelings just like you or anyone else. If I want a man "between my legs", as you so delicately put it, I'll not ask your permission.'

He raised a hand as if to strike her and Arian faced him squarely. 'No more of that, Dad, or I'll walk out on you right now.'

He moved towards her. Arian stood her ground, facing him, her hands on her hips. 'You dare hit me, ever again, and I'll leave you for good. You'll never see me again. I mean it.'

She watched as her father lowered his hand and sank into a chair. 'I don't know what the world is coming to,' he said in a low voice. 'I'm your father, you should have respect.'

'I'll have respect when you stop pickling your liver in brandy.' Arian didn't know where she found the strength to speak to her father the way she did. Was it the knowledge that Eddie wanted her, would take her away if only she gave the word? But no, it was some deeper instinct than that; it was as though she had suddenly left girlhood behind and become a woman.

'Arian!' Her father looked up at her in disbelief. 'I drink because I'm alone, you must understand that.'

'No, Dad,' she said, 'you are not alone. If I walked out on you, *then* you'd be alone.' She paused to take a deep breath. 'And as for the drinking, you drink because

212

you're weak and you are filled with bitterness. For heaven's sake, why don't you pull yourself up by your bootstraps and be a man? Then I would show you all the respect in the world.'

'Have you quite finished, girl?' he asked in a dull voice.

Arian nodded. 'I'm going to my bed now, and if you need the bottle so badly, there's a new one in the kitchen, and you can go to hell your own way.'

She walked through the large, shabby hallway and up the curving staircase to her room. After a few minutes, she heard her father come upstairs behind her. She smiled; for tonight at least, he was not having any more to drink. It was a small but significant triumph.

When she was in bed, Arian thought of the moments she'd spent with Eddie out there on the banks of the pool. They had been filled with magic, those moments, filled with desire and longing and curiosity, and perhaps spiced a little with love.

Her mouth curved into a smile. Dad might have stopped her knowing Eddie's love for now, but when the time was right she would know it, and then she would go to Eddie, and she would learn what it was like to have a lover.

She had meant what she said. She wouldn't marry Eddie, not while her father needed her, but there were joys to be tasted that didn't need the words of a preacher or the presence of a gold ring to make them more precious.

At last, Arian fell asleep, and she dreamed of Eddie and his touch on her breasts. She woke to the silent darkness of the night, and there were foolish tears staining her pillow.

CHAPTER SEVENTEEN

'That's it, then.' Calvin smiled down at Eline, his handsome face alight with happiness. 'It's decided; we'll be married the last day of November, just before the rush for Christmas begins.'

Eline felt her heart contract with apprehension. Now was the time to tell Calvin she was not sure, she was having doubts about the wisdom of marrying a man she didn't love. And yet what else lay before her?

She thought of Will with a sense of unhappiness. He had betrayed her; he had taken Gwyneth Parks to his bed, given her his child. Was this the act of a man who loved her?

'Yes, that's a good date.' Eline forced herself to smile up at Calvin as he stood in the window of the gallery, staring at her anxiously.

'Eline, you are sure, aren't you?' he said, crossing the room to where she was sitting and taking her hand in his.

Eline's lips were dry. Now was the time to give voice to her doubts and fears, to be honest with the man she was taking for her husband. And yet Calvin knew she didn't love him, had told her he had enough love for both of them.

The door-bell rang at that moment, and Eline looked up, grateful for the interruption.

'Hari!' she said warmly. 'Welcome to the gallery. It's an honour to have your patronage.'

Hari looked doubtfully towards the couple; her sharp eyes had taken in the way Calvin was holding Eline's hands in his, and the glitter of the diamond ring on her finger.

'I hope I'm not intruding,' she said quickly. 'I just wanted a word with you, Eline.'

'That's quite all right,' Calvin said, his smile warm. 'There's a great deal for me to do, arrangements I must make; it's about time I moved myself and went into town.'

There was silence in the gallery after Calvin had left. Eline sensed what Hari had come for, and she wanted to keep the words at bay for as long as possible.

'Please, sit down,' she said. 'I'm afraid I can't offer you any refreshments; Calvin has neglected to keep anything in the cupboard.' She shrugged deprecatingly. 'Being a man, he'd much rather go out to his club or to one of the restaurants, instead of making himself a cup of cordial.'

'Eline,' Hari said softly, 'you must know why I've come.' She arranged her elegant skirts around her legs as she seated herself on one of the carved chairs. 'It's Will. He's so unhappy, and he won't talk to me about it. Do you know what's wrong?'

Eline looked directly at Hari for the first time, and her heart seemed to lurch at the very mention of Will's name.

'Yes, I know what's wrong.' She heard the bitterness in her own voice with a sense of helplessness. She was bitter, and who could blame her?

'He's been spending time with Gwyneth Parks,' she said at last, feeling that some explanation was called for. Hari should know the truth; she cared about Will, and yet she was fair-minded enough to see Eline's point of view.

'I see,' Hari said slowly, but Eline broke in quickly.

'It's not just that,' she said defensively. 'I wouldn't be *that* childish, to be jealous over a few hours spent in another woman's company, but it's more. She's expecting Will's baby.'

215

She saw the shocked expression on Hari's face with a sense of despair. 'It's true, unfortunately,' Eline said. 'There's no doubt about that.'

'Oh, my God!' Hari put her hand to her cheek. 'Poor Eline! Will doesn't come out of this very well, does he?'

She rose and walked to the window. 'What on earth came over Will to do something like this?' she said softly. 'Are you absolutely sure, Eline?'

'Yes.' Eline nodded miserably. 'And I have to say that Gwyneth was going to release him from any responsibility. She was actually considering having an illegal abortion.'

Eline looked down at the glittering half-hoop of diamonds that Calvin had put on her finger, and twisted it without thinking, as though to remove an unwanted shackle.

'In any case,' Hari continued, 'think very carefully before you marry a man you don't love.'

She held up her hand as Eline would have spoken. 'I know it's none of my business, but I can't help speaking my mind. I *know* you love Will, and he loves you, whatever else has happened. Do you really think you could be happy married to Calvin Temple, fine man though I'm sure he is?'

Eline looked up at her, knowing that Hari was giving voice to the doubts that had haunted her ever since the marriage had been arranged.

'Perhaps not,' she said in a strangled voice, 'but I don't know how to get out of it now. It wouldn't be fair to Calvin; he would be humiliated.'

'Would it be fair to Calvin to marry him under false pretences? That's what you must ask yourself.'

'He knows I don't love him, and he's prepared to accept me as I am,' Eline said defensively, but she knew in her heart that Hari was talking cold common sense.

'I *do* have doubts,' she admitted suddenly, 'but I'm

wondering if I have the courage to face Calvin and tell him it's all been a terrible mistake.'

Eline fell silent. She'd been married to a man she didn't love once before and it hadn't worked. What made her think that this time it would be any better?

'You will always love Will,' Hari said softly. 'I can see it in your eyes, hear it in your voice. You *must* see him, talk it over with him. Please, Eline, for your sake and Will's, don't rush into a marriage you might regret.'

'How can I talk to him?' Eline said, the pain apparent in her voice. 'I want to be with him, I want to love and trust him, but there's nothing he can say to put things right.'

She paused in an effort to control the threatened tears. 'Hari, thank you so much for your concern, but, really, I've gone over and over it all in my mind. Will must feel the only honourable thing to do is to marry Gwyneth. There is no alternative.'

'Perhaps,' Hari said. 'One more thing and then I'll shut up. There is the possibility that Gwyneth Parks is mistaken; emotional upsets can have a physical effect on women. Have you thought of that?'

Eline was silent, but into her mind came a picture of Gwyneth's face, pale and so lined with worry that she knew Gwyneth was not mistaken.

'See Will, at least,' Hari repeated. 'Talk to him and then at least perhaps everything will be out in the open.' She forced a smile. 'I think I'd better be going, I've meddled more than enough all ready.'

Will got off the train at Swansea and stared around at the familiar landscape. The smoke from the works along the river bank filled the air, and yet to the south there was the cleaner air of the seaside.

Hari Grenfell wanted to see him again, urgently. The messenger had come to Cardiff bringing the letter by hand. It explained very little, but William knew something must be very wrong if Hari had sent for him in that peremptory way.

On his last visit, there had been little time for discussion; Hari had been too busy preparing for the return of her husband, who had been away on business, to pay much attention to Will's reports. In any case, Will's visit had, of necessity, been a fleeting one. There were problems in the shop in Cardiff that needed immediate action. A pipe had burst, destroying one of Eline's displays, and Will needed help with sorting out the ruined stock.

Hari was waiting for him now, seated in her elegant drawing-room, a tea tray ready before her. As always, she'd known what he was thinking, known he would come on the first train into Swansea.

'What's wrong, Hari?' he asked anxiously, searching her face.

She smiled reassuringly, gesturing for him to sit down. 'I'm going to be an interfering old busybody,' she said. 'Gwyneth Parks is saying she's expecting your child. Is it true, Will?'

He was taken aback by her abrupt question, and for a moment was at a loss how to answer.

'I realize this has nothing to do with me,' she continued in a rush. 'But it *is* something to do with Eline Harries. She's so unhappy, Will, so in love with you, that she's cut to the quick by all this.'

Hari sighed. 'She intends to marry Calvin Temple on the rebound, and I thought you should be here to sort things out.'

Will felt shock hit at the pit of his stomach like a pain. He should have expected it, of course. Calvin had never concealed the fact that he wanted Eline. And Gwyneth, having a baby? It just couldn't be true, could it?

'This is the first I've heard of any baby,' he said. 'Surely Gwyneth would have come to me, told me about this . . . this condition she's supposed to be in.'

'How could she?' Hari said. 'She was probably going to see you on your last visit to Swansea but, if you remember, it wasn't a very prolonged one.'

She was right. Unless Gwyneth travelled up to Cardiff, what chance would she have of talking to him? The full import of Hari's words hit him then.

'Christ!' he said. 'Gwyneth pregnant, and Eline intending to get married to Calvin Temple! What's happening to my world, Hari?'

'Is it true, then, Will?' Hari urged gently. '*Could* this girl be having your child?'

He felt sick and defeated. He knew that Gwyneth loved him to a point past understanding. She would never have given herself to another man.

'It must be true,' he said. 'If she is with child, then I'm the father, no doubt about that.'

He felt plagued with a mixture of emotions. He knew he must see Gwyneth Park, sort this mess out, learn the truth from her own lips; and yet he wanted to rush to Eline, beg her not to marry another man. He sighed heavily.

'Come on, now, love,' Hari said softly. 'It can't be all that bad, can it?'

When he didn't reply, she continued speaking. 'Even if Gwyneth is expecting, you could support the child. You needn't throw away your life by marrying a woman you obviously don't love.'

But she was wrong, and Will knew it in his bones. He could not simply pay for his mistake with blood money, leave Gwyneth to the scorn of her neighbours, and allow his child – *his* child – to be brought up with the stigma of illegitimacy hanging over its head.

'What a sorry mess!' he said, rubbing his eyes. 'What a stupid fool I've been, taking my pleasure and not thinking of the consequences.'

Hari smiled. 'That's the nature of man, my love. No good blaming yourself; you must just try to make the best of the situation now.'

He met her eyes. 'I'll have to marry Gwyneth, if only for the sake of the child; you above all people will appreciate that, Hari.'

'Look, don't go making rash decisions,' Hari said. 'Find out for sure if Gwyneth is with child before you do anything hasty. She could be . . . be mistaken about all this, you know.'

Will felt a momentary lifting of his spirits. Hari was right; it could all be a false alarm; these things did happen. But, then, Gwyneth was from a large family of women; they would have advised her to see a midwife, to make sure of her facts.

He rose to his feet. 'I'll go down to Oystermouth now,' he said. 'I'll talk to Gwyneth; it's the only thing I can do.'

'And Eline?' Hari asked quietly. 'What about her? She loves you, Will; she knows she's made a mistake with this man Calvin Temple, and I think she'll call off the marriage if you go to her.'

He sighed heavily. 'I would like nothing more than to go to her, to beg her to forget all that's gone and to take a chance on marrying me. I have regular employment now, and though I'll never be wealthy, at least I could support her, give her a home, love her; but I've made too many mistakes, it's far too late for that.'

Hari rose and hugged him, and for a moment Will buried his face in her hair, feeling the warmth and love that came from her, the love that required nothing in return.

On the train to Oystermouth, Will stared back across the bay towards Swansea. The twin hills of Kilvey and Townhill rose protectively around the huddled town, and edging the shoreline the sea washed inwards in a gentle curve.

He sighed heavily; such a lot had happened in the last few months. His business had failed, he'd taken Hari's

220

offer of a job in Cardiff, he had made Gwyneth Parks pregnant, and he had given up the only woman he could ever love. For he *had* given her up; once he took to Gwyneth Parks' bed, he had forfeited all rights to Eline's love and trust.

Will stared out fixedly, longing to cry out his tears of frustration and despair; but men didn't cry, did they?

Oystermouth bay was filled with billowing sails; the oyster boats were going out to dredge for the harvest of oysters that was the lifeblood of the village. It was the strange, temperamental waters of the bay that had caused Joe Harries's accident and ultimately his death. Why hadn't he stepped in then, Will thought in anger, claimed Eline as his own?

He had wanted to offer her the best of everything, a thriving businessman for a husband, a life of ease and luxury; instead he'd become a failure, and too proud to ask her to share that failure. Now it was too late; he had obligations elsewhere, and there was no-one to blame except himself.

He alighted from the train, feeling as though he had wept a thousand tears. The truth was that his eyes only burned from the dust thrown up by the horses' hooves from the well-worn track to Oystermouth. Or at least that's what he told himself.

He paused outside the gallery, and a feeling of nostalgia filled him as he remembered being inside the light, airy rooms with Eline, watching her plan her future.

He paused, seeing that the window was filled with an enormous canvas, a rich painting of the bay with a sailing ship unloading sheep on to the still wet sand. It was an effective and moving picture, and, from the price ticket above it, it would need a very wealthy client to buy it.

The knowledge that Eline was a success filled him with a sense of renewed despair. Everything she touched went well; her designs for shoes were much sought after, and now her gallery was flourishing, with the help of Calvin Temple of course.

No doubt Eline would be better off married to such a man. He was rich, influential; and Eline deserved the best. Slowly, Will turned away.

'William!' The voice reached out to him softly, like a hand touching his shoulder. 'Will, please don't walk away.'

He turned to face Eline. She was looking at him longingly, and if ever he'd doubted her love he couldn't doubt it now.

'Come inside,' she said. 'I'm here alone; Calvin's in London on business. I was just closing up.'

He went with her and watched as she shut the door and firmly locked it. She turned then and held out her arms and he went into them readily, holding her close.

'You know?' he whispered, and she touched his cheek with her hand. 'You know what a stupid, thoughtless fool I've been, throwing away my chance of happiness with you?'

'I know,' she replied. 'Hush now, don't say another word. Just kiss me, Will! It will be our farewell to each other.'

He touched her mouth with his, losing himself in the sweetness of holding her, feeling her body pliant against him, relishing the soft swell of her breasts against his chest. His blood seemed to turn to water. He could die at this moment, here in her arms, and be happy.

After a long moment, Eline moved away from him. 'I love you, Will,' she said. 'I suppose I'll always love you, but I know you well enough to understand that you have to go to Gwyneth Parks. She needs you now.'

His hands dropped to his sides. 'Will you marry Calvin Temple?' he asked, knowing he had no right to question her, but driven to it by the jealousy that tore at him.

She shook her head. 'I don't know, Will. I don't love him, but he understands that.'

She moved away, as though putting as much distance between them as she could. 'I suppose this is my last chance to live a normal life, to have a family – oh, I don't know!'

The words were anguished, and Will felt a great burden of guilt. It was his fault, all his fault. He had given in to the weakness of the flesh; his need of a woman had driven him into a corner, and here he was now, faced with the irrevocable results.

'I can't tell you how sorry I am,' Will said. 'Damn! The words sound so hollow, so meaningless, and they don't begin to express what I really feel.'

'I know,' Eline said, 'and I understand, Will. We all make mistakes. I made my biggest mistake when I married Joe Harries just because I was afraid of life, afraid to be alone.'

'Then don't make the same mistake again,' Will said softly. 'I've no right to even think that sort of thought, but I can't help it, Eline.'

'Go now,' she said turning away from him and slowly, Will obeyed knowing there was nothing else he could do.

'Will!' The name was torn from Eline's lips. 'Hold me just once more, please.'

They clung together like children drowning in a remorseless sea, and Will longed to fling her down and possess her, put his mark on her, make her truly his. It was ironic that he had never possessed the woman he loved more than life itself.

He released her suddenly and made for the door, afraid to stay any longer. As he hurried out into the street, he could hear the soft sound of Eline weeping.

He walked away, up into the hills of Mumbles, trying to regain his composure. He stared down at the foaming waters rushing in against the cliffs and wondered what it would be like to simply fall into the depths of the sea. It would be a blessed release, and yet he knew in his

223

heart it was a coward's way out, and one he could not take.

It was perhaps an hour later that he returned to Oystermouth, calmer now, his chaotic thoughts tamed into some semblance of order.

Gwyneth looked pale and sick when she opened the door to him. She stared at him for a long moment before stepping back to allow him to enter.

Nina Parks took one look at his face and then rose to her feet. 'I'll be in the parlour if you want me, love,' she said to her daughter, and the look she gave Will dared him to hurt her daughter even more than he already had.

'How are you?' he said softly, pityingly.

Gwyneth lifted her head. '*Duw*, I'm all right. Girls like me always get by, mind,' she said, with a touching air of defiance.

'Gwyneth,' Will said more firmly. 'I want you to marry me.'

The words hung in the air between them, and Gwyneth stared at him, her eyes huge in her pale face.

'You don't mean that, do you?' she said. 'You are just doing what you think is right; you don't love me.'

He felt pity tear at his heart, and, on an impulse, he took her into his arms, folding her against him, smelling the salt of the sea in her hair.

'I think a great deal of you, Gwyneth,' he said, 'otherwise I wouldn't have taken you to my bed, would I?'

She sighed heavily. 'I want to believe you, but I know you love Eline Harries. You do love her, don't you, Will?'

'It's possible to feel . . . affection for more than one woman.' Will avoided a direct answer. 'I certainly enjoyed making love to *you*, Gwyneth, surely you must realize that?'

'You've never made love to *her*?' Gwyneth asked, with something like disbelief in her voice.

'Never,' Will said emphatically. 'Come on, Gwyneth,

you know there's no other way. We will get married, have our baby, and live happily ever after.'

She relaxed against him then. 'I'm too tired to argue with you. I want you so much that I'll have you on any terms, and if I have to be second choice because Eline is marrying that Calvin Temple, then I'm content with that.'

'I would want to marry you anyway, Gwyneth,' Will said gravely, 'even if Eline never married the man. I know you need me, and our child needs me. There's no question of you being second choice.'

Nina Parks came back into the room. 'Stop arguing with the man and just be glad he's come to you when you need him.'

She pushed the kettle on to the flames of the fire and then turned to Will. 'I'll say this, you are a real gent, and what's more you got guts.' She folded her arms across her full breasts. 'Some would have run a mile where there's a babbie concerned, and I know what I'm talking about.

'Now, let's sit down and have a cup of tea and talk about practical things, shall we?' She smiled and rested her hand on Gwyneth's shoulder.

'There's a lot to arrange for a wedding, mind, and not much time to do it in if your belly isn't going to go before you down the aisle of the church.'

They were married quietly three weeks later. The November rain had set in, and a mist hung over the parish of Oystermouth, but Gwyneth Parks was radiant as she walked up the aisle of All Saints, her head held high.

All around her were her family, proud and happy to see Gwyneth marrying William Davies, who when all was said and done was quite a toff.

Sal hung on to the arm of her husband, her round face smiling with pleasure, glancing down at her little Fon with Jamie big and handsome at her side.

Nina was dressed in her Sunday best, with a fine new hat perched on her greying hair, and she nodded encouragement to Gwyneth as she swept up the aisle on the arm of her new husband.

No-one noticed Eline Harries standing on the perimeter of the sightseers – no-one, that is, except the groom, who for an unguarded moment looked as though he was not celebrating his wedding but going to his own funeral.

CHAPTER EIGHTEEN

'I know you are going to be the happiest girl alive.' Fon embraced her sister warmly. Around them in the small back room of the Smith's Arms, the sound of voices rose and fell. Glasses were being emptied; the small celebration lunch was almost finished.

The bride looked tearful, and yet she was smiling. It was clear that Gwyneth was going through a mingling of emotions, which was exactly the way Fon herself had felt on the day she was married.

She released Gwyneth and glanced up lovingly at Jamie, who was talking to Will Davies, man to man, without the deferential air people usually adopted with Will. But, then, she knew her husband's views on life very well, any man might be as good but no man was better than Jamie O'Conner.

'I can't help feeling I'm second best,' Gwyneth said softly, her eyes brimming with tears.

'I know what you are going through,' Fon said quickly. 'Wasn't I haunted by the ghost of Jamie's first wife?' She squeezed her sister's arm. 'But love comes, when you lie with a man every night you become . . . close, so close.'

Gwyneth smiled suddenly. '*Duw*, who'd have thought my little sister would have been giving me advice about men?'

Fon's colour rose. 'Don't tease, Gwyneth, girl; I'm an old married woman, and don't you forget it.'

Will had come to stand behind Gwyneth's shoulder. 'I think it's time to go, Gwyneth.' He spoke quietly; there was no light in his eye, no upturning of his mouth. He looked like a man who was doing his duty and nothing more, and Fon felt a tingling of apprehension. She knew in that moment, she felt it in her bones, that no good was going to come from the union of Will Davies and her sister Gwyneth.

She forced herself to smile brightly as she hugged Gwyneth close. 'Take care of her,' she said, looking over her sister's shoulder into the face of Gwyneth's new husband.

'I will, don't you worry,' he said, and Fon believed him. Will Davies was an honourable man. He would keep his word, whatever happened. And what could happen? Surely her feelings of gloom were misplaced?

As Jamie drove Fon homeward, up the hill from Swansea towards the farm, she leaned against his shoulder, grateful for his nearness. It was only now and again, when he seemed preoccupied with the past, that she doubted his love. His desire for her was evident; he made love to her with joy and vigour, but he rarely put tongue to his feelings, he wasn't that sort of man.

'Well, I think I've got a buyer for that piece of land, Fon,' he said, looking down at her. 'I was hasty spending out for it in the first place.' He smiled ruefully. 'The time wasn't right for expanding; you were wise enough to know that, colleen, and I wouldn't listen.'

'But you will make a handsome profit now, when we most need it, so it turned out right for us after all,' Fon said reassuringly.

'Aye,' Jamie said, 'and I won't have to sell the Black Devil; that's one consolation.'

'Who is buying the land?' Fon asked, moving even closer to Jamie, feeling the heat coming from his skin with a sense of pleasurable belonging.

'It's a consortium,' Jamie said. 'It seems that the project is so big that several of the Swansea businessmen have got together over the deal, which makes sense.'

Fon sighed. 'What if there's a roadway running past the farm; will that do us any harm?'

'I can't see it doing anything but good,' Jamie replied. 'We will be able to shift the crop by road so much more easily, not to mention the bringing in of new machinery.'

'So we'll be all right now, will we?' She looked up at her husband and saw the smile curving his mouth. On an impulse, she pulled his head down to hers and kissed him.

'Hey, that's no way for an old married woman to behave! Sure it's a brazen hussy I've got for my wife.'

'I'll give you brazen hussy!' Fon said. 'Wait till I get you home, and then I'll show you how brazen I really am.'

In the farmhouse, Eddie was just ladling out a bowl of *cawl* for Patrick; thick slices of bread were piled up on a plate, and Eddie looked flushed from the heat of the fire.

'Thank goodness you're back.' His tone was heartfelt. 'Give me farm work to looking after children any day of the week; it's easier. Where's Jamie?'

'Washing at the pump,' Fon replied, turning her attention to Patrick. 'Been naughty, have you?' she asked lightly.

Patrick shook his head. 'No, not naughty, I been a good boy. Eddie said I been good.' Patrick beamed.

'He's been good all right,' Eddie agreed. 'No tantrums, nothing like that; it's just that he's so curious that he's into everything.'

Fon smiled. 'Don't I know it!'

She sat next to Patrick and helped him to some of the soup. 'Come on, love, it's nice dinner,' she encouraged, but Patrick turned his head away.

'I think he's eaten enough,' Eddie said sheepishly. 'I took him out for a picnic, and we had bread and cheese and some of the cakes that you left in the pantry.'

Fon looked at him with a smile curving her lips. 'You didn't happen to meet up with Arian Smale, did you?'

Eddie actually blushed. 'Well, yes, I did,' he said. 'By accidental design, I suppose you could call it.'

'More design than accident, if I know you, Eddie.' She patted Patrick's shoulder. 'Right then!' Fon put down the spoon she had been holding to Patrick's lips. 'Off you go then, boy; you can leave the table if you've finished your meal.'

Patrick climbed down from his chair with alacrity and went out of the open door into the garden.

'Getting keen on Arian, are you?' Fon asked quietly. 'She's a lovely-looking girl, but be careful, mind.'

'No good telling me that, Fon,' he said. 'I've fallen for her, hook, line and sinker. I'd marry her tomorrow if I had prospects and if she'd have me.'

He grimaced at Fon. 'Her father has other ideas, of course; my back is still smarting from the whipping he gave me.'

'Awful man!' Fon said feelingly. 'He doesn't deserve a daughter like Arian.'

Eddie leant forward, his elbows on the table. 'If only I could make my fortune, I could persuade her to marry me, I'm sure.'

Jamie came into the kitchen. He was stripped to the waist, his hair glistening with water from the pump outside. 'What's this talk of marriage, my man?' he asked, sitting at the table and taking the bowl of soup that Fon offered him.

'Just dreaming,' Eddie said ruefully. 'I'm not in any position to take a wife, but I wish I was.'

'It'll come soon enough.' Jamie assumed an air of sheepish submission. 'Then you'll be sorry! Bowed down with care you'll be, with a woman's sharp tongue giving you hell night and day.'

Fon made a face at him. 'And all the wife gets is washing and cooking and hard work from morning till night,' she retorted.

Jamie leant forward and pulled at her hair. 'Ah, but

when night comes, think of the rewards of being married to a lusty man, and you, my lady, have got yourself a real man of vigour.'

Fon blushed. 'Hush, don't talk like that in front of Eddie,' she said, half-smiling.

'Why not?' Jamie said. 'Wasn't the man all set to be a doctor? Him knowing more than me, I dare say.'

Eddie laughed easily. 'In theory, perhaps, but in practice you'd have me beaten hands down.' He rose from his chair and glanced affectionately at Fon. 'I know a fulfilled and loving wife when I see one. You are a lucky man, boss.'

'If you say so.' Jamie's voice was casual, but his hand touched Fon's cheek lightly in a gesture of great tenderness.

The small house nestling in the folds of Kilvey Hill was washed silver by the moonlight. From one window came the dull gleam of an oil lamp casting a soft glow on to the grass outside, outlining the tall figure of a man.

Will Davies, hands thrust into his pockets, was staring out across the valley below, at the silver water of the docklands and the haphazard building of the town beyond. He felt trapped, closed into a world of domesticity from which there was no escape.

Within the house, his new wife waited for him. He felt her uncertainty with a tightness of pity in his gut, and yet he needed these few moments alone to come to terms with himself.

He needed to reconcile himself now to a life with a wife and to the fact that he must forget the woman he loved.

He smiled sadly into the darkness; he had never possessed Eline Harries, though he had loved her for ever, or so it seemed. Now he would never possess her. His life and hers would take separate paths, never to join together in union.

231

Sighing, he turned and went indoors, closing the latch against the world. He squared his shoulders and made his way upstairs; and there, in the dimness of the lamplight, Gwyneth was waiting.

Her hair spilled around her shoulders; the white of her gown covered, with a touching display of modesty, the fullness of her breasts. Her eyes searched his face, and Will saw with a feeling of pain that her condition had given her an ethereal quality, a paleness of skin that was almost transparent, and a shadowing of her eyes that made them appear huge.

'Will!' She held out her arms in a gesture of supplication, and he went to her and held her close, his head resting on her hair. She should never know what it cost him to put Eline out of his life, he vowed. His wife would bear his child, and he would do his utmost to make them both secure and happy.

'Come into bed with me, *cariad*,' Gwyneth said softly. 'Love me, just a little.'

He undressed swiftly, pulling his shirt over his head and unfastening his belt with an air of unreality. Where was the passion that had brought him to this? Why did he feel cold as ice as he entered his marriage bed?

Gwyneth's arms closed around him; she buried her face in his neck. 'I love you, Will,' she said softly, 'and I know I can make you want me, even perhaps love me, in time.'

Her hands stroked and caressed him intimately, and in spite of his pain, Will knew that he was becoming roused. He would be less than a man if he remained unmoved as Gwyneth slipped off her chaste nightgown and leant close to him, her full breasts, milky in the moonlight, tipped with pink.

They were close to his face, an invitation that he could not resist. He leant towards her and as her hands grasped him he moaned with pleasure. He knew that he needed

232

some kind of peace, that his body, so long denied, cried out for release.

'That's it, my love,' Gwyneth whispered, her mouth against his neck. 'Make me spin with love and happiness, as only you ever could.'

Her words were a balm, as, in his heart, he knew they were meant to be. Gwyneth was not a stupid woman; she was sensual and quick-witted, and she knew how to please. She flattered him with soft words and all the time her body arched towards him, waiting for his passion.

Will held back until he could no longer contain himself, and then he took her, feeling with each movement of his body that he was betraying Eline.

'My love, that's so wonderful,' Gwyneth gasped. 'That's right, come on, take your fill of me, for now you have the right; you are my lawful wedded husband.'

The words rang hollowly in Will's mind, and for a moment he almost withdrew himself from her. But Gwyneth, sensitive as ever, closed her milky thighs, trapping him in a sensation so erotic that he felt the life force flow through him.

Even as he reached the heights of his passion, one part of his mind looked down objectively at the man labouring on the bed and thought him a fool.

It was some weeks later that Will was approached in the street by a man he scarcely knew.

'Bob Smale.' The man held out a hand and, with surprise, Will took it.

'I am joint owner of the *Cambrian*.' Bob Smale was smartly dressed, his linen clean, his coat well cut and expensive. He smelled a little of claret, but then most of the better-off families took an after-lunch drink.

'And you are, I believe,' he continued, in a pleasant voice, 'Will Davies, businessman.'

'That's right,' Will said, not bothering to explain his exact situation as employee to Hari Grenfell or to conceal his surprise. 'What do you want with me?'

'Well, I'm sorry to approach you in the street in this way' – Bob Smale smiled with a deprecating manner – 'perhaps you'd come into the Burrows Arms for a drink. I'd like to talk to you about a bit of business.'

'I'm not really a businessman, you know,' Will said, bluntly. 'I simply work for Hari, Mrs Grenfell.'

'I'll explain over a glass of port.' Bob Smale led the way into the warmth of the back room of the inn and lifted a finger to the barman. As if by magic, a bottle of port and some glasses appeared on the dull surface of the table, and Will realized that Smale was obviously a very good customer here.

'What's the business?' Will said, not inclined to give up too much of his time. He was on his way to see Hari; he longed to talk to her, to hear her common-sense views on the way his life was moving. He found it more than a little wearing commuting between Cardiff and his home on Kilvey Hill, and it seemed Hari had come up with a solution. Recently, he had been given promotion; it seemed Hari and Mrs Bell from the Cardiff emporium had got together and talked about his future, coming up with startling results.

'I want you to act for me in a business venture. I'm part of a consortium, you understand.'

'I'm not quite sure what you mean?' Will said, his eyebrows raised. 'Why should you need me? This isn't crooked, is it?'

'Of course not,' Bob said smoothly. 'I'm a respected citizen of Swansea; I couldn't afford to be mixed up in anything the slightest bit crooked. No, it's just that there's been a clash of personalities, you might say.'

'I'm waiting.' Will took the glass of port the man handed him and watched him over the rim of the glass as he drank.

'I wish to buy a certain piece of land,' Bob Smale continued. 'Unfortunately, though all I would like is to be friends with the vendor, he simply does not like me. I believe he would refuse to sell me the land, just out of stubbornness on his part.'

He shrugged. 'Still, the consortium in which I'm involved does not care about personalities; all they want is to pay a fair price for a fair deal.'

He eyed Will shrewdly. 'You are at liberty to look over all the relevant documents, just to assure yourself it's all above board. Jamie O'Conner would be getting a good deal, and you could be the one to help him.'

'Jamie?' Will said. 'Surely you don't find him unreasonable?'

Bob Smale smiled wryly. 'He is where I'm concerned. His stubbornness is doing him out of a good price for the land; he wants to sell it, I know he does. And,' Smale continued, 'there would be a nice little sum of money by way of commission for you.'

Will rubbed his eyes. He wasn't really interested in Bob Smale's problems. 'Look, if Jamie doesn't want to sell, there's nothing I can do,' he said, wearily.

'You are a trusted man in these parts,' Bob Smale said persuasively. 'And I'm sure you want what's best for your kin, don't you? Jamie could do with the money; we none of us can afford to turn down a good deal. Look, there's five per cent of the sale price as remuneration, a respectable sum in anyone's book.'

Will looked up at Smale, studying his face carefully, but there was no sign of avarice; the man seemed genuine enough. He paused; the money would certainly make a difference to him.

'I'd like to know a lot more about the deal before I make a decision,' he said at last.

'Quite right too.' Bob Smale smiled, leaning back in his chair. 'I'm sure that, after due consideration, you'll see that everything is fair and above board.'

Will tipped up his glass; he didn't like the idea of pulling the wool over Jamie's eyes, even for a short time,

235

and for his own good. The matter would need careful thought, but if, as Smale claimed, this was just a case of personal dislikes and Jamie was cutting off his nose to spite his face, then perhaps he should step in.

'All right,' he said. 'I suppose it's for the best.' He wanted out of the pub, away from Smale's persuasive voice; Will wanted to be alone with his own problems – he had enough of them, goodness knows.

'Fine!' Bob Smale seemed well pleased, and so, in theory, should he himself be, Will thought; and yet there was a feeling of uneasiness about the whole thing that rang warning bells in his mind.

Perhaps he was being over-cautious; his judgement at this time was not too finely honed. He sank back in his chair and took another drink; to hell with reservations. It was about time he made some money for himself, instead of relying on others to put him on course.

He thought of Mrs Bell, urged on, no doubt, by Hari. She'd already hinted that she wanted a branch of her emporium opened in Swansea, and Will would be the obvious one to run it.

Run it – the words echoed in his mind. He was a little tired of running other people's business, and now, with only a little capital, perhaps he could have a stake in the business, buy in as a partner, if only in a small way.

He lifted his glass as if in a toast. 'To the success of your consortium and to my five per cent,' he said, almost in a mood of resignation. He tossed back his head and drank the sweet liquid from the glass in one swallow.

Fon sat at the table, a large platter of bacon and eggs steaming before her. 'Will Davies must be all right to do business with, mustn't he, Jamie?'

'It's not Will Davies I'm concerned about,' Jamie said. 'It's the fact that he doesn't seem to know who exactly is behind this consortium that bothers me. There's a doubt niggling at the corners of my mind.'

Fon sighed. 'Well, it's either sell the land or the Black Devil.'

'Perhaps I could sell my wife,' he paused, head on one side.

He pulled her close and rested his head against her breast. 'I suppose you still have your uses,' he said, his mouth nuzzling the buttons of her bodice. 'Perhaps I'll keep you a little while longer.'

'Let me go, and behave yourself! The boys will be in any minute for breakfast.'

'Shrew,' Jamie said, releasing her. 'I'll just have to contain myself in patience until later, then, will I?'

Fon ignored his smile and pushed the kettle on the hob, where it immediately began to issue steam from the blackened spout.

'What are you going to do about the land, then?' Fon asked, making the tea in the huge brown pot.

'I suppose I'll sign the documents when someone brings them over this evening,' he said. 'But I do wish I knew who the consortium consisted of.'

'Well, at least it can't be one owner,' Fon reasoned, 'so it will take a group decision to do anything with the land.'

'Still, I'll insist I know the names of the people involved in the deal as part of the agreement,' Jamie said. 'I don't want just anyone owning the land; the Lord only knows what would be done with it in the wrong hands.'

'It couldn't harm us, could it?' Fon asked, putting the cups together and pouring the tea. 'I mean, could it be used against us in any way?'

'Possibly,' Jamie said, taking his cup from her hand. 'I suppose, if it wasn't a roadway that was planned but a coalmine, the damage to our land could be disastrous. Our ponds and streams could be choked up, for a start.'

'Aye, but it was Eddie who found out that a road was planned. He's a sensible man, he wouldn't be easily fooled.'

'I know,' Jamie agreed, 'but you mustn't believe everything you read in a newspaper, especially one part-owned by Smale.' He smiled. 'That's why I've done a bit of checking on my own account.'

The door opened and Eddie came into the room on a blast of cold, damp air. His face was reddened by the wind, and his hair, beneath his cap, was plastered on his forehead.

'Ploughing's bloody hard work.' He glanced at Fon. 'Excuse my language; I didn't mean that to slip out.'

'Sit down and have some bacon and eggs,' Fon said, smiling to show he was forgiven. 'You'll feel better when you've got some good food inside you.'

Eddie sat in a chair and rubbed the splattering of earth from his face with the back of his hand. 'Well,' he said, 'I've found out something this morning, something I think we should all know.'

Fon saw the sparkle in his eye and felt instinctively he'd been talking with Arian Smale. She felt a sudden knotting of her insides; she knew that what Eddie was about to say was something she wouldn't want to hear.

He leant forward, his face earnest. 'If we sell the strip of land bordering the farm, you know who will own it?' He paused a moment for effect. 'It's that bastard Smale. He's the one behind the whole deal; he must really want that piece of land.'

Jamie smiled enigmatically. 'Well, in that case,' he said slowly, 'we must make sure the man gets just what he wants.'

He looked at Fon and winked, and she realized that, whatever was happening, her husband had everything under control.

CHAPTER NINETEEN

Eline looked down at the books resting on the desk before her and saw, with no sense of satisfaction, that the profits from the gallery were excellent and improving day by day.

She sighed and glanced through the gallery window at the snowy landscape spread before her. The trees glittered whitely against the pale sunshine, and across the road the seashore held drifts of untrodden snow right to the water's edge.

She closed the books. It was time she was getting back to Swansea, to the big house she'd rented on Mount Pleasant Hill, where there would be cheerful fires in the grate and she would spend the evening working on yet another design for winter boots.

It was strange, Eline mused as she rose to her feet and moved closer to the window, the way that success bred success, for not only was the gallery flourishing, with Eline's reputation for handling only the finest painting spreading across the country, but her footwear designs and her window-dressing talents were now almost as much sought after as were those of Hari Grenfell. Eline was, if not rich, at least comfortably placed. But she was not happy.

Earlier today, as she had travelled on the Mumbles train down the curving coast from Swansea, memories had swamped her, memories of her abortive love affair with Will Davies. She smiled ruefully; it hadn't even been an affair, not really. They had never touched, intimately, never become lovers; and now she wondered at the foolishness that had kept them apart. What good

239

was chastity, when it left nothing to hold on to, not even memories? If only she and Will had consummated their love, given everything to each other, at least now she would have memories, real memories that she could take out like precious jewels and examine in the loneliness of night.

Suddenly her attention was caught by the sight of two figures bent close together. With a leap of her heart, Eline recognized Will's tall frame bending protectively over Gwyneth Parks. No, not Gwyneth Parks; she was now Mrs Davies. Eline's heart contracted with pain.

'Eline!' Calvin came into the room on a gust of wind. She was startled; she had not seen him enter through the gallery door. Snow lent a white frosting to his hat and fringed his moustache, and she drew herself upright, forcing a smile even as she attempted to push away the image imprinted on her mind of Will and Gwyneth so close together.

'Calvin, it's good to see you!' She felt a throb of affection for the man who had accepted with good grace her decision not to marry him, loving her enough to let her go.

'Eline, my dear girl, I'm sorry I wasn't here to meet you; you must have had an uncomfortable journey in from town.' He shrugged out of his coat. 'But what are you doing here so late?' he said in concern. 'You are not going to be able to return home tonight; all the roads to Swansea are closed.'

Eline shrugged. 'It doesn't matter. I'll take a room in one of the lodging houses, I'll be all right.'

Calvin took her hands and drew her towards him. 'Poor little love, you're so unhappy; coming here always affects you that way.'

She looked up at him. He was so strong and yet so sensitive; why couldn't she just fall in love with him and have done with all the torment of longings for a man she could not have?

240

'What's upset you now?' Calvin put his finger beneath her chin and looked down at her. 'You seem more edgy than usual.'

'I saw them, together,' Eline said with difficulty, 'Will and Gwyneth.'

Eline took a deep breath, trying to force back the pain that the sight of the couple arm in arm had aroused in her. 'Her child must be due very soon now.'

Calvin drew her close. 'Eline, I've respected your wishes, accepted your decision not to marry me, but look, you can't stay alone all your life; you are a flesh-and-blood woman, you can have children of your own, a family – our family – at least you won't be on the outside looking in for the rest of your days. Won't you reconsider?'

Eline leant against him, warmed by his concern, feeling, in spite of her success, an emptiness inside her that cried out to be filled.

As she struggled for a reply, Calvin spoke again. 'You know how I feel about you,' he said softly, his mouth against her hair. 'I'd always care for you, respect your every wish; I'd be good to you, Eline.'

She looked through the window at the snowy scene outside, and she shivered.

Calvin held her closer. 'Come into my sitting-room,' he said softly. 'You haven't seen what I've done to the attic rooms, have you?'

Eline felt strange as she mounted the stairs beside Calvin. She knew she was playing with fire as he led her from the impersonal gallery rooms to his own quarters.

'There!' He opened the door, and Eline drew a deep breath at the cosy atmosphere that was generated by the cheerful fire burning in the grate and the oil lamps strategically placed around the room.

Heavy curtains were drawn against the cold, and the entire effect was of a cocoon of warmth and secrecy, a haven from the world outside.

241

'It's only for when I'm spending time in Oystermouth,' he said, quickly, 'but wait until you see the house I've bought on top of Mumbles Hill; the view is fantastic, and when I've finished making improvements to the building it will be very comfortable indeed. I wish you would share it with me, Eline.

'I'm sorry' – he rushed on – 'you're shivering! Sit by the fire; I'll bring you a glass of port to warm the blood.'

She looked round, feeling suddenly lethargic, as she leant back in the comfort of a high-backed chair. She watched as Calvin filled two glasses with liquid that gleamed ruby in the firelight, and a sense of peace seemed to permeate the room.

'You must stay here tonight,' he said. 'I'll go along the road to the club and find a bed; I can't have you walking the streets in this weather.'

It was good to have someone take charge, Eline thought, wearily. It was all very well and good to be self-sufficient, strong, in charge of her own destiny – how many women would give the world to be in her position – but she was tired, so tired.

'Thank you, Calvin,' she said humbly. She sipped the warming liquid, and it spread through her like a panacea, easing the pain a little. She held out her glass for more, and Calvin obligingly filled it.

He looked down into her eyes, and she saw the admiration there with a feeling of gratitude; she was desirable, wanted by a man and a good man, a handsome man – why was she holding back, for what?

She had held back with Will, had cared more for her reputation and conscience than for her love and desire; what good had come of it?

'Calvin . . .' she said tentatively, 'I want you to stay with me tonight.'

If he was surprised, he concealed it well. He smiled down at her, his eyes bright with sudden hope. 'I do believe you are serious, Eline,' he said softly. 'You know

242

I've wanted you for such a long time, and if you are offering what I think you are, then please make sure you mean it; I'm only human, remember.'

'I'm not teasing,' Eline said quietly. She put down her glass and moved from her chair, making her way the few paces across the room to where he was standing pouring a drink from a crystal decanter.

Slowly she took the glass from him and stood it carefully on the tray and then, as if in a dream, she put her arms around him. 'I am serious,' she said. 'I've never been more serious in all my life. I want you to make love to me, Calvin; is that putting it plain enough?'

He took her in his arms then and his face was alight with happiness. Eline sighed as his hands gently began to unfasten her gown. She was committed now; there was no turning back, not now, not ever.

Gwyneth, pale and tired, had retired to bed and William sat before the fire, head in hands as he fought against the feelings that threatened to swamp him in self-pity. He had seen her, Eline, framed in the light from the gallery window, as beautiful and unobtainable as one of the paintings that hung about the room behind her.

'Damn,' he said softly. If only he could forget her, put her right out of his thoughts, then he could almost be happy. He poked at the embers in the fire, and a blaze of sparks rose up as though in anger before the coals shifted lower into the grate.

He sensed someone standing behind him and turned to look into the face of his mother-in-law. 'Nina,' he said, 'I didn't realize you were there.'

'You're in torment, aren't you, Will?' Nina sat down beside him and put her hand on his knee. 'I know it's hard, being here, seeing *her*; it's only natural to feel bad, you can't help it.'

'I think the world of Gwyneth,' he said desperately. 'I

want to look after her and our child, and yet I can't help but feel . . .'

'I know, *cariad*.' Nina shook her head. 'I wasn't always an old woman.' Her eyes became dreamy. 'Not so long ago I had the love of a fine man; I loved Joe Harries more than I can ever say in ordinary words.'

She sighed, her eyes clearing. 'But I lived with Kevin, my husband, until he died, brought up our children, and all the time I pined for Joe.'

She spread her work-roughened hands wide. 'I had him then, for a short time, after Eline had left him, that is; and we found a joy and a happiness of sorts together because it was meant to be.'

She sighed heavily again. 'The most comforting thing I can say is, what's for you, you'll have; the good Lord evens things out – joy, suffering, happiness, unhappiness, he does the best he can to give us something of each.'

Will rose to his feet. 'You are a good woman, Nina,' he said, smiling down at her.

She burst into a spontaneous laugh, her mouth curving, her eyes merry; and for a moment Will could see the beautiful, sensual woman she must have been.

'*Duw*, no-one's ever accused me of being that before,' she said. 'Wicked and wanton were the words most of the people round here would have used.' She straightened her shoulders. 'And proud I am of it too, mind.

'Well' – she stared up at him – 'where are you going to try and drown the devils within you? The tap-rooms will all be closed now.'

'I'm just going to walk along the sea front,' Will said softly, 'see if the salt air will clear my mind.'

'It isn't your mind that's the trouble, Will, it's your heart.'

She rose and stood before him. 'Look, I'm older than you, much older in years and experience. Try to be

244

content with what you have right here, a good woman, a child on the way and' – her face brightened – 'you've had promotion, and now there's a chance of a bit of money coming your way, if I'm not mistaken.'

Will paused at the door, his eyebrows raised. 'There's not much you miss, is there?'

'Well, Fon is my daughter too, mind,' Nina said, 'and she seems all excited about this land her husband is selling. Put them right, it will. Jamie's been having a bit of a difficult time, see, some fool trying to ruin him.'

Will turned away from the door, his spine suddenly tingling. 'Ruin him, what exactly do you mean, Nina? I think you should tell me all about it.'

'Right, sit down, then, have your walk later. This story will take a bit of telling.' She smiled at him. 'Why don't I bring out the rhubarb wine?'

Will settled himself in the armchair, his own misery forgotten. There was something strange about the consortium, about Robert Smale and the whole set-up, and Will had the feeling he was going to find out just what it was.

It was perhaps an hour later that he walked out along the sea front of Oystermouth, his hands thrust into his pockets, his brow furrowed. It was clear now to Will that this man Smale had some sort of grudge against Jamie O'Conner and wished him more harm than good. Well, as soon as it was light, Will would take a trip up to Honey's Farm and warn Jamie of what was afoot.

Jamie was an astute man, but then so was Smale. Who would suspect Fon's brother-in-law of being engaged in underhand dealings? No, Smale had chosen well when he approached Will in the street.

Will thrust his hands into his pockets. He would like to teach Smale a lesson, give him the hiding he deserved; how dare he involve Will in one of his schemes?

He paused outside the gallery, his senses longingly tuned in to Eline. Was she still in there, behind the stone walls and the cold staring eyes of the windows?

As if in answer to his question, a light was turned on in one of the upstairs rooms. Against the light, Will saw the outline of a woman, and he drew a deep ragged breath, shock surging through him like a poison, for there, just beyond Eline's shoulder, was another shadow – that of a man.

Jealousy hit Will like a sudden blow as the two shadows seemed to merge into one. They moved away from the window, and then the light was extinguished.

'Eline!' Will whispered into the dark. 'Eline, you can't do this to me.'

The silence around him was intense; it filled the whole world, so that Will felt trapped in an oasis of darkness and despair. He wanted to break the spell by rushing inside the house, taking Eline in his arms and making her his own. But he had no right; he was a married man, he had responsibilities, and nothing could ever change that. Slowly, hopelessly, he turned away and walked towards the darkness of the sea.

Eline closed her eyes for a moment as the light was extinguished, leaving her and Calvin alone in the warm womb of the darkness. She felt his hands on her breasts as his fingers fumbled with her buttons, and she forced herself not to panic but to remain quiescent. All around her were the scents of him, for this after all was his bedroom. Here Calvin stayed when he had extra business at the gallery.

'Eline, my sweet girl.' Calvin had freed her breasts; he caressed them gently, and now Eline could see the outline of his broad shoulders as her eyes became accustomed to the gloom. He bent his head and captured her nipple between his lips and, almost against her will, Eline found herself responding. It was so long, too long, since she'd been in a man's arms.

Slowly, Calvin undressed her, taking his time to

246

remove each of her garments. He was practised, and Eline could tell he'd had numerous lovers.

Once she was naked, he knelt beside her, just looking down at her skin, pale in the moonlight. 'Beautiful,' he breathed, 'more beautiful than even I had imagined.'

Quickly, he took off his own clothes, and he stood proud and tall, his body eager for her. But still he took his time; he was a man of experience, and he knew that anticipation was all part of the building excitement.

He stretched out beside her on the bed and gently drew her close. His lips found hers, and he kissed her with such tenderness that Eline felt suddenly she was cheating him. She wanted him now, with an urgency that surprised her, but it was not his love she wanted, just the satisfaction of release from the tensions within her.

But no, that was not quite true, she reasoned; she needed his adoration as a thirsty flower needed water. She had been starved of the emotions so dear to a woman; she felt the need to be desired, and Calvin was more than fulfilling that need.

Delicately, he smoothed her thighs, his fingers expertly advancing and retreating. Eline found her arms winding around his shoulders, drawing him down to her; she wanted to be pierced, to be possessed, to feel like a woman once more.

As though sensing her readiness, he moved above her; for a moment he was poised and then he was taking possession of her body, making it his, setting his mark of ownership unmistakably upon her.

She moved against him, clearing everything from her mind but the needs of the moment. She no longer thought rational thoughts; she simply let the sensations roll through her, sweeping her away on a journey of discovery.

Never before had she been loved with such finesse, such expertise; she had known only the mundane couplings of her marriage bed. Joe Harries had never been blessed with finesse. Vigour he had in abundance, but he had been a straightforward man, uncomplicated in his love-making. Calvin was of a different breed.

She felt herself surrender to him; the delights he was bringing like gifts to her were too much to resist. She knew that in this moment he could ask of her what he wanted, and she would give it to him.

It was as if he sensed her inner feelings, for he paused in his stride and his rhythm was broken for a fraction of a moment.

He caught her face in his two hands and forced her to look at him. 'You are my woman now, Eline, and don't you ever forget it.'

His sudden movement brought a gasp from her, and then he was driving hard, his hands gripping her waist. She cried out, and for a moment it was as though time ceased. Then came the rushing cascade of sensation that spread like wildfire through her blood, pounding from her thighs to her breasts and filling her head until she thought she would die of it.

She clung to him, holding him to her, pressing him closer as the ripples reached a crescendo. Then she fell back against the pillows, her eyes closed as she struggled for breath.

Calvin held her close, still possessing her; he kissed her breast and she ran her fingers over his back, down towards the strong buttocks that curved pleasingly beneath her hands.

'Eline!' he said hoarsely. 'I love you.' The words fell like pieces of ice into her mind; the picture of Will flashed before her eyes.

She would have drawn away from him, but she was aware that he was growing aroused once more. 'This time it will be more gentle,' he whispered against her ear. 'It will be slower, quieter, but afterwards you will never want to leave me.'

248

As he began to move once more and Eline felt the overriding need for his body to assuage the heat in hers, she knew a mingling of sadness and joy; she wanted Calvin, there was no denying that she wanted him, and yet her spirit, her inner core, cried out for Will to be the one holding her close.

Even as the ecstasy began to grow within her, Eline felt tears of sadness running down her cheeks and falling salt into her mouth.

It was morning when she woke. Eline stretched her arms and turned over in the bed and saw that it was empty. From downstairs, she heard the sounds of the maid putting coal on to the fires in the gallery rooms. She became aware of the aroma of coffee and sat up, looking around her, as though awaking from a dream.

'Calvin!' She looked down at her naked body, and the colour stained her cheeks; she had lain with Calvin, enjoying his love-making with what she could only describe as a feeling of shameless lust, for she didn't love him; that much was clear to her even now.

He entered the room, and he looked handsome in a scarlet silk robe tied loosely around him. He was carrying a tray laden with a pot of coffee and two cups, and his eyes searched her face. Instinctively, she covered her breast and, smiling, he put down the tray and came over to the bed, drawing the sheet away from her fingers.

Lightly, he traced the outline of her body from breast to thigh. 'Mine,' he said with satisfaction. He sat down beside her and poured the coffee, and when he handed her a cup, she held it between them like a barrier.

'You are going to marry me, Eline Harries,' he said casually, but his eyes were clear and direct.

She shook her head. 'No, Calvin, I'm not going to marry you.' She spoke quietly but calmly, and there was no doubt that she meant what she said. 'But I'm yours whenever you want me.' She looked up at him in surprise as he took the cup of coffee from her and stood it on the table beside the bed.

'Well' – he paused – 'we'll talk of marriage later; in the meantime,' he said, with a smile around his eyes, 'I shall take up the option on that offer straightaway.'

Slowly he began to untie the belt of his robe as he advanced towards the bed.

CHAPTER TWENTY

Eline sat up in bed and stared around her, feeling suddenly cold. She shivered; she had spent another night with Calvin, enjoying an almost wanton abandon in his arms. He had made her feel like a woman again, there was no denying it. Calvin, though she didn't love him, had woken in her a sensual passion she had known herself capable of. And yet absurdly, she felt, each time she had lain with Calvin, that she had been untrue to Will, Will who was married now, his wife expecting a child – how foolish of Eline even to consider him.

She had spent the night hours, once the glow of love-making had worn away, in sleepless remorse. She had lain beside Calvin's unfamiliar form and hoped he would wake and take her in his arms, make her forget everything but the brief sensations of being aroused to the heights. But the coming down again was all the more bitter.

The bed beside her was empty now; she must have fallen into an exhausted sleep by the time he'd silently left the room.

She felt tears on her lashes, blurring her vision; guilt etched a sharp pain through her body, and she felt, deep within her, that she had betrayed everything she held precious.

It was so foolish to have regrets for the wasted year, all those years she had longed for Will to hold her in his arms and make love to her. Why, she asked herself now, had she denied herself and Will the joy of being together? Why had she insisted that they must hold their feelings in check until the moment was right, everything perfect?

So why had she allowed Calvin to take her to his bed when she didn't even love him? And yet she knew the answer; there had been a need within her to restore her lost pride. She needed the knowledge that she was precious to someone, if not to Will Davies.

She felt the hot colour flame in her cheeks. She had enjoyed Calvin's love-making, she couldn't deny it; she had thirsted for love, her starved body overcoming her mind that had urged caution.

The sheets slipped from her shoulders and she glanced down at her nakedness with a sense of despair.

Hurriedly, she rose and washed quickly in the water from the jug on the table. She dressed with shaking fingers, and all the time she wanted to cry out her shame and her sorrow, regretting now the indiscretions of the night.

There was no sign of Calvin downstairs, and it was with relief that Eline let herself out into the street. She turned from the door to hurry away from the gallery, and she felt the colour drain from her face as she came unexpectedly face to face with Will.

She could tell from the look on his face that he knew. How, she wasn't sure, but there were lines of pain around his mouth and his eyes, and she looked away from him quickly.

'Why didn't I make you mine when I had the chance?' he said dejectedly, and Eline shook her head.

'I know,' she said in a small voice. 'I was stiff-necked and full of pride, and now I regret it.' She sighed heavily. 'There's so much I regret, Will.'

'Me too.' He didn't touch her, and she bit her lip; there seemed no more to be said.

'Goodbye, my love.' Her words were softly spoken, but he caught them and his face twisted as though he would cry.

'Goodbye, Eline.'

He walked away swiftly, and Eline watched his tall

252

figure with a feeling of sorrow aching within her. She longed to run after him, to cry out his name, beg him to forgive her; but it was useless. He was married, he had responsibilities; their lives were no longer entwined.

She caught the train without a backward glance at Oystermouth, and yet every jolt of the wheels against the rails felt like a blow. Life would never be the same for her, not now. She had committed herself to Calvin; he had made that quite plain last night.

Eline turned to look at the sea without really seeing the pewter waves washing against the shore. She was remembering Calvin drawing back the sheet, staring down at her nakedness and running his finger over her body, declaring it was his.

And where had he gone this morning, she wondered with a small dart of apprehension. What was he planning? Because he would no longer be content to stand by and let her have all her own way; he was not that sort of man.

She alighted from the train in Swansea and stared around at the grey rain-soaked streets with a feeling of dismay; here, in the bustling town, her actions of the previous night seemed even more bizarre and out of character. What on earth had possessed her? She must have been deranged with unhappiness.

She walked along more purposefully now; she had decided, some days ago, to look for new premises for her boot-and-shoe store and had arranged to see a shop on the outskirts of Swansea. Somehow she must begin to make some sense of her life; she was a working girl, not cut out for the idle life of a rich man's paramour.

The building she was to view was an old one, but there was plenty of room for the installation of machines as well as for a cobblers' workshop. And she could well afford to expand now; what with the success of the gallery and her regular wage from Hari Grenfell for the window-dressing, there was no shortage of funds.

She felt a little comforted; at least she could do some good for children with foot defects. A surge of excitement filled her; hope began to replace the gloom of earlier that morning. Perhaps she could find fulfilment in her work at least.

She planned to start a savings club, enabling parents to pay a small sum each week towards the cost of a pair of boots. The profit would be slow coming in, but what did that matter? She had enough money, more than enough to live comfortably these days.

She squared her shoulders, determined to put Calvin Temple and all thoughts of sharing his bed out of her mind. He didn't own her; nobody owned Eline Harries, she was her own woman. Then why did she have the uncomfortable feeling that Calvin would not share her point of view?

'Why are you giving the man what he wants?' Will sat opposite Jamie O'Conner in the tap-room of the Burrows Inn and sized him up, liking what he saw. The man was honest, and yet he was no fool; he was outspoken, and the thrust of his jaw showed determination.

'It's not what he wants, it's only what he thinks he wants.' Jamie smiled. 'Bob Smale believes there is going to be a road running through the piece of land he's put you up to buying for him.' He smiled without humour. 'But I've made it my business to find out more about the scheme.' He lifted his glass of ale to his lips, and his eyes were full of laughter.

'Plans have changed, then?' Will said. 'And now you intend to sell the land?'

'The plans have been shelved indefinitely. I don't think there will be any call for that stretch of land, not in my lifetime. In any case, I have to sell that land,' Jamie confessed. 'I need the influx of capital into the farm, thanks to the work of Bob Smale and his cohorts.'

He lowered his glass. 'Though for sure he'd never have got it from me if there *had* been a road going there. Oh, no, I'd have made myself a tidy profit on it.' He shrugged. 'As it is, I'll have to be content with a modest gain, though the knowledge that I've made a fool of the man will help.'

Will leaned back in his chair, staring down for a moment into the liquid in his glass. He admired Jamie; he didn't blame him one bit for turning the tables on Bob Smale, and yet the man was a bad enemy; that much was clear.

'Well, Smale will continue to believe that you are ignorant of his identity,' he said, 'I will have my commission, and we'll all be happy.'

But would he ever be happy again? Will thought. He was tied to Gwyneth now; he was her husband for better or worse, and though he had tender feelings of affection for her and vowed that he would care for her always, his gut cried out in anguish for Eline.

Knowing that she had gone to the bed of another man had made him sad at first; now anger and bitterness had replaced his sadness. Why hadn't Eline become his? She had held out against him, and he had respected her wishes; and what good had it done him? If he and Eline had been lovers, he would never have taken Gwyneth to bed, and all the resulting chaos would have been avoided.

He became aware that Jamie was speaking again. 'Then you'll be seeing Smale later on today to conclude the deal, I take it? Good.' He drained his glass and put it on the table and held out his hand to Will. 'I'll thank you for your cooperation, and perhaps some time we'll do business again.'

Will rose and took the proffered hand. 'My pleasure,' he said. He watched as Jamie left the pub, his hair gleaming brightly as he stood in a patch of light outside the door. Then the man was gone and Will was alone

255

in the noisy, smoke-filled room – alone, he thought ruefully, except for the thoughts of what might have been that plagued him.

But now he must be positive. He must plan for his future; he would have a small capital to start a business of his own, and, though he was grateful to both Hari and Mrs Bell for their faith in him, he knew he couldn't work for other people all his life.

He had opened the branch of the Bell Emporium in Swansea a week ago, and it was doing well. The goods imported from Cardiff were proving a novelty, and the windows dressed by Eline were a joy to behold.

She had been reluctant, at first, to handle the dressing of a window with clothing, protesting that shoes were her business. But it seemed that, with her artistic flair, Eline could do no wrong. She had successfully set out the window with an array of nightwear that had enchanted the public of Swansea.

It seemed everyone wanted Mrs Bell's quality goods, goods bought on Eline's advice to replace the dusty stock that Mrs Bell had been so fond of.

Eline! How Will ached for her. She seemed so pale and so sad, even though her new venture with remedial boots and shoes, like everything else she touched, had flourished over the past weeks. She would become a very rich woman; she had the flair for making money at whatever she turned her hand to. But it was her vulnerable side that Will saw when she didn't know he was observing her.

Sometimes, when she was filling a window or selecting goods, he would catch a sense of something like panic in her eyes, and then he wanted to take her in his arms and hold her close and protect her – though protect her against what, he didn't know.

He glanced at the clock on the wall and then rose and left the tap-room and made his way to the solicitors' office on the High Street. He was to meet Bob Smale there and finalize the sale. Then, with his commission safely in his hands, he would put his own plans into action.

He hunched his shoulders against the coldness of the day and stared ruefully at the big shops flanking the roadway. He would have to start very modestly, and in the only business he knew, that of cobbling.

He would go back to his grass roots; from manager he would become nothing more than a workman at the bench again, moulding the leather, binding and stitching and cutting. The awl and the dog would be his tools, and his skill would at least make him a living; he would be independent, his own man. The thought brought him a grain of comfort as he strode through the winter streets towards the centre of town.

'I love you, Eline,' Calvin said, 'and this is my gift of appreciation to you.' He waved his hand around the large, empty sitting-room of the house he had bought her.

'You must furnish it as you wish. I will foot all the bills, and please don't protest – you know as well as I do that I have money to spare.'

Eline looked at him, wondering what she could say to turn down his offer but with graciousness.

She saw him smile. 'You are not allowed to refuse,' he said softly, his hand touching her hair. 'It's what I want to do, Eline; please don't be difficult.'

She lifted her hands in a gesture of defeat. 'Thank you, Calvin, you are too generous.'

And yet she felt bound, tied to him, by yet another invisible cord. His sexual demands she had acceded to, feeling she owed him that much. It had been she who had led him on, she who had instigated their first night of passion, and she realized she had turned on a tap that she could not simply turn off again.

And, to be truthful, she enjoyed his love-making just

257

as much, if not more than, she had that first time; but afterwards, each time, she felt the same sickening feeling of betrayal.

He seemed to sense her thoughts. 'Come upstairs,' he said quietly, taking her hand and leading her to the wide curving staircase. 'I've something to show you.'

Her feet echoed against the bare wood of the treads, and, glancing through the window, she saw, far below the sweeping tree-lined hillside, the wash of the sea against the grey, winter shoreline.

'I have taken the liberty of furnishing one of the rooms myself.' Calvin smiled, his handsome face alight with merriment. 'I must admit to having an ulterior motive, but you'll forgive me for wanting you so much, won't you?'

The master bedroom was high-ceilinged and gracious, the silk hangings on the wall tasteful and expensive. Elegant paintings graced the chimneybreast, and Eline had to admit that Calvin was possessed of exquisite taste.

The huge bed dominated the room, a four-poster with silken drapes sweeping down to the raised dais on which it stood. Scattered over the deep carpet were rich Indian rugs in jewel colours that brought brightness to the dullness of the day.

'It's beautiful!' Eline said in admiration. 'I congratulate you, Calvin; I couldn't have chosen better myself.'

Against a long wall stood an elegantly carved cabinet, and Calvin moved towards it, opening one of the doors and drawing out a silver tray set with small covered dishes.

'I have brought us a picnic,' he said, smiling like an excited boy. Eline was touched by his obvious pleasure.

'Come, sit on the bed, let me wait on you.' He bowed mockingly and Eline joined in the spirit of the occasion by kicking off her shoes and climbing into the deep silk of the bed.

258

'I feel like a queen,' she said, smiling. 'You spoil me, Calvin; you shouldn't be so generous.'

'I have no-one else to whom I wish to be generous,' he said softly. 'You have become my life, Eline.'

She thrust aside her uneasiness and laughed as he poured champagne into tall glasses that sparkled like diamonds. 'Here, my lady,' he said, handing her a glass.

He poured his own and climbed on the bed beside her. 'This is a celebration,' he said, 'as if you haven't guessed.' He sipped his champagne and smiled down at her.

'What sort of celebration?' she asked, carefully, her senses heightened as she waited for his reply. It was not what she expected, and she sighed in relief.

'An old, not very close uncle has gone to the great mansion in the sky,' he said, calmly refilling her glass. 'And that means that from henceforth I am no longer plain Calvin Temple, but Lord Temple, with even more lands and houses and wealth.'

He leant forward and kissed her mouth. 'And what am I to do with it all, I who have no kith and kin to leave it to?'

He took her glass from her hand and placed it on the side table. 'Eline, don't answer straightaway, think carefully about what I am going to say: I want you to marry me, I want that above all – but even if you refuse, I shall name you as my next of kin. You shall inherit my own private fortune.'

'No, Calvin!' Eline said quickly. 'Please don't put such a burden of responsibility on me; I can't accept.'

'Of course you can,' he said, his hand unfastening her neckline. 'You are my concubine, and even if you won't be my wife, all I have is yours, and nothing will ever change that.'

He touched her breasts with delicate fingers, his breathing becoming ragged. 'I can't live without you,

259

Eline. I love you so much; I have loved you from the first moment I set eyes on you.'

He kissed her mouth and then her throat. 'Why fight it? What is there for you in spinsterhood? Who and what are you waiting for, Eline?'

'No-one,' she agreed dully. He was right; who was there in her life now? Will was married, about to become a father; what use was there in fighting Calvin's wishes?

'You know you don't like being a mistress,' Calvin said, persuasively. 'The irregularity doesn't sit well upon you, does it?'

She shook her head dumbly as he continued to undress her. 'I would be so good to you, Eline, I would care for you and protect you with my dying breath.'

The silk beneath her was cool against her bare skin. She watched as Calvin quickly took off his own clothes, and objectively she looked at his fine strong body and handsome face. She wondered what was wrong with her that she did not leap at the chance of being his wife.

He was against her then, holding her close, his expert fingers caressing, bringing her desire to life in spite of her disquiet.

She moaned softly, and he laughed. 'You see, you want me; isn't that enough to be going on with, my darling?'

'Let me think . . .' she whispered, but he didn't hear her; he was intent upon giving them both pleasure. Slowly Eline relaxed against the softness of the bed, emotions taking over from rational thought. She closed her eyes as he possessed her, his finesse combined with young, healthy vigour stirring her passion.

She felt her arms close about his smooth back, she stroked the back of his neck, feeling the hair curl against her fingers with a dart of tenderness. Calvin was a good man, an ardent lover; what more did she require in a husband?

Love, came the traitorous thought, darting into her

head like a blade of a knife. But love was denied her; her love, her William, was out of reach. They had said goodbye once and for all and now, it was time that she thought about herself.

It took only a few weeks to arrange the wedding. It was winter, with snow dusting the trees, but Eline, in her soft satin gown, was too nervous to feel the cold.

Inside the pretty church of St Paul, she made her vows to love and honour and obey, and it struck her that this was the second time in her still young life that she had given her vows to a man she didn't love.

Outside, the grounds were filled with well-wishers and guests; the huge wedding breakfast was to be held in the fine rooms of the Mackworth Hotel. Calvin had seen to it that the entire building was theirs for that day and for their wedding night. Tomorrow, they would go home to the enormous house on the hill, to The Crest, and to a life of luxury and ease.

And yet she must pursue her career as a designer of shoes; Calvin had promised her that he would not interfere. But already he had discarded the small premises she had planned for herself in favour of larger, more substantial buildings.

As the couple emerged into the open air, a flurry of snow fell over them, almost, Eline thought, like a benediction.

She smiled up at Calvin, and he squeezed her hand gently. 'My wife,' he said. 'At last, Eline, you are really mine.'

CHAPTER TWENTY-ONE

Will sat in the small workroom and sighed heavily. The boot he was mending stood on the iron last in front of him; the bench was littered with pieces of leather, and the smell of it, fresh cut, reminded Will of his apprenticeship with Hari.

In those days he was an uncomplicated, innocent boy who was grateful for a roof over his head and food in his belly. Grateful too for the affection Hari unfailingly showered on him, her love wiping out the pain of losing his family to the yellow fever. Hari had shown him what happiness was, and now, somehow, he had lost it all.

He rose to his feet and removed the leather apron. The sky was darkening outside the window; a flurry of snow flew against the windows. It was high time he was getting home.

Home! The word rang hollowly in his mind; home was now the modest cottage at Oystermouth, for, with Gwyneth sickly with her pregnancy, Nina thought it wise that her daughter should be where she could keep an eye on her.

He pulled on his topcoat and picked up the parcels, gaily wrapped, from the table. Gifts to put under the tree, small gifts from himself, a pair of slippers for Gwyneth, sturdily fashioned to keep out the chill of the flagstone floor, and stout boots for Nina, who good-naturedly did the shopping now that her daughter was heavy with child.

And in the mound of parcels, gifts from Hari, toys for the expected baby and a pretty nightgown and woollen bed-wrap for Gwyneth. For William there was an envelope containing money; it would be more useful, Hari insisted, than any other gift.

He had balked at first, his pride rearing up to deny that he needed funds, but Hari had simply touched his cheek and smiled. 'Let me do this, Will,' she'd pleaded softly. 'I have too much money, and you are the little brother I never had, remember.'

He sighed heavily. Would he never be free of petticoat tails? Well-meaning as they were, the women in his life seemed destined to keep offering him a helping hand. Still, he would have no need to walk the five miles tonight; because of Hari's generosity, he could afford to treat himself to a ride home on the Mumbles train.

Home, he thought ruefully, was a place which sheltered the people you loved; he was fond of Gwyneth, sorry for her sickness and obvious discomfort now that the birth was near, but his love was all given to another woman, to Eline, who had become the wife of one of the richest men in the town.

He must stop these feelings of self-pity, he rebuked himself angrily. He wasn't badly off; he had banked the commission paid to him by Bob Smale, and that, for now, was his nest-egg, his small bit of security. As for the rest, he was making a living, his workshop practically rent-free.

It had been Eline who offered him the accommodation in the building she had planned to use for her own business before her husband had insisted on a fine new workshop that would be worthy of her standing in the town.

Eline had taken him round the building, offering him the low rent with the excuse that she had paid out half a year's rent in any case and this way, she argued, she would at least recoup some of her losses.

Will believed that Eline's new husband had no knowledge of the arrangement, and he felt a small glow of triumph that, at least in this, Eline shared something, some small part of herself, with him.

The door opened and a large figure stood framed against the light. 'I hope you are proud of your part in all this!' The words were harsh, a challenge.

Will put down his parcels and took up a hammer as he faced the red, angry countenance of Bob Smale. 'What are you talking about?' he asked, pretending innocence but knowing exactly what the man was talking about.

'The roadway, it isn't going through that parcel of land I bought after all. It's a useless burden now, just more space for the weeds to grow.'

'Sorry,' Will said cheerfully, 'but it wasn't part of our bargain that I survey the land or find out what it was to be used for. You didn't confide that much to me, remember?'

For a moment Bob Smale appeared nonplussed. 'Well, common sense would tell you that I wouldn't buy the ground unless there was something in it for me.'

'Quite,' Will agreed. 'In which case I'd have thought it was in your own interests to check the plans before you put out any money.'

Bob Smale, defeated, made for the door, but before he left he swung round to face Will, his face even redder, his eyes blazing.

'I don't care what you say,' he snarled, 'you were part of this – this outrage – and I thought you were a man to be trusted.'

Will raised his eyebrows in mock indignation. 'What outrage?' he enquired. 'You asked me to front a consortium buying a piece of land from Jamie O'Conner, and I did exactly that; where is your quarrel with me?'

Bob Smale swung away, slamming the door shut with a bang that reverberated through the building. Will smiled to himself; the man had got only what he deserved. But Will was wise enough to know that he, as well as Jamie, had made an enemy of a dangerous man.

Will let himself out into the darkness and locked the door of the workshop carefully; there was no telling what a man like Bob Smale would do once angered.

Sitting in the cold leather seat of the Mumbles train, Will stared out into the darkness, seeing the twinkling lights of the houses on the perimeter of the bay with no sense of comfort. He dreaded going back to the small cottage where he and Gwyneth slept in a cramped bedroom together, of necessity unable to be apart. But he had made his bed, and now he must lie on it.

The cold wind was rushing in from the sea when Will alighted from the train, and he was thankful to reach the shelter of the cottage. He pushed open the door and stared round at the familiar kitchen, with the fire burning cheerfully in the grate and the small tree decorated bravely with paper chains, and his throat constricted. Gwyneth had done her best to make their first Christmas a happy one.

He placed the parcels carefully round the base of the tree and looked around, wondering where everyone was. He glanced at the back of the door and saw that Nina's coat had gone. A chill of apprehension touched him; there was only one reason why Nina would go out so late and in such weather – the birth of the baby must be imminent.

He took the stairs two at a time and moved quickly into the bedroom.

'Will!' The gladness in Gwyneth's tone brought a searing guilt that was difficult to contend with; he should have been here, with her, he knew it was near her time, the least he could have done was to leave work early.

'What's this, then, idling in bed while your husband slaves to bring in the bread! What sort of wife are you?'

He crossed the room and took her hand, seeing, with sympathy, the sweat beading her forehead and upper lip.

'Is it very bad?' he asked quietly.

265

He sat on the chair beside her and smoothed her wrist, and Gwyneth forced a smile.

'No worse than for other women,' she said bravely, 'and if they can do it, so can I.'

Her face crumpled, and her mouth was pursed into a circle of pain. Her eyes were closed, and beneath the bedclothes her body stiffened.

Will was at a loss. Memories of his mam, straining on the bed, and him crouched in the corner, listening in mute terror to her moans, filled his mind. For a moment he was back in the past, in the hovel that had been his home. Then he shook his head as though to clear his mind and held his wife's hand, waiting for the pain to pass.

When Gwyneth rested, finally, he smiled down at her, brushing the damp hair from her forehead. 'Can I fetch you anything?' he asked softly. She shook her head. 'Mam's gone for the midwife,' she said. 'Once the new young nurse is here, I'll be all right, you'll see.'

Will marvelled at the fortitude of women, who endured the agony of birth not once but several times in their lifetime. The procreation of the species must go on at all costs, he mused with some bitterness.

It was with a sense of relief that he heard the door bang downstairs and the sound of footsteps coming steadily nearer.

'Out of here, Will Davies,' Nina said, her voice full of false cheer. 'This is women's work; you did your job when you planted your seed, my fine man.'

Downstairs, he made some tea, feeling it a useless gesture but knowing he must occupy himself with something or go mad. Was this the agony that came then from a few moments of thoughtless passion? The tearing of a woman's body to produce a child? The one comforting thought was that it was something women experienced all the time, something they apparently wanted.

He tensed, almost dropping the cup as he heard

Gwyneth scream out in agony. He gripped the edge of the table, his knuckles white. God! He had done this to her, foisted on her a baby, brought her nothing but pain. He rubbed his hand over his eyes and sank into a chair, and then he became aware that Nina was in the room, her face ashen.

'Something's wrong,' she said in a small voice. '*Duw*, had babies, me, and not felt such pain as my girl is suffering.'

'What can I do?' Will asked, looking up at Nina uncertainly.

'Only one thing,' she said. 'Fetch my girl a doctor before it is too late.'

Fon turned over in bed and saw the white of the snow against the window with a feeling of contentment. Jamie in the bed beside her was still asleep, a rare occurrence on a farm where, in the normal course of events, work began at an early hour. But this was Christmas, and even Jamie had decided to lie in bed for a while.

As if aware of her scrutiny, he opened his eyes and immediately reached for her, his hand seeking and finding her naked breasts.

'Behave!' Fon said in mock anger. 'Don't you ever think of anything else?'

'Not often,' Jamie agreed, drawing her close. She felt the heavy weight of him against her and smiled happily, knowing he was aroused as always by her nearness. One thing she could be certain of, Jamie's desire for her was total and undiminished by the familiarity brought about by the closeness of their marriage.

'I've got you a lovely present,' Fon said dreamily. 'I'm sure you'll love it; I can't wait for you to open it.'

He nuzzled her neck. 'I can give you yours right now, if you like,' he said, coaxingly.

'Hush!' she said good-naturedly. 'I can hear Patrick getting out of bed.'

She sat up, her breasts proud against the coldness of the morning. 'He'll be so excited,' she said. 'I can't wait to see his little face. Come on, Jamie, rouse yourself.'

He made a face at her, and she laughed at her own foolish choice of words.

'All right, you cruel woman, I'll get out of bed, if you insist.'

He slipped from beneath the blankets, and Fon immediately felt the cold seeping into the bed. She looked at him, tall, his hair dark, with hints of red, and his manhood standing proud and him unashamed of it.

She sighed. 'I regret being so hasty.'

Her voice was soft but he caught her words. The door sprang open and Patrick came into the room, clutching a brightly painted toy train.

'Look what I got, Fonny!' He held it out to her. 'Lovely puffa train.'

'Daddy Christmas been, then?' Fon said, hugging the little boy. 'Come on, get in bed with Fon. Your father can light the fire today as a treat for us.'

She sank back against the warmth of the pillows and watched as Patrick, well wrapped up in his flannel night-shirt, ran the train along the folds and dips of the patchwork quilt. She closed her eyes and must have dozed, because she heard Jamie's voice calling for her to come down.

In the kitchen, the fire was blazing cheerfully and the table was laid with a succulent dish of bacon and eggs surrounded by bread fried in the fat.

'Starving,' Patrick said, and climbed up on to his chair.

Jamie poured the tea and sweetened it liberally with sugar. 'Eddie and Tommy will be here soon.' Jamie sat at the table and began to eat, and Fon, watching his even, white teeth bite into the bread, felt love surge through her.

'Aye, well, I've got each of them a small gift,' Fon said happily. 'They're good boys, both of them.'

268

'I have something for them too.' Jamie was smiling. 'I've deliberately kept it back until today.'

'What is it?' Fon asked. 'You've paid them up to date, haven't you?'

'Oh, aye, but I thought a little bonus might not go amiss.' He helped himself to more bacon. 'As you say, they are good lads, and I intend to keep them.'

He leant big elbows on the table. 'Now that the land is sold, we have enough money to buy in seed for the spring sowing. We'll put down more swedes this year, and a good couple of fields of potatoes.'

'Is all the ploughing done, then?' Fon asked, drinking her tea, grateful for its warmth. She was glad that Tom had the task of milking the cows this morning and Eddie would see to the laying hens.

'Most of it,' Jamie said. 'And it's a good feeling to have money in hand again.' He smiled suddenly. 'I can't forget the look on Bob Smale's face when he found out the road wasn't going through here at all.'

'Serve him right,' Fon said feelingly. 'He's an awful man; he deserved all he got.' She looked anxiously at Jamie. 'But it won't end there, mind. Smale isn't the sort to forgive and forget; he'll be an even worse enemy from now on.'

'I can handle him,' Jamie said easily, 'but you must be extra vigilant. You must keep the farm door closed and the gun at the ready, just in case.'

'I know,' Fon said softly. 'I'll be all right, Jamie, don't you worry.'

The door opened on a rush of cold air. 'Merry Christmas, boss!' Eddie entered the room, blowing on his reddened hands. 'That's the milking all done, thank the Lord.'

'Sit down and eat,' Fon said. 'I'll throw more bacon into the pan. My husband seems to have a good appetite this morning.'

'And why not?' Jamie said, smiling, his eyes warm as

they rested on Fon. 'I work hard enough, don't I? I think I deserve a good hearty breakfast.'

'All right' – Fon held up her hand in mock surrender – 'I was only saying, mind.'

It was half-way through the morning when Eddie handed Fon a parcel, wrapped in plain brown paper but with Eddie's scrawled handwriting wishing her compliments of the season.

'What's this?' Fon asked. 'You affording presents, Eddie – how did you do it?'

He winked. 'Open it and you'll see.' He sank into the chair nearest the fire and pulled off his cap; his hair seemed frosted with silver from the cold.

Fon opened the paper quickly and held up a pocket of linen that exuded the sweet scent of dried lavender. She held it to her face and breathed in deeply.

'That's lovely,' she said. 'The smell of summer on a cold winter's day! You are clever, Eddie.' She turned the pocket over. 'But how did you manage the sewing? These stitches are beautiful.'

'I was going to be a doctor, remember,' Eddie said. 'I've done a bit of stitching, believe me.'

Fon rose and took a gift from under the tree. 'Mine isn't nearly as imaginative,' she said, 'but it's given with good heart and in gratitude for all you've done for us.'

Eddie's face lit up. He tore the parcel open with almost childlike delight, and a brightly coloured scarf fell into his lap.

Laughing, he wrapped it around his neck. 'It's splendid!' he said. 'I don't think I've ever had anything made especially for me before. It was good of you, Fon.'

'It's nothing,' she said shyly. 'I've made Tommy the same thing – couldn't manage anything more elaborate.'

'No need for anything elaborate!' Eddie said quickly. 'This has been one of the best Christmases I've known for a long time; it's been lovely except . . .'

'Except that you haven't been able to see Arian.' Fon finished his sentence for him.

'No,' he sighed. 'That father of hers is keeping her well hidden. Indeed, I'm more than a little worried. I'm going up there, this evening; I *must* assure myself that she's all right.'

'I'm sure she is.' Fon spoke comfortingly, but she wasn't sure at all; with a man like Bob Smale as a father, anything might happen.

'I'd better get some work done, then.' Eddie rose to his feet. 'I'll mend that fence up on the top field; might as well get it all done before spring.'

Fon smiled. 'You're turning into a real farmer, Eddie. I'm proud of you.' She moved to the door behind him. 'I'll see you later, and we'll have a big dinner, with plum pudding to follow; we'll be together like a real family.'

On an impulse, Eddie bent and kissed her cheek. 'You and Jamie are a very happy couple,' he said. 'Anyone with half an eye could see that. And if I could have anything in the world I wanted, I would choose marriage like yours to the woman I love.'

Then, as though embarrassed by the expression of his innermost thoughts, Eddie hurried away across the windswept yard, pulling his scarf around his neck.

Watching him, Fon smiled. He was right; she and Jamie were close and very happy. And yet, now and again, the ghost of Katherine came to haunt them, especially now, near the Christmas time, for it was then that Katherine had died.

Quietly, Fon closed the door and went inside. It was time she started the evening meal; there was plenty to do without wasting her time delving into the past. Anyway, she told herself, she must count her blessings, be happy with all that she had.

'Thank you, whoever is up there,' she whispered and moved purposefully towards the pantry.

* * *

271

The wait for the doctor seemed endless. Anxiously, Will kept vigil in the window, his heart leaping with every cry from the room above.

At last, the doctor's carriage pulled up outside the door, and even before he had alighted into the street Will was dragging at the latch, anxious to let him inside.

'She's in a great deal of pain, doctor.' He took the man's coat, shaking it free of snow before hanging it on the latch behind the door.

'Women in childbirth usually are in pain,' the doctor said dryly, hoisting his bag into a more comfortable position in preparation for climbing the stairs.

Will noticed, irrelevantly, how shabby was the worn lino on the treads, how it cracked and groaned beneath the combined weights of the doctor and himself.

'The first room on top of the landing,' Will directed, wincing as Gwyneth's cry, nearer now and filled with anguish, rang out, seeming to surround him, to fill him with despair.

'Go back to the kitchen,' the doctor advised. 'You'll only be a hindrance; boil up some water, make tea, anything to keep yourself occupied and out of my way.'

The door was opened briefly and Will saw Gwyneth, her knuckles white as she clutched the bed posts above her head. Her face was screwed up, almost unrecognizable in her pain, and then, mercifully, the strong wood of the panelled door was closed, shutting him away from the harrowing scene of the childbed.

He returned to the kitchen and pushed the kettle on to the flames. The tea in the pot had grown cold and stewed, and he made fresh, not caring that it too would doubtless be wasted.

The screams continued, for what seemed to Will to be endless hours. Finally, his wife's voice seemed spent, and the only sounds emanating from the bedroom were soft, hoarse moans.

'Christ almighty!' He hammered his fist against

the scrubbed boards of the table. 'Is it never going to end?'

Into the suddenness of his silence came another silence. Will realized that the sounds from the bedroom had ceased. It was, for a moment, as if time stood still. Then, with a dipping of his heart, he heard the soft, pitiful sounds of a woman weeping.

Will pushed himself upright, brushed back his hair and made for the stairs. Something was wrong, terribly wrong. Tentatively, he opened the door to the bedroom. The first person he saw was Nina, and she was holding a shawled bundle in her arms.

Behind her, the doctor and midwife worked over his wife, and Will realized that the weeping was hers; the sound, low and despairing, tore at him.

Nina looked up. Her eyes were dry but full of anguish. 'All for nothing,' she whispered brokenly. 'All that pain for nothing.'

Will moved forward and stared at the child in her arms – a perfect child, with waxen features and closed eyes. The baby was still, too still, and Will felt the breath leave his body as the truth dawned on him.

'Your son was stillborn.' Nina spoke with difficulty, her mouth trembling as she fought to bring out the words. 'It was a difficult birth, and it was all too much for the little mite.'

She held the baby towards Will, and he took the child, staring down into the small face, not believing that the baby could have died so easily.

'Think of a name for him,' Nina urged. 'Give him a little bit of dignity.'

Will's mind was blank. He could not think rationally; he stared down at the child, so light and insubstantial in his arms, and felt despair wash over him.

From the bed came Gwyneth's voice, shocking in its weakness. 'I want him called Kevin, after my father, please, Will.'

273

'Yes, we'll call him Kevin.' Gently Will returned the child to Nina, as if even now the baby was a precious thing that could be hurt.

'Gwyneth!' He looked to where the doctor was bent over his wife. The man turned, and his eyes, meeting Will's, were full of sympathy. He shook his head. Will, uncomprehending, went to his wife's side.

'There's sorry I am to let you down, Will.' Gwyneth's hand, frail and white, was resting in his own.

Will controlled his tears, smiling down at her with difficulty. 'You didn't let me down, Gwyneth,' he said, forcing himself to speak. 'You worked hard, you did your best; it was fate, that's what it was.'

'But why *my* baby?' Gwyneth said, her voice thread-like. 'I wanted him so much.'

'You are young' – Will rushed out the words, wanting to comfort – 'you can have plenty more babies.'

He looked to Nina for support, but she did not meet his eyes. As if drawn, he turned towards the doctor, and the man gestured for him to come outside.

'I won't be a minute, love,' Will said, tucking the bedclothes around Gwyneth, as though the warmth could ease her pain. 'I think the doctor deserves a cup of tea, or maybe something stronger.'

Outside on the landing, the doctor took a deep breath. 'Your wife is sick,' he said, 'very sick.'

Will's mouth was dry. 'What do you mean?' he asked, fear clutching him with cold hands.

'I mean she has lost too much blood, and the birth, it has sapped her strength beyond endurance. It's doubtful if she will see morning. I'm sorry.'

Will found himself, idiotically, thanking the doctor. 'You did all you could,' he said. 'I'm grateful.'

'Go to her, spend some time with her; it's all you can do now,' the doctor said softly.

Will sat through the dark hours beside Gwyneth's bed. She slept fitfully, her hands seeming to pluck at the bedclothes, her eyelids twitching spasmodically, as though she was being plagued by bad dreams.

Near dawn, she woke and looked at Will with a clear gaze. 'Hold my hand,' she said, her voice little more than a breath. 'I don't want to leave you, Will; I love you.'

He took both her hands in his as though he could warm life into her by the sheer strength of his will.

They sat thus for what seemed a long time and then Gwyneth sighed softly, just once, and Will knew that she had relinquished her slender hold on life. He bowed his head over her hands and wept.

CHAPTER TWENTY-TWO

Fon stared up at the light slanting across the ceiling and felt the chill of the morning air on her face. Outside, the ground was hard, lying beneath the cold rime of frost. But soon spring would come; the drilling of early potatoes would begin, and then the lambing season would be upon them, and for a time life would be hectic.

Cautiously, Fon turned to look at Jamie. He was still asleep, his strong arms above his head, his breathing quiet, regular and even. How she loved him!

Turning, she snuggled against him, and he stirred, his arms folding around her. Even in his sleep, he was roused by her nearness. Fon lay for a long moment, savouring the closeness of him, the warmth of the bed and the sweet sensation of being alone in the world with the man she loved. Then, smiling, she crept out of bed and, shivering, picked up her clothes.

She would light the fire and cook the breakfast before Jamie was up and about, make life as easy as she could for him. She dressed on the landing and, twisting her hair into a knot at the back of her neck, she made her way downstairs. It was cold in the kitchen, the flags of the floor striking a chill into her bare feet.

Quickly, she knelt before the fire; the ashes had been riddled the night before, and so she placed sticks and paper behind the black leaded bars, arranging them so that they formed a crisscross pattern, a platform on which she could arrange the coals and cinders.

The cheerful flame shot up through the paper, and, though having no real warmth, the sight cheered her.

Carefully, as the fire took hold, Fon placed coals in strategic positions over the fragile glow.

Afterwards, Fon was to remember every detail of her morning with exact precision, just as though it was marked down in her mind as the momentous and tragic occasion that it was to prove. But for now the kitchen was a cheerful place, and it was soon resounding with animated talk as Eddie and Tommy joined Jamie at the table, faces aglow with the cold.

Fon ladled out bacon, egg and fried potatoes, knowing the men needed good, warming food inside them to prepare them for the work ahead.

It was when she was alone, with Patrick still asleep in his bed, her hands plunged into the bowl of hot water as she washed the dishes, that the knock on the door came. She froze for a second, and only when Patrick made his way sleepily into the room, rubbing his eyes, did she move towards the kitchen door, stopping to pick up the gun from its usual place in the porch.

'Fon, it's me, Mammy.' Nina's voice sounded strained, and at once it was obvious that something was very wrong. Fon replaced the gun and opened the door quickly. She saw at once that Nina's eyes were red with weeping. At her shoulder stood Will Davies, white-faced and haggard.

'It's your sister,' Nina said. 'Oh, Fon, my little love, something terrible has happened.'

'Come inside, Mam,' Fon urged. 'Sit down, and I'll put the kettle on the fire. We'll all have a hot cup of tea – you look frozen.'

She knew she was babbling, and she dimly recognized that her chatter was a futile attempt to put off the evil moment when the bad news could be suppressed no longer.

Nina held out her arms. 'Fon, I got to tell you straightaway, Gwyneth's gone, her and her baby son died in the night. I came straightaway, I just had to get away

277

from the cotttage. Say I can stay up by here for a bit, for I can't face going home, not yet!'

'Oh, God,' Fon said hoarsely, holding her mother close. 'I can't believe it – our Gwyneth dead, her baby too – it can't be true.'

Gwyneth was the one who was always bursting with health; she had a fine big-boned frame and full, rosy cheeks. She was the girl who could handle a sack of oysters as well as any man.

'Fon,' Will said, '*is* it all right for Nina to stay with you, just for a while?'

'She can stay as long as she likes,' Fon said and her mind raced, rearranging the bedrooms, putting out the best bed-cover, filling her thoughts with trivia, avoiding for as long as possible the full import of what her mother had told her.

Suddenly, she sank into a chair; her hands were trembling, and after a moment tears, hot and bitter and totally useless, sprang to her eyes.

'Will, I'm so sorry.' She held her hand out blindly and Will took it, his fingers strong around her wrist. Her heart went out to him; he had lost his wife and his son, he must be bereft, and yet here he was comforting both herself and Nina, acting more like a son than a newly acquired in-law.

'I'll make the tea.' Nina seemed glad of something positive to do, and Fon watched as her mother performed the familiar tasks, swishing hot water round the china pot, warming it before adding the precious quota of tea leaves.

Nina allowed the kettle to sing and dance on the flames, the fine gust of steam penetrating the cold air, before at last adding the boiling water to the pot.

She searched, with a helpless gesture, for cups. Fon pointed. 'In the cupboard, on your right, Mam.'

Patrick came and stood beside Fon, resting his arms in her lap, his face anxious. Fon attempted to swallow her tears, and they seemed to lie in a hard knot within her chest.

'What went wrong?' she said, when at last Nina and Will were seated with her at the table. It had to be talked about, every detail must be brought out and examined, before belief could become a reality.

'She was brought to her childbed,' Nina said. 'Her pains were bad, worse than I've ever seen.' Her voice broke for a moment. Then, struggling for composure, Nina continued. 'She was brave, mind, very brave, and Will' – she turned to him, her hand on his arm – 'he spent most of his precious savings on the doctor's bill.'

She shrugged. 'Not that it did no good, mind. The babbie went first, and then, as though she'd given up all hope, Gwyneth slipped away.'

Nina swallowed hard. 'Will was at her side, as a good husband should be. There is nothing but praise for our Gwyneth's man.' She looked at Will. 'Whatever your life holds now, my boy, you can say you did right by our Gwyneth, and I'll always be grateful to you for that.'

Will bit his lips and shook his head, and Fon saw how shocked he had been by the events of the night. He had been there with Gwyneth, witnessed her pain, and he must be feeling as though nothing in his life would ever be right again.

Now, Fon thought, she was without her sister; there was no more Gwyneth, no more the cheerful, flirty girl who breezed about the house, acting the expert on men, but who in reality loved only one, her husband.

'What will *you* do, Will?' Fon asked softly. 'Where will you stay?'

He seemed to rouse himself from depths of thought that darkened his eyes. 'Oh, I'll be all right,' he said quickly. 'There's a small room at the back of my workshop; I'll live there for now, it will be convenient at least.' He smiled without humour. 'I think the best thing to do is immerse myself in my work, such as it is.'

'Remember,' Nina said suddenly, 'I shan't be staying up by here with Fon for ever and my home is your home, whenever you need it.'

Will didn't reply; he simply rested his hand on Nina's shoulder and smiled with infinite sadness.

Fon rose to her feet. Activity was the thing to keep their minds off the tragedy that had fallen upon them so unexpectedly.

'Come on, Mam,' she said. 'We got work to do, mind; there's beds to be made and rooms to rearrange, and then I must see to the chicks; they want their food whatever happens.'

Will nodded at her in silent approval, and he pushed away his chair, standing tall and somehow distant, a far-away look in his eyes.

'I'll get back to Swansea, then,' he said quietly.

Nina turned to him and, putting her hands on his cheeks, kissed him soundly. 'God go with you, Will Davies,' she said quietly, and Fon bit her lip to stop the threatened tears as Will turned away, his shoulders hunched in misery.

'Look after yourself,' he said, 'and don't worry, I'll see to . . . everything.'

'I know you will, love,' Nina said, 'even though the cost of it all will take most of the money you've got left. But you'll see our Gwyneth out of this world right, and I thank you for it.'

When Will had gone, there was silence in the kitchen for a long moment; then Fon silently held her arms out, and her mother, all her bravado gone, went to her daughter gratefully.

'Why don't we just run away?' Eddie said, his arm around Arian, holding her slim form close to him in the darkness of the barn.

'I don't see why I should have to hide what I feel for you from my father,' she said. 'And, anyway, I promised

280

I would always be here when he needed me; and it seems he needs me more than ever since that deal with Jamie O'Conner went wrong, blast the man!'

'That's not fair.' Eddie felt bound to defend his boss; it had been Bob Smale's intention to take the land away from Jamie under false pretences and then sell it at a vast profit. All that had happened was that Smale got his just deserts.

'I know it really,' Arian conceded. 'But when Daddy's hurt, I feel hurt.'

'I'm not surprised,' Eddie said dryly. 'The way he talks to you when he's in drink makes me see red.'

'He doesn't mean it,' Arian said, softly. 'Deep down he loves me; it's just that he can't seem to face reality.'

'Well, the land is worthless now it's not required for road building,' Eddie said, 'and your father is stuck with it; there's nothing he can do.' He paused. 'He could farm it, of course, instead of letting all his land go wild.'

'He hasn't the money,' Arian said reasonably. 'It would take many men and horses to get all that land into shape in time for the spring planting. In any case, he hasn't the interest; he's never been a working farmer, you know that.'

'Well,' Eddie said slowly, 'you have to be allowed to live your own life at some point; you can't be his little slave for ever.'

'I *can* be your little slave, though, can't I?' Arian's mood had changed suddenly; she was coquettish. Her lips parted invitingly as she tipped back her head. 'Kiss me, Eddie.'

He felt the familiar rising tide of emotion as he held her close, and when he tasted the sweetness of her lips, he knew he'd kill to have her.

'Stop teasing me,' he whispered, his mouth moving to her throat, 'or one day my feelings will get the better of me and I'll tear off your clothes and rape you!'

'I can't wait.' Arian's hands moved to his belt and it

was several moments before Eddie realized her intention.

He tipped her face up, his hand beneath her chin. 'Arian, are you sure?' he asked.

She smiled up at him. 'Hurry up, before I change my mind, you big oaf.' She lay back in the hay, her skirts falling back to reveal shapely legs.

'You wanton little hussy!' Eddie said thickly. 'I'll ravish you until you cry for mercy.'

'We'll see who cries for mercy,' Arian said, and, reaching up, she bit at his neck, her mouth hot, her hands helping him with the buttons of his trews.

It was the moment he had waited for all his life, or so it seemed to Eddie; and he was determined to make it an occasion to remember for the rest of his life.

The funeral of Gwyneth Davies and her infant son brought the villagers of Oystermouth out in force. The church of All Saints was crowded to the doors, and even the weather, cold and damp, seemed to conspire with the general atmosphere to mourn the passing of a young woman and her child.

Will was grateful for the presence of Hari Grenfell at his side; her arm was through his, and her eyes beneath her dark bonnet were filled with love and sympathy.

'I'm sorry Craig is away on business, love,' she said softly. 'He wanted to be with you now, I know he did.'

Will squeezed her arm. 'You are here,' he whispered, 'as you always are when I need you.'

Will stared straight ahead as the vicar spoke honestly and sincerely about Gwyneth and her family; but all the time he was talking it seemed to Will as though he was an onlooker, not a participant in the sad drama that was unfolding around him.

He caught his breath as the two coffins were carried outside in preparation for the journey to Oystermouth Cemetery. The impossibly tiny cask of his baby son followed that of Gwyneth, who had been wife and

mother for so short a time. As Nina had wished, Will
had seen his family depart with as much dignity as he
could afford.

'It will be over soon, love,' Hari whispered, 'and then
you can mourn in private; chin up.'

Will smiled at her, grateful for her no-nonsense sympathy. As always, Hari knew instinctively that he wished
to be alone, to lick his wounds in solitude, and perhaps
then, after a time, he could begin to come to terms with
his loss.

The funeral seemed to drag on and on; the damp, cold
cemetery was swept by winds from the sea and the earth
seemed heavy and forbidding as his wife and child were
laid to rest.

Nina had insisted, with tears in her eyes, that there
must be a funeral luncheon; it was tradition, she said.
There would be hams and oysters and crusty bread and
frothing ale to serve to the mourners; it was just one
more ordeal to endure, and Will squared his shoulders.

It was when he was leaving the cemetery that he saw
Eline. She had remained in the background, but now
she stepped forward and put winter roses on the fresh-
dug earth. Will felt tears constrict his throat as, for an
instant, their eyes met over the crowd. He was grateful
to Eline for coming to pay her respects and more grateful to her for keeping her distance from him. Now,
they had no common meeting ground, their lives had
moved them both in different directions; he was a
widower, and she the wife of one of the richest men in
the country.

He remained in the cottage at Oystermouth for an
hour, enduring the sympathy and the platitudes, well
meant but meaningless; but at last he felt able to accept
Hari's offer of a lift into Swansea.

There was silence in the carriage except for the clop
of the horse's hooves against the wet roads. Hari rested
her hand lightly over Will's, and he smiled at her.

283

'I'm all right,' he said softly.

Hari lifted her hand to brush a strand of rain-dewed hair away from his forehead. 'Well, you don't look all right. Why don't you come home with me, if only for a few days?' She paused for a moment, watching as Will shook his head.

'I know you need time to be alone, and you *will* have it, I promise you; but at least let me be sure you are well fed and warm.'

'I'm not a child any longer, Hari,' he said softly. 'I know that from your seven or eight years' seniority I must seem it, but I'm a man well able to stand on my own two feet now.'

'You're right, Will,' Hari agreed, 'but I can't help wanting to look after you; it comes naturally to me.'

He hugged her for a moment and as the carriage came to a halt outside his workshop she held on to his arms.

'It looks so dismal and depressing!' She gestured towards the building, and Will smiled down at her.

'No more dismal and depressing than your place in World's End was, Hari, my love.'

She sighed heavily. 'I suppose you are right.' She kissed his cheek. 'You'll make a great success of your business, I just know you will; it's in you, that need to get on in life.' She kissed his cheek again. 'You have the dream and the drive, and I love you for it.'

Inside the building, it did indeed appear dreary; rain ran along the windows and the fire was grey and dead in the grate. Will took off his coat and set to work; he'd build up the fire and then cook himself a light meal, for he had eaten nothing of the feast Nina had prepared.

Then perhaps it would be a good time to begin work on the big boots for the coalman, who wanted them tapped urgently, seeing as he only had the one pair.

He sighed, and it sounded loud in the silence. He was alone, as he'd wanted to be, but now his stomach

284

turned over as he realized he was destined to be alone all his life.

The second time Eddie made love to Arian, he was more controlled. To his chagrin, he had been too quick the first time, overawed by Arian's pale, naked beauty and by the sweetness of possessing her.

'That's it, my darling.' Arian moved with him, rocking her hips towards him, clinging to his neck, her head flung back, her eyes closed. 'I want you, Eddie, I want you so much.'

He felt the fire move in his gut and his loins; he held her close, her breasts full and yet yielding under his hands. He breathed raggedly and then the world exploded around him, within him, and he cried out her name.

They lay side by side in silence for a long while, and then, anxiously, Eddie raised himself on his elbow and looked down at her fine-boned face. The alabaster skin beneath the cascade of silver hair seemed to glow with inner light, and her sweet mouth curved into a smile.

'Come away with me, Arian,' he said softly. 'I'll be good to you, I'll care for you always.'

As if given a signal she did not wish to receive, Arian rose to her feet and began to dress, her hands steady, her hair flowing down her back.

'Don't go, please,' Eddie said. 'I want you again and again – I can't get enough of you.'

She did up her bodice, covering her lovely breasts, and her teeth were white as she laughed at him.

'You must contain yourself in patience, my lad,' she admonished him. 'You are not the only man in my life, you know.'

He was on his feet in an instant, holding her close, his hand tangled in her hair as he forced her head back.

'If any other man came near you, I'd kill him,' he said. His voice was quiet but he meant every word he said.

285

She touched his cheek. 'You will be the only one, I promise,' she said, and then added teasingly, 'I shall only have one at a time.'

'I'll give you one at a time! I'll thrash you within an inch of your life.' Eddie pulled her down into the hay once more. 'And I'll show you who is master.'

He tumbled her on to her back and pushed up her skirts. 'When I say I want you now, I mean I want you now.'

Playfully, she fought him off, her hands tugging at his hair, her lithe body twisting and turning as he straddled her.

'Leave me be, you wretch,' she said and slipped away from him, panting a little, her eyes bright with laughter.

Eddie lunged for her, and she dodged him easily. He fell to the floor, and immediately she was upon him, holding a small gleaming knife to his throat.

'Now who is in control?' she asked triumphantly. Eddie saw the whiteness of her thigh with a surge of his blood; she was so beautiful, so desirable – would he ever be satiated with her?

He groaned. 'Don't torture me, Arian,' he said, his body seeming to vibrate with longing for her.

She rolled away from him and was on her feet, laughing, with her head thrown back and her hair swinging over her shoulders.

He closed his eyes, pretending to rest, and then, so suddenly that she was taken off guard, he caught Arian's ankles and she fell back in the straw, her hair spread around her like a cloak, the knife falling from her hand.

He could wait no longer; he took her as she was, fully dressed, and she remained soft and still beneath him, content to allow him his pleasure.

'I love you so much, Arian,' he whispered. 'I want you and need you, always.'

She wound her arms around him then and held him close to her while the sweet fires raged through him, so

286

that he shuddered in her arms and for a moment it seemed he almost lost touch with conscious thought.

Neither of them saw the big figure of her uncle, Mike the Spud, in the doorway, his hair wet with rain, his eyes alight with mischief, his big hands clenched so tightly that his knuckles gleamed white.

In a few seconds, he had disappeared, and the barn was empty except for the two lovers, who were unaware of the intruder, wrapped as they were in each other's arms.

CHAPTER TWENTY-THREE

The white snows of winter were thawing now, the pale sun coaxing forth the first few crocuses to give brightness to the dull days. The sky was warming earlier from cold dawn to sunrise, and, though the weather was still chill, the promise of spring was everywhere.

Eline sat in the huge drawing-room of the new house Calvin had bought her after their wedding and stared around at the unfamiliar drapes and hangings with a feeling of unreality. There had been nothing wrong with the first house he'd given her, but that lay empty now, its rooms silent, the small staff of servants the only inhabitants. It was not grand enough, so Calvin claimed, for the wife of a lord.

Stormhill Manor, on the other hand, was perhaps the grandest, most elegant house in Swansea; its walled gardens encompassed an apple orchard and a sweetly running stream, as well as being home to a herd of timid deer.

The large, ornate doors of the drawing-room stood open, leading on to the hallway with the enormous sweeping staircase rising from the centre of the marbled floor. How had she come, Eline thought, from a humble fisherman's cottage to all this grandeur? And was it what she really wanted? She seriously doubted it.

The house seemed full of servants: footmen, cooks and a plethora of maids moved about silently, and the unwritten pecking order below stairs was a constant source of confusion to Eline.

Calvin, of course, handled the staff with complete aplomb; he was used to having his every wish met, his every whim catered to. His easy but authoritative manner made him a popular, respected master, and Eline admired him, his sophisticated attitude to life, as she enjoyed his physical nearness, his thoughtful ardour. But love was absent from their marriage, and that made her sad.

She knew that all he wanted now was for her to give him a son, an heir to all he owned; and yet motherhood, it seemed, was not for her. She had been Joe's wife for long enough and had not conceived, even though her first husband's fruitfulness was without question. And lately, to her shame, she had begun to make excuses when Calvin came to her bed. She often found herself imagining being in Will's arms, but that was an impossible dream.

As for children, she mused, perhaps there was something deep within some women that rebelled against motherhood unless it was entered into with the right man. Or perhaps, more simply, she was barren. In any event, she felt she was failing Calvin in the very thing he most desired.

She rose to her feet and sighed heavily. She must get out of her silken cage, walk around the busy streets of the town. Perhaps with the sights and sounds of Swansea all around her, she would be stimulated into taking an interest in the business of designing and making shoes once more.

It was not that Calvin deliberately prevented her from working, but his unspoken disapproval was difficult to ignore.

As Eline stepped outside, the pale sun dappled through the trees lining the drive, and she waved away the servant anxiously enquiring if she needed the coach brought round.

'I'll walk,' she said, knowing that Calvin would have dismissed the man with charm, while not bothering to explain his reasons to the servants. 'The exercise and

fresh air will do me good,' she added, recognizing the
note of rebellion in her voice with a sense of dismay.
What was she turning into? A spoilt, inconsiderate
woman who sulked at the luxuries provided by her
husband instead of enjoying them.

The walk into Swansea was invigorating. Eline felt the
pale sun on her cheeks and breathed in the scents of
early spring with a feeling of growing excitement. She
felt suddenly alive, freed from the velvet confines of the
huge house – a woman again, not a cosseted doll to be
brought out when her husband needed her.

Immediately she felt guilty. Calvin was so kind and
thoughtful; he did not patronize her or treat her as
anything less than an equal, but his ardour and his
protectiveness were sometimes stifling.

The town of Swansea was busy with afternoon traffic;
vans carrying all kinds of goods were pulled along by
weary horses, while the high-stepping, glossy-coated
animals drawing rich carriages trotted along the cobbles,
heads raised proudly, their burdens light.

The gulf between rich and poor was great indeed,
Eline thought, and was highlighted in the appearance of
the animals they drove.

She realized then the main reason for her discontent.
Her own small enterprises, though successful, every one
of them, seemed insignificant and almost unnecessary
beside Calvin's great wealth. Calvin, in loving her, giving
her everything, had taken away her ambition; she had
no goal, no star to aim for.

Almost unconsciously, she squared her shoulders,
deciding that she would not live the rest of her life as a
plaything, an ornament gracing Calvin's home. If he
loved her, he must accept that she had to lead her own
life, and that meant working at what she loved best.

She looked around her; perhaps she should think
of renting new premises somewhere in Swansea? The
ones Calvin had provided for her were all wrong, too

290

luxurious, too clinical. In any case, she would need to make her own plans, because if she confided her ideas to her husband, he would take over again. With the best of motives, he would erode her plans, making them his own. That was the last thing she wanted.

Eline sighed. She had been remiss in not putting her plans into action long since. Her wish to make shoes for children with foot defects seemed to have been shelved along with the plans to begin a savings club.

Eline thought of the original premises she'd planned to use; they were let now to Will Davies, and at the thought of him Eline's heart moved within her. She felt suddenly faint and ill.

She pushed the thoughts away; her life and Will's had taken different roads, they might as well be living on separate planets. She would do no good at all to think about him.

She moved around the streets with purpose now, her mind sizing up and discarding various sites. She must place her shop somewhere accessible to the poor people of the town; the premises must be humble enough not to frighten off prospective customers. It might well be that she herself would have to take a back seat, for most people knew Eline, now Lady Temple, by sight.

Perhaps, she thought, she should employ a young woman to work in the shop for her – several young women if necessary. She smiled. She was rushing ahead; as yet she had no premises, nothing to offer anyone but the ideas in her mind. She looked at the buildings around her, and suddenly she realized why they appeared familiar; they were the ones she had once planned to use, and there was the worn, crumbling façade of the building where Will worked.

'Eline!' The voice was low, and she turned sharply and came face to face with Will Davies. Her heart contracted. He looked awful; he was pale and there were lines running from his nose to his mouth. His hair was a touch long to be fashionable, and over his thin frame hung the leather apron of the cobbler.

Pity swept through Eline; she reached out and touched his hand. 'Will, I'm sorry, your wife and baby – I don't know what to say.'

And suddenly she ached to take him in her arms, to wipe away the air of sadness that hung almost tangibly around him. 'You been working today?' She gestured to the doorway behind him, knowing that the question was banal, the words she longed to say dying on her lips.

He nodded. 'I work and live here now. It's my shop, my home; it's all I have.' He smiled down at her, and she saw the old Will still lived; life had taken a hand against him, but he still had his spirit.

'May I see it? I'm suddenly hungry for the touch and the smell of leather,' she said; but she was hungry for much more.

'Come inside.' He led the way indoors.

At the bench Eline stopped and picked up an awl, staring at it as though it was a precious gem. 'How I miss it all,' she said. 'But I intend to do something positive about it.

She felt suddenly that she wanted to confide her plans in Will; he if anyone would understand. 'I'm tired of doing nothing,' she said. 'I must work at my designs, otherwise there's no reason for living, no reason at all.'

Will was leading the way into the back room. 'I'm just closing up the shop,' he said. 'I'm going to make some tea; like some?'

'Yes, please.' Eline felt as though she was a little girl out on a treat. She sat near the bright fire and watched as Will removed his apron and hung it behind the door.

'You are too thin,' she said, and then she felt the colour rise in her cheeks; what he looked like was no concern of hers.

He didn't appear to notice her confusion. He placed

the cup before her and stood at the end of the table, looking down at her. 'So you are weary of being lady of the manor, are you?'

There was a note of derision in his voice, and Eline looked up at him defensively. 'Not exactly,' she said, 'but I do want to continue with my own work.'

'Why?' Will said challengingly. 'You'll only be taking bread out of the mouths of cobblers who really need it.'

Eline rose and pushed away her cup. 'I see I was wrong,' she said, her voice trembling. 'I thought you of all people would understand my need to . . .'

Will moved closer to her. 'Your need to what? To play the grand lady stooping to help the poor? How laudable!'

'I didn't mean that at all!' Eline said hotly, suddenly realizing that Will was deliberately baiting her.

'But that's what all the rich do, isn't it?' he said. 'Play at helping those less fortunate, it's expected.'

'I'm not like that,' Eline said.

Will smiled, but without humour. 'You don't think so? You married for money a man you didn't even love – do you deny it?'

'And *you* married because you were unwise enough to get the girl pregnant!'

He caught hold of her wrists as she lifted her hand to push him away, and then he was shaking her, his face bitter and angry.

'Get away from me!' Eline said. 'Take your hands off me.' But her voice held little conviction. Suddenly, without realizing it, she was in his arms, held against him, and she could feel his heart-beat, loud and fierce, as though it was her own heart.

'Oh, my God, Will, I love you so much,' she said in anguish.

He kissed her mouth and her eyes and her throat. They clung together then, in silent misery, just holding each other, without passion, like bereft children.

Finally, Will released her. 'Go on home to your

293

husband,' he said softly. He sank into a chair and covered his eyes with his hand.

'My God, talk about history repeating itself!' He spoke harshly. 'I've said those words to you so many times before, and all that's changed is that you now have a different husband to go home to, a rich husband.'

He gestured around the room. 'I'll never be rich – you are well out of it.'

'Did I ever ask for riches, Will?' she said quietly. 'I only wanted you. Together we would have made a good life for ourselves, only you were too proud. You had nothing to offer, so you said, but we had love, Will, we had the most precious thing in all the world.' She paused. 'If only you'd made love to me, held me in your arms, made me forget everything but that we cared about each other; it would have been a memory to cherish.'

'It's too late to talk about it now, isn't it? Go home, Eline – forget me.'

She moved to the door. 'I'll never forget you, Will,' she said. 'I think I'll love you till the day I die.'

Out in the street, she stared around her with a feeling of confusion; her optimism had faded and given way to a sense of dull determination. She could not have Will, but she could have a goal in life; whatever anyone thought, she would open her shoe shop, she would help people, especially the children.

She needed to walk, to clear her mind; she could not go home to Calvin, not yet, not with her flesh still tingling from Will's touch, even though he had touched her in anger. She made her way through the winding streets of the town and towards the sweet open hills where she had once lived. She would walk around the perimeter of Honey's Farm, think about her childhood and try, somehow, to find peace.

'I will not go to Auntie Maisie's house!' Arian stood facing her father, ignoring the packed bag at her feet

294

and trying not to be frightened by the look on his face.

'I want you out of my sight,' he said, 'before I lose control and kill you with my bare hands.

'Anyway,' he added dully, 'you need looking after – a woman's touch – and Maisie will give you that.'

'I *am* a woman, Father,' Arian protested. 'I have feelings just as you have, and I can look after myself.'

'You might have to; if you give Maisie any trouble, you'll be out on your backside!' he said through his teeth, and Arian knew that his control was beginning to break. 'I want you out of the way, and I will see to it that the rutting pig of a man you were with gets his just reward.'

Arian was suddenly chilled; while she was not frightened for herself, she feared what her father might do to Eddie.

Behind her the door opened and her Uncle Mike came into the room, his big arms folded across his chest.

'I got the cart ready, Bob,' he said. 'I'll have the girl over to our Maisie's before you can snap your fingers.'

'I'm not going,' Arian said, her chin lifted, 'especially with a man like you who spies on people and then tittle-tattles to others about what he's seen.'

Mike grunted, lifted her in his big arms and threw her, like a sack of potatoes, over his shoulder. He picked up her bag and left the house, kicking the door shut behind him.

'Now we can do this hard, or we can do it easy,' he said, dumping her into the cart. 'You can be tidy and behave yourself, or I can tie you up like a crazy animal; which is it to be?'

'I'll be quiet.' Arian had no intention of being quiet, but neither had she any intention of being hog-tied to the cart.

She folded her skirts beneath her legs and stared around her at the open land she loved. She was supposed to submit peaceably to living with her auntie in the suburbs of Swansea. Well, wild horses wouldn't make her do what she didn't want to.

Mike climbed up to the front of the cart and clicked his tongue at the horse, urging the creature into movement. The jolt threw Arian off balance and she fell back, her head catching the edge of the wooden rail.

'Damn and blast!' Her voice rang out. 'What do you think you're doing, Uncle Mike?'

He grunted. 'Nice language for a lady, I must say.'

He didn't turn to look at her, and as Arian righted herself, she poked her tongue out at his unresponsive back.

'You know I'll run away from Auntie Maisie's the first opportunity I get, don't you?' Arian said defiantly, and Mike shrugged is big shoulder.

'There'll be nowhere to run to, my girl,' he said, laconically.

'I'll go home,' Arian said reasonably, wondering what on earth Mike was talking about.

'Won't be no home to go to,' Mike said quietly. 'Your father has lost everything; the bank has called in the loan he took out to buy that useless piece of land. Your father's flat broke.'

'No!' Arian pushed herself up on to her knees and looked over at the uneven ground beneath the wheels of the cart. She had to get back to her father; he would be in despair. No wonder his control was so thin; whatever he did now, he had nothing to lose.

'Whatever he did . . .' She uttered the words out loud, and a great fear filled her. Lightly, she poised herself on the edge of the cart, and when Mike slowed for a slight rise in the land, she leaped downwards and outward to avoid the small hunched patches of rock.

She hit the ground and rolled over, grazing her legs, but she looked after the retreating cart with a sense of triumph, knowing that Mike, always slow-witted, would not realize she'd gone – not yet at least.

She ran back towards the farm, but as she neared the outbuildings, she saw her father mounted on the grey, a gun under his arm; and he was heading towards Honey's Farm.

'Oh, my God – Eddie!' Arian cried out loud, a sudden fear paralysing her limbs. She stood uncertainly for a moment, trying to sort out her confusion of thoughts. Then she began to run.

Eddie was working in the barn, pulling down a bale of hay from the diminishing store of winter fodder. He glanced up through the open door, just in time to see Bob Smale cross the yard and enter the cottage, where Fon was busy working in the kitchen. His gut tightened; he had caught sight of the barrel of a rifle protruding from under Smale's arm.

Slowly Eddie moved towards the door and glanced about him. He had to make sure that Smale was alone; usually he took the precaution of having company when he went out looking for trouble.

The yard was empty. Jamie, Eddie knew, was gone to the market in Swansea, and Tommy with him; in all probability they would not be back till sundown. Whatever was to be done, Eddie must be the one to do it.

He made his way cautiously across the yard; every snapping twig, every loose stone, sounded like a crack of thunder. His heart was beating swiftly. What he would do when he reached the cottage he wasn't quite sure; but one thing was clear, he could not leave Fon to the devices of the crazed Bob Smale.

The kitchen was empty except for young Patrick, who was lying flat out on the floor. There was a small bruise on the boy's temple, and Eddie felt fury burn within him; the man must be a maniac to attack a child.

Quickly, Eddie knelt beside the boy. He seemed to be all right; in any case, there was nothing Eddie could do but wait for him to recover consciousness. In the meantime, where was Bob Smale? And where was Fon?

He picked up the huge poker from the fireplace and moved slowly and cautiously towards the stairs. From the room above he could hear Fon's voice.

'I will not strip!' Her voice was like ice. 'You'd have to kill me first.'

There was the sound of tearing cloth, and Eddie bit his lip, resisting the urge to fly up the stairs. His only advantage was the element of surprise, and he would do little good by throwing it away.

At the door of the bedroom, his first fears were confirmed. Fon was standing before Bob Smale, her bodice hanging in tatters. Her face was white but defiant. Her eye was beginning to turn black, and, even as he watched, Eddie saw Bob raise his hand to Fon again.

'Are you going to do what I say?' His voice was almost unrecognizable, and Eddie felt fear tear at his gut; this man had no feelings, he would plunder and destroy with no compunction.

'No, I am not.' Fon sounded calm by comparison, though Eddie could see that she was trembling. Admiration filled him; Fon was a fine woman, a brave woman – but Bob Smale would not be denied.

His hand came down with such force that Fon staggered backwards, crashing against the china washbasin, which fell to the floor and shattered into pieces.

Bob Smale was, for a moment, distracted, and it was then that Eddie lunged forward, the poker held high. He brought it down hard, aiming for the base of the man's skull; but some sixth sense warned Bob Smale and he half-turned, the blow landing on his shoulder.

The gun was knocked from his hand and skidded across the floor.

'Get out!' Eddie shouted to Fon, and she rushed past him, her skirts flowing behind her as she ran.

Eddie raised his arm to strike again, but Bob Smale

298

hurled himself forward, his weight and strength bearing Eddie to the ground.

'I'll kill you, you bastard!' Smale ground out the words. 'Fool with my daughter, would you? Well, I'll show you who has the last word on that little matter.'

The man's illogical words told Eddie just how crazed Smale was; he, who had been on the point of raping Fon, was prepared to beat a man to death for making love to his daughter.

Eddie scrambled to his feet and launched himself down the stairs. He dimly saw Fon bending over Patrick, and then Bob Smale was upon him, bearing him to the floor, the rifle pointing at Eddie's head.

Smale squeezed Eddie's throat with one hand, but while he had breath, Eddie called to Fon in anguish. 'Run!' he gasped, as he twisted and turned, trying to suck air into his lungs. 'Take Patrick with you and get help!'

He lashed out and the rifle clattered to the floor.

Fon, as though galvanized into action, picked up the rifle and tried to steady it. Smale released his grip on Eddie and lashed out, felling Fon easily with the back of his hand.

Eddie drew rasping breaths and tried to rise to his feet, but then Bob Smale had picked up the gun and was pointing it again at Eddie's head.

'Don't!' Fon cried, and Bob Smale looked at her, his face twisted.

'Save your pity for yourself! You'll be going the same way – after I've finished pleasuring myself with you.' He laughed.

'All your husband will find when he gets back is two people who have died violently. It will all look like a lovers' tiff! He'll feel betrayed – but only for a moment, before I kill him too.'

His finger was closing round the trigger of the rifle.

Eddie held his breath, frozen in a moment of horror when he knew he was about to die.

'Put it down, Daddy.' The voice was low, cajoling, and Eddie turned in disbelief to see Arian standing in the doorway.

'I'm going to kill the bastard!' Smale ignored his daughter, and realigned his sights menacingly.

'No, Dad, don't, please don't shoot!' Arian's voice was low but composed. Bob Smale took no notice; the rifle spat fire, and Eddie felt as if someone had hammered his shoulder.

He heard a woman scream, and then Arian had thrown herself forward on to her father. There was another crack of rifle-fire, and Eddie winced, waiting for the pain.

Slowly, Bob Smale toppled forward, sinking to his knees. 'Arian . . .' he said in a thick voice. 'Arian!'

His eyes glazed over and he slumped to the floor. Bob Smale was dead.

CHAPTER TWENTY-FOUR

Eline had decided to call in at Honey's Farm, just for old times' sake. As she was so near, it would be silly simply to turn around and walk back to town. In any case, she was thirsty; she would beg a drink of water drawn from the sweetness of the well, the well that once, when she was a child, she used to believe was a magic one that would grant her every wish.

The only wish she had now was to make herself useful in some way, use her skill for the benefit of children who would think it a miracle to walk straight. She bit her lip. Perhaps, if she was honest, there was another wish, an impossible wish that involved Will Davies. She thought of him holding her in his arms so tenderly; they would have been so right together, and yet, foolishly, she had allowed herself to quarrel with him. Why couldn't she have left well alone?

Eline was almost at the door of the farmhouse when she heard the sharp retort of a gun. It echoed on the still air, sending the ravens flying from the trees in a dark ragged cloud.

Eline began to run. No-one on the land used a gun anywhere near the house – not unless something was radically wrong.

She drew nearer to the doorway of the kitchen, once so familiar to her. The sound of a woman weeping softly brought chills to her spine.

Eline stopped short, hands resting on the wooden door jamb. A child sat on the kitchen floor, his eyes wide as he stared at her.

Eline hurried into the kitchen, her heart beating

swiftly. What tragedy had been played out in the sleepy peace of Honey's Farm?

Clear of the door, she stopped short, her gaze drawn at once to the man lying on the floor, blood flowing from a wound in his chest.

Eline, on a sharp intake of breath, recognized the dead man as Bob Smale, and, as though in a nightmare, she saw Smale's daughter kneeling over him, her slim hands covering her face, her shoulders shaking.

On the floor, close to the distraught girl, lay a rifle, menacing and gleaming evilly in the light from the window. Beside the bowed figure of Arian Smale, a young man was standing, his face puffy, as though he had been hit many times, his hands hanging uselessly by his sides. He was clearly at a loss what to do. Behind him was Fon O'Conner, her face white with shock.

It was as if the appearance of Eline galvanized the small tableau into movement. The young man helped Arian Smale to rise to her feet, and gently he took her in his arms.

'I killed him, my father,' Arian said brokenly. 'How could I do such a thing to my own flesh and blood, Eddie?'

'It was an accident,' he said softly. 'You snatched at the rifle to protect me, and it went off; you couldn't help it. He would have killed me, and after that it would have been Fon's turn to die – Jamie's too, when he came home. Your father was out of his mind, Arian, he didn't know any more what he was doing.'

'I know you're right.' Arian's voice was a little stronger now. 'He had gone quite wild with the pain and grief of losing everything; as you say, he no longer knew what he was doing.'

It was Eline who took control of the situation. She spoke gently to Fon, whose bodice was hanging around her slim body in tatters. 'I'll fetch the doctor. You go outside, get some fresh air; you've had a terrible shock.'

With touching dignity, Fon held her bodice around her and spoke firmly, though her voice trembled a little. 'There's nothing a doctor can do; Bob Smale is dead.' She paused. 'I wish Jamie would come back from market; he'd know how to deal with all this.' She waved her hands, encompassing the dead man and the others in the room.

It was strange, Eline thought, that Fon didn't question the appearance of Eline so unexpectedly or the fact that she seemed to be organizing everyone. She simply crossed the room to where Patrick was sitting and clasped him tightly in her arms.

Eline took it upon herself to fetch a blanket from the cupboard on the stairs and cover the still form of the dead man with it.

Fon took a shawl from the back of the door and draped it around her shoulders to cover her breasts, and then, in a gesture of determination, she pushed the kettle on to the flames.

'Do you think we should call in the constable?' she asked of no-one in particular. Then she turned to Arian. 'There will be an awful scandal.' She shook her head, as if attempting to clear it. 'You must prepare yourself for it; all sorts of stories will go around the town.'

'Oh, God! I don't care about gossip for myself!' Arian Smale said. Her beautiful eyes, filled with the horror of what had happened, turned to Eline in supplication. 'But I don't want everyone to know that my father had turned into a rapist and was intent on murder.'

'Let me go for my husband,' Eline said softly. 'Calvin has a great deal of influence in the town; he'll know just how to handle this.'

Fon put some cups on the table. 'We'd be grateful for any advice,' she said. 'None of us know what we should do next.'

'My father will be branded a madman and a killer,' Arian said softly. 'I know what he was doing was wrong,

303

but I don't want his memory besmirched with malicious gossip.'

It was Eddie who rose to his feet, wincing a little as he moved. 'I'll go into town,' he said. 'If you'll tell me where I might find your husband?'

Eline frowned. 'But your shoulder, it must be . . .'

'It's all right – just a graze,' Eddie said quickly.

After a moment's hesitation, Eline gave him directions in soft tones. 'Tell Calvin what's happened, he'll know what to do.'

'Don't worry,' Eddie said reassuringly. 'I won't be long, and then we'll have all this nightmare taken out of our hands.'

There was silence for a moment after he'd gone, and Eline watched as Fon reached out and covered Arian's hand with hers.

'Thank you for saving my life,' she said simply. 'I realize what courage it must have cost you to tackle your own father, especially the . . . the way he was.'

She paused and took a deep breath. 'You know you have a home here with us for as long as you want it.'

Arian's face crumpled. 'You're kind and generous, but I couldn't stay here now, not where I . . .' Her voice faltered. She put her head down on her arms as they rested on the scrubbed boards of the table and she wept.

Eline was proud of the way Calvin sorted out the problem of the death on Honey's Farm; the killing was, he said, clearly a sad accident. With the help of one or two of his magistrate friends, the entire affair was hushed up. All that the townsfolk knew was that Bob Smale had died suddenly in an unfortunate shooting accident.

Eline sat in her newly acquired workshop and looked across the table to where Arian was gamely trying to cut a piece of leather into the shape of a boot sole.

Arian glanced up and shrugged ruefully. 'It's good of you to give me work,' she said, 'but I don't seem to be very good at this.' Her hands dropped dejectedly into her lap.

'You show great promise,' Eline replied. 'No-one can learn a trade in five minutes. Give yourself time. You are already good at selecting the best leather; you seem to have an aptitude for it.'

'Well, that's something,' Arian said, smiling. 'At least I'm not entirely useless.'

Eline studied Arian as she returned doggedly to her task. The girl had spirit and courage; how much courage it must have taken to pull the shattered threads of her life together after the dreadful experience she'd gone through up on the farm, only she would know.

The girl was very lovely. Her hair was looped up now in silver coils about her face, which was, perhaps, a little too thin and, in repose, quite melancholy – a fact that added to Arian's ethereal quality. But she was tough, Eline knew that already; the girl would never do anything she didn't want to. She needed to be led, not driven: something any man in her life would need to learn.

'Know me next time, will you?' Arian said, her eyebrow raised.

Eline laughed. 'Sorry, was I staring?' She put down the drawing she had been making. 'Let's break for a cup of tea, shall we?'

'I still can't believe that I did it,' Arian said as, a few minutes later, she sipped tea from the cup Eline had handed her. 'Killed my father, I mean.'

She shook her head as if to free her mind from the terrible memories that filled it. 'A daughter raising her hand to her own flesh and blood, it's unheard of.'

'No, it isn't,' Eline said. 'It's often within the family that the greatest violence takes place. In any case,' she continued, 'you had no choice. It was an accident; you snatched for the gun and it went off.' Eline paused. 'Look,' she said, 'it was quite obvious that your father meant to leave no-one alive, not even the little boy.'

305

She leant across the table. 'He wasn't himself; he was disturbed, that's the only way you can think of him with any peace of mind.'

'I know.' Arian looked down into her cup. 'But unfortunately I know my father; I think he was quite clear about what he was going to do.'

Eline watched the girl, sensing her anguish, knowing she must speak out, clear her mind of her nightmare thoughts, however much the words hurt her.

'I know you are right. I believe Dad would have raped Fon and then killed everyone, including Fon's husband. Then, only then, when he felt he'd had his revenge, he would have turned the gun on himself.'

Eline saw that Arian's mind was crystal-clear. The girl faced life head on; she would not be content fooling herself with comforting half-truths.

'Well, in that case, you did the only thing possible to avoid an even greater tragedy; you must see that.'

'Oh, I do,' Arian said. 'My head accepts it, but my heart, my soul, whatever it is that lies deep within me, still says I killed my father, and somehow, some time, I will be punished for it.'

Eline sat back in her chair. She knew it was useless to protest further; Arian's views were unmovable. She would always regret what she had been forced to do, but she would survive, because she was strong.

'Please, Arian.' Eddie was lying beside her on a sweet bed of hay. She was naked as a baby, her slim body lying close to his, so close that he could reach out and touch her. He could even take her again, make her moan with desire and fulfil that desire; but what he couldn't do was make her love him.

'No, Eddie,' she said flatly, with the ease of practice. 'I have no intention of marrying you or anyone else.'

She turned laughing eyes towards him. 'You men are useful, *very* useful, I won't deny that; but I don't want to live with one. Less do I want to be married to one. Forget it, Eddie' – she turned to him, pressing herself against him – 'let's just make the most of the moment, shall we?'

Later, Eddie went back to Honey's Farm and made his way to the room above the stables. Tommy was there, sprawled out on his bed, his hair tousled as though he had been rubbing his hands through it.

'Been out tom-catting again, have you?' He sat up on one elbow and stared at Eddie enviously.

Tommy was still a pimply youth, with a strong but too thin body. However often Eddie assured him that the pimples would go if he only left them alone, Tommy despaired of ever being attractive enough to get himself a woman.

'You needn't answer that,' Tommy said. 'I can see by the look on your face that you've had enough oats to keep you happy for a week, lucky bastard.'

He spoke without rancour and fell back against his bunk. 'Well, I suppose at least my sister'll be safe with you; she's still a kid yet.'

'Your sister?' Eddie undressed and sank on to his bed, kicking off his boots.

'Aye,' Tommy said laconically. 'Mam's feeling bad, so April is coming to stay up by here with Fon for a few weeks.'

'Oh?' Eddie's thoughts were still full of Arian, her lovely body, her passion, her total refusal to be his wife. But he didn't wish to hurt Tommy's feelings by showing a lack of interest in his affairs.

'What's wrong with your mother, then?' he asked, stretching his arms behind his head and staring up at the dark beams of the ceiling.

'Some women's trouble,' Tommy said vaguely. 'Don't really know. Anyway, it seems April's getting in the way down at my auntie's place; causing a bit of bother, she is, and Mam can't cope.'

'I see,' Eddie said, but his eyes were closing; sleep was claiming him. He turned over on his side and pulled the covers up over his naked shoulder.

'Lucky bastard!' Tommy said again, and Eddie smiled to himself. He *was* lucky, even if Arian did refuse to regularize their affair; at least there *was* an affair, and for that he should be heartily thankful.

'Night, Tommy,' he said slowly, as sleep closed his eyes and dulled his senses, drawing him into a net of sweet darkness.

In the morning he met Tommy's sister at breakfast and saw at once why she had been sent away for causing trouble at home. She was about eight years old, skinny, but with a startlingly white skin against an unruly mop of dark hair. There was a sullen expression on her face.

'Morning,' Eddie said pleasantly, sitting opposite the child and smiling.

In reply, she kicked him fiercely beneath the table.

'Little horror,' Eddie said calmly and turned his back on her. She made a soft raspberry sound with her lips, but Eddie took no notice.

'What's for breakfast?' he asked and Fon looked up at him, laughter in her eyes; she'd not missed the little scene between him and April.

'The usual,' she said, 'bacon and eggs and fried bread. I see you've met our new guest.'

'You could say that.' Eddie didn't look at April. 'Perhaps I'm wishing I hadn't.'

'I don't like you,' April said, leaning forward.

Eddie barely glanced at her. 'I don't think I like you very much either.' He moved from the table to take the large dish of bacon from Fon's hands.

The door opened and Jamie entered the kitchen on a rush of soft spring air. 'God, something smells good!' he said, and moved towards Fon, kissing the back of her neck.

'Cupboard love,' Fon said laughing. 'Sit down and eat, there's a good man.'

She glanced at Eddie. 'Where's Tommy? He should be back from the milking by now.' She smiled down at April. 'You can go with him tomorrow, learn how to handle the beasts. You'll enjoy it.'

'Shan't,' the girl said, looking down at the plate Fon had set before her as though it contained poison.

'Nevertheless, you'll do it,' Fon said calmly, but with such authority that the child remained silent, even though her eyes gleamed angrily.

'He got up a little late,' Eddie said. 'But, knowing Tommy, he'll be here as soon as he smells food.'

Looking round at the peaceful breakfast scene, it was hard, Eddie mused, to imagine the violence and the horror of the moment, almost a month ago, when Bob Smale had come charging into the place brandishing a gun and bent on murder. Now the man was buried in Dan-y-Graig Cemetery, his passing scarcely causing a ripple on the surface of the town's awareness.

If nightmares still haunted any of them, it was never spoken of. These days even Arian scarcely made any reference to her father.

The room where the killing had taken place had been scrubbed within an inch of its life. New mats had been placed on the boards, even new drapes had been hung in the windows. The kitchen seemed a bright place, Eddie thought, if he could forget his nightmares.

He glanced at April and smiled ruefully; it would be a brave spirit that would manifest itself to such a wilful child. Not that Eddie believed in such things as hauntings, and yet he rubbed his sore shoulder and shivered.

It was as if Fon read his thoughts. She looked up at him, and her eyes were clouded.

'How is Arian getting along these days?' she asked softly. 'I do hope she's managing to get over . . . things.'

309

'I think she is,' Eddie said. 'She seems quite happy working for Eline Temple – *Lady* Temple, I should say.'

'Good woman that,' Jamie broke in. 'Thank God she came on the scene when she did.'

'I agree,' Eddie said, 'but it was Arian who stopped Bob Smale; otherwise I think the madman would have killed us all.'

Jamie met his gaze; his knuckles were white. 'It still frights me to think about it,' he confessed. 'It would happen when I wasn't here, wouldn't it?'

Fon reached out and covered his hand. 'It's over now, love, over – we must forget it.'

'Sure, I know you're right,' Jamie replied, taking her hand and kissing the palm. 'But I shudder when I think of the danger you were in, all of you.'

Eddie pushed away his plate; he was no longer hungry. 'I'll get out to the fields,' he said. 'My shoulder's healing nicely; I can do a little bit of preparation work at least.'

Jamie nodded. 'If you're sure, lad,' he said. 'There's a lot to do, I must say, but are you ready for it?'

'I'm the doctor, remember?' Eddie smiled. Outside, he breathed in the soft scents of spring, the first flowers, the clear air, the smell of earth waiting to receive its early seeds. It was as if all the world knew that this was a time of regeneration and was receptive to it.

His heart lightened as he strode across the fields. Tonight, he would be with Arian, he would hold her in his arms, taste her sweetness; he could not get enough of her. And yet would he or any man ever possess the inner core of her? He doubted it.

But Eddie was whistling as he climbed the stile and made for the stretch of land where the potatoes would be planted. All in all, it was a good world, and he was glad to be part of it.

'Eddie is a good man, but I've no intention of marrying him.' Arian shaped the leather with deft movements of

310

her fingers and took up the dog to crimp the upper to the sole.

'Why?' Eline smiled at her and put down the large boot she had been measuring.

'I don't want to be tied to any man,' Arian said. 'I had enough of that with my father.'

'But Eddie is a very clever man,' Eline said. 'I'm surprised he's just a farm labourer.'

'He was going to be a doctor,' Arian said. 'He'd begun his training but, when his father died, apparently there was no money left for Eddie to go on.'

'That's a shame,' Eline said at once. 'I think he would make a very good doctor; he certainly has the mind for it.'

Arian looked up at her as Eline stood and stretched her arms above her head. 'You haven't really seen much of him; how can you say that?' she asked curiously.

Eline smiled. 'I pride myself on being a good judge of people,' she explained, 'and you only have to talk to Eddie for a few minutes before you realize how intelligent he is.'

'I know you're right,' Arian said, and indeed, she entirely agreed with Eline; but what could Eddie do? He had only his small wages to keep himself, he could never afford to train. But there, she thought wryly, people like Eline who had money could never understand those who did not.

One day, Arian promised herself, she would have money in abundance; she would be free then, really free. In any case, one thing was certain, she was never going to rely on any man, nor be obligated to any man. Her father had taught her a sharp lesson and one she was never likely to forget.

CHAPTER TWENTY-FIVE

The sun was streaming in through the grimy windows and Will realized, quite suddenly, how dirty the glass was – so dirty he could hardly see the streets outside. Later, he would get a bucket of water and wash the windows down; otherwise his handwritten advertisement for boot-and-shoe repairs would not be decipherable to anyone on the outside, he thought ruefully.

But for now, there was an urgent job he must be getting on with; he needed to finish mending the boots that Glen the baker needed so desperately.

Will rubbed at the leather. The boot was still coated in the white dust from the bakery; the flour had encrusted the eyelets of the laces and clung to the stitching around the worn sole.

Will scratched his chin, and his fingers met rasping stubble. His beard badly needed trimming and so did his moustache, but Will was too busy to care much about his appearance – which, perhaps, was a mistake. Customers wanted a clean shop and a neatly dressed proprietor to greet them when they entered it. He smiled to himself a little wryly; perhaps his present customers wanted only cheap and good service, and to hell with appearances.

He looked along the shelves lined with good heavy working boots, some of them tapped, some still awaiting attention. He was managing at least to make some sort of living, keeping a roof over his head; that, and having a little food in the pantry, was all he really needed.

He thought of Eline, and there was a sudden ache in

his loins – no, not all: there was the love of a good woman, something he would never have now.

It took him almost an hour to complete the repairs on the baker's boots, and then he took up a cloth and began to polish them so that they shone like new.

Glen would be eager to have them back; perhaps it would be just as well to take the boots over to the bakery straightaway. It would at least get him out of the workshop for a while.

It was sunny and fresh, with the promise of spring in the air, as Will stepped out of his workshop. The street was busy with traffic, and all around him people seemed to be in a hurry, eager to get somewhere. Not like him; he had nowhere to go, no-one to go to.

He smiled wryly; feeling sorry for himself was futile and weak and he seemed to be doing quite a lot of it this spring morning. Introspection was a luxury he could not afford. Will squared his shoulders, glancing back at the tall building where his shop was housed; it was not much but soon, if he wished, he would have enough money to put down a deposit on it and own rather than rent it. He had plans for leasing out the rest of the building to other aspiring shopkeepers, make a sort of hodge-podge of goods available to the poorer population of Swansea. He had already been approached by Amos Fisher, who wanted to start up his own pawnbroker's shop – a service that would be used frequently enough, if Will was any judge.

Glen was standing at the long table that filled the bakery, his apron hanging round his thin frame, a great mound of dough before him, which he was kneading with an expertise born of long practice.

He glanced up as Will entered and smiled a welcome. 'Thank God you've brought my boots back! My feet been killing me. Been wearing my brother's old cast-off boots, I have, and they pinch like hell.'

The atmosphere in the bakery was overpowering;

313

the great ovens seemed to shimmer with heat, and the scent of newly baked bread teased Will's empty stomach.

'*Duw*, you look like you could do with a good feed, man,' Glen said cheerfully. 'Come home with me and have some dinner.'

Will shook his head, his first instinct to refuse; and then he thought better of it. 'Thanks,' he said. 'I'll take you up on that.'

Glen looked at him with some sympathy. 'It's a hard thing for a man to lose his wife and child,' he said, 'but now's the time for you to look for a new woman to fill your life. You can't mourn for ever, mind.'

He grinned then, and deftly cut the dough into pieces before shaping it into loaves. 'And I think I know just the girl for you.' His grin widened, showing a great gap in his teeth. 'My Rita, pretty as a picture, but that shy with the boys, can hardly speak to them without blushing. Sixteen, she is, and her afraid to move from her mam's skirts.'

Will smiled wryly. 'Thanks for the honour, but your daughter will think me an old man. In any case, I'm not ready for marriage, not yet awhile.'

'*Duw*, you're only a boy, yet,' Glen said easily. He opened one of the ovens and manhandled a huge tray into the gaping mouth, heedless of the blast of hot air that issued round him.

Glen closed the oven and then squeezed the dough from between his fingers. 'We'll go back into the house, and our Rita can check on the loaves for me.'

He led the way out of the bakery and round to the front of the building, grinning at Will as he went.

'I'll be glad to get these lousy boots off my feet and get into a pair that fits me.'

Glen's house was typical of the area, tall and gloomy, with dull windows staring sightlessly into the mean court outside. Little sun penetrated between the buildings, and

314

even on this bright spring day the houses appeared to be in darkness.

Inside the kitchen was another picture, one of brightness and warmth, with a good fire in the grate and a clean, fresh tablecloth set for dinner. The appetizing smell of roasting rabbit permeated the room, and suddenly Will realized how long it was since he'd had a decent, cooked meal.

Kerry was a tall, red-haired Irish woman, and she greeted Will with a warm smile, just as though she'd been expecting him. With little fuss, she set the table with another place and then took the boots from Will, studying them with bright, laughter-filled eyes.

'Watch out,' Glen said, humorously. 'Gimlet eyes, has my good wife; spot a bad job a mile off.'

'Aye, but this isn't one of them,' Kerry said cheerfully. 'This is as fine a bit of cobbling as I've seen; nearly in bits were these boots, and now shining like the day they were bought, so they are.'

She disappeared into the parlour, and Glen winked. 'Going to raid her hidden hoard of money now, mind,' he said. 'Don't let on to me where she keeps it, in case I take it into my head to have a jar or two down the public.'

The sound of voices filled the passageway outside and Will froze. He glanced at Glen, who shrugged.

'Sounds as if we got another visitor,' he said. 'Eline Harries, as she was, come to see our Mickey and his bad feet, I spects.'

Will felt the blood pound in his head. Eline here, in the same house as he was? It was more than he could have dreamed of. He moved out into the passage, without noticing Glen's expression of surprise, and was drawn towards the front parlour, where he guessed the voices must be coming from.

At the doorway of the parlour, he paused, taking in at a glance the old polished piano, the worn rag mats and

315

the table, covered in a lace cloth. Lastly he looked towards the sofa, where Eline sat alongside a small boy, who was staring in wonder at the pair of boots Eline held in her hand.

Eline looked up and her eyes met Will's; he almost flinched at the naked joy he saw in her face, mirroring his own.

'Will!' Her voice shook a little. 'How are you?'

He became aware, with a sudden sense of shame, that he was looking far from his best. 'Well enough, and you?' he asked, though the question was superfluous. She was as beautiful as ever, her hair shining, her eyes clear, her clothes immaculate. But then, he thought ruefully, she had servants to do her every bidding; she did not bend over a tub scrubbing at her clothes the way he did.

'Will, I'd like your opinion on these boots I've made for Mickey,' she said quickly, as though reading something of his thoughts. 'Mickey's foot was just a little bit twisted, and I hope these special boots will help correct it.'

Drawn almost against his will, he bent down on one knee near the boy and the scent of Eline drifted over him, plaguing him with desires that were as futile as they were painful.

'They'll do the job, right enough. Here, let me help you put them on, Mickey.'

The small boy sat quietly until Will had tied up the boots securely, and then, urged by Will's hands, he stood up and took a tentative step forward.

'Excellent,' Will said softly. 'You're doing well, Mickey, atta a boy!'

With growing confidence, Mickey walked about the small room, his face alight, and after a moment, he stood before Eline, holding out his small hand to her.

'Thank you, miss,' he said gravely. 'My foot don't hurt no more, I can walk like the other boys.'

Eline sighed. 'I'm glad,' she said softly. 'I was

316

afraid I might have made a mistake with your boots, Mickey.'

Her humility touched Will, and he resisted the urge to take Eline in his arms. He rose to his feet abruptly, his hand inadvertently brushing Eline's hair. He sprung back as if stung, and Eline stared up at him, her eyes full of misery.

'Sure, mother of God bless you, miss,' Kerry said quickly, sensing some of the tension that had sprung up between her visitors. 'Now, how much is it that I owe you?'

Eline delved into her bag and brought out a list. 'Let me see now,' she said softly, 'you've been paying into the club for some weeks, haven't you? Ah, yes, I can see you don't owe very much at all.'

She tucked the paper away and smiled. 'In any case, Arian Smale will be coming around, as usual, collecting your club money every week, if that's more convenient for you.'

'To be sure, I'd be glad of that,' Kerry said, the relief in her voice evident. 'I've our Glen's boots to pay for this week, worn to the bone they were.' She smiled at Will. 'You and Miss Eline should go into business together, you're both such clever people.'

Will felt at a disadvantage; he too would have liked to waive payment, but unlike Eline he simply couldn't afford the gesture. He glanced away from Eline's steady gaze; her eyes, somehow imploring, seemed to be looking into his very soul.

'I'm sure Eline does very nicely on her own.' Will tried to speak lightly, but his words came out all wrong; it sounded like pique on his part.

'You'll stay and have a bit of dinner with us, Miss Eline.' Kerry filled the awkward silence. 'It's lovely rabbit, done in the oven with herbs and spices, a good hearty meal for anyone.'

To Will's surprise, Eline accepted. 'That would be

lovely,' she said warmly. 'The smell of it is making me hungry.'

It was strange to sit at the same table as Eline, and Will could not help glancing at her covertly when he thought she wasn't looking. But somehow he knew that she was as aware of him as he was of her.

On his right sat Glen's young daughter. As the baker had said, Rita was shyness itself, her eyes downcast, her whole attitude self-effacing. And yet she was a beautiful girl, with her mother's flame hair and her father's dark eyes, an enticing combination.

'Did you help your mother cook this lovely meal?' Will said, determined to draw her out. 'I can't tell you when I tasted rabbit like it.'

Rita blushed a fiery scarlet, and her eyes met his for a brief instant. 'Yes, I skinned the rabbit and rubbed in the herbs,' she said, her voice barely audible, 'but Mammy showed me how.'

As the meal progressed, Will found Rita warming to him and, as her confidence grew, she began to talk to him quietly. He found she had a quick mind and a fine sense of humour.

Will, looking across yet again at Eline, met her eyes, and the sadness he read there cut him to the quick. An air of unreality gripped him; here he was breaking bread with Eline, sitting so close to her that he could have reached across the table and touched her hand, and yet they were poles apart.

After the meal had finished, Glen rose and rubbed his hands down his trousers, a smile on his thin face. 'I don't know about you people,' he said, 'but I've got work to do. Did you take the bread out of the oven for me, Rita?'

'Yes, Dad.' The girl seemed to retreat into her shell once more, as though aware of the other people in the room. 'Shall I come and wash the tins for you?'

'Aye, good girl, that would be a great help,' Glen said, and, crossing the room, he held out his hand to Will.

'And thanks, lad, for a fine job. I can't tell you what a relief it is to get a good pair of boots on my feet again.'

Eline rose too and smiled at Kerry. 'Can I help you clear away or something?' she volunteered.

Kerry shook her head quickly. 'No, you and Will are visitors; I don't expect you to help me. But thank you anyway.'

'In that case, I'd better be going,' Eline said, smiling warmly, 'and thank you for the best dinner I've eaten in ages.'

'Can I see you home?' Will found himself making the offer with a sense of surprise.

He stared down at Eline and his heart lifted with joy when she nodded. 'That would be very kind of you.'

Then, with Will scarcely remembering how, they were out in the street together, walking side by side as if it was the most natural thing in all the world.

'I love you, Eline.' Will said the words softly. 'I've never stopped loving you.' He held up his hand. 'Please don't say anything; I know I can never have you. You are far out of my reach, but I can't help what I feel.'

Eline stopped walking and turned to him. 'Invite me in, please, Will,' she said softly, and he realized they were outside his shop. Eagerly, he opened the door and led the way through the workshop to his living-room at the back of the building.

In the living-room the fire was still burning in the grate; the kettle hissed on the hob and Will was somehow acutely aware of his surroundings, as though he wanted to imprint the scene on his consciousness.

'I want you, Will,' Eline said, standing before him, her eyes looking up into his.

'This is playing with fire,' Will said hoarsely. 'Your husband will be expecting you home . . .'

He stopped as Eline put her hand softly over his mouth. 'No,' she said. 'He's away on business; no-one is expecting me anywhere.'

319

Will was swamped by the scent of her, the closeness of her, and desire flared through him, so that he felt drunk with it. 'Eline,' he said thickly, 'Eline, my love.'

'Will' – she moved closer – 'do I have to *ask* you to make love to me? I'll beg, if that's what you want.'

'Eline, if you don't mean it, please . . .' Will stopped speaking as she reached up and, standing on tiptoe, pressed her mouth against his.

'We can have this one afternoon, Will,' she whispered. 'Is that too much to ask of life?'

'Eline.' His arms were around her, holding her close, his mouth warming to her kiss, his arms tender as they held her, knowing that this was a dream he thought would never come true. He would not think beyond the moment; he would take what Eline was offering him, her love for a few short hours.

They kissed softly, experimentally, as though tasting each other. Will felt a bursting of passion that threatened to overwhelm him as he allowed his hands to stray to her breasts, touching softly, as if even now fearing rejection.

'I won't break,' Eline said, opening the bodice of her gown. 'I'm a flesh-and-blood woman, Will; treat me like one, I beg of you.'

He picked her up in his arms then and carried her through to his bedroom. The curtains were closed against the outside, spreading a dim, romantic glow over the shabby furnishings.

Gently, he set her down and lay beside her, catching her waist, drawing her close to him. His body longed to take her, to own and possess her, but he knew he must savour the experience; it would never happen again.

Her lips were like butterflies, kissing his eyes, his mouth, his throat. 'I've wanted this for so long, my darling,' she breathed. 'I've dreamed of you, of being in your arms, of being yours so many, many times. I can't believe this is really happening.'

320

Her body, when he undressed her, was milky white in the dimness; she was perfect, the way he'd expected her to be, and for a moment he stared at her, drinking her in, imprinting the sight of her on his memory.

'Eline, you are so beautiful,' he said raggedly, and she touched his cheek.

'Hush, don't talk, not now.' Her eyes were half-closed; desire gave her a dreamy, ethereal look, and suddenly Will wanted her so fiercely that he thought he would die.

He touched her reverently, and in response her hands were running over his naked body as if to own every part of him. Little did she know that she owned his very soul.

He could bear his restraint no longer and, moving delicately, he became one with her, so easily that they might have been fashioned for each other. He could scarcely believe the wonder of it all, the sweet hot sensations of possession, the feeling of power and yet overwhelming tenderness that filled him as she moaned softly beneath him.

She was his, his very own woman, at least for a few hours. Will closed his eyes and gave himself up to the passion that held the both of them as though in a brilliant rainbow of light.

They slept in each other's arms, and Will woke first, feeling her softness against him with a sense of wonder. It was dark now, with only a sliver of moonlight shining through the opening in the curtains.

Then she too was awake; her arms reached up for him, and she pressed herself close to him with an urgency that sent the blood coursing through his veins.

'Please, Will . . .' she breathed, and he took her then with all the vigour of his pent-up longings. It was as though he must find the deepest recesses of her, to own her, to put his mark indelibly upon her. They cried out together, and it was a cry of happiness and triumph.

★　　★　　★

321

Eline sat in the elegant drawing-room of the house Calvin had bought for her, staring into the fire without seeing anything of the flames. Some weeks had passed since she'd lain with Will, and yet the residue of the passion she had shared with him remained with her, along with her awful sense of guilt.

She sighed wistfully. She had never felt like this before; loving Will was an intoxication, and Eline wondered if she could live without it now she had tasted it.

She closed her eyes, seeing again, in her mind's eye, Will, naked in her arms. He was too thin, of course, and the urge to hold and protect him was as strong in her as desire.

She opened her eyes and rose restlessly from her chair. She felt trapped, as though she had been here before, in exactly the same situation; and of course she had. Except that she had honoured her marriage vows to Joe, but not to Calvin. She had cuckolded the man who had given her everything, and she was ashamed.

Calvin entered the room and he was smiling, his handsome face full of happiness. He came towards her holding out a great bouquet of flowers, and Eline felt her throat contract with unshed tears.

'What are these for?' she asked softly. 'What have I done to deserve such a wonderful gesture?' She buried her face in the soft blooms to hide the blush of shame that tinged her cheeks. She only prayed that Calvin could not read her guilt in her eyes.

'This is the happiest day of my life,' Calvin said gently. 'I've just seen Dr Ferguson, and what he had to say was just what I was longing to hear. You are a clever girl, do you know that, Eline?'

A cold hand of fear gripped her as Calvin led her to a chair and gently pushed her into it.

'You know I insisted on calling in the old quack when you had that funny turn? Now we know what caused it.'

Eline took a ragged breath, her hands flying to her

322

cheeks. 'No, it can't be . . .' she said, her voice scarcely audible.

'It *can!*' Calvin said in delight. 'Eline, we are going to have a child! I shall have an heir, and I can't tell you what it means to me.'

'But I'm barren!' Eline said flatly. 'If I'm not, why have I never conceived before? There couldn't be some mistake, could there?'

'There is no mistake,' Calvin said softly. 'Eline, you *are* pleased, aren't you? You did want a baby?'

'I don't know,' Eline said, her heart beating fast. Not now, her mind cried in protest, now when I have lain with Will. 'I can't believe it's really true,' she said lamely.

He took her gently in his arms, holding her close. 'It is true, my love. The doctor is quite sure, and I'm so pleased I would give you the moon if you wanted it.'

Eline closed her eyes as Calvin held her close; her head rested against his shoulder as she sought to clear her mind. She was going to have a baby, after years of barrenness – but, a small voice of doubt said in her head, which man was the father?

Suddenly she longed to rush out of the house, to escape from the cloying love Calvin was showering upon her; and, most of all, she wanted Will to be holding her, Will, not Calvin.

Oh, God, she'd got herself into a terrible position; and right now there seemed no possible way of escape.

CHAPTER TWENTY-SIX

Fon looked out at the fields, rich and green now with the promise of a good crop of corn later on in the year. On the top field the men were transplanting the cabbages, putting them down into land that had been cleared of early potatoes.

Eddie was out with the men. He was almost recovered from the shot that had grazed his shoulder at dangerously close quarters. He'd been lucky that he'd known how to handle the wound, which surprisingly had bled very little, and that there had been no resulting complications. Eddie, though his arm was a little stiff, had insisted on going back to work as soon as possible; he knew full well that there was a lot to be done.

The farm, Fon felt, was flourishing; and yet a sense of unease hung persistently over her as she stood now in the kitchen window, her hands covered in flour, the smell of baking permeating the room.

From the garden she could hear the sounds of happy laughter and her tense expression relaxed. Tommy's little sister might be a handful, but April was certainly good for Patrick. She loved him dearly, adopting him as her baby brother, and her attitude was proprietary to say the least.

Fon's attention was caught by the sight of a horse and cart just rising over the crest of the hill. The cart, bumping and clattering its way along the rutted track towards the farmhouse, held just one figure, hunched rather awkwardly in the driving seat. For a moment, she grew tense, and then, as the cart drew closer, she saw that the driver was a woman and she relaxed, smiling at her own foolishness.

She opened the door wide. 'April, your mother's coming,' she said cheerfully, and April looked up, her face suddenly alight. The small girl rushed forward, her arms outstretched.

'Mam!' April's voice was full of happiness as she helped her mother down from the cart.

Fon was shocked to see how thin Mrs Jones had become; her shoulders beneath the cotton bodice were bony and angular, her face elongated, with lines running from nose to mouth.

Fon remembered Mrs Jones as she used to be when she lived on the land adjoining Honey's Farm, a plump, healthy woman, lively and intelligent, her eyes clear and full of humour. Now she was shadowy, insubstantial, and Fon had the feeling she had come back to the land once more by way of a goodbye.

'Come inside, Mrs Jones,' she said warmly. 'Sit down and have some cordial; you look a bit tired.' It was an understatement, but Fon smiled as though she'd noticed nothing amiss.

'Where's our Tommy?' Mrs Jones sank gratefully into a chair. 'Working in the fields like a good boy, is he?'

'Aye.' Fon poured a long drink of dandelion and burdock and handed it to her visitor. 'I don't know what we'd do without him,' she said, smiling. 'He's such a good worker.'

'He loves the land, all right,' Mrs Jones said softly. 'I hope you will keep him here with you, Fon.'

'We will,' Fon said emphatically. 'We couldn't manage without him.'

'That's good.' Mrs Jones picked up her glass with a hand that shook, and Fon could not help noticing how thin was the woman's skin, so thin that the blue of her veins stood out in sharp relief.

'And our April, is she giving you any problems?' Mrs Jones sounded anxious, and Fon shook her head.

'Indeed, she's a great help.' She smiled at the girl who was still standing at her mother's side, leaning against the thin shoulder. 'You look after Patrick for me, don't you, April?'

'When can I come home with you, Mam?' April ignored Fon's remark and turned to her mother, her rosy lips pouting.

'You like it here, don't you, love?' Mrs Jones asked quickly, and April nodded.

'I like it fine, but I miss you, Mam.' She spoke softly, and Fon was taken aback by the change in April's attitude. Usually she was brisk, almost impudent; but now it was as if all her defences were down.

Mrs Jones put her arm around her daughter, but Fon couldn't help noticing that she winced as the girl leant against her breast.

'And I miss you too, my lovely.' Mrs Jones's eyes filled with tears, even as she forced herself to smile. 'But we are all in the hands of the good Lord, mind, we can't always have what we want.'

Fon caught the woman's eye, and, with a sinking of her heart, she felt that history was repeating itself. Mrs Jones was very sick, just as Katherine O'Conner had been when Fon first came to Honey's Farm. And Fon felt instinctively that, like before, she would be asked to become a substitute mother, both to April and to Tommy who, although he was almost a man, needed a family behind him, a guiding hand, Jamie's hand.

April, at last giving in to Patrick's insistent demands to go outside, left her mother's side, and Mrs Jones leaned towards Fon, the expression on her face grave.

'I'm not going to beat about the bush, Fon,' she said firmly. 'I'm a dying woman, and I've come to ask a great favour of you.'

'I know,' Fon said quickly. 'I think I knew the moment I set eyes on you.' She forced a smile. 'And of course

326

Tommy and April will always have a home on Honey's Farm.'

Mrs Jones nodded and then reached into her bag. 'Here,' she said, putting a brown parcel tied with string on the table before her. 'This is all the money I have in the world, the money I've saved since my husband's death, the money your good man paid me for the land.' She sighed. 'It's everything I own, and I have no need of money where I'm going. I want you to take it and use it wisely to pay for my children's keep.'

'But, Mrs Jones,' Fon protested, 'Tommy pays his own way. We don't need money, I promise you we don't.'

Mrs Jones smiled wryly. 'Well, what use will I have for it, Fon?' She shrugged her thin shoulders. 'My funeral expenses are taken care of; there's nothing I need, not now.' She pushed the packet towards Fon. 'Take it for the sake of my children, please.'

Fon rose without another word and took the packet, placing it in the drawer of the dresser. 'I'll look after the money until Tommy and April need it,' she said quietly. She smiled down at Mrs Jones, who was leaning back in her chair, her mission accomplished.

'You are very brave,' Fon said. 'These hill farms must give birth to a very special breed of woman; I can't say how much I admire your courage.'

'It's not courage, lovely,' Mrs Jones said softly. 'It's acceptance, acceptance of what is inevitable.'

She rose to her feet. 'I'll be getting back to my sister's house now.' She paused at the door, as though to gather her strength. 'I doubt I'll see you again.'

Fon rested a hand on the older woman's shoulder. 'Don't you want to see Tommy, to say goodbye?'

Mrs Jones shook her head. 'I want my boy to remember me the way I was.' She made a gesture of helplessness. 'I don't want him to see me like this. Perhaps you'll tell him that I came here, after . . . after it's all over?'

Outside, the sun was shining and the birds were singing. There was no sign of April or Patrick, though their voices could be heard clearly on the quiet air. Mrs Jones climbed up into the cart with a pitiful slowness; she seemed weak and tired, and Fon felt instinctively that she would find death a welcome release.

She watched as the woman drove the horse and carriage away from the farmhouse. Mrs Jones did not look back, and the last glimpse of her Fon would ever have revealed a sick but determined woman, whose back was straight and whose head was held high.

There was a constriction in Fon's throat as she returned indoors. She sank down into a chair, her head resting on her hands; life was full of joy one minute and full of sadness the next. She sighed heavily, pushing herself to her feet. There was work to be done; nothing would be achieved by sitting here moping. And yet even as Fon returned to her chores, the tears spilled over, running down her cheeks and tasting salt on her lips.

Eline stared down at the small girl sitting before her, thin legs hanging like threads over the edge of the chair.

'Well, Jessie, we'll have to see what we can do for you, won't we?' She spoke softly, her mind racing, trying to sort out the complex problem with which she was being presented.

Jessie Kennedy had a condition that had wasted the muscles of one of her legs. No ordinary pair of boots was going to help her walk straight and strong.

'Can you do anything?' Jane Kennedy's hands were twisted together almost pleadingly, and Eline hadn't the heart to confess that she had very little idea of exactly what could be achieved.

'I'm certainly going to try,' she said, smiling. 'Give me a few days to come up with some drawings, and then we'll talk again.'

'Thank you, and God bless you,' Mrs Kennedy said.

Eline bit her lip. 'I can't promise results,' she cautioned, 'but I will try my level best to help. *That* I can promise.'

She watched as Mrs Kennedy took her daughter's hand and helped the girl down from the chair. She handed Jessie a carved stick, and the child leant against it heavily, her weak leg twisting as she put her weight on it.

Her progress from the workshop was slow and painful, and Eline felt determination rise within her. She *must* think of something, some design that would support the little girl's leg as well as her ankles and feet. She picked up a pen.

Eline lost track of time as she covered the paper with drawings, scratching some out, circling others with a ring and the words 'might work'.

It was only when the door sprang open and Calvin stood framed against the dying light that Eline realized the time. She shuffled her papers together almost guiltily.

'Come on home,' Calvin said, smiling. 'No-one should work these hours.'

Eline returned his smile. 'You're right. I'm a slave driver – but only to myself, mind.'

She was suddenly tired and climbed readily into the carriage waiting outside. The leather seats creaked and the coach groaned as Calvin climbed in beside her.

'I'm taking you out to dinner,' he said. 'We've been invited to the home of Hari Grenfell, and I thought it one invitation you would be pleased to accept.'

Eline smiled. 'Of course. Hari is always interesting to talk to; she loves the shoe business even more than I do.' And, Eline thought, pushing away her tiredness, perhaps Hari would come up with some ideas for helping little Jessie Kennedy.

As Eline bathed at leisure, luxuriating in the hot scented water, her mind was worrying at the problem of a boot that would support Jessie's thin leg without restricting it too much. The structure must be light; the girl had little strength in her limbs, and so the design would need to be strong too.

As she stood before the mirror, towelling herself dry, eyeing her still slim body, Eline's thoughts turned to the one thing she had been trying to avoid thinking about – the child she was carrying.

She had not dared tell Calvin that she was uncertain about the baby's father; was it her husband's child or that of her lover, Will, with whom she had shared one afternoon of happiness?

Should she tell Calvin? Could she tell him? It was a dilemma that seemed to have no solution. She sighed, staring at her still slim waist, and yet her breasts were fuller now, the veins showing through the thin, creamy skin. She supposed that, to the eye of an expert, she was obviously in the first stages of motherhood.

She still could not believe it. Perhaps she simply did not wish to believe it; she pushed the thought away impatiently.

She dressed quickly in the clothes the maid had set out for her but discarding the tight, laced corset. She was not used to her body being restricted, and in any case she had no time for a fashion which dictated that a woman should be tied up like a sack just to look shapely.

The maid came into the room and made no comment as her glance slid over the corset lying brazenly open on the bed. She took up a brush and began to attend to Eline's hair in an authoritative manner that somehow irritated Eline.

'It's all right, Maggie,' she said, trying to be pleasant. 'I'd prefer to do it myself.'

'But, madam,' the girl protested, 'it's not seemly for a lady to attend her own toilette.'

Eline waved her hand. 'I'm used to caring for myself,'

she said firmly. 'Please, Maggie, go and find something else to do.'

Eline could have sworn that the girl sniffed disdainfully as she left the room, but she didn't care. She hated being fussed; it was not the sort of thing she was used to, and she was not going to be treated like an imbecile or a child at this stage of her life.

Eline smiled ruefully. What would the ladies of Oystermouth make of it all? Nina Parks, Carys Morgan and the others – how they would be impressed by all the show of pomp that Calvin's servants were so fond of. And yet, like Eline, they would all have balked at being treated as a useless ornament.

At last, she was ready, and she didn't look too bad, she decided. The blue gown suited her and the rouge she had rubbed into her cheeks took away the pallor of tiredness that had made her look worn and a little unwell.

Calvin came through from his dressing-room, and Eline was struck afresh by his immaculate taste in clothes and the handsomeness of his bearing. He was a fine man, a man any woman would be happy to have for a husband. So why wasn't she the happiest woman in all of Swansea?

He held her in his arms and then stood back to admire her. 'Lovely,' he said, 'so lovely. I'm a lucky devil, Eline, have I ever told you that?'

She smiled and hugged him. She was fond of Calvin; but 'fond' was a watered-down sort of love, and he deserved better than that.

Later, as the carriage drew to a halt outside Summer Lodge, Eline saw that all the lights were ablaze; this was apparently going to be a large supper party.

Eline stepped into the spacious hallway and looked around at the rich wall hangings and the well-polished woodwork with a critical eye. At one time, all this grandeur would have overawed her, but now, used as she was to Stormhill Manor, the house seemed small in

331

comparison. Though, she conceded, everything in it reflected Hari's impeccable taste.

Hari and her husband Craig were waiting to welcome their guests, and once the formalities were over, Eline spoke quietly to her hostess.

'Could I talk to you, some time soon? I want to ask your advice about a little girl with foot problems.'

'Of course,' Hari said at once. 'I'll come to your workshop tomorrow; would the afternoon suit you?'

'That would be lovely.' Eline smiled, and, as she moved away to make room for more newcomers, she wondered at the warmth of an important woman like Hari Grenfell, who was never too busy to give a helping hand to anyone.

Calvin left her side to get a drink and Eline turned, glancing round the room with covert curiosity. Most of the women were dressed in rich silks, with gems blazing at wrist and throat. There must have been a fortune there in emeralds, diamonds, pearls and sapphires, Eline thought ruefully; enough money to set up clinics all over town for children like little Jessie Kennedy.

Suddenly, Eline froze as she caught sight of a tall figure coming through the crowd towards her. The sight of him brought the blood pumping through her veins; her head pounded as her heart-beats quickened and her mouth was suddenly dry.

'Will!' She breathed the name and then he was standing beside her, and it was as if they were the only two people in the room.

'Eline,' he said, 'I can't get you out of my mind, not since that day . . . it seems so long ago.' His voice trailed away and he glanced around him anxiously, careful not to be overheard.

'Eline, I can't stand being parted from you like this! God, I want you so much, it's like a constant pain that just will not go away.'

'Hush, Will,' she said quickly. 'We can't talk, not

332

here.' She put her hand on his arm just as Calvin returned to her side.

'What's this?' he asked. 'Making overtures to my wife, are you?' He was teasing, but there was an edge of anger in his voice that Eline was not slow to notice.

'It's me,' she said, forcing a laugh. 'I was begging some advice from Will. I have this little customer, Jessie, she has a wasted leg, I want so much to help her.'

'This is not the time or the place for talking about work,' Calvin admonished. 'Come along, Eline, we have to find time for my friends too, you know.'

He drew her away and moved easily into another group, joining the conversation about politics and the state of the government with ease born of long practice.

Eline was afraid to glance back at Will. Calvin did not hesitate to speak his mind, and she was lucky that he had accepted her explanation so readily.

The gong sounded for supper, and groups of people began to drift into the long dining-room. Eline found herself seated between Emily Miller and Craig Grenfell, and she breathed a sigh of relief. At least with her two supper companions she had something in common; they were as involved in the shoemaking business as she was.

But still it proved to be a long and trying evening. Eline studiously kept her eyes turned away from Will, while all the time she knew he was silently begging her to look at him. There was a respite when the women withdrew to the drawing-room, but Eline found the general gossip trivial to the point of boredom.

When the men joined the ladies, Eline found Will beside her once again, his eyes drawing hers irresistibly.

'I love you.' He mouthed the words, his head turned so that only she could see, and the tell-tale colour rose to her cheeks.

She became aware of a hand gripping her arm firmly. 'I would appreciate it' – Calvin's voice was low but had an edge of hardness to it that chilled Eline – 'if you would keep away from my wife. I won't tell you again.'

He drew her away and Eline, fearing a scene, kept her eyes firmly on the carpeted floor.

It was a relief when Calvin announced that it was time to take his wife home. 'I must look after her, you know,' he said softly to Hari, but clearly enough for his words to carry to where Will was standing nearby. 'She doesn't realize quite what a delicate condition she is in.'

As if on cue to his words, Eline felt herself awaying as a whirling darkness pressed down upon her. She was aware of Calvin leading her to a chair and of Hari brushing the hair back from her forehead.

'You see, my darling, you need me to look after you.' Calvin's voice seemed to come from afar, and Eline made an effort to pull her thoughts together.

'I'm all right, really I am.' She was aware of faces staring in her direction and a hot colour suffused her face; now everyone knew that she was with child. She looked across the room to where Will stood alone, suddenly still, like a graven image, his face pale with shock.

She longed to run to him, to throw herself into his arms, to ease the pain that etched his mouth with deep lines. But it was too late for that; Calvin was helping her to rise and was leading her towards the door. They were outside then, and in the splash of light thrown across the driveway he was taking her in his arms, kissing her mouth.

'This, my dear Eline,' he said softly, 'is the proudest moment of my life.' She knew then that she couldn't speak out, couldn't tell Calvin of her awful doubts.

She sank into the carriage that was taking her towards home, towards all the silk and luxury that suddenly seemed little more than a golden cage. And somewhere there, back in the house that was rapidly fading into the distance, was the man she loved with all her heart, the man whose dreams had just been shattered.

CHAPTER TWENTY-SEVEN

They were having their first real row. Fon faced Jamie, her hands gripped to her sides, her mind reeling with the anger that washed through her.

'Didn't you want me to take care of April, then?' she demanded. 'Was I supposed to tell Mrs Jones to take the girl away, and damn the consequences?'

'There is no need to swear.' Jamie's eyes rested on her as though she was a stranger who had suddenly come into his home. He ran his hands through the dark curls and stared down at Fon, a strange expression on his face.

'Can't you see,' he said, 'I don't want you and me to be simply substitute parents. We should have children of our own. *I* at least want children of my own, a healthy family of boys and girls filling the house with their noise.'

He paused and moved to look through the window. 'I need children who will take over the place after me; a farm needs a big family living on it.'

Fon felt a pain within her. 'You have Patrick, remember,' she said, her voice low now. 'He will take over after you. Only one son can inherit the farm, so why do you want more?'

She couldn't tell him that she didn't want children. The feeling had crystallized in her of late, in spite of the brave words she had used when talking to Jamie about having sons. The truth was, she was afraid of childbirth, afraid of becoming like her mother.

Fon had stood on the sidelines and watched as Nina had conceived children by two different men. Nina had gone through enough pain and suffering to try the strength of a lesser woman. Fon had suffered with her,

335

borne the shame of seeing her mother walk about the streets of Oystermouth with her swollen stomach and no husband to call her own. But worst of all was Gwyneth's death; her sister, who was still young and beautiful, she had spent agonizing hours in labour only to lose her child after all her pain. Gwyneth had survived her baby by hours, slipping away from life, at last beaten and defeated.

'Look, Jamie,' she said, 'I'm young yet. There's plenty of time for children of our own.' She put her hand on his shoulder, but he did not respond; he might have been made of stone for all the notice he took.

'All right, then!' She was angry again. 'Behave like a big child yourself, but remember, I can't help it if I can't conceive, can I?'

'No, but you needn't be so *happy* about it.' He left her then, without another word, and she sank down at the kitchen table, biting back her tears. She felt a hard anger towards Jamie; he was selfish, he wasn't thinking of anyone but himself and what *he* wanted. Well, he would just have to put up with it; she couldn't help it if babies didn't come along, could she? Anyway, she was still young, there was time enough for her and Jamie to have a family. But in her heart she felt sick and afraid. All her protests were excuses, and she knew it.

It was quiet in the kitchen, and Fon was thankful that the children were playing in the fields. April had buttered some fresh bread and cut a piece of cheese and wrapped them, along with a bottle of water, in a cloth which she slung over her shoulder like a traveller. Clutching Patrick's hand, she had gone off across the fields, her bare brown legs deliberately adopting a slow pace so that the boy could keep up with her.

Fon rose from the chair. It was time she began her chores; there was a great deal to do before she went out to the fields and did an honest day's work on the land.

She looked round at the neat kitchen, the well-stoked

fire, the big pan of scrubbed potatoes ready for boiling. Why wasn't Jamie content with what they had?

Abruptly, she drew her thoughts into order. She must get on. She had to stuff the fresh-killed chicken and put it in to roast; the beds must be made; the sheets washed; then and only then could she go out into the fields.

Fon sighed heavily. Life was hard enough, goodness knows, without a brood of children round her skirts. 'Forget it!' she told herself harshly, and yet a tinge of guilt continued to tug at the corners of her mind.

She supposed, in all fairness, she was not being a good wife to Jamie; a good wife would *want* her husband's child. Was she, by deliberately setting her mind against the idea, preventing the very thing that her husband most desired?

'To hell with Jamie's desires!' she said, and then she laughed suddenly at the sound of her own voice filling the empty kitchen.

In bed that night, Fon lay awake waiting for Jamie to come upstairs. For the first time since she'd been at Honey's Farm, she had not stayed to help him with the books. She was tired; her back ached from bending over the grass that had doggedly refused to be cut. And yet the men, even Eddie, with his damaged shoulder, had wielded the scythe with ease leaving a swath of neat grass behind them as they moved steadily forward.

She tensed as she heard Jamie's footsteps on the stairs. He came into the bedroom and closed the door quietly behind him. She watched him remove his clothes and stand for a moment naked, the pale light from the moon revealing his readiness to make love to her.

He slid into bed beside her, his hand, as always, cupping her breast as he drew her back towards him. Fon, instead of turning to him with her usual eagerness, remained still, not drawing away but unresponsive to his caressing fingers.

'Fon, my lovely,' he said, 'sure and there's daft we were to quarrel.'

She didn't reply. Jamie kissed the back of her neck, pushing aside the heavy plait of her hair, his mouth warm. Undeterred, his hands slid down her back and round to her thigh.

She held herself rigid, anger pouring through her like wine; he wanted her, and so he was being kind just to achieve his desire. Well, she could not get over their differences that quickly; she was not to be humoured by his overtures that were driven by need rather than by any wish to make up their quarrel.

'What's wrong?' He leant on his elbow and looked down at her.

Fon hunched her shoulders against him. 'I don't want to . . .' Her voice trailed away, and she heard Jamie's sharp breath with a feeling of triumph.

'You mean you are refusing me?' He could scarcely believe it; she who was always so ready to please him was turning away from him. Well, she was not in the mood to please him right now; he must learn that he could not always have his own way.

He was shaking. He fell back on to the pillow, and, startled, Fon looked over her shoulder to where her husband lay against the pillows. His face was contorted, his shoulders shaking. With a shock of amazement and anger, Fon realized he was laughing.

She sat up abruptly. 'What's so funny?' she demanded.

Jamie turned his face into the pillow to stifle the gales of laughter, but his shoulders continued to shake.

Angrily, Fon climbed out of bed. 'How dare you laugh at me?' she said, and, grasping the quilt, pulled it from over his shoulders. She threw it down on the floor and wrapped herself up in it, trying not to hear his laughter.

She forced her eyes shut, knowing her face was red with humiliation; she had refused her husband, and he found it all highly amusing.

Fon heard the creak of his feet against the bare boards of the floor and then he was kneeling beside her, tugging at the quilt, drawing it away from her.

'Fon!' He cradled her in his arms. 'You funny little thing, if you don't want me to make love to you, then I won't; there's no need to give up your soft bed for a place on the floor.'

She felt foolish, as though it was she who had been acting as a spoiled child, not him. He lifted her in his arms and held her close to his bare chest, and her face was in the warmth of his neck.

Suddenly, against all reason, she desired him, with a fierce need that shook her.

But when she was in bed once more, Jamie turned his back and, tucking his arm beneath the pillow, was quickly asleep. Beside him, Fon listened to his even breathing and felt the silk of his back against her body and knew that she had been a fool. She had, as her mother would have put it, cut off her nose to spite her face.

She wound her arms around Jamie's waist, her hands smoothing the flat of his stomach, feeling beneath her fingertips the strength of his thighs and the hardness of him that even in his sleep showed his arousal.

He turned to her quite suddenly and then, without warning, he was within her, his arms encircling her, his lips fierce against hers.

'Jamie!' She fought her mouth free of his and stared up at him, trying to see his expression in the darkness. 'You weren't asleep at all, were you?'

He didn't answer. He moved slowly at first, and she gasped, wanting him to take and plunder and make her lose her senses in a welter of sensation as he always did.

'You are my slave, aren't you, Fon?' His body teased hers; he withdrew from her, and she clasped him, drawing him close once more. 'Say it, my colleen' – his voice was thick with emotion – 'say you are my slave.'

'I am,' she gasped, joining in the game of love that Jamie played so skilfully. 'I am your slave, Jamie, now and for always!'

He filled her and encompassed her; he owned her, he dominated her, and Fon cried out in the passion of the moment, knowing that the sweetness he gave her stemmed from love as well as desire.

She touched his face with her hands. 'Jamie, my love, if you want sons, then I am ready.' She closed her eyes and flung back her head and knew that, when she was loved the way Jamie loved her, she *was* ready, ready to do anything he wanted of her.

Eddie eased his shoulder, rubbing it with the tips of his fingers. He was still a little sore from the gunshot wound inflicted by Arian's father. Still, he mused, he was lucky to be alive; if Bob Smale hadn't been distracted by the arrival of his daughter, Eddie might not be here right now.

He drew his clean shirt around him and did up the buttons with a feeling of anticipation. He was meeting Arian; it was her day off from work, and Jamie had obligingly given Eddie the day off as well – about time too, Eddie thought good-naturedly.

He went to the mirror to adjust his tie and saw, with a start of surprise, how much his body had filled out since he'd worked on the farm.

And yet the hankering to be a doctor was always there. The love of books was inherent; he took to studying as other people took to breathing. He grimaced at his reflection. 'Be glad of what you've got, lad,' he admonished himself. 'You could be starving in the mean streets of Swansea somewhere.'

The walk down the hill towards town was a pleasant one; a soft breeze was coming in off the sea and Eddie felt it ruffle his hair. He felt alive, full of vigour; he was happy with the anticipation of meeting Arian.

340

She was waiting for him in the gardens of Victoria Park. Her moonlight hair, caught back in a ribbon, was hanging down her back in soft waves; Arian had never cared for fashion or convention.

She looked up and smiled as he sat beside her on the bench. She put her hand in his and his fingers curled warm around her slender wrists.

'Watch my callouses,' she said, laughing. 'Making shoes isn't easy work, believe me.'

'I do,' Eddie said solemnly, 'but you obviously enjoy it.' He lifted her hand and kissed it.

Arian drew away, embarrassed at his gesture. 'We've got a new customer,' she said quickly, 'a sweet little girl named Jessie. She has a withered leg, and Eline is trying to sort out some kind of boot that will support it so that she can walk more easily.'

Eddie was interested. 'I wonder if I could help,' he said. 'I admit to knowing nothing about shoemaking, but I *do* know a little about anatomy.'

Arian looked at him thoughtfully. 'That's true. Perhaps you'll walk with me to the workshop, talk to Eline – though I must admit she seems a little distracted right now. I do hope she's not sickening for something.'

'Come on, then,' Eddie said, good-humouredly. 'I might as well see this Eline of yours and find out what sort of work she does.'

He glanced at her sideways. 'Nothing better to do if you are not going to let me make love to you.'

Arian's pale eyebrows rose. 'And who told you those lies?' Her smile widened, and Eddie felt love rise within him like a tide. Arian was lovely and desirable, but she had a fine mind, too, and an ambitious streak that he found irresistible.

'Am I mistaken, then?' He pretended to leer at her. 'Am I going to get my wicked way with you, after all?'

'Perhaps,' Arian said softly, 'when it's not quite so sunny and bright.'

'We could always go into the dunes,' Eddie said. 'We'd be hidden from view there on the beach.'

'No thanks!' Arian spoke emphatically. 'I don't want the skin sanded off my backside.'

'*My* backside wouldn't mind a bit of sand,' Eddie said, the corners of his mouth twitching into a smile.

'Forget it,' Arian said, 'we're going to the workshop, remember?'

They walked along the edge of the shore, not touching but very close, and Eddie, glancing up at the blue skies of late summer, felt at peace. It was a lovely day, Arian was beside him; what more could he ask?

Eddie's first impression, when he saw Eline sitting on a stool near the bench which was littered with tools and off-cuts of leather, was that she was far too pale. She looked up and smiled as Arian entered the workshop.

'What are you doing here? I thought it was your day off.' She put down the boot she had been working on and straightened her back.

Eddie could see at once that she was not well; there were lines of strain at the corners of her eyes and mouth.

'I wanted Eddie's opinion on the boots we're making for Jessie Kennedy,' Arian said. 'Eddie was training to be a doctor – I think I told you about it – *and*,' she rambled on, 'he knows all about anatomy.'

'Not all,' Eddie protested wryly, 'just a little, perhaps enough to help with the construction of the boot.'

'I'd be glad of any help I can get,' Eline said. 'I know shoemaking but I can't quite make out how to support the little girl's leg without making the whole thing too constricting.'

Eddie looked down at the drawing at Eline's side and frowned. 'I don't think a boot made entirely of leather will work,' he offered diffidently. 'Perhaps some struts of iron along the side and then a double layer of leather around the calf would do it.'

342

'I thought of that,' Eline said, 'but I decided it wouldn't look very elegant.'

'It wouldn't,' Eddie agreed, with more confidence. 'But it would support the weak leg.'

'How about struts of iron covered with leather to make it look part of the design?' Eline asked, looking up at Eddie as though expecting him to have all the answers.

'That would work,' Eddie said. 'But how about getting the boot on and off?'

'I'd make a front opening,' Eline said, 'with buttons, just like any other boot.'

Eddie felt admiration growing for the dedication of the woman who had everything money could buy. She was a lady of title, living in the grandest manor house in the area, and yet she was concerning herself with the problems of a child whose parents would probably never clear their debt to her.

'The cost of the boots in materials and time might be prohibitive,' Eddie said.

Arian dug him rudely in the ribs. 'There's long words, then.' She lapsed into the Welsh accent that she used when teasing him and Eddie tugged at her long hair.

'Shut up, ignoramus,' he replied. Her eyes met his, and he knew that she had been impressed with his suggestions. It took a great deal to impress someone like Arian, and the sensation Eddie had was of swallowing too much wine, heady and confusing.

Eline looked up at them. 'Why don't you go and enjoy what's left of your day off?' She smiled. 'I think I've picked your brains enough for now, Eddie. Thanks so much for your interest.'

Suddenly, Eline swayed and would have fallen from the stool if Eddie had not stepped forward and caught her in his arms. He held her tilted forward, talking softly, in the professional manner of a doctor.

'Take it quietly, now, you're going to be all right, just a little dizzy, it's quite normal in your condition.'

343

'Condition?' Arian whispered, looking down at Eline in surprise. 'What are you talking about, Eddie?'

Eddie ignored her and rubbed Eline's wrists. 'It will pass. Just give it a moment, and then you'll begin to feel much better.'

After a moment, Eline looked up and, though she was still very pale, she was smiling. 'Thank you, again, Eddie.' Her voice was low. 'You've missed your vocation, haven't you? If anyone was meant to be a doctor, you were.'

'Come on,' Eddie said, 'we'll take you home. I think you've done enough work for today.'

'Yes, doctor,' Eline answered meekly. She looked at Arian. 'I should have told you before this; I didn't mean to upset you. I'm fine really, it's just that I'm going to have a baby.'

'Congratulations, I suppose,' Arian said softly, 'if it's what you want?' Arian was looking shrewdly at Eline.

Eddie saw Eline shrug. 'I wasn't prepared – it was a bit of a shock, but I'm sure I'll warm to the idea, given time.' She smiled, as though to soften her words, and yet Eddie felt she had serious reservations about her condition. In any case, that was her own business. His business was to get her home safely.

Stormhill Manor reminded Eddie of his old home on the outskirts of Cardiff. It was large and airy, with well-proportioned rooms and high ceilings, and the house had the advantage of spectacular views over the bay.

'It reminds me of my old home,' he said, and he felt Arian looking up at him in surprise. Eddie smiled. 'You don't know *everything* about me, madam,' he said to her.

Eline led the way through the broad entrance hall towards the sitting-room and Eddie opened the door for her. He was amused to see Arian still standing in the hallway, gazing in awe at the curved staircase and the huge landing above, with the brilliant stained-glass window casting a rainbow of colour over the carpets.

Calvin Temple was reading the paper, his feet stretched out before him. He rose hurriedly when he saw Eline. 'What is it?' he asked. 'What's wrong?'

'Nothing's wrong,' Eline said quickly. 'I just felt a little faint, what with the heat in the workshop and . . .'

Calvin led her to a chair. 'Come and sit down. I *told* you not to work in your condition.' His handsome face was anxious, and Eddie realized that Calvin Temple loved his wife very much. He warmed to the man as Calvin offered him his hand. 'I see, you brought my wife home. Thank you very much, both of you.'

'It was nothing,' Eddie said quickly. 'My pleasure.'

'No,' Calvin insisted, 'it was very kind of you.' He paused. 'Perhaps I could give you . . .'

'Eddie was going to be a doctor,' Eline interrupted swiftly, and Eddie hid a smile; Calvin had been about to offer him some money, a gesture that Eline felt would cause offence.

'He grew up in a house just like this one,' Eline continued. 'It was a shame, Eddie' – she turned to look at him – 'that you had to give up your training.'

'What happened?' Calvin asked, and Eddie could see he was genuinely interested.

Eddie shrugged. 'My father was improvident,' he said. 'He lost all his money, and the only way to settle his debts was to sell Brookland House. I had to forget my training in London and try to find work where I could. In the event, I came west, to Swansea, and now I'm labourer for Jamie O'Conner on Honey's Farm.'

Calvin studied him for a long moment. 'How would you like to resume your training?' he asked.

Eddie smiled. 'I would love it, if I had the money,' he said, 'but, as it is, I'm lucky to have a roof over my head.'

'What if I made you a loan?' Calvin said, turning to Eline for support. 'Don't you think it would be a good idea, darling?'

345

'I do,' Eline said at once. 'Eddie offered some sound advice on a special boot I was making. I'm sure his talents are wasted where he is now.'

'I agree,' Calvin said. 'Once you were earning, you could pay me back a little at a time; you doctor chaps earn a fair bit of money, I understand.'

'Eventually,' Eddie said, 'but it would take some time, years, in fact; and perhaps I would never be in a position to repay you.'

He could see Arian making faces at him, apparently urging him not to be such a fool. He ignored her.

'Look,' Calvin said briskly, 'I can afford to lose some money; this tax business, you know, helps me out really. I would be delighted if you would look on my proposal as a business venture on my part, one from which I hope to reap rewards once you are qualified.'

'It's kind of you, but it's out of the question,' Eddie said, smiling. 'It's taking too much of a risk, though I appreciate the offer, sir.'

Calvin inclined his head, and Eddie moved towards the door. 'I hope you'll soon be feeling better,' he said, and Eline smiled at him warmly.

'Goodbye, Eddie and thank you. See you in the morning, Arian; be at work bright and early, mind.'

Once outside, Arian clutched his arm. 'You're made up, my boy!' she said. 'You're on your way to being a doctor. Congratulations!'

Eddie smiled down at her in amusement. 'Didn't you hear me refusing Lord Temple's offer?' he said.

She laughed up at him. 'I heard, but you must think again. You owe it to the ordinary people out there to become a doctor; you're needed, don't you understand? Promise you'll think about it.'

'I promise I'll think about it.' He tugged at her hair, and she pulled away, poking out her tongue at him. She ran along the street and Eddie chased after her, watching as the wind caught her skirts, lifting them to reveal a shapely pair of ankles. All thoughts of Calvin Temple's offer were erased from his mind.

Arian was proved right and, once the money was at his disposal, Eddie knew, deep within himself, that he would take the opportunity presented to him and take it thankfully. And if it meant taking the rest of his life to pay Calvin Temple back, then so be it.

CHAPTER TWENTY-EIGHT

Arian missed Eddie; she didn't deny it. She missed his intelligence, his dry humour and, most of all, she recognized wryly, she missed his passion.

He had gone to London, after much persuasion on her part and string-pulling by the indomitable Lord Temple, and had resumed his training in a big teaching hospital somewhere in the city.

Eddie had attempted to persuade Arian to go with him; he had held her in his arms, his mouth close to hers, and begged her softly, with love in his eyes, to go with him, as his wife. Two, he said, could live easily on the generous allowance put at his disposal.

Arian appreciated the honour he did her and would have accepted the difficulties readily; but she had envisaged endless days spent in some faceless boarding house while she waited for Eddie to spare her a little time from his work. That, she had told him firmly, was not for her.

'But you could learn more about shoemaking' – he'd held her closer, his taut, strong body against her offering a potent inducement – 'with the extra experience you would gain from working in London you could come back and take up a high position in Eline Temple's scheme of things.'

She had touched his face lightly. 'Eddie' – she'd spoken softly but emphatically – 'I'm not the do-gooder you seem to think me. I'm a young girl out to suit herself in life, that's all.'

He had made love to her then, with great tenderness and a feeling of saying goodbye for ever. It had been good, very good, a memory that Arian treasured; but it was not the love of a lifetime, and the sooner Eddie realized that, the better.

Arian looked up. The workshop had been extended; new, more efficient machines, recently acquired, had been placed in the room at the back – a room full of inhuman monsters that seemed to dominate the building with their noise. Even now they clattered busily, a strange, unreal sound but one that, strangely, pleased Arian, gave her a sense of power.

In the workshop itself, a small staff of three lady cordwainers and four cobblers worked easily, talking to each other over the noise of the machines as busy hands shaped and cut and fashioned the shoes that Eline Temple had designed. Some of them were making remedial footwear, but many of the shoes Eline was producing now were new and innovative designs, eye-catching and lovely. The patterns, when translated into leather, would hit a market ripe for change, and Eline would become even more rich and famous.

The door opened from the street and Arian sat up straighter as one of the new young cobblers entered the workshop. He paused, the light behind him emphasizing his broad shoulders and slim hips; and her eyes kindled.

Price Davies was a beefy, handsome young man, with more brawn than brains but with a fall of dark, straight hair across his brow and incredibly bright blue eyes. And, as if his looks weren't attraction enough, he was an extremely talented shoemaker.

'Got the leather we wanted,' he said. 'Good stuff, last us a couple of weeks.' He was no silver-tongued charmer, not up to Eddie's standards when it came to conversation and quick repartee; but he had other attributes, Arian thought with a wry twist to her lips.

She nodded to him and indicated that he should come closer to the workbench. 'I want to know how to choose good leather,' she said bluntly. 'Seeing as Eline has put me in charge, I need to know all about the job of shoemaking. I'd like you to teach me all you know, Price.'

He rested his hand on her shoulder. It was hot through the material of her bodice; he had read more into her words than she'd intended him to. She looked up at him, frowning but without a word.

Swiftly, he removed his hand. '*Duw*, Arian, the way you look at a man is enough to freeze the balls off him.'

' "Miss Smale" to you,' she said, 'and we can do without vulgarities, if you please.'

He was open-mouthed at the reproach, and suddenly Arian smiled with all the charm she could muster. 'Come on, Price, show me how skilful your hands can be; show me how to feel and judge the leather the way you do.'

He rubbed his hand through his hair. 'You got me beat, Arian . . . Miss Smale. I don't know what to make of you.'

She was well pleased; that's exactly what she had intended. While she might consider having fun with him out of hours, in work he would treat her with respect.

She followed him outside to the store room, and the smell of new leather swept over her. It seemed, as always, to bring her a sense of excitement. She knew, in her bones, that this was going to be her life from now on; she would make it her business to know everything about leather, from choosing the best, to cutting and shaping, moulding and stitching. She was greedy for knowledge.

'See' – Price took up a piece of leather – 'when you buy it first off from the tanner, it stinks to high heaven. But it's then you'll spot the best stuff; it must be firm, but not too unyielding, and don't touch any stuff that's ragged on the edges.'

He became engrossed in his appraisal of the leather, and Arian listened intently, drinking in the knowledge that it had taken Price five years to assimilate.

She found him, in that moment, incredibly attractive;

she admired his expertise, wanted to graft it from his mind to her own.

He seemed to sense her feelings, because he stopped talking and looked up at her. 'Arian . . .' His voice trailed away, but the desire in his eyes was unmistakable.

'No,' she said flatly, and then she smiled again. 'Later, maybe.'

And maybe not, she added silently; but for now, she chose to humour Price, she needed his knowledge, she thirsted for it. She was using him shamelessly, she was aware of that; but then men were so gullible. Tempt them, as Eve did Adam, and they would give you the earth.

'Go on,' she said. 'Tell me more about the leather; I want to know it all.'

And she did; she would learn the business from the workshop floor to the management of the books and the running of the finances. And, she promised herself, she would be independent; she would not be subjugated to any man, not now, not ever.

Arian shuddered as she thought of her father, of his beatings when he was in drink. She remembered with a sense of horror the moment in the farmhouse when her father had cold-bloodedly shot Eddie. She had battled with her father then for the last time, and the cold metal between them had spat fire and her father had died. It was like a nightmare that would never completely go away. No, Arian would trust no man, depend on no man; she would be alone, and alone she would succeed beyond her wildest dreams.

She clenched her hands into fists. She would make it happen; she would shape her own future, and no man would stand in her way. So she smiled at Price Davies even while her mind was fixed on the goal that was ahead; and in that moment she had invited the very thing she vowed never to endure again, the violence of a man.

★　　★　　★

351

Fon was perplexed and very relieved. In spite of Jamie's efforts to make her with child, there was still no baby on the way. Her mouth curved into a smile; the trying was good – the loving that Jamie showered on her was the very breath of life to her.

She loved him more with each passing day, and yet sometimes, like now, she felt a sense of guilt wash over her. Was it her fault that no baby came from their love-making? Was her reluctance to be a mother not smothered, as she'd thought; was it preventing the very thing that Jamie most desired?

She stood in the window and looked out at the land spread out before her, O'Conner land, Jamie's land. Mists rose from the damp morning grass, swirling upwards in delicate drifts. Out there, somewhere in the morning air, was her husband, lifting the late potatoes; and alongside him, Tommy and the new boy, Cliff, who had come to replace Eddie.

Fon thought of Eddie with warmth. She was glad for him, glad that he was to finish his training as a doctor. After all, his talent had been wasted on the farm. And yet his presence had been reassuring; he was thoughtful, intelligent and had proved a companion for Jamie.

'Can I have some pencils, Fon, and some paper? I want to show Patrick how to write his name.'

April stared up at Fon with large eyes, her thick dark hair hanging around her face in wild curls. She was going to be a beauty when she grew up.

Fon smiled at her affectionately. 'There's a soft question,' she teased. 'Of course you can have pencils, and there's some paper in my drawer. Go on, you get it, there's a good girl.'

Fon watched as April opened the drawer and took out the paper, caressing it, almost as though it was a thing of beauty. April loved writing and spent a great deal of her time showing Patrick how to form his letters.

Fon sighed. April really should be going to school; she

352

must see about it, it was only proper. The girl was intelligent; her usual belligerence had given way now to an attitude that could almost be described as amenable. Schooling would suit April; in any case, it was what Mrs Jones would have probably wanted for her daughter had she been well enough to deal with the child herself.

Fon looked through the window again. Soon, the sun would take away the mists, the land would warm, and then she and the children would go out and help with the potato picking.

The children. The phrase rang in her ears; what would she feel like when she had her own brood around her? Would she be happy and fulfilled, or would she feel that her happiness with Jamie was being threatened?

She was about to move away from the window when she saw a horse and rider coming along the rutted track towards the farmyard. Fon grew tense; even since the day that Bob Smale had arrived at the farmhouse intent on his thirst for blood, she had feared strangers.

Constantly on her mind was the knowledge that out there, somewhere, was Mike the Spud. He might never bother them again, but the man was unpredictable, a thug with little intelligence. Fon glanced towards the rifle, kept always by the door, and she shuddered.

She often thought of the moment when Eddie had been shot, when Arian had struggled with her father for possession of the rifle and it had gone off, killing Bob Smale. Awful as the thought was, if Mike, Bob's brother, ever came to the farmhouse seeking revenge, it might be necessary for Fon to use the gun; and the thought frightened her.

The rider came nearer, and she saw it was a young man, straight and tall in the saddle, and she relaxed as she saw the white collar of the priest.

He reined the horse near the railings of the yard and swung himself down with the ease of practice. He doffed his hat as Fon opened the door to him.

353

'Morning, Father,' Fon said, smiling a greeting and wondering if this was a social call or if the priest had any business with Jamie.

But it was Tommy he'd come to see. 'It's bad news, Mrs O'Conner,' he said, standing in the warm kitchen, his ruffled hair giving him an impossibly young appearance.

Fon knew instinctively that he must be new to the position, and she smiled encouragingly. 'I'll send April to the fields to fetch him.' She glanced at the small girl, who was engrossed in her writing, head bent over the paper, oblivious even to Patrick's busy chatter.

'April is Tommy's sister,' she said warningly. The priest inclined his head and waited in silence until Fon had spoken to April, asking her to fetch Tommy in from the fields.

'Take Patrick with you, April, there's a love,' Fon said encouragingly and April studied the priest, her expression solemn.

'It's about Mammy, isn't it?' she asked, and before the priest could answer, she had grasped Patrick's willing hand and urged him outside.

'The child is quite right,' the priest said softly. 'I'm Father Murphy, and it is about Mrs Jones – God rest her soul – that I have come.'

Fon, not being Catholic, was at a loss how to treat the priest. She indicated a chair uncertainly.

'Would you like to sit, Father Murphy? Have a drink of tea with us, I'm sure you're tired after your ride.'

He took a seat and smiled up at her. 'I'd love a cup of tea and with lots of honey, if I may. I have a good thirst on me this morning, and I've been up all night, you see.'

Fon pushed the kettle on to the flames and busied herself in silence, warming the pot and carefully spooning in just enough tea leaves to make a decent brew. 'I know it's none of my business, but Mrs Jones – she's

354

'. . . she's . . .' Fon's words trailed away as the priest nodded.

'Aye, she slipped away into the night, poor lady. A brave woman, was Mrs Jones, and her not wanting her son to see her *in extremis*.'

Fon poured the tea and sat opposite the priest. 'And now you have the awful job of telling Tommy the bad news,' she said sympathetically.

'That's part of my duties,' he agreed. 'Is Tommy likely to take it badly?'

'He's a sensible boy,' Fon said hesitantly. 'I think it will upset him, of course it will; but he is very stoic, very brave, just like his mother.

'April, though' – Fon bit her lip – 'I'm not so sure about her; she's only a child, and she *was* very close to her mother. She seems to know what's happened, but she's acting so calmly, I worry about her.'

'Children are often the most resilient of folks,' the priest said. 'They have acceptance, which is just what is needed right now.'

It was about half an hour before Tommy came in from the fields, and Fon saw that April was lingering with Patrick outside in the yard, reluctant to come indoors. The sun was brighter, now, dispelling the last of the morning mists; it was a lovely day but one that was to be for ever a painful memory for both Tommy and April.

When Tommy saw the priest he made the sign of the cross and stood head bent, waiting for the father to speak.

'I'm sorry, Tommy.' Father Murphy's voice was kind. 'It's bad news about your mam.'

'I know,' Tommy said. 'I guessed that, Father.' He was suddenly pale and Fon went to his side and instinctively put her arm around his shoulder.

'She passed over in her sleep, Tommy,' the father continued. 'Peaceful it was, at the end; you can be sure of that, for I was with her to the last.'

355

'She knew it was coming,' Tommy said slowly. 'She didn't want me to see her sick and ill.' He swallowed painfully. 'I'm glad she went peaceful-like.'

He turned beseechingly to Fon. 'You'll tell April, won't you? It would come better from you – begging your pardon, Father,' he added quickly.

'Yes, of course I'll tell her,' Fon said reassuringly, though she was quite sure the girl knew already.

'You'll come down to town for the funeral, of course?' the father said softly.

Tommy nodded. 'Aye, I'll pay my last respects to Mam.' His voice broke, and he moved towards the door. 'If you'll excuse me, Father, I'll go outdoors, be by myself for a bit.'

'Go with God, Tommy.' The father nodded and watched as the gangling youth moved away across the farmyard, stopping only to ruffle his sister's dark hair before loping away across the fields.

The father sighed heavily. His eyes met Fon's, and he smiled suddenly, a wan, rueful smile. 'First time I've had to do that,' he said, and Fon lifted the teapot from the hob.

'Well, you'd never have thought it, Father. Another cup of tea?' She paused, silent for a moment, and when the father was drinking thirstily, she looked across the table at him.

'I want your advice about April, Father,' she said softly. 'I think it's time the girl went to school.'

Telling April that her mother was dead was more difficult than Fon had anticipated. She spoke haltingly, not knowing much about the Catholic faith, but trying to instil some sort of hope in the child that some day she would see her mother again.

'I knew Mammy was dead,' April said when Fon's voice had trailed into silence. 'I knew as soon as I saw the priest.'

Her composure was staggering, and Fon realized that

356

April had probably cried her tears alone at night in her bed; the thought was painful, and on an impulse she reached out and hugged the child.

'Don't be sad for me,' April said, her arms around Fon's neck. 'I know Mammy wanted to go; she was hurting, and I'm glad she'll be hurting no more. But, Fon, I don't want to go to the funeral. You won't make me go, will you?'

'Of course I won't make you go,' Fon said stoutly. 'You will stay by here with me. You'll always be with me and Jamie and Patrick; you're part of our family now, aren't you?'

It was then that April began to cry, large gulping sobs that shook the thin frame. Tears of pity formed in Fon's own eyes.

'I'll look after you, my lovely, don't you ever doubt it,' Fon said, and it was as though she was making a vow before God, a vow which Fon knew she would simply have to honour, whatever it cost her.

Arian sat on the bed in the new rooms Eline had provided for her. The boarding house was respectable, set along the sea front in Swansea, a large dwelling house with seven lady boarders. Men were not encouraged over the threshold, and that suited Arian; it gave her an excuse to keep the eager Price at arm's length.

And yet Price had taught her a great deal. She knew the difference now between properly cured leather and shoddy workmanship. She had entered the stinking world of the tanneries without blanching and in total ignorance; but now she felt that, at last, she was coming to grips with the whole business of shoe-making.

She glanced in the mirror, adjusting her bonnet. She intended going for a stroll along the sea front, and the damp, misty air would curl her hair into a fuzz of ringlets. She jammed the unfashionable bonnet over her hair

357

impatiently and frowned at her reflection; how she hated to conform.

But, God, did she love the shoe business; the workshop was somewhere she could be herself, without having to act the simpering miss. The only part of the leather world she didn't like was the business side, the interviews with prospective buyers, the dressing up. She was used to riding bare-headed and bare-backed over the fields, used to dressing in loose skirts with no undergarments to hamper her movements. Now she was pushed into stays and buttoned into tight bodices, and the fact that she had chosen to act like a lady did not lessen her sense of discomfort.

The hallway was redolent with the smell of beeswax; the wooden banisters shone with much diligent cleaning. The soft light from the gas lamp washed down on the faded carpet, giving it a gentility that was only an illusion. Still, Mrs Maitland provided a good table, she made sure the bed linen was clean, and, though treating the young ladies in her house as children, she was none the less a sensible, dependable landlady.

Arian let herself out into the street. It was quite warm, in spite of the thin mist coming in off the sea, and she took a deep breath of the salt air. She walked briskly past the Bay View hotel and heard the sound of voices singing inside with a feeling of being an outsider, looking in on the world.

She *was* alone; she had no-one now that Eddie had gone away, no-one to care if she lived or died. Eddie, maybe, *had* cared, but then he was in London, completing his training. His life was mapped out for him now, and it did not include her.

She pondered on her family; the only one remaining was Uncle Mike, Mike the Spud, as he was known locally. She made a wry grimace; Mike wouldn't give a damn for her well-being. In all probability he blamed her for her father's death.

'Arian!' The voice jolted her thoughts back to the present. Arian saw the misty seashore, the ghostly image of a sail, and, standing before her, the tall, masculine figure of Price Davies. She smiled with more warmth than usual, her feeling of being disembodied from the world disappearing under his admiring gaze.

'What are you doing here?' Arian asked. 'It isn't your day off, is it?'

'No, boss,' he said laughingly, 'but I was told to make some deliveries and then go home, so that's where I'm going. Come with me?'

Warning bells rang in Arian's mind. It was dangerous to be alone with a man like Price; he was filled with energy, his blue eyes even now appraising her.

And yet the thought of walking on alone, or returning to the boarding house, did not appeal to her. 'Who'll be there?' she asked cautiously, and he smiled.

'Well, my brother and sister-in-law, for a start, and probably their brood of kids: should be enough to chaperon even Helen of Troy, don't you think?'

She felt silly then, as though she was setting herself up as the most desirable woman in town. 'I'll come home with you,' she said, 'on condition that you make me a nice hot cup of tea.'

'Done.' He pulled her arm through his, and Arian, feeling a little self-conscious, walked along the narrow road from the beach into the back streets of the town.

The house where Price lived was typical of the buildings sprawling through narrow courts and cobbled roadways. Ragged children played in the streets, and the smell of rotting garbage pervaded the air.

It was all a far cry from the green fields and open countryside where Arian was brought up, and she could think of nothing worse than to have to spend her life in the poor streets bordering the town.

'Not quite what you are used to, I'm afraid,' Price

359

said, but he was smiling, in no way apologizing, and Arian liked him for that.

'Well, I grew up in the countryside above the town,' she explained. 'I don't suppose I'll ever get used to busy, crowded streets such as these.'

The house was spotless inside, the furniture well polished, the floors swept and scrubbed. There was a smell of cleanliness about the place, and Arian felt a respect for Price's sister-in-law.

'By the way, where's your family?' she asked, as the silence penetrated into her consciousness.

'Come upstairs,' Price said, and before Arian could protest he had taken her arm and was propelling her upwards.

It was only when she found herself in his bedroom that Arian realized how gullible she'd been.

'Your family are not here.' It was a statement, not a fact. 'You fooled me, Price, you damn well fooled me.'

'And you knew it,' he said, laughing. 'Come on, you've wanted me as much as I've wanted you. Don't think I haven't noticed you looking me over as if I was a prize stallion in a show.'

She felt her colour rise; she couldn't deny it. 'I thought you were going to make me a cup of tea?' She tried changing the subject, but he wasn't having any.

'Later,' he said. 'But now just get your clothes off.' His hands were on the buckle of his belt. 'Let's get down to business. That's what we're here for, we both know that, so let's not have any beating about the bush, is it?'

Arian shook her head. 'I don't want . . .' she began, but in a moment she felt her arms held in a steely grip.

'Don't play with me, Arian,' he said warningly. 'Or is it that you like a bit of rough stuff, is that it?'

'No!' she said, deciding to play along with him. 'I like to be treated like a lady, that's what I like. I thought you'd be more romantic in your approach, Price, that you'd show more finesse.'

'Oh, finesse, is it? Well, pardon me. I'm a man, not a ruddy fop.' He snatched at the buttons of her bodice and roughly pulled at the cloth, sending a button flying to the floor.

'Damnation!' He cursed when he saw the corset laced around her like an armour. 'Are you going to take it off?'

She put her arms around his neck and breathed heavily, an idea of how to ward him off springing into her mind. 'Get me a knife,' she said softly. 'I'm going to cut the laces, otherwise we'll be here all day.'

He drew a knife from his boot and, to her chagrin, began cutting through the laces himself. After a few seconds, the corset fell from her and her breasts were free.

'That's better.' He stood back, looking down at her. 'Very nice, very nice indeed.' He breathed. 'You're better-looking even than I'd imagined.'

She fell back on the bed. 'Come on, then,' she urged. 'Take my skirts off for me; you might as well finish what you've started.'

She watched as he placed the knife back in his boot and pulled at her petticoats. She would make a pretence, she thought, of caressing him, and then, when she had a chance, she would take the knife and show him just where he stood with her.

He fell upon her then with such ferocity that the breath was knocked from her body. She tried to reach down, to grasp at the knife, but he was ruthless, forcing her back on the bed, his mouth pushing at hers, his tongue probing.

She tried to twist away; she heard her petticoats tear; his arm was across her throat, holding her down. She felt her eyes begin to mist, she could scarcely breathe.

There was no time for thought, or action, he was forcing himself upon her defenceless body, plunging, bruising, violating her without mercy. She gasped with the pain and indignity of it all, her mind refusing to

361

believe what this monster was doing to her. She tried to struggle away from him as one of his hands bruised her breast. She managed to get her arm up and to pull at his hair, but he reared above her and lunged at her, a demonic glow in his eyes.

His hand caught and held her arms in a cruel grip as she would have pushed him from her. 'Don't pretend you are not enjoying it,' he gasped, increasing the power of his movements so that she cried out in agony.

Outrage filled her, rising like a tide of blood to her head so that she wanted to kill him. She wanted to be free of this torture that he was inflicting on her, but she could do nothing except endure the brutality that seemed to go on endlessly. But at last he fell away from her, his clothing in disarray around him. His mouth was twisted in a grin of triumph as he turned his head to look at her.

'Give me a minute,' he said, 'and I'll give you the treat of your life. I'll show you things you never dreamed of. I'll make a real woman of you before you leave here tonight, and you'll be begging me for it.'

She was on her feet in a moment. She had the knife in her hand, poised above his heart. Her arm plunged downwards, and he moved sharply, crying out in surprise at her action.

The knife grazed his arm and drew blood. She plunged again and it caught his wrist, held up in defence. Again she lifted the knife, and it sliced his cheek from eyebrow to chin.

'You bitch!' he cried. 'I'll swing for you!' He was up from the bed then, his powerful cobbler's hands gripping her throat. She felt a blackness spin around her; breathing was impossible, and then she fell into a dark, merciful oblivion.

CHAPTER TWENTY-NINE

Fon watched as April curled up in an armchair, her nose buried in a book. The little girl was engrossed in the story, and Fon marvelled that, without any schooling, April was so bright and intelligent, so clever at her letters and figures.

'Who taught you to read, April?' Fon asked, putting down her sewing and staring across at the girl.

April looked up at her with sombre eyes. 'My mammy showed me letters and numbers when I was little,' she said, with dignity. 'Mammy came from a rich family, mind, but she married beneath her.' She frowned. 'At least, that's what my posh grandmother used to say. What's "beneath her" mean, Fon?'

If Fon was surprised at the revelation that Mrs Jones had been born of a 'posh' mother, she concealed it well. 'It means that your gran thought your father wasn't good enough,' she said gently, 'but lots of mothers think that, it's quite natural really.'

'Gran ran the big house for the priests,' April said. 'Mammy used to take me there when I was only a baby. The priests taught Mammy to read and write and she taught me.'

She chewed her nail thoughtfully. 'I don't suppose Gran was posh really, but she talked nice, all English-like. I don't remember Grandad at all. A sailor he was, so Mam said. Never came home one day, and that was that; Gran had to go out to work to keep her family.'

'So your mother married a farmer,' Fon said, smiling, 'and came to live up on the hill. That's where you were born, April, a real little country girl.'

April studied Fon for a moment, as if suddenly seeing her as a person for the first time. 'Are you a country girl, Fon?' she asked, her head on one side.

Fon laughed. 'Oh, no, far from it. I was born Irfonwy Parks, down in Oystermouth, alongside the sea. I used to sort out the oysters, put the little ones on perches to grow, and take the rest for market.'

'That sounds lovely,' April said wistfully. 'I'd like to see Oystermouth.'

'I'll take you there,' Fon said, 'one day when we're not too busy on the farm. You can meet my family, then, my mam and my sister Sal – they're all I've got left now.'

April put down her book and rushed across the floor to hug Fon. 'You've got me,' she said, holding Fon tightly around the neck, her small cheek soft against Fon's.

'Hey, don't choke me, then,' Fon laughed. 'Of course I've got you, and Patrick and Jamie.'

'And my brother Tommy,' April added conscientiously. 'You've got a lot of us to love you.'

'Quite right.' Jamie swung in through the door, bringing with him a hint of mist and rain. 'Lots of us love our Fonny, don't we, April?'

He kissed the little girl on top of her dark curls and then bent and kissed Fon's mouth.

'Ugh!' Fon said, grimacing. 'You smell like a beer barrel.'

'Well,' Jamie sat in the chair near the fire and stretched his long legs before him. 'Me and Tommy been out to the public; the boy needed a bit of diversion.'

'I suppose so,' Fon said softly. It was only a few weeks since his mother had been buried in the windswept cemetery at Dan y Graig, and Tommy was bound to be feeling a little lost.

'I saw the priest in town,' Jamie said. 'He was talking about you, April; he said you should be going to school any day now.' He winked at her. 'St David's has a place for you where you can learn to be a scholar.'

'She's a scholar now,' Fon said. 'But I think it's high time you went to school, April; you're a clever girl and I don't want you to grow up at a disadvantage.'

April's eyes widened. 'I *want* to go to school,' she said, positively, 'then I can be a teacher, or perhaps even a nun.'

Jamie laughed. 'I wouldn't think that far ahead yet, madam. Let yourself live a little before you even consider shutting yourself away in a convent.'

'She has plenty of time,' Fon said gently, 'and April can be anything she wants. She has a very sharp mind.'

Jamie leant back and closed his eyes. 'And your husband has a very great appetite,' he said lazily, a playful edge to his voice. 'But I don't suppose I'm going to get any supper.'

'There's cold meat and some crusty bread in the pantry,' Fon said, trying not to laugh. 'Now Patrick's in bed I've got a chance to mend his clothes, and you are big enough to see to your own supper.'

'I'll do it,' April said eagerly, and with a shy glance at Jamie she busied herself in the kitchen, clattering dishes with more gusto than finesse.

Fon looked after her thoughtfully. April was growing up, she admired Jamie, wanted his approbation; and he wasn't a bad figurehead to fuel a young girl's future dreams.

Eventually, April emerged from the kitchen, bringing with her the half-cut loaf and a dish of butter. Balanced precariously on her arm was a plate of beef and a small cut of salted pork. She placed them proudly on the table with an air of having produced a fine meal.

'Do you want a bit of the beef, or would you rather the last bit of pork, Jamie?'

She sounded so grown-up and serious that Jamie winked covertly at Fon and leant forward thoughtfully.

'Let me see now. The beef, I think; it looks good and lean, and I could just manage it, with a bit of home-made pickle to go with it.'

April hacked at the beef inexpertly, and Jamie rose and guided her hand, showing her how to slice the meat thinly and neatly.

'Perhaps you are going to be a cook and look after a big house like your gran,' Fon said playfully.

April shook back her dark hair. 'No fear! I'd rather read and write any day than stand in a hot kitchen cooking.'

Fon sighed. 'I know how you feel, April.' The light was fading and her eyes were tired. Fon put down Patrick's half-mended trousers and rubbed at her face.

'Tired, colleen?' Jamie asked softly, his hand resting for a moment on her shoulder.

Fon put her hand over his and smiled up at him. 'Not *too* tired,' she said, her mouth twitching into a smile. 'But I have had enough of sewing for tonight. That boy of ours is always tearing his trousers; I don't know what he gets up to half the time.'

'He needs a hoard of little brothers to play with,' Jamie said, 'keep the rip quiet.'

'He's got me,' April said stoutly as she carried the plate of food to Jamie. 'But then, if I'm to go to school, he *will* need some brothers and sisters. What do *you* think, Fon?'

'I'll do my best to oblige,' Fon said, and yet a cold hand of fear gripped her. She was afraid of the pain, afraid of being big and ugly, and most of all afraid of the responsibility of bringing up a baby of her own.

Jamie's hand touched her cheek. It was as though he'd read something of her thoughts. 'Plenty of time, colleen,' he said, reassuringly. 'You are only a little bit of a thing yourself, yet; and you'll know when you're truly ready.'

She smiled up at him gratefully even as she wondered what was wrong with her. When had this strange fear

366

begun to manifest itself, or had she always, secretly, been afraid?

She well remembered her wedding night; she'd been afraid then, too. Jamie had been loving and patient, and her fears had slowly been dispelled, to be replaced with the passion that seared her whenever she was in her husband's arms.

But childbearing was something different; a new being might come between Jamie and her, spoil the closeness they had come to enjoy.

She caught Jamie's hand and held it to her lips. Nothing must ever come between them, she thought fiercely – nothing.

The mists were slowly clearing from her mind. The darkness was rolling away, and Arian found she was staring up at a barn-like ceiling that loomed above her like a menacing, shadowy barrier between herself and the open sky.

She heard the hooting of a tug and then, as her ears became accustomed to the nearby sounds, she recognized the wash of the waves against the stone sea wall. She was, she guessed, in a warehouse on the docks, and, from the rancid smell, the stock around her was composed of animal skins.

She tried to sit up and realized that she ached from head to foot. Her throat was constricted, and she put up her hand to feel the weals embedded in her soft skin.

She pushed herself upright against a stack of boxes and saw that she was half-naked, her clothes hanging round her in shreds; and the memory of what had happened swamped her mind.

She felt a moment of pure hatred for the man who had violated her. Her hands clenched into fists, and her nails cut into the soft skin of her palms.

It took several moments for her to climb to her feet, holding on to the boxes and forcing herself up. She felt ashamed of what had happened, appalled at her own foolishness in being alone with Price Davies, a man she had known, deep within her, could be dangerous.

Her body burned with pain and humiliation. She felt bruised and battered and knew with deep bitterness she had only herself to blame. Perhaps the worst insult of all was that the coward had used her and then dumped her like a sack of potatoes, to face God only knew what fate at the dockside.

After a moment, she drew her tattered skirt around her and tied the edges together so that at least she was decently covered. Somehow she must make her way home, hide herself away until her wounds were healed.

Price would not get away with what he had done; but she would take her revenge in her own way and in her own good time. No-one else would ever know what had happened to her tonight.

The journey through the docklands was a nightmare. Once she was stopped by a drunken sailor and offered a handful of coins for a cheap stand-up. She stood her ground, staring at him with such hatred that after a moment the sailor had put his money away, appalled by her ferocious, almost deranged appearance.

How she reached her lodgings without being seen was a miracle, but at last Arian was safely indoors, the door locked and bolted behind her.

The first thing she had to do was to wash away all the dirt and the shame she felt at Price's treatment of her. She knew she would never cleanse herself of the feeling of being used, half-killed just to satisfy a man's lust.

The huge bath was a monument of luxury, an indication of the richness her employer had brought into Arian's life. Eline Temple, along with her husband, owned half the county, and she wasn't mean to those who worked for her.

She had been kind and thoughtful, finding Arian accommodation with just the right kind of genteel respectability and with a good landlady in the person of Mrs Maitland to chaperon and care for her boarders.

The disaster that had befallen Arian had been of her own making, brought about by her foolishness in consorting with a man she didn't trust.

It was a luxury to lie in the warm water, feeling the smell and the touch of Price Davies washing away from her. Arian looked down at her body in dismay; she was covered in bruises that were slowly turning black. Her throat ached; but, as she felt her face gingerly with her fingertips, she came to the conclusion that there was no bruising to her eyes or nose. He had spared her that at least.

Later she lay in bed, wide-eyed, reliving the nightmare of the past hours, the violence of the rape, the awakening in the dark womb of a warehouse on the docks, the painful walk back to her lodgings. She vowed to punish Price even if it took the rest of her life.

Arian returned to work the next day. In her belt was a sharp-bladed knife. As she walked into the shop, she was acutely conscious of Price standing at the bench, one foot raised on a stool as he worked.

'Morning,' he said softly, and there was a hint of menace in his voice. 'I see you found your way home, then; I knew you would.' His mouth curled. 'Sluts usually do.'

'You have a bad problem; you have made an enemy of me,' she said, anger pouring through her like wine. 'I tell you this, you come near me again and I'll kill you. I mean it.'

His eyes glinted. 'You enjoyed it as much as I did,' he said. 'It was only your foolishness in attacking me that spoiled a perfectly good rogering.'

She was incredulous. She stared at his eyes, and saw that Price really believed what he was saying.

'I'm more than capable of killing,' she said coldly. 'I shot my own father at point-blank range, so I wouldn't

369

hesitate to get rid of scum like you.' It wasn't quite an accurate account of what had happened that awful night at Honey's Farm, but Arian hoped it would be enough to put the fear of God into Price.

It did no such thing. 'Tut, tut, temper.' He seemed unmoved by her revelation; perhaps he did not even believe her.

She turned away. Well, let him lay a finger on her again, and he would learn the truth.

Arian did not look at him after that; not once during the morning did she show even by a flicker of an eyelash that she was aware of his presence like a threat, hanging over her. She worked diligently on the built-up shoe she was making for a four-year-old child, trying to push all thoughts of Price Davies from her consciousness.

Eline came into the workroom and paused beside Arian, head on one side, a shawl draped about her shoulders and swamping her thickened waistline.

'You're looking peaky, Arian,' she said in concern. 'Are you sure you should be in work?'

'My throat' – Arian heard the croak in her voice with dismay – 'it's a little bit sore, but I'm feeling all right, really I am.'

'I think perhaps you should take the rest of the day off,' Eline said quickly. 'I don't want you going down with a fever.'

'I'll take Arian back to her lodgings,' Price said, his voice casual.

Arian met his eyes, hoping he would take the venom in hers as a warning. 'No,' she said. 'I don't want anyone to walk me home, thank you. I can manage quite well on my own.'

'It's no trouble.'

Price's brazenness amazed Arian. Anger and disbelief at the man's attitude warred within her, and for a moment she was at a loss for words.

'No,' she said flatly at last, and Price shrugged and returned to his bench.

Eline accompanied her to the door. 'Is anything wrong?' she asked, quietly. 'Has Price Davies been pestering you with his attentions?'

Eline was an astute woman, and Arian recognized that she would have to tread carefully if she was not to give away too much.

'I just don't like him very much,' she said, in a low, hoarse voice. 'I'd rather not have him too close to me.'

'I thought you were getting on rather well,' Eline said. 'Perhaps his . . . his attempts to begin more than a working relationship are an embarrassment to you?'

'Yes,' Arian agreed. 'That's it. I don't want any involvements, not at the moment.'

'Well, take a couple of days off,' Eline said. 'Give yourself a chance to get over your – your sore throat. Then come back to work when you feel ready. And remember, Arian' – her voice was low – 'you have the power to hire and fire whom you choose.'

It was clear Eline suspected there was more under the surface than Arian was prepared to reveal, but she was not a woman to pry.

'That's quite all right,' Arian said. 'I don't want to go home, but I'll bear in mind what you've said.'

And she would; the thought of getting rid of Price Davies was the only thing that would keep her sane. Too long spent on her own, thinking of the revenge she would like to exact on Price, would drive her mad.

It was a few days later that Eline approached Arian and invited her into her private sitting-room. Arian was prepared for the worst, a grilling about Price, a demand for an explanation as to why the workforce was not in harmony any longer, for the cordwainers had become aware of the tension.

'Please sit down,' Eline said. Arian obediently sat on

371

one of the soft upholstered chairs that graced the sitting-room.

Eline sank thankfully into a chair and, not for the first time, Arian noticed that she was looking pale and tired. The shawl she continually hugged around her had fallen open, revealing Eline's swollen figure.

'I'm going to take time off soon,' Eline said. 'I need to rest before the baby is born.' She seemed sad rather than elated, her eyes shadowed, her mouth etched with lines of weariness.

'I'm sorry,' Arian said quickly. 'I don't think I realized how far along you are – I mean the baby – it will be born soon?'

'Quite soon,' Eline agreed, 'and in my absence I want you to take complete and sole charge of the workshop and the other workers.'

She smiled, and her features softened. 'You are young, but already you have an air of authority, and you know how to manage people. You are quick to learn, and I want you to have your chance to rise to the top of the cordwaining profession. There will be a substantial rise, of course, and a house and staff of your own.'

Arian felt elated. This was something she had not imagined in her wildest dreams. 'I'm honoured,' she said quickly, 'if you really think I can do it.'

'I do, or I wouldn't be offering,' Eline said firmly. 'Now, one thing, what's really happened between you and Price? Is there a problem?'

Arian looked at Eline thoughtfully. 'Yes, I'll admit there is a problem, but one I'd much rather deal with myself.'

Eline seemed to relax. 'I hoped you'd say that.' She smiled. 'That's the stuff good managers are made of.' She pointed to the desk. 'Now, I think I should show you all the account books. You must see what we are owed by our various customers. You will be responsible

372

for keeping the records of what is paid into the club each week.'

'Not enough is paid in, that much is obvious to me,' Arian said quickly.

Eline returned her smile. 'No, not enough,' she agreed, 'but the object isn't really to make money.'

'I realize that,' Arian said. 'The object, as I see it, is to provide shoes for those who can't really afford them while letting them keep their pride.'

'Perhaps,' Eline said, 'but I want you to organize things better for me. At the moment it is all rather haphazard; payments come in irregularly, and it's difficult to keep an accurate check on it all.'

Eline smiled. 'My husband looks on the business as a way of saving some of his taxes, because the workshop does not make a profit, you see.'

Arian didn't see, but she would, she vowed; she would learn the entire business from the inside out.

Eline took a red book out of the drawer and spread it open on the table. 'Have a look, at your leisure,' she said. 'I've got a carriage coming to take me home in about half an hour, and I'll tell you something, I'll be glad to have a rest; my back aches like toothache.'

She handed Arian a bunch of keys. 'These are yours to take charge of, and, Arian, I have every confidence in your ability to run a first-class enterprise.' She smiled. 'I wouldn't be surprised if somehow you managed even to make a profit.'

Arian felt elated. 'Why are you doing all this for me, when you have other, more experienced shoemakers working for you?' she asked.

'Perhaps because I see a little of myself in you, perhaps because I'm pleased to see a woman making a success of things; but most of all because you have the ability to assimilate all aspects of the shoemaking business.'

'I'm not quite sure what you mean by that last statement,' Arian said thoughtfully.

373

'Some people are cobblers, some designers, some only see one straight track before them. You have vision; I think you will make a name for yourself some time in the future. You have courage, Arian, and I admire that.'

Eline rose. 'I'm going to talk to the others in the shop, tell them what I've decided. They won't like it, I warn you of that now; but it's up to you how you handle things.'

Arian looked down at the keys in her hand and for a moment she was frightened. Of all the staff who worked for Eline, Price was the one she most feared trouble from. She squared her shoulders; she could handle Price Davies, she told herself. But a cold hand of doubt reached out and touched her shoulder. Arian shuddered; she *could* deal with the situation, she must – she had no option.

CHAPTER THIRTY

Eline sank on to the bed and closed her eyes. It was so good to rest. She felt tired and disillusioned with life, and it seemed she was in a trap with no way out. Here she was expecting a baby, the child of the man she really loved; but that man was not her husband.

As for Calvin, he was looking forward so much to having an heir, a son who would some day take over the Temple empire. His delight only served to fuel Eline's terrible feelings of guilt; how could she let him believe that everything in the garden was wonderful when it was all a lie?

'My darling!' The door had opened and Calvin appeared at the side of the bed as if in answer to her thoughts. He fell on to his knees and took her hand tenderly in his. 'Are you all right? Are you having pains? Is the baby coming?'

She smiled and touched his cheek. 'No, silly, it's not due for a few weeks yet.' She looked up at him, but her eyes failed to meet his. 'I'm just a bit tired, that's all. I'll sleep for a while and then, I'm sure, I'll feel much better.'

'My dear girl, whatever you want.' Calvin kissed her forehead, pushing aside a stray curl, his mouth turning up into a smile. Eline touched his cheek briefly, the words of her awful confession trembling on her lips; and then, wearily, she closed her eyes.

When Eline awoke, it was to find that she'd slept for longer than she'd intended. She sat up and stared around the elegant room, feeling disorientated, wondering, for a moment, where she was. Then, remembering, she covered her eyes with her hands as a feeling of unhappiness swamped her. She was living a lie, and she felt she couldn't bear it any longer; she must tell Calvin the truth, that the baby she was carrying might not be his. Any decision he might make then, she would abide by. Anything was better than this awful, tearing unhappiness and guilt. In any case, her disturbed emotions could not be doing her child any good.

She slid from the bed, staring out of the window unseeingly for a moment, undecided what to do next. A nice warm bath and a change of clothes might make her feel better, she decided; then, perhaps, a walk through the gardens to blow away the cobwebs that clouded her mind?

Eline reached out to ring the bell for the maid, and it was then that the pain caught her. She doubled up, clutching her stomach, gasping as the pain strengthened and tightened around her body. It was as though an iron hand was wrapping itself around her, gripping mercilessly.

But it was too early for the baby to come – weeks too early, she thought in panic.

With an effort, Eline pulled at the silken rope that hung beside the mantelpiece, and somewhere in the deep kitchen regions of the house she knew a bell would ring and bring someone to help her.

She slumped back on the bed and bit her lip to stop herself from crying out. How did women bear this tearing pain, time after time, giving birth to a brood of children?

Eline closed her eyelids tightly together, feeling sweat bead her brow; she heard a low guttural moan and knew with surprise that it was her own.

When the pain receded, she became aware of the frightened face of one of the maids staring at her from the doorway. The girl bobbed a curtsey, unsure what she should do next.

'Send Lord Temple to me,' Eline gasped, trying to

resist the panic that was deepening as her pains increased.

'He's gone out, my lady.' The maid bobbed a curtsey once more, her face white. 'But I'll tell the housekeeper to come, shall I?'

'Just see that the midwife and the doctor are sent for.' Eline regained some of her composure; there was no point in giving in to the fear that beat through her at the thought of being alone in her ordeal, with only strangers to tend her.

The maid disappeared and shortly afterwards the housekeeper knocked on the door. 'Everything is under control, my lady.'

Mrs Mort was the antithesis of all her name suggested. She was plump and smiling, her cheeks pink, her eyes those of a startled baby, wide and blue. And more, Eline saw with a sense of relief, she was the embodiment of reassurance.

'Come, my lady, me and Bella will change you into a fresh gown and get you as comfy as we can by the time the midwife comes.'

She talked smoothly and quietly, her smile motherly, and Eline was suddenly aware of how little she'd been involved with her staff. She had been remiss, had failed to get to know the people who worked in the house, and it was a wonder that she was being shown such kindness now.

'Thank you, Mrs Mort,' she said breathlessly. 'I'm very grateful.'

'No trouble at all. Fetch a basin of warm water, Bella!' Mrs Mort addressed the maid a little sharply, for the girl was standing around, arms hanging at her side, as though she was at a loss what to do next.

'Move, girl!' Mrs Mort carefully undressed Eline, her hands gentle. 'I'll give your face a little swill,' she said. 'It will freshen you up a bit, make you feel better.'

Eline grimaced. 'I don't think anything is going to

377

make me feel better. I feel already as if I've been wrung out through the mangle.'

'Don't you worry,' Mrs Mort said. 'More women have babies than you'd imagine; they do it every day – can't be anything to it. Never had any myself, but then it's a natural enough happening, so it can't be all that bad, can it?'

Eline felt like telling Mrs Mort that she should try childbirth herself before being so confident; but another pain washed over her and she bit her lip, lowering her chin against her chest, eyes tightly closed.

It was a relief when the midwife came bustling into the bedroom, her tall, imposing figure swathed in white, a large bag under her arm.

'Good evening to you then, Mother,' she said, briskly. 'Let's clear this room and see what's happening, shall we?'

Underneath the cover of the sheet, the midwife prodded and probed and emerged satisfied. 'Right, we're doing fine.' She smiled rather grimly as she patted Eline's stomach with little respect. 'Coming a bit early, isn't it?' Her voice held a note of accusation, as though Eline had been a disobedient child.

'I think so,' Eline agreed unsteadily. 'Will it be all right – the baby, I mean?'

'Well, I didn't think you meant next door's cat,' the midwife said acidly; but she didn't, Eline noticed, answer the question. She folded her arms across her thin chest. 'I'm Mrs Conran,' she introduced herself. 'I believe Dr Mayberry is attending you?' She sniffed. 'He's very *young*.'

She uttered the word 'young' as though it was something contagious, and Eline half-smiled before another band of pain began to tighten around her body.

'Breathe easy, now,' Mrs Conran urged. 'Don't fight against the pain, just let yourself go with it, and it'll all be over before you know what's happened.'

378

Eline moaned softly. The pains were rapidly in-
tensifying; she didn't think she could bear it, and she
sucked in her breath sharply.

The midwife urged her to lean forward and proceeded
to rub Eline's spine in a way that was strangely comforting. 'Come on, now, you can do this; it's nature's
way, after all, nothing to worry about.'

Eline's head began to spin. In her mind she was
confusing the midwife with the housekeeper, though
Mrs Mort and Mrs Conran couldn't have been more
different from each other.

Eline wished Calvin would come home. His presence
was always so reassuring; she always felt that he was in
complete control of every situation. But what he could
not help her with, she told herself ruefully, was this
struggle that was going on within her. She alone was
responsible for bringing a child into the world, a child
whose parentage was in question.

When the doctor arrived, he took charge and in-
structed Eline to kneel on the bed with her hands
grasping the brass bedstead for support. The midwife
clucked her tongue in disapproval, but Eline's only
concern was that she had gained a little comfort from
the new position.

When the pains started to come at rapidly decreasing
intervals, she tried to relax, to go with the flow, as Mrs
Conran had told her; but it was becoming more and
more difficult to keep a hold on reality. Images danced
before her closed eyes, images of Honey's Farm, of the
wide rolling spaces on the hilltop. Then, as though
chronicling her life, she saw images of Joe, of the oyster
boats, of Nina Parks stealing her husband from her. And
Gwyneth, dead now, arm in arm with Will.

'Will!' The name was torn from her lips as a surge of
strength forced the last effort. There was a sudden
silence, and then the angry cry of a baby.

'Good girl!' Mrs Conran enthused, but there was an

379

odd note in her voice. 'It's over.' Eline knew the woman must be wondering why a woman would call out a name at the moment of childbirth that was not her husband's.

'Let's just see what you have here, Mother. Well, now, it's a fine handsome son, a small but perfect little boy; your husband will be pleased.'

She wrapped the baby in a sheet and held him up. 'Just look at him and *listen* to him! Fine pair of lungs he's got; aye, he'll do.'

Mrs Conran was as proud as if she'd borne the child herself. She gently wiped the baby's mouth and eyes, her smile broad.

'Here,' she said to Eline, 'hold him while I see to the rest of the job.' She glanced up at the doctor, as though his presence was superfluous, as indeed it was.

'No need to hang around, Doctor,' she said firmly. 'I'll see to Mother now.'

Eline looked down at her son as he nestled in her arms. She searched the screwed-up face, and her heart lurched as she saw, immediately, a great likeness to Will. The hair, the thrust of the chin, the shape of the eyebrows shouted the baby's paternity. Or was it, Eline thought, all a product of her guilty conscience?

By the time Calvin returned, Eline was propped up with a multitude of pillows, the baby, neatly wrapped and dressed, lying against her breast.

Calvin came towards the bed, his expression one of wonder and delight. 'We have a boy!' he said, his voice breaking. 'You have given me the most precious gift of a son.'

He kissed Eline's forehead and then drew the soft white blanket away from the infant's face. Eline held her breath. Would Calvin see what she had seen, the incredible likeness to Will Davies in the small features?

Calvin was still smiling as he took the baby in his arms and held him proudly. 'My son,' he said in wonder. 'My

380

very own son and heir! I don't think I'll ever forget this moment, not if I live to be a hundred.'

Eline felt a pain sear her at the joy in Calvin's face. A tear trembled in his eyes as he stared down at the baby, and the words she longed to say died on Eline's lips. She had wanted to confess it all to Calvin, her uncertainty, her fears that he might not be the father, that Will, in their moment of illicit passion, had filled her with his child.

She looked down at her hands, so white against the covers, and she held her tongue, not daring to destroy Calvin's dreams.

'We shall call him Jonathan Frederick,' Calvin said softly. 'The names have always been in my family, for as long as I can remember; do you mind, Eline?'

She shook her head. She felt numb and tired, so very tired. She closed her eyes, and immediately the midwife took charge.

'Let's give the new mother some rest, shall we?' Mrs Conran's voice made it plain that her words were a command, not a request.

Reluctantly, Calvin handed the baby to the midwife, then bent to kiss Eline's forehead. 'I'll be back, when you've rested.' He smiled. 'For now, I think I'll go out and tell everyone I've got a son.'

Eline held up her hand, and he took it and kissed the palm. To her dismay, she saw there were tears trembling on her husband's lashes.

She watched with a feeling of deep unhappiness as Calvin went out of the room, closing the door gently behind him; and then she gave herself up to the blessed sweetness of sleep.

Will's business was steadily improving; his name was synonymous with good but reasonable workmanship, and now he had to employ a cobbler to help him. He doubted he'd ever be rich, but he would always make his way in life; he would never have to starve.

He had put a deposit on the house he wanted. There was a small workshop attached to the side of the modest building that was more than adequate for his needs; and, though it would take Will a little time to pay back what he owed on the property, it would at least one day be his.

He strode along the street now towards Hari Grenfell's house and looked down at his neatly pressed suit, a small smile crossing his face; Rita was looking after him well.

The daughter of Glen the baker came round to Will's rooms several times a week and, for a few pennies, cleaned and cooked for him.

Glen was hoping, as Will well appreciated, that Rita would become so important to Will that one day he might even marry her. And, he thought, he could do worse.

His spirits suddenly sank. The only one he wanted to be with was Eline, the woman he had loved and lost. They had shared each other for a brief time, such a short interlude of love and passion, and then she had virtually disappeared from his life.

Except for that awful night at Hari's, when Calvin had announced that his wife was expecting their child and he had looked into her face and seen her pain – that was when Will knew that it was finally over. The last shred of hope that he and Eline could be together had vanished then for ever.

He kicked savagely at a stone as he made his way along the drive of Summer Lodge. He was a failure, for all his improved conditions; he was still a failure in comparison to the woman he loved.

The lights of Hari's home splashed out into the driveway; the door stood open revealing the large, impressive hallway. Why was it, Will asked himself, that the women in his life were destined for success, while he had made little or nothing of his talents?

Hari welcomed him with her usual warmth, her arms hugging his neck, her soft mouth pressed against his cheek.

'Will, you are looking so much better,' Hari said, 'so elegant and smart.' She smiled up at him. 'Could it be that you are in love again? I've heard the tales of a certain young lady who wants only to look after you.'

Will shook his head. 'Rita, you mean? Well, she's a sweet girl but . . .'

Hari put her soft palm across his lips. 'You don't have to explain anything to me,' she said quietly. 'I only want what I've always wanted, for you to be happy.'

As she drew Will into the crowded drawing-room, he smiled ruefully. 'But you have lowered your sights a bit,' he chided. 'Once you wanted me to marry a lady of quality, but now I'm a widower and a poor cobbler, I suppose I must take what I can get.'

'Don't be silly!' Hari pinched his cheek. 'You could have any woman you wanted, you handsome man.'

'Except the only woman I ever really wanted,' Will said softly. 'Go on, Hari, talk to your other guests. I'll find something to entertain me, or some*one*, if I'm lucky.'

He stood in the shadow of the window, staring out into the night. Moonlight bathed the garden in silver, and dark shadows lay beneath the trees. Most of the leaves had fallen now, and bare, skeletal branches pointed towards the skies.

'Why so pensive?' The voice was soft, well modulated, and Will turned to look into the smiling face of Emily Miller.

'I don't know,' Will said honestly. 'I suppose I was adding up my regrets.'

'At your age?' Emily said, eyebrows lifted. 'But, Will, you are a young man; you have your whole life before you.'

'Sometimes I feel that all my best experiences are behind me,' Will said. He studied Emily. She'd changed more than a little from the grand lady he'd known when he was apprenticed to Hari some years before. Then she had been proud and haughty, despising those less fortunate than herself. Now she was married to a cobbler, and John Miller had made her more human and somehow more vulnerable. That's what love did to people, Will thought, made them vulnerable.

'You've drifted away again,' Emily said. 'Penny for them.' She smiled to soften her words, and Will returned her smile.

'I was thinking of the good days,' Will said. 'Remember when you had the yellow fever, and Hari nursed you back to health?'

Emily laughed. 'I remember, but I'd hardly call those the good days.'

'No, but many of them were good days,' Will said softly. 'I had my dreams then, my ambitions; but now . . . ' He shrugged apologetically. 'I must be feeling sorry for myself,' he said. 'I expect I sound like a weakling.'

'We all had dreams then,' Emily said, 'different ones to what came later, I suspect.'

'What did you want most of all?' Will asked, curious.

Emily pulled a wry face. 'I thought I wanted to marry Craig,' she admitted. 'I was engaged to him, after all.' She glanced across the room to where Craig was bending attentively over Hari, his hand lightly resting on her shoulder.

'They make a lovely couple,' Emily said. 'They were meant for each other, and I – well, I found my wonderful John, so it all turned out for the best. Things usually do.'

'I wish I could think like that,' Will said quietly. Suddenly he could bear the crowded room no longer. He excused himself and went into the garden, staring up at the brilliant stars in the cold night sky.

Had he ever been as lonely as he was now, he wondered. What had he to strive for, what good was there in making a go of his business, when there would never be anyone to share it with?

The bell echoed through the big house and out of the open front door to the lawn where Will stood, hands thrust into his pockets. With a sigh of resignation, he went indoors and forced a smile as he met Hari's questioning eyes. 'I'm all right.' He mouthed the words and moved towards the dining-room.

The meal seemed endless, and it became clear to Will during the course of the evening that Hari, in spite of her teasing about Rita, had taken it into her head to try a bit of match-making.

The pretty young lady at his side had been introduced to him as Madeleine Grenfell, a fourth daughter of one of Craig's many distant relatives. She spoke intelligently, and the attention she paid him was very flattering; but he wondered if she knew he was a poor cobbler, with little or no prospect of ever becoming anything else.

'You are very quiet, Mr Davies,' Madeleine said, leaning closer to him. He caught the aroma of her perfume and wondered at the way parents had of doing their daughters up like a lamb going to the slaughter, just to attract a husband. Suddenly he found himself in the ludicrous position of feeling sorry for Madeleine Grenfell.

'I was listening with great interest to what you had to say.' He smiled. 'It seems your time is very much taken up with doing good and charitable works – very worthy.'

'And very boring.' Madeleine smiled back, and her cheeks dimpled.

Will warmed to her. 'Why do it, then?' he asked, his eyebrows raised, giving Madeleine all his attention for the first time.

'I suppose because it's expected of me,' Madeleine said. 'That and meeting eligible young men seems to be just what my parents want.'

'And you?' Will studied Madeleine with fresh eyes.

She was more than just pretty; she had large eyes fringed with heavy lashes, and her hair hung around her face in soft dark curls.

'And me?' Madeleine said. 'Well, all I want is to be allowed to get on with my own life. However well-intentioned Papa is, I won't have him pushing me into a marriage I don't want just because it's convenient for him.'

'Well said.' Will's words were quietly spoken. 'You wait until the right man comes along, and then grab him with both hands.'

She leant back in her chair, her big eyes fixed on him. 'I just might do that,' she said, and her dimples were in evidence again. 'If only there was a yardstick to tell a girl who *is* the right man.'

'You'll know,' Will said firmly, and Madeleine leant towards him.

'I'm intrigued,' she said. 'I take it you *have* met the right woman, which I confess is a bit of a blow to me.'

'I *did* meet the right one,' Will agreed, 'but I let her get away. She's married now to another man.'

'I expect you mean Eline Temple – *Lady* Temple,' Madeleine said, and shrugged. 'I'm afraid people do gossip. She's just had her baby, I understand; that must be very painful for you.'

'Eline has had her baby?' Will felt as though the bottom of his world had suddenly dropped away from beneath his feet.

'Didn't you know?' Madeleine's voice was full of sympathy. 'She's had a son, and I gather Lord Temple is like a dog with two tails.' Madeleine put out her hand and touched his briefly. 'I'm sorry.'

Will sank back in his chair, a hollow feeling in the pit of his stomach. Eline had borne Temple a son. Suddenly a great sadness filled him. It was all over now; there was no hope of ever winning Eline back. No longer could he cherish dreams that were doomed to failure.

He turned to look into the large sympathetic eyes of Madeleine Grenfell. 'I'm sorry,' she said again, in what was almost a whisper. 'I'm so sorry to be the one to tell you.'

Will put down his napkin and rose to his feet. 'If you'll excuse me,' he said, turning to Hari, 'I'm not feeling very well.'

Then he was out of the roomful of people, who suddenly seemed to have prying, curious eyes, all focused on him. He strode out into the darkness of the night, wanting to put as much distance between himself and the roomful of people as he could.

A soft drizzle was falling and touched Will's cheeks, and the coldness of the rain mingled with his tears.

CHAPTER THIRTY-ONE

The workshop was alive with excited chatter. The cordwainers, seated together in a huddle, marvelled that Lady Temple had given birth prematurely to a son and heir. More intriguing to the ladies, whose work was neglected for the moment in favour of gossip, was the fact that Arian Smale had been left with sole responsibility for the entire shoemaking enterprise. She, apparently, had the power to issue orders to her elders and betters, the power to hire and fire as she so wished.

'It's not only the four cobblers here whose noses will be out of joint,' one of the cordwainers said quietly. 'But there's we three ladies, all of us older than Arian.' Sophie Pope clucked her tongue in annoyance. 'That a *girl* has been put in charge of the machine shop, and all the finance as well, is just unbelievable!'

Unnoticed, Arian had entered the workshop. Her leather apron had remained on its hook, her neat blouse and skirt an unspoken mark of her new position.

'Well, Mrs Pope,' Arian said smiling, 'you'd better believe it, because it's true; I *have* been put in charge, and I'm afraid you'll have to put up with it – or leave.'

Sophie Pope looked flustered. 'Oh, sorry, I didn't see you there,' she said uneasily. 'No offence intended; it's just that you are so *young*.'

'That's all right,' Arian said smoothly. 'There was no offence taken, and I'm sure that we'll work as well together as we've always done.'

'I'm sure,' Sophie Pope agreed, casting a doubtful look at her friends.

'I'll be in the office, if anyone needs me,' Arian said,

and, even as she walked from the workshop, she heard one of the women sniff scornfully.

Before she could close the door, Price Davies was standing with his foot in the gap. He was smiling insolently. Behind him, the other workers were watching with avid curiosity. Arian felt a prickling of her scalp. She was being tested; she knew it, and so did the other workers.

'Can I come in, or do you want to talk about our affair in front of everyone?' Price spoke easily, every line in his body exuded confidence.

'I beg your pardon?' Arian's mind was racing. How should she deal with the situation? How could she get out of it with grace and dignity? Anger rose within her that this man, who had violated her once, was attempting now to humiliate her in front of the other workers. She forced herself to be calm, she must not lose her nerve now.

'Well, we have been . . . close, haven't we?' Price was smiling and Arian held the door wide, facing him squarely, knowing that everyone was hanging on her words.

'Close? Oh, I suppose you mean the night you tried to get me into your bed?' Arian was smiling, her eyes deliberately mocking. She looked past him at the ladies, who were agog with the excitement of it all.

'Poor Price,' Arian continued. 'I'm afraid I need a real man, not one who has to try to force a woman into submission instead of using a little natural charm.'

She turned to the cordwainers. 'A woman needs gentleness, doesn't she, ladies?' Arian tossed her head. 'I'm afraid, Price, your feeble attempt to make love to me resembled a clumsy bull trying to cover a reluctant cow!'

It was Sophie Pope who was the first to laugh. She tried to smother her giggles with her hand, but gave up when the rest of the workers joined in the laughter.

One of the men called jeeringly to Price Davies, 'So you are not such a hot shot with the women then, Price – all lies was it, boy?'

Price Davies stared down at Arian in a moment of pure hatred. 'You bitch!' he said hoarsely. 'I should have finished you when I had the chance.'

'You didn't even start with me, Price Davies,' Arian said emphatically. 'As I said, I need a real man, not an apology for one.'

He raised his hand as if to strike her. Arian stood her ground, staring him out.

'Don't be a fool, man,' one of the cobblers called out anxiously. 'We don't want the constables down on us, do we?'

Arian smiled sweetly. 'As you are clearly not happy working under the new management,' she said, 'I'm afraid I've no alternative but to let you go. Your wages of course will be paid up to the end of the week.'

She closed the office door and sank down into a chair, aware that she was trembling. It had been an ordeal; but Arian felt she had come out of the confrontation with Price Davies with her dignity intact. No-one, now, would lend credence to his claims; only she and Price himself would ever know the truth of the night he had raped her.

After a moment, Arian opened the order book. The stocks of leather needed building up; she would, she realized, miss Price's expertise when it came to buying the finest skins, but she would simply have to find someone else to work with, someone she could rely on wholeheartedly.

At least she had learned one thing; it didn't do to try to mix business with pleasure. From now on, she would keep her love affairs right away from the workshops.

It was later, when Arian was walking home and darkness was beginning to close in, that she saw Price Davies again. He was just entering the doors of the

Castle Hotel, his big frame washed with light from the doorway. Arian drew a sharp breath as she saw the man he was with; it was her uncle, Mike the Spud, and from the way the two men had their heads together, they were not planning anything good.

Arian shivered and crossed to the other side of the road. Uncle Mike on his own was bad news, but, together with Price Davies, he would be a force for evil. Arian felt, instinctively, that from now on she would have to be extra vigilant, or her safety would be in jeopardy.

'Come here, my colleen.' There was a dreamy look in Jamie's eyes that Fon recognized. She smiled, eluding his searching hand, and slipped out of bed, her toes curling against the coldness of the floor.

'Too much work to do, *boy bach*,' she said softly. 'Anyway, Patrick's awake. I can hear him pottering about; we'd have no peace.'

Jamie sighed. 'It's terrible to have a disobedient woman for a wife, a shrew who won't give her husband his dues.' He fell back against the pillows, his hands over his eyes. 'I think I should take my belt to you, colleen.'

'Huh!' Fon threw a pillow at him. 'Just try it, my lad, and see where it gets you.'

He leapt out of bed so suddenly that Fon was taken by surprise. He was naked, and his desire was evident. 'You witch!' he said, holding her close, his hands on her breasts. 'I think I'll ravish you whether or not you want me to.'

His mouth on hers was sweet and hot with passion. Fon clung to him, suddenly wanting him with a fierce longing.

'No need for any ravishing,' she whispered in his ear and, tugging his hands, she drew him down on to the bed, eager as always to have his love. She sighed softly as his sweet weight pressed against her; it was going to be another beautiful day.

It was later, when the men were out in the fields, that Fon looked up from her baking to see a large figure blocking out the light. She felt chilled as she recognized the rough hair and big shoulders of Mike the Spud.

'What do you want?' she demanded, her eyes going to the rifle placed behind the door, too far away for her to reach it.

'I mean no harm, missis.' The man's tone was whining; he was crushing his cap between his fingers. 'I just wanted to know if there was work here for me.'

'You can't mean it?' Fon's tone was incredulous. 'I wouldn't give you work if there was no-one left to farm the land.'

'Please, missis.' Mike smiled ingratiatingly. 'I need money real bad, like, and I've changed, I'm not a villain any more. I'll prove it if you'll only give me the chance.'

He looked at the tray of cakes cooling on the table, and Fon could tell that the man was genuinely hungry.

'I can't possibly take you on here,' she said. 'My husband would never allow it.' Her voice softened. 'But you can have something to eat before you go on your way.'

'Thank you kindly, missis.' Mike sat eagerly at the table, and Fon poured him some tea and pushed a plate towards him.

'Help yourself,' she said. 'The tea is a bit stewed by now, but it's been on the hob, so it should be hot at least.'

She edged around the table, picked up the rifle and held it against her breast, glad of the reassuring feel of the metal beneath her hands.

'No need of that, missis,' Mike said. 'I'll eat up and go, if there's no chance of work. I won't pester you any more.'

Nevertheless, Fon kept the rifle close to her until Mike the Spud had eaten his fill and pushed away his chair.

'Thank you, missis.' He suddenly swayed, and, putting his hand up to his eyes, moaned softly.

'What is it?' Fon asked. 'Are you sick?' She moved carefully towards him, the rifle still clasped firmly in her hands. 'Do you need a doctor?' she persisted, as Mike couldn't or wouldn't answer. Fon bit her lip, not knowing what to do.

He moved so swiftly that she was unprepared. His big fist seemed to come from nowhere and exploded into her face; she thought she heard the rifle clatter to the floor, and then a total blackness blotted everything out.

Fon awoke slowly to a feeling of unreality. She was in an unfamiliar room, tied hand and foot to a chair in which she had been dumped unceremoniously, to judge by the dishevelled look of her apron and skirts.

One eye would not open, and Fon guessed that the pain on that side of her head was from the blow that Mike the Spud had dealt her. She sat up straighter and tried to look through the dusty curtains covering the window, but only a chink of light pierced through the folds.

A quick look round the room told her that she was in an unused farmhouse. Hooks jutted from thick beams, and it was clear they once held salted pork hung out to dry in the heat from the fire. And, as she breathed in, the scents of the land were all around her.

She struggled to free herself. Where was Mike the Spud, and what on earth did he think he was up to? Jamie would kill him when he found out what had happened.

A cold chill spread through her. How would Jamie know where to look for her? He had been out in the fields when Mike had come to the farmhouse, and the children had been with him. All he would see when he returned home was her unfinished baking on the table.

Mike would more than likely have left things tidy in

393

the kitchen; he was cunning enough not to leave any evidence that he had been there.

A sense of despair swamped her. She would never be found; she would be at the mercy of a maniac like Mike the Spud for ever. Fon swallowed her fear, along with the tears that threatened to spill over. Panic would be of no use now; she must keep a cool head and think things out quietly.

It was dark by the time the door opened and two men entered the room. Fon looked up and tried to peer through the gloom. She recognized Mike's big rough build, but the man with him was a stranger to her.

'Well, Price, how much should I ask for her, do you think?' Mike said, staring down at Fon with a blank expression on his coarse-featured face.

The man came up to Fon and tipped up her face, staring down at her in a way that made her flesh creep. 'Not a bad looker, is she, except for the shiner you've given her?' The man's hand slid down her neck, caressing her skin with slow deliberation. She shrank back, but remorselessly his hand dipped into her bodice. With a sense of outrage, Fon lashed out with her foot. In retaliation, the man squeezed her breast until the pain made her gasp. Fon knew then he was merciless; she could never appeal to his better nature, for the man lacked any finer feelings.

'Bitch!' he said softly. 'I know just how to deal with you. A good man between your legs is what you need.'

Fear brought a sickness to the pit of Fon's stomach. The man's hand was on his belt; his look was speculative, as though he intended to put his words into action right away.

'Come on, Price,' Mike the Spud broke in. 'We've got to see to that other little matter, haven't we? I thought it was urgent, like.'

'You're right.' Price's smile was suddenly charming. He leant forward, lifted Fon's chin and pressed his

394

mouth to hers, forcing his tongue between her teeth. She tried to twist away, but it was impossible; he was holding her too cruelly.

When he released her, she stared up at him, frozen with horror. 'Don't worry,' he said. 'I'll be back to finish what I started.'

He moved to the door, speaking to Mike as though Fon was not within earshot. 'We'll bleed the husband dry,' he laughed. 'He's probably anxious to get his sweet bundle of charm back in one piece, and he'd pay whatever we asked.'

He clapped Mike on the shoulder. 'He won't need to know that I've taken a drink of nectar from his own little flower cup, need he?'

Mike looked uneasily back towards Fon. 'I'd be careful if I were you. Jamie O'Conner can act like a madman when he's roused.'

Price took a long knife from his boot and rubbed his finger along the sharp blade. 'I can handle him.' He spoke scornfully, and Fon shuddered, closing her eyes against the sight of the shining blade.

When the men had gone, she tried again to free herself from the twisted rope that bound her, but the friction burnt her skin, and, after struggling for what seemed an eternity, she slumped back in the chair, defeated.

It was quite dark now, and the heavy blackness closed around her. All she could see were the shapes of the furniture in the small glimmer of light that pierced the slit of open curtain.

Suddenly Fon was angry, so angry that her vision blurred. She pushed her feet against the floor, and the chair moved a little. She looked up; if only she could get to the window, kick it open, perhaps she could call out and attract attention. With renewed energy she began to move.

Reaching the window was the easy part, although it took the best part of an hour, as far as Fon could judge.

It was when she got as far as the deep sill that she realized the window was too far away, too high in the wall, for her to reach.

With her head she moved the curtain aside and looked out into the darkened landscape. It was then she realized where she was. Mike had taken her to the farmhouse once owned by his brother, Bob Smale; and there, just over the rise of the hill, was her own home, her home – and her husband Jamie.

The thought of Jamie's bewilderment and panic did to Fon what fear for her own safety had failed to do. Tears came to her eyes and, unchecked, ran down her cheeks and fell salt on to her lips.

'Where can she be?' The little girl's voice broke into his thoughts, and Jamie did his best to speak kindly to her.

'I don't know, April, but I intend to find out.' He was pulling on his coat as he spoke, ready to rejoin the search of the gulleys and rocks around the farmlands. All the men he could muster were out there with torches and dogs, combing every inch of ground in an effort to find Fon before the cold hours of dawn set in.

If she was lying somewhere injured, which seemed to be the most likely explanation for her disappearance, it was imperative to find her, and soon. But Jamie felt in his bones that Fon had not simply wandered outside, leaving her baking half-done; no, there was something more sinister at work here.

Jamie frowned. There was only one man who could answer for what had happened to Fon, and that was Mike the Spud. He was the one with the greatest grudge against Jamie. Mike probably blamed him, not only for taking his brother's land but for causing Bob Smale's death as well.

Jamie turned at the door to look at the woman who had volunteered to look after the children while he continued the search.

'I'll try not to be long, Mrs Morris,' he said, 'and thanks for your help. I'll always be grateful.'

'Take as long as you like,' Mrs Morris replied. 'Your wife must be found, whatever, and the little ones will be quite safe with me.'

Jamie stepped outdoors. The light had faded now to almost complete darkness; even the moon seemed to have deserted the land and was hidden behind a thick mass of clouds. Soon, it would rain; the earth would be soaked, and any trace of footsteps or signs of a struggle would have disappeared.

Jamie searched the ground outside the farmhouse yet again. There were cart tracks, of course, and marks of the horses' hooves; and here, he crouched lower, it looked as if the earth had been swept or, he thought with dismay, something or somebody had been dragged along the rutted path towards the gate.

He straightened and stared into the blackness. Where could he start to look for his wife? *Fon*, his mind cried, *I love you, my Irfonwy, I can't lose you the way I lost Katherine.*

The silence pressed in around him as he moved towards the gate. The other searchers would be giving up until morning light; nothing could be discovered in the pitch blackness of the night. But he would go on; he couldn't stop, not now, not ever, not until he had his wife home safely with him once more.

'What are we going to do next then, Price, boy?' Mike the Spud sat in the public, drinking the frothing ale and belching inelegantly.

'I thought we'd find the bitch in her lodgings,' Price said quietly. 'She had to be out, didn't she? Well, I won't be defeated; we'll go back later, see if she's back.'

'What has this woman done to you, then?' Mike leant across the table, his big belly resting on his huge thighs.

'She's got me the order of the boot, that's what,' Price

said fiercely. 'Done me out of my job.' He shrugged. 'I gave her a good rogering one night, and because I didn't want her after that, she turned against me, as women will.' He leant back in his chair, scowling. 'Think they can have what they like from you, then turn nasty; well, no-one makes a fool of me, not twice they don't.'

Mike swallowed hard. There was something about Price Davies that scared him; big and rough though he himself was, Mike would think twice about crossing a man like Price.

'What will you do with her, then?' Mike said. 'Ask for some money for her, like I'm going to do with the missis of the high and mighty Jamie O'Conner, is it?'

'No money to be made out of the bitch, not directly anyway,' Price said. 'But if I keep her away from the job for long enough, Eline Temple will have to take me back, put me in charge of the place; I'm the most experienced man she's got.'

Mike grinned unpleasantly. 'That'll be an eye for an eye, all right, won't it?' He supped his ale with a slurping sound and banged the empty glass on the table meaningfully.

'Get your own soddin' beer,' Price said. 'You are the one making money, not me.'

'Yes, 'course, boy, I'll get the drinks in all right,' Mike said hastily.

When he returned to the table, Price looked up at him, and he was smiling with the strange charm that he could exert whenever he chose.

'This farmhouse a safe place, then, is it?' he asked. 'We don't want anyone finding the booty, do we?'

'Aye, it's safe for a while at least,' Mike said. 'The land been standing idle since Bob died; I don't think anyone is likely to go there for any reason.'

'Quiet, is it? Far away from any other houses? I don't want anyone hearing any screams.'

Mike suddenly felt cold. 'What do you mean,

screams?' he asked. 'You're not going to harm the women, are you?'

'All depends on what you mean by harm,' Price said easily, still smiling; and the smile brought goosebumps out on Mike's skin.

'I'll just have a bit of fun with them,' he said. 'I quite fancy that farm girl with her lovely skin and her soft little mouth.' He stretched his legs beneath the table. 'I think I'll have her for dinner, and then Miss high and mighty Arian Smale for afters.'

Mike's mouth was suddenly dry. Arian, his brother's girl – a right little minx, if ever there was one, but could he stand by and watch one of his kinsfolk being hurt by the sadistic man sitting before him?

He glanced at Price; he was drinking his beer and hadn't noticed Mike's sudden silence. Mike realized with a prickling of fear that he would have to play along with the man for the moment at least; he knew little about Price Davies except that they had got drunk together one night in the public bar and had slept together like friends on the bed in Mike's shabby lodgings.

Foolishly Mike had told Price of the plan to take Fon O'Conner and hold her till her husband paid up. Now Price had a game of his own to play, and Mike wasn't sure just where it would lead.

'Come on.' Price rose as if suddenly restless. 'The bitch must be home by now. Let's go and show her what we're made of, shall we?'

He wiped his mouth with the back of his hand and smiled. 'She'll be pleased to see me, I'm sure; and, as for me, I can't wait to see *her*.' He moved to the door. 'Arian Smale,' he said softly, 'you are about to get everything you've been asking for.'

Standing behind him, Mike shuddered. There was something within this man that frightened him, something beyond evil. It was as if Mike had set in motion a series of events over which he now had very little, if any, control. For a moment, Mike was tempted to run, to put as much distance between Price Davies and himself as he could. Then his big shoulders slumped. It was no good running from such a man; he would just have to go along with whatever it was Price Davies had planned.

CHAPTER THIRTY-TWO

'Don't you think it's a little chilly to take the baby out today, Eline?' Calvin's voice was solicitous, and Eline bit her lip on the irritable answer that she'd been about to make.

'He's well wrapped up.' She hoped her voice sounded reasonable; she needed to get outdoors, away from Calvin's almost constant presence. Ever since the baby had been born, Calvin had been at her side, pampering her, indulging her and crooning over the baby.

He meant well, Eline knew that better than anyone; but Calvin's pride in the boy he believed was his son twisted like a knife in her heart. His joy shone in his face, and Eline knew in her heart that one day she had to destroy that joy with just a few words of truth.

'In any case,' Calvin continued, 'the baby has a nurse to take him out. It's not seemly for you to be carrying the boy in the shawl, Welsh-fashion, in the manner of the poor people.'

'It may not be seemly, but it's what I want to do,' Eline said, 'and since when have you been such a snob?' This time her voice was edged with an impatience she couldn't conceal. 'I came from the "poor people", if you remember.'

'All right!' Calvin held up his hands in a gesture of mock defeat, his good humour unshaken. 'I realize my lady wife is not like other women but is an independent soul with a string of successes to her credit.'

He came to her and held her in his arms, kissing her neck and then her lips. 'I love you very much, my darling,' he said. 'Never forget that.'

401

As if she could; his attentions were cloying at times, and, although Eline knew she was being unreasonable, she could not help resenting the constant pressure on her to play the role of a good and loving wife.

It was with a sense of relief that she said goodbye to Calvin as he stood in the doorway of the grand house. He watched as she walked down the drive, and, turning, she gave him a perfunctory wave.

She breathed deeply and looked around her, glad to be out of the house and in the real world again. Anything was preferable at this moment to remaining in the house; any diversion that served to take her mind away from Calvin and his devotion was more than welcome.

The trees were bare now, the earth hard with frost, but soon the spring flowers would burst through the soil, thrusting shoots upwards, heralding a new beginning. But not for her. Eline sighed heavily, wondering how long she could keep up the pretence of being a good and loyal wife.

She paused and drew back the checked woollen shawl, staring down at the baby's sleeping face. He was more like Will than ever, with a slight frown on his tiny forehead as he struggled against the sudden intrusion of the light into his comfortable sleep.

Already, a lick of dark hair hung forward over his brow, giving him an earnest, scholarly appearance. A smile softened Eline's features. How she loved her son; she could, she vowed, endure anything so long as her child grew up in a secure background. And what, she reasoned, could be more secure than being heir to Calvin Temple?

Doubts assailed her on the other hand. Could *she* survive the long years ahead, years of Calvin's cloying attention, years of living a lie? For the fact that her son was not Calvin's child was becoming more and more apparent to her as every day passed.

The streets of the town were crowded, and Eline

mingled with the crowds, glad to be anonymous, un-noticed. She would call at the workshop, she decided, see how Arian was coping.

Eline allowed herself a small sense of triumph; she would help Arian Smale the way she herself had been helped by Hari Grenfell. Arian had the wits and the courage to rise high in the leather business; she learned quickly and had a forcefulness that commanded attention.

A ragged boy edged past Eline without even looking at her, a strange feeling indeed; she realized that, with the Welsh shawl wrapped around her, she looked just like any other working woman of the town.

When she reached the workshop, she pushed open the door and heard the hum of machinery from the back room with a feeling of satisfaction. The smell of leather permeated the air, and on the bench lay a half-finished remedial boot, one she herself had designed.

Price Davies came forward and smiled his charming smile, drawing a stool from under the bench for Eline to sit on.

'Where's Arian?' Eline asked, aware of the quiet that had descended on the workers. There was a feeling of tension in the air, as though something untoward had happened.

'I'm sorry, Lady Temple,' he said, with just the right touch of deference. 'No-one seems to know; she hasn't been in to work for several days.'

Eline frowned. 'Why didn't someone inform me of the situation?' she asked, and she saw Price hesitate before answering. Eline was puzzled. She'd believed Arian was going to get rid of the man, and yet here was Price Davies running the place.

'Well, no-one felt it was right to tell tales out of school, if you'll pardon me saying. We just thought she needed a few days off and we were sort of covering her tracks, so to speak.'

403

Eline considered his words in silence, biting her lip. Workers stuck together against bosses, that much was true; she hadn't forgotten that, had she?

'I suggest you send someone round to her lodgings,' Eline said more easily, 'find out if Arian is sick.'

'I'll go myself,' Price offered. 'It's not far; it will only take me a few minutes.'

'On second thoughts,' Eline said, 'I'll come with you.' She felt uneasy; it wasn't like Arian to abdicate her responsibilities, not without very good reason.

In the street, Price measured his step with hers. He was deferential and charming, and Eline wondered why she couldn't quite trust the man.

'Did Arian seem all right last time you saw her?' Eline asked, frowning, and she saw Price smile.

'She was in fine fettle,' he said. 'Talking about some young man who seemed to have taken her fancy, she was.'

Strange, Arian didn't seem the sort of girl to let her heart rule her head, Eline thought; but then, who was to tell what a woman in love might do? Look at her own tangled life.

The landlady at the boarding house sniffed as Eline enquired about Arian's health and invited her into the parlour with due deference.

'Gone, she is, without a word,' Mrs Maitland said when Eline was seated in one of the uncomfortable horse-hair chairs. 'Wouldn't have thought it, mind, of a young lady like that.'

'What wouldn't you have thought?' Eline asked, a little impatiently.

'Well, it's not my place to gossip about my ladies, but Miss Smale had a *man* in here, against all the rules. Saw her from the window, I did, leaving, leaning all over this . . . this *person*. If you ask me, both of them were worse for liquor.'

'I don't believe it!' Eline exclaimed.

Mrs Maitland sniffed again. 'I'm not in the habit of telling falsehoods, my lady, with all due respects,' she said.

'No, I'm sure,' Eline replied. 'It's just that it seems so out of character for Arian to behave in that way.'

'I know,' Mrs Maitland said, 'but then who's to tell what can happen when a man charms his way into a woman's heart?'

'Did you get a look at this man?' Eline asked, and she sensed Price moving impatiently beside her. She looked up at him, but his expression was bland.

Mrs Maitland shook her head. 'Only the back side of him; rough chap, big, with shoulders like a barn door. Looked too old for a young lady like Miss Smale, I'd have thought.'

Eline felt defeated. There was not a great deal she could do at the moment; it was clear the landlady knew very little about Arian's disappareance.

'I shall see that the room is paid for,' Eline said, 'and please keep it free for Miss Smale. I'm sure there's some perfectly good reason for all this mystery.'

Mrs Maitland's expression suggested that she knew the reason and didn't much like it; but she inclined her head in agreement. Lady Temple was a force to be reckoned with.

'What shall we do now?' Price asked when he and Eline were in the street once more.

She shrugged. 'I don't know, I'm completely at a loss.'

'Perhaps she *has* run off. What about that fellow she had who went off to London to be a doctor; might he have sent for her?'

Eline shook her head. She doubted it, but it was a possibility; Arian was young and impressionable – but *not* irresponsible, her mind insisted.

'What about the workshop?' Price asked, with seeming innocence. 'Would you like me to take charge, just until Arian comes back?'

It was the most sensible solution. Price was probably the most experienced man in her employ, Eline thought; in any case, his fellow workers seemed inclined to follow his lead.

'That's very kind of you, Price,' Eline said, feeling somehow that she had been manipulated. 'You will have a rise, of course; and, who knows, I may be in a position to make the opening a permanent one some time in the future.'

She left Price at the workshop and began the trek back home, feeling suddenly tired. She had walked much too far, and the baby was heavy now in her arms.

She made her way into Victoria Park and sat down on the bench, staring out at the pond, where the ducks dipped and glided on the still surface, searching for food. It was peaceful here, and her chaotic thoughts began to sort themselves out a little.

There must be some rational explanation for Arian's disappearance. And yet Arian did have a wild streak that might cause her to behave irrationally.

But doubts persisted. Eline couldn't believe Arian would have left the job without any notice; she was proud of her work and had always been anxious to get on in the world of shoemaking.

A shadow fell across her face and, looking up, Eline drew a sharp breath. 'Will!' She spoke the name softly, as though not quite believing he was really standing there before her.

'Eline.' His tone was polite, nothing more, and there was a pain in his eyes that he couldn't quite conceal.

'Are you all right?' he asked stiffly. 'I mean, it's strange to see you alone like this, with the baby wrapped in a Welsh shawl. Where's your fine carriage? Why are you sitting here in the park – is anything wrong?'

'I'm all right,' Eline said quickly, hugging the baby to her, afraid that Will might see her son's face.

Will sat down beside her, abruptly. After a moment,

he leant over the child in her arms, his hand gently pulling the shawl aside.

There was a long moment of silence and then Will lifted his head. His eyes met Eline's, and she knew in that instant that Will had realized the truth.

'He's mine,' he said flatly, his tone brooking no argument. 'This child is mine; do you deny it, Eline?'

She looked directly into his eyes and knew she could not lie to him – not about this. 'I don't deny it, Will. How can I, when he looks the very image of you?'

Will rubbed his hand over his face. Slowly, a smile began to light his eyes and reached his mouth. 'Let me hold him, please, Eline,' he said softly. 'It's not much to ask, is it?'

She sighed and, after a moment's hesitation, handed him the baby, their son. She drew a ragged breath at the joy in Will's face, and her smile was brilliant as she looked at the two beings she loved most in all the world.

'Why didn't you tell me?' Will asked, and then he looked away from her. 'Of course, I know why. Temple could give the boy everything, when I could offer him nothing.'

'It isn't that, Will,' Eline said. 'But Calvin was so joyous, so proud, I couldn't find the words to tell him the truth.'

'You didn't want to hurt him?' Will asked. 'And yet you would hurt me; how could you think like that?' His voice was edged with anger. 'I could have borne it if you'd wanted our son to have every advantage in life, but I don't understand how you could keep silent out of pity for Temple – or was it love, Eline? Have you fallen in love with him after all?'

She shook her head in dumb misery. 'Don't, Will. What was I to do?'

He stared down at the boy in his arms, and there was a longing in his eyes that tore at Eline's heart. 'He's a fine child.' Will's voice was tender. 'A son any man could be proud of.'

He looked up at Eline then. 'It seems I'm destined not to have any sons I can call my own, doesn't it?'

'Will, Will! Don't torture the both of us,' Eline said. 'It can do no good.'

'I know, but I ache for you,' Will said. 'You occupy my thoughts every minute of every day. I can't seem to function without you; I have no ambition any more.'

Eline began to cry. Tears rolled down her cheeks, and she tried to dash them away, impatient with any sign of weakness in herself. She needed to be strong, for her son's sake if for no-one else's.

Will put his arm around her and drew her head down on to his shoulder. 'I'll savour this moment,' he said softly, 'the moment when I held my two loved ones in my arms. It will never come again, because I'll go away, leave you in peace and leave my son to be brought up with every privilege he could wish for.'

Neither Eline nor Will saw the figure of Calvin Temple standing a short distance away, watching the small tableau, his face filled with sadness. After a moment, he turned and walked away, and there was purpose in the way he strode out of the park and climbed into his waiting carriage.

Fon's arms ached. The ropes bit cruelly into her wrists as she struggled yet again to free herself. Across the room Arian was slumped in her chair, her face red from the slap administered by Price Davies before he'd left them.

'It's no use struggling,' Arian said slowly. 'We have no strength to resist these awful men, so we will just have to outwit them.'

Fon looked at her hopefully. 'You've got a plan?' she said, her voice cracking with fatigue and fear.

'I'm going to try to lure Price into the bedroom,' Arian said, in a matter-of-fact tone, as if she was simply talking about going to the shops to buy some groceries. 'While I'm there, talk Mike into letting you go free; he's frightened by what Price intends to do, I can see it in his face.'

'But you *can't* go into the bedroom with that animal,' Fon protested. 'You know what he'll do to you.'

'I know.' Arian shrugged. 'But what's the alternative?' She pursed her lips as the silence lengthened.

'He'll rape the both of us, whatever we do,' Arian said at last, 'so in my own case I'll only be getting the ordeal over more quickly.'

She paused for a moment and chewed her lip. 'I think there's a strong possibility he might do more than harm us . . .' Her words trailed away.

'You mean he might . . . might kill us?' Fon felt a wash of fear as she looked into Arian's eyes. She felt in her bones that Arian was right; Price Davies intended at the very least to violate them both. It had been quite clear what Davies had in mind when he thrust his hand into Fon's bodice. As for letting them go after that, it was doubtful he would compromise himself by letting them complain about his brutality.

'I think you're right,' she said, remembering how cruelly Price had slapped Arian's face before tying her into a chair. 'But what makes you think Mike the Spud will listen to me?'

'There's just a chance he might help,' Arian said. 'You must convince him that Price wants us dead, and I know that's not what Mike wants. He's my uncle, remember, and for all his badness I think he'd stop short of murdering me.'

'I don't like to think of you sacrificing yourself to that terrible man,' Fon said quietly. 'Do you think that when you get him alone you could outwit him?'

'I could try,' Arian said ruefully, 'but when I tried that before, he was too quick for me.'

She smiled reassuringly. 'Don't worry, it won't be the

first time I've lain with a man; and, though I detest Price Davies, I would prefer what he would do to me to being dead.'

Fon bit her lip. It seemed a hare-brained, dangerous scheme, but, as Arian had pointed out, they had little alternative. She was quite sure Jamie would have instigated a search by now, but in all probability no-one would come looking for her in the empty farmhouse adjoining her own land.

'We *must* give it a try,' Arian urged. 'It's the only way, I promise you.' She sighed heavily. 'With two of them together, I don't think we'd stand a chance; Mike's too afraid of Price to defy him openly.'

The two women fell silent, both of them contemplating the coming ordeal. It was growing dark, and Fon, tired to the bone, felt her eyelids begin to droop.

She was awakened by the door being swung roughly open. She sat bolt upright, blinded by the light held high above the man's head. For one crazy moment, she thought Jamie had come to find her, and then Price Davies spoke.

'Well, my sweet little bitch.' He stood in front of the chair where Arian was tied, his legs astride, the lantern held high. 'I've sewn you up good and proper. I've got your job, the job I should have had from the beginning.' He sniggered. 'I spun the yarn that you've run off with a man. Your precious boss has lost faith in you, so the job is mine – mine for good.'

Arian stared up at him, her face unreadable. 'Well, perhaps you did deserve the job, no-one can question your expertise with leather,' she said in a deliberately subdued voice.

'You said it, woman,' Price answered boastfully. 'I think that our boss has recognized that at last.'

Fon, watching, saw Mike enter the farmhouse and close the door carefully behind him.

410

'Watch that light, Price,' he warned. 'We don't want anyone coming up here, do we?'

'Pull the curtains, man,' Price replied shortly. 'I'm not going to spend the night in the dark.'

He held the lantern up and looked from one woman to the other consideringly.

'Now which one of you beauties shall I take to my bed?' he said speculatively.

Fon shrank against the chair, her scalp prickling with fear. She couldn't bear it if this man so much as touched her again.

'I shan't let you take advantage of *me* again,' Arian said quickly. 'You did it once, but you won't do it again. You're not man enough for me, don't you understand that yet?'

'Who says?' Price hovered over her menacingly. 'If I want you I shall have you; I'll show you how much of a man I am.'

'No,' Arian said, 'you won't make me do what you want a second time. You don't know how to show a girl a really good time – you are inadequate, incapable of satisfying me.'

Fon saw Mike put his hand over his mouth to conceal his coarse laugh; but he shut up abruptly when Price turned venomous eyes on him.

'Untie her,' he commanded, pointing to Arian. 'I'll show this piece of baggage what respect for a man is all about. By morning I'll have her broken, or I'll know the reason why.'

As Mike bent down beside Arian's chair, he spoke to her softly. 'It's only a little bit of fun, it won't hurt you, will it, you not being chaste-like.'

'Shut up,' Price said, and seized Arian's wrists. She struggled, kicking out at him, and Fon, watching in horror, marvelled at the girl's courage and tenacity.

Price twisted both Arian's hands behind her back and held her wrists between his big fingers. With his other hand, he caught the front of her bodice and tore it downwards.

Fon looked away in fear and pity for what Arian was going to endure. She knew, with a sudden, sickening surety, that if she couldn't convince Mike the Spud that she must be released, she would be in for the same fate.

'Good night, folks.' Price smiled his charming smile and dragged Arian towards the bedroom. 'Sleep tight.' He looked back at Fon. 'Don't worry, sweetheart, you won't be neglected. You shall have your turn, all in good time.'

The bedroom door slammed. There was the sound of a vicious slap; Arian screamed, and then there was nothing but an ominous silence.

Fon closed her eyes. She wanted to scream; she was living in a nightmare and she didn't know if she would ever wake up from it. 'Arian,' she whispered, 'oh, Arian! What is going to become of us both?'

Eline left the park aware that it had grown dark. She hurried, knowing that Calvin would be worried about her; indeed, she was surprised he had not come looking for her already.

The baby was heavy in her arms, and Eline felt the dampness of tears against her cheek. Will, poor darling Will, he'd been so hurt she would probably never see him again. She had burnt her boats now, where he was concerned.

She had hated telling him she must stay with Calvin; it had hurt, the pain had gone deep, and her words of farewell had been spoken in despair.

But she owed Calvin a great deal. He was kind and considerate, he loved her and adored the child he believed was his; how could she tell him the truth now? It was too late for that, far too late.

She reached the gates of the manor with a sigh of relief. Her whole body seemed to ache and her legs were

412

trembling; she realized she was not recovered yet from the birth of her son.

The lights in the porch were ablaze, and, to her surprise, the carriage was outside the door, the driver standing at the head of the animals as though ready to make a journey. Could Calvin be going away on business?

The front door resisted her efforts to push it open, and, impatiently, Eline rang the bell.

Behind her, the coachman coughed.

'Beggin' your pardon, my lady, I've had my instructions to take you to a lodging house in the town,' he said slowly, and she heard pity in his voice.

'What do you mean?' she asked. 'Where's my husband?' She felt a sense of unease grip her. 'Lord Temple hasn't been taken sick, has he?'

The man held out a long envelope and Eline opened it quickly, holding it under the lamp hanging above the porch, straining her eyes to read the scribbled message. It was short and to the point.

It became only too clear as she read the note that Calvin had seen her with Will in the park, had heard some of her conversation, had gathered the truth about the child he had called his own son.

Calvin stated in no uncertain terms that he would have nothing more to do with her; he would divorce her, in spite of the scandal it would cause, and he never wanted to see her again.

Wearily, Eline climbed up into the coach and nodded to the driver. 'Let's be on our way,' she said softly, and the tears that came to her eyes were for the kind man she had called her husband, the man she so badly betrayed.

CHAPTER THIRTY-THREE

Arian wakened, consciousness returning slowly, and she stared in bewilderment at the bedroom that had once been hers. It was as though time had lost its meaning and she was still a child, living here under the protection of her parents.

Once, a long time ago, she had been happy here, happy to ride free across the wild grasslands, happy to share her life with her father. But that was before he began drinking heavily and slapping her every time she displeased him. At those times, Bob Smale had been a monster, a man she didn't know; and now he was dead and she was being held prisoner in what was once a safe haven.

And now it was another man who had hurt her. Price Davies had used her, for several nights had forced her to share his bed. In that moment, Arian hated Price Davies more than she had ever hated anyone.

She turned her eyes cautiously towards the pillow beside her. It was empty, and relief swamped her, so that Arian felt faint and weak. She lay for a moment gathering her strength before sitting up. Under the tangle of bedclothes, she was naked, her body marked with bruises. She shuddered.

She tensed as she heard the latch of the door being lifted and then she eased herself back against the pillows, closing her eyes in feigned sleep.

She heard a coarse laugh. 'Let her sleep it off.' It was Price's voice. 'She'll give you no trouble today, Mike, I've taken all the spirit out of the bitch.'

Anger brought tears to Arian's eyes, but she forced

herself to remain still. She heard Mike's voice, a little truculent as he rebuked Price Davies in an uncharacteristic mood of rebellion.

'I hope you are not being cruel to the girl. She's my brother's child after all, mind,' he said. Arian felt a small flame of warmth, her uncle had some humanity left then.

The hostility in Price Davies's voice brought chills to her spine. 'She had it coming; took my job from under my nose, didn't she? Well, what I've done to her is not punishment,' he said crudely, 'it's more like pleasure, I'd say.

'I'm going to work now, so watch her! Watch both of them; we can't have them slipping the net, not now. Things have gone too far for that. I can't be here all the time. I don't want to lose my job, not after all I've done to get it back.'

Arian lay still for a long time. She could imagine how Price would have blackened her name with Eline Temple. She shuddered; but he would pay for what he'd done, oh, yes, he would pay, one way or another.

She remained quiet until she heard the outer door of the farmhouse closing. Then she breathed more easily, knowing that Price had left for work.

She roused herself to climb painfully from the bed and, looking round, realized that Price had removed her clothes from the bedroom; he was taking no chances.

Arian strode into the kitchen and, ignoring Mike's gaping mouth and shocked eyes, pulled on her clothes. She flashed Fon a look begging her silently not to move or speak.

'*Duw*, girl, he's beat you bad. There's a bastard the man is,' Mike said angrily.

Arian pulled on her shoes while Mike looked at her helplessly. 'I'm going to wash,' she said coldly. 'I feel dirty after sleeping with that pig.'

She opened the door to the back yard and was outside

in the cold clearness of the day before Mike had time to gather his thoughts.

Her spine tingled as she climbed over the fence and quickly hurried across the fields, wondering if Mike would come after her. She knew every inch of the farmlands where she had lived and, provided Mike did nothing to stop her, it would be an easy task to make her way to Honey's Farm and find help before it was too late.

There had been no possibility of freeing Fon; she would have to hope the girl would be safe until she returned. Mike the Spud, rough though he might be, was not the animal that Price Davies was; but neither could he protect the woman once Price had made up his mind to do his worst.

She stared across at the open lands beyond the trees and knew that stretch could be clearly seen from the front of the house. She would just have to take her chances that Mike would be otherwise occupied and wouldn't notice she was taking a long time over her supposed wash outside at the pump.

She took a deep breath and braced herself to run across the clearing, looking ahead to where the fields sloped away from the farmhouse. Once there, she would be hidden from sight; and from there on, it was only a matter of a few miles to Honey's Farm and safety.

She was almost clear of the open stretch of land when, with a suddenness that made her cry out, cruel arms caught and held her and her hair was grasped in a painful hold.

'Thought you could put one over on me, did you?' Price rasped into her face. His eyes were blazing, and in that moment Arian knew with a sickening certainty that he was not quite sane.

'I turned back for my tools,' he said, smiling unpleasantly, 'and I watched you leave the farmhouse, bold as brass.'

416

He laughed and tugged at her hair, forcing her head backwards. 'You have to get up very early to catch me out, madam.'

He slapped her face and then dragged her back across the ground, not caring that cruel stones dug into her flesh or that her body ached from the beating he'd given her. It was almost a relief when they reached the farmhouse door and he flung it open, throwing her inside.

She fell on to the stone floor, her hair falling over her face, her breathing laboured. She heard Fon gasp with shock and looking up saw the horror in the girl's eyes.

'Tie her up,' Price growled at Mike. 'Or do I have to do everything round here?' He stood menacingly before Mike, and the man cringed.

'I didn't know she'd gone,' he lied. 'I was busy clearing the place up.'

'Shut your mouth, you stupid oaf!' Price said fiercely. 'And hurry up and get that note over to Honey's Farm. Leave it where that blasted Irishman can find it for sure this time, do you hear? If you fail, it will be the worse for you.'

He left then, slamming the door shut, his feet crunching the hard ground and fading away into silence.

'Poor girl.' Mike helped Arian to her feet. 'Not even your daddy beat you this bad; you don't deserve this.'

'Look, Mike,' Arian said, 'he means to kill us. You've got to let us go before it's too late.'

Mike was staring at her, his hands hanging to his sides, a hopeless look in his eyes. 'I can't let you go again, girl, he'd kill *me* for sure. He won't go that far with you two; he wants to get money for this one.' He gestured towards where Fon was sitting.

'And what about me?' Arian asked. 'I'm no use to him now; he's got what he wanted, my job at the workshop and my total humiliation. I'm no further use to him now, you must see that.'

'He'll just let you go' – Mike was almost pleading – 'you'll be in disgrace with your boss, and that will be that.'

Mike's eyes flickered away from Arian's direct gaze. 'You'll soon find another job, girl.'

'Don't be silly, Mike!' Arian's voice was sharper than she'd intended. 'Price can't afford to let us go. We'll talk, tell everyone what he's done. *He'll* be the one who's disgraced.'

She saw at once that she had made a mistake. A stubborn look came over Mike's face, and his eyes had a closed look that she recognized from the old days, when she used to plead with him to help her father. He hadn't wanted the responsibility of being involved then, and he certainly wasn't going to go against his own interests now.

'I'll have to tie you up again, girl. Sorry I am but there's nothing else for it.'

Mike pushed her into a chair and twisted the rope around her body. Arian, for a moment, felt like weeping, her pain and the humiliation of the last few nights had been nothing but a useless ordeal. She had not escaped as she'd hoped; she was back where she had started.

'I'm going out for a while,' Mike said. 'Don't try to get away, right?'

He left them, and the sound of his footsteps could be heard fading into the distance.

'Are you all right?' Fon's voice trembled, and Arian attempted to smile.

'Aye, I'll live,' she said ruefully. 'But I didn't do us much good by running away, did I?'

'You look awful,' Fon said, and the sympathy in her voice brought fresh tears to Arian's eyes.

'Well, thank you kindly.' She forced a dry note into her voice. 'I've known times when I've felt better, mind.'

'Oh, God,' Fon said softly, 'is he going to do that to me when he comes back tonight?'

418

It was a fair bet, Arian thought; but she forced herself to speak reassuringly.

'I shouldn't think so,' she said. 'You know he's afraid of your husband; I imagine he'll treat you with a bit more respect than he's treated me.'

'Aye, we might be safe until Jamie gets this note they were on about,' Fon agreed. 'But once they get the money, if Jamie will give them any, what then?'

Arian shrugged. She didn't have to think very hard to make a good guess, but she wasn't going to reiterate her fears and make Fon feel as hopeless as she did now.

She stared towards the light from the window. The clouds were lifting now, promising a fine, if cold, day. Arian tried to draw hope from the lightening skies, and yet she knew within her heart that there was very little real hope, either for Fon O'Conner or herself.

Jamie was cooking the breakfast for his son and the little girl, both children looking up at him with large eyes.

'Is Fonny coming home soon?' April asked timidly, for she was half-afraid of the stern-faced man Jamie had become within the last few days.

Jamie was forced to think of a reply. 'We'll see.' He knew his voice was hard, but the pain bit deep, and anger was making him feel sick and helpless.

The door opened and Tommy came into the kitchen, smelling of the fields.

'*Duw*, it's been a funny morning.' Tommy took off his boots and left them near the door, padding across the cold slate on feet encased in two pairs of thick socks.

'Funny?' Jamie didn't think anything was funny, not since Fon had disappeared; the dull sense of anger burned in him, giving him no rest. But he had waited, knowing that sooner or later a sign would come from the men who had taken his wife.

'Aye,' Tommy said, scraping his chair against the floor in an effort to draw nearer to the table. 'I saw that Arian

419

Smale, you know, the girl with the silver hair? Flitting across the fields up top there she was, like a ghost. Then I got distracted, and when I looked away there was no sign of her.'

Jamie contained his impatience, waiting for Tommy to get to the point.

'And then I found this note pinned to my coat. She must have put it there.'

'Note?' Jamie's tone was sharp. 'What does it say?' He put down the skillet with the sizzling bacon in it and gave Tommy his full attention.

'I haven't read it, boss,' Tommy said. 'You know I'm not so good at letters, but I could see it's got your name on it, so I came back to the farmhouse. I thought it might be important.'

Jamie took the note and tore it open. It contained only a few lines, blunt and to the point, asking Jamie for money in return for his wife.

'I'm to leave a hundred guineas in a bag,' he said, slumping into a chair. 'As if I could raise a hundred guineas just like that.'

'But, boss, you'll have to get it if the missis is to be allowed to come home,' Tommy said, with an unshakeable faith in Jamie's abilities.

Jamie felt a cold touch of fear. 'There's no signature on this,' he said, waving the note in the air. 'The bastard who's got Fon isn't giving much away, is he?'

'You'll pay it though, boss, somehow,' Tommy said quietly, his young face creased with worry.

'If I pay it, Fon will never be returned to me. Dead women can't talk, sure you must see that, lad?'

For a moment, Jamie felt anger and panic cloud his mind and then he forced himself to think clearly. 'Arian Smale,' he said suddenly, 'where did you see her, *exactly* where, think?'

'Not far from the old farmhouse,' Tommy said, his mind forced into sudden clarity by the urgency in Jamie's voice. 'Aye, the land that used to belong to Bob Smale, that's where it was. I didn't think anyone was still living there.'

'I see.' Jamie sat back in his chair, deep in thought. Arian Smale – what was she doing up on the land so early? The place was deserted now.

The idea exploded into his mind with a suddenness that brought excitement tingling through him. The farmhouse! *That* was where Fon was being held, he was sure of it. What better place? It was remote enough and yet right under his nose; the crafty bastard who had taken Fon was not stupid by any means.

His first instinct was to get on his horse and ride up there, a shot-gun at the ready; but in that way he would be putting Fon's life at risk. No, he must move carefully, stealthily; he must outwit this man.

'What you going to do, boss?' Tommy asked. 'You can count on me to come in it with you, whatever it is.'

'Arian Smale,' Jamie said, 'she's definitely the girl you saw up near the farmhouse – you are sure?'

'Dunno,' Tommy said. 'I thought it looked like her; but, come to think of it, when I was in town Saturday, the gossip was she'd buggered off with some fellah, not been in work for a while, and that Price Davies cockahoop because he had her job and was having it cushy-like.'

'That's very interesting,' Jamie said, his uncertainty turning into a gut feeling that Fon was being held up on the deserted farm. And this Price Davies, what was his involvement in all this? Was he in cahoots with Arian for some reason? The gossips were linking their names together, at any rate.

'Go up to the farmhouse, Tommy,' Jamie said. 'Prowl around, try to find out who's there. Be careful you don't arouse anyone's suspicions, mind. If you are spotted, say you're looking for some stray cattle or something.'

Tommy looked regretfully at the pan of bacon and then rose to his feet. 'Right, boss, I'm on my way.'

He ambled towards the door, pushed his feet into his boots with what, to Jamie, was maddening slowness and left the kitchen.

'I'm starving hungry, Daddy,' Patrick said plaintively, and Jamie forced himself to smile at his son.

'Right! Sure your breakfast is coming up in two minutes, my boy. Just hold your horses and give a man time to draw breath.'

He returned to the pan of bacon and forked the slices on to a plate, then cracked some eggs into the fat and watched the transparent whites become opaque in the heat.

Fon – his heart lurched – Fon, my colleen, when I get the bastard who did this thing I'll strangle him with my bare hands.

For a moment, in the silence of the kitchen Jamie wondered if he'd spoken the words out loud. He looked at the children, but they were sitting quietly, waiting for breakfast to be put before them.

He handed April the plates and sank down into a chair. Taking the note from his pocket, he read it again and again, as if it could tell him more than the words written on it.

'Bastard!' It was only when April giggled that he realized this time he *had* spoken his thoughts out loud. He ached for action, to get up and wreak vengeance on someone, anyone – but that was not the way to win. He must go carefully and outwit the man who thought he held all the cards in his grubby little hand.

Fon's arms were numb. She glanced across at Mike, who had returned from delivering the note to Honey's Farm and had been in a mood of taciturn silence ever since.

Fon had searched his face for any evidence that he had seen or spoken to Jamie, but she knew in her heart

422

that he had not. She almost smiled, in spite of the pain, as she imagined Jamie throwing himself bodily at Mike the Spud and demanding to know where Fon was being held. No, there was no way Mike had confronted Jamie in person; otherwise he wouldn't be standing there now in good health.

'When are you going to see sense, Uncle Mike?' Arian's voice, harsh with anger, broke the silence. 'Price is going to kill us – you too, maybe – and then there will be no witnesses.'

'Shut up, woman!' Mike said in irritation. 'You are talking a lot of nonsense.'

'Am I, Mike?' Arian said softly. 'Am I?' She relaxed a little in her chair; her barb had been shot.

Fon looked at Mike intently, and she could see he was rattled in spite of himself. He knew Price was a man not to be trusted, a man with a gleam of madness in his eye that superseded all finer instincts, and he feared him.

Perhaps that was all to the good, Fon thought hopefully; perhaps Mike would be convinced that it would be just as well to release them and to get out of the place himself while he had the chance.

Suddenly Mike gave a bellow that frightened Fon so that she jumped, almost tipping her chair. He rushed to the door, and it banged open as he darted outside.

There were sounds of a scuffle and a cry of pain, and Fon's mouth was suddenly dry.

'My God, what's happening?' she said in a whisper, her eyes wide as she looked at Arian. 'Do you think Jamie has come for me?'

Mike fell into the room, swearing and cursing, and he was holding a thin, unconscious figure in his big arms.

'It's Tommy!' Fon said. 'What have you done to him?' She heard the near-hysteria in her voice and tried to calm herself, but questions were racing through her head.

423

'Keep your mouths shut,' he warned quietly, 'for the boy's sake if not your own. Do you understand?'

Fon exchanged glances with Arian, and it was clear that they both understood perfectly. Tommy's safety depended on their silence; once he knew they were there, he would be as much a prisoner as they were.

'We'll be quiet,' Arian said and Fon bit her lip, fighting the feeling of unreality that was clouding her mind.

Mike scrambled to his feet and dragged Tommy outside once more, shutting the door firmly behind him.

'Come on, boy!' Mike's tone sounded muffled. 'Wake up! I didn't hit you that hard.'

Fon heard Tommy moan, and then there was a sound of cloth tearing; it seemed that Mike had taken the boy by his shirt collar and was shaking him.

'Now, what are you doing here?' Mike was demanding. 'Why are you spying on me? The truth now, or I'll break your neck!'

'*Duw*, I'm not spying – I was looking for some stray cattle, that's all, man.' Tommy's voice was shaking. 'Fence broke, see, and the cows got out. Boss will be on my tail if I don't get the beasts back safely; good milking cows they are.'

'The note,' Mike said, 'what did you do with the note?' His voice had an edge to it and Fon felt sorry for Tommy, who wasn't very brave at the best of times.

'What note?' Tommy sounded genuinely puzzled. 'I didn't see no note.'

'I pinned it on to your coat, boy!' It sounded as if Mike was shaking the hapless Tommy until his teeth rattled.

'I haven't seen any note,' Tommy persisted. 'Honest, Mike, I haven't seen it.'

'Hell and damnation!' Mike shouted. 'Bloody thing must have blown away.'

Tommy was silent, and then Mike spoke again. 'You get out of here and stay out, or it will be the worse for you, right?'

424

'Right.' The relief in Tommy's voice was evident.

Fon felt the urge to call to him to help them, but she knew she couldn't do that to him. She heard the sudden silence and she knew Tommy had gone.

She looked at Arian. 'Did you hear that?' she asked. When Arian shook her head, she took a deep breath. 'Tommy didn't find any note.' She felt despair creep over her, paralysing her. 'Jamie doesn't know we're here – nobody will come to help us!'

Her voice broke. 'I'm afraid of Price,' she said softly. 'I'm not afraid of death so much as of what he'll do to me before . . .' Her words trailed away, and she bit her lip.

'We'll just have to think of a way of escaping by ourselves,' she said, suddenly angry. 'Look, your chair isn't far from mine; perhaps we can edge together and untie each other's ropes.'

'It won't work,' Arian said softly. 'The ropes are too tight.'

'Let's try it,' Fon said, hope springing within her. 'It's a chance; at least it's better than doing nothing.'

Before she had finished speaking, the door was flung open, and, with a feeling of alarm, Fon heard Price's voice, shouting so loudly that it was obvious he was in a raging temper.

'Blast the woman!' he yelled. 'Got kicked out by her husband for cuckolding him!'

Price strode into the room, his face red with anger, and Mike followed him. 'Eline bloody Temple!' He kicked at the leg of the table. 'She's only gone and had a bastard child by another man! Who'd have believed it? And her acting the Miss High and Mighty with me.

'Well, she's no different to any other woman, and now she's out of her husband's bed, she's finished. He's divorcing her, and what's more he's closed down the workshop, sent everyone packing, me included.' Price

425

Davies thumped a great fist on the table, taking out his rage on the scrubbed boards.

After a few moments, he spoke again. 'What's been happening here? I know something has gone on, so don't lie.'

He spun round to look at Arian. 'This one hasn't been giving any more trouble, has she?' His hand snaked out and caught Arian around the throat.

'No, it's not her, it's that kid from Honey's Farm, been up here looking for cattle, so he said.'

Mike was all set to continue with his garbled explanation, but Price bellowed out again, his voice almost hysterical. 'Christ almighty, is nothing going right?'

He flung Mike up against the wall. 'You can't be trusted with anything, you stupid bastard.' He shook Mike roughly, and the big man stared at him, almost without comprehension.

'Come on, man,' Mike said pleadingly. 'Calm down! We got things to do, mind. We got to figure out how we can get out of all this mess.'

Price turned away. His voice when he spoke was thick with rage. 'Aye, mess that you got us into, you fool! I'm going for a pint of ale. I can think better then.'

He slammed the door shut, and Fon breathed a sigh of relief. Price had been too distracted to pay any attention to her. She had been given a reprieve, for now; but the day of reckoning would come, and then what would she do?

426

CHAPTER THIRTY-FOUR

'Everything's gone wrong, man.' Mike was standing near the doorway, staring out in the silent fields. 'Why don't we get out of here, while the going is good?'

Price Davies swung round. He was smelling of ale, and his face was contorted with rage.

Mike visibly paled. 'I only meant that . . .'

Price grabbed him by his collar. 'You only meant what?' His voice was dangerously quiet. 'You were a fool not to keep that boy up here. You're *sure* he didn't see anything or suspect the women were here?'

'I can't be sure of that,' Mike said, 'but I think the sooner we're out of all this, the better. For all we know, the constables might be on to us by now.'

'Or worse,' Fon said. 'Jamie O'Conner might be riding up here right now with a gun in his hand.'

Mike glared at her. 'I'm all for taking the women as far up as we can into the barrenness of the Bwlch Mountain and turning them free,' he said flatly. 'They're more trouble than they're worth, if you ask me.'

'I didn't ask you,' Price said, glancing at Fon. 'And you, shut your mouth! If the note had got to him, O'Conner would have been here straightaway. He wouldn't have waited this long.'

He was right, Fon realized with a sinking of her heart; Jamie would have ridden up to the farmhouse in a fierce rage, he would have confronted both Price and Mike the Spud without any thought for his own safety.

'I must think,' Price said, rubbing his hand over his eyes. 'I can't just let these women go now; it's one of the daftest ideas you've had.' He spoke uncertainly for the first time, and Arian, with a courage Fon admired, spoke up.

'It would be best to set us free right now,' she said. 'So far you have only held us here against our will; you have not harmed Fon O'Conner, and, as for me, well, I will get over it, I suppose. Isn't it better to get away now, while you don't have our blood on your hands?'

'Shut up!' Price moved abruptly, waving his hands in anger. 'For Christ's sake, get me something strong to drink,' he snarled at Mike. Fon heard the chink of a bottle against a glass; both men had their backs towards her.

Arian shook her head in warning as Fon made to speak. It was best to remain silent for now; all the talking had been done.

'Come on, man!' Mike was pleading with Price. 'As the girl said, no real harm has been done; we could put it all down to a bit of fun, like; no-one could take that seriously, could they?'

'Do you think O'Conner is going to take it as a bit of fun? Shut up, man, and let me think this thing out. Perhaps I can still salvage something from the mess *you* have made of it all.'

Fon felt a sickening lurch of her stomach. What did Price Davies have in mind for them now? She bit her lip and turned towards Arian with questions trembling on her lips.

Pity filled her as she saw the blackened bruises around Arian's eyes. Arian's cheek too was bruised and swollen, and her mouth was cut. She had been ill-treated enough by that oaf Price Davies, and yet Arian had not lost her spirit.

Fon realized she could not – would not – have endured the vile attentions of Price Davies, the beating, the humiliation. She knew with certainty that she would have killed herself first.

'Perhaps we can take them away from here,' Price

428

said, glancing to where the two women were crouched in the corner.

'Now you're talking, man,' Mike said eagerly. He glanced at Arian with a gleam of triumph in his eyes that quickly disappeared as Price spoke again.

'Aye, dump them somewhere so that their bodies would never be found. *That's* what I mean. No-one could prove anything, could they?'

Price's voice was becoming slurred, and Fon realized he was drinking heavily. Arian was aware of it too; her mouth was pressed into a hard line, but whether it was from anger or fear Fon didn't know.

'Na,' Mike said, obviously trying to reason with Price, 'don't take the risk, man. We'd be burdened with them; they'd give us all sorts of trouble on the way. We'd be better off getting on out of here without them hanging round us.'

'They couldn't give us much trouble if we killed them here, could they?' Price said slowly.

He turned towards Fon, his hand on his belt, and she shuddered. 'But first I mean to have my way with Miss High and Mighty, here.' He smiled unpleasantly. 'I always keep my promises.'

Fon shrank back against the wall as far as she could go, trying to make herself invisible. But it was no use. Price was coming closer, and there was a manic gleam in his eye that brought terror into Fon's heart.

Jamie had checked his rifle and then fingered the ammunition in his pocket. His anger, held in check for so long, burned within him, steady and fierce as a forest fire in summer-time.

'Can't I come with you, boss?' Tommy asked, his thin frame tense, his shoulders hunched.

Jamie glanced at him and then shook his head. 'You take care of the children,' he said firmly. 'Make sure

429

nothing happens to them; it's very important that you be here.'

Jamie forced a smile. 'I know you've got guts, lad; you don't have to prove it to me. But this job is a one-hander; we don't want to alert the bastards that we're coming.'

Tommy nodded, resigned to the sense of Jamie's argument. 'The only thing, boss,' he said, 'there's two of 'em up there with the women. Price is the worst of the two, but Mike the Spud is no weakling either.'

'I know,' Jamie agreed, 'but as they don't know I'm coming for them, I'll have the element of surprise on my side.'

'That's true,' Tommy said thoughtfully. 'I'm pretty sure Mike believed me that I'd not seen the note, otherwise he wouldn't have let me go so easily.' He rubbed his neck where Mike's thick fingers had gripped him. 'I hope he hasn't hurt the missis.'

Jamie's grip on the gun tightened. 'He'd better not have.' He moved towards the door. 'But it's the other one who's the danger,' he said. 'I think the man's insane.'

Tommy followed Jamie and stood in the doorway looking out at the darkening landscape. This had been one of the longest days of Jamie's life. He breathed deeply; knowing his wife was up there, within the old walls of the deserted farmhouse, in the hands of a maniac like Price had made him cold with fear. And yet there was nothing to be gained by rushing in half-prepared and giving the two villains a chance to over-power him.

One consolation was that Arian Smale was probably up there too, for Tommy had seen her near the farm-house. Arian was Mike the Spud's niece, and it wasn't clear what her part in all this was; but it was almost a certainty that, if she could, she would bring a calming influence to bear on her Uncle Mike.

Jamie gritted his teeth. If Price had so much as laid a

430

finger on Fon, he would suffer the torture of the damned before Jamie strangled him with his bare hands.

'Cool head, now,' Jamie warned himself out loud. 'Got to keep a clear mind.' He turned to Tommy. 'If I'm not back in an hour, send the constables in, right?'

'Right, boss.' Tommy nodded emphatically. 'I'll take care of everything this end, don't worry.'

Jamie mounted his horse and rode uphill away from Honey's Farm. He would have to keep to the perimeter of the land if he was not to be spotted by Price or Mike the Spud.

The clouds were closing in overhead and the moon was obscured much of the time, which was all the better, Jamie thought in satisfaction; the growing darkness would contribute to his element of surprise.

As he drew nearer to the run-down farmhouse, Jamie dismounted from his horse, speaking softly to quieten the animal. Then, gun in hand, he moved soundlessly over the grass, aware of the faint gleam of lamplight through an opening in the curtains.

He'd get the bastards; he'd shoot them both dead if necessary. Jamie gritted his teeth and crouched lower, his every sense alert as he listened to sounds within the house.

Until now, he had not realized how much he loved Fon; she was his life-blood, part of him, as though her blood ran in his own veins. That was something he must tell her, as soon as he could. He would hold her in his arms and never, ever, would he let her out of his sight again.

'I'm not staying to help you any longer.' Mike the Spud's voice was edged with desperation, and Price stopped in his tracks, his hand gripping Fon's shoulder tightened.

'What did you say?' Price ground out the words, and Fon flinched as his fingers bit into her flesh. She glanced up at him; his red, angry face and burning eyes seemed to hover above her like a vision in a nightmare.

'It's madness to stay here, man,' Mike said. 'I don't want to go to jail. Come on, see sense, Price! Let's get out while the going's good.'

Price strode across the room and slapped Mike several times across his face. 'Shut up!' Price sounded beside himself. 'Stop snivelling like a child! Where are your guts, man?'

'I'm not lacking guts.' Mike sounded angry too now, his pride doubtless hurt by the blow Price had given him. 'But I'm not crazy either. This thing has gone wrong; let's face it and get out.'

'Are you calling me crazy?' Price demanded, his voice low now. 'Don't ever call me that, you scum.'

'I've had enough,' Mike said. 'I'm going to get out of here, and you can't stop me.'

Mike moved suddenly, bending down towards his boot, and then there was a knife gleaming in his hand.

Fon screamed out a warning as Price flung himself on Mike.

'I'll kill you before I'll let you walk out on me!' he shouted. 'A knife doesn't make you any more of a man; I'll best you yet, you bastard.'

The two men rolled across the floor, Mike's foot connecting with Price's head. For a moment, the man lay still, and Mike, breathing heavily, got to his knees.

Fon held her breath. Was the fight over? Would Price crumple under the force of Mike's superior strength? Fon knew that for Mike to win the fight was her only chance. Mike rolled across the floor, blood running from a wound in his chest. Price was on his feet in an instant, the knife in his hand.

Fon stared in horror; Mike lay as if mortally wounded, his eyes wild with pain and fear, his big hands clenched.

Price turned on her then, the knife poised, and Fon tasted the bitterness of fear like bile in her mouth.

He fell upon her, gasping loudly, pulling at the ropes that bound her, and, once she was free, he pushed her to the floor, dragging at her clothes with his bloody hands. Fon screamed.

The door shot open with a resounding crash, and Fon, using all her strength, pushed Price away from her.

He staggered, looking wildly towards the door, and Fon drew in a sharp breath as gladness filled her. 'Jamie!' she cried.

He was in the kitchen then. He seemed to fill the room with his anger; he radiated strength, and his eyes burned in his face as he looked towards where Price was now standing.

In his hand was a gun; but, even as he raised it, Price lunged forward and grasped the barrel.

'Jamie! Look out!' Fon called.

But Jamie didn't hear her; he was locked in a silent struggle with Price.

A table crashed over and the oil lamp fell to the floor. Immediately a trail of spilt oil caught fire, and the flames seemed to engulf the small kitchen.

Fon screamed and then crawled towards Arian, tugging with frantic fingers at the ropes that bound her. Arian was on her feet at once, grasping Fon's arm. 'Let's get out of here!' Arian said urgently.

Jamie half turned, and it was then that Price caught him a blow to the side of the head that sent him reeling.

The flames caught the curtains and they blazed bright against the dark windows, turning acrid and black in seconds. The heat was becoming unbearable.

Fon, in the doorway now, resisted Arian's urgent hands, heard the sound of an explosion, and saw the shattered fragments of an oil can fly across the room like fiery missiles. In a panic she spun round, her eyes searching through the smoke and flames for sight of her husband.

She put her hand over her mouth, tears streaming

433

from her eyes. She tried to peer through the debris, her ears straining for sounds of life, but there was only the roaring of the flames as they took a greater hold on the building.

'Jamie!' Fon called in anguish, knowing that if he was dead, she wouldn't want to live. The flames could consume her too, extinguish her life, and it would be a blessing.

Through the smoke, a figure suddenly appeared, the broad shoulders and the strong neck so sweetly familiar to her that Fon gasped in relief. Then Jamie was at her side, drawing her away from the heat of the blaze, his face blackened with smoke.

He swung her into his arms and they clung together, both of them gasping for fresh, cleansing air.

'Are you all right?' Jamie demanded, and then, as Fon nodded, he moved away from her towards the farmhouse, intending to re-enter the inferno. Just then a ball of flame exploded upwards, and the roof of the farmhouse, with a sound like a scream, caved inward.

Fon held on to Jamie with both hands. 'It's too late to save anyone,' she gasped, 'much too late.'

She swayed against him, and Jamie clasped her in his arms, his breathing ragged. 'You are safe now, my colleen, safe. Don't cry.' He tipped her face up to his. 'Did that bastard . . . ?'

His words died away into a choked silence, and Fon shook her head. 'He didn't touch me,' she said, and for the first time in hours she smiled. 'I think he was too afraid of you for that.'

As Jamie led her away from the blazing farmhouse, Fon paused, looking up at him. 'Arian . . . where is she?'

'Here I am!' Arian appeared, leading Jamie's horse. 'I thought I'd go into town, report the . . . the accident; someone has to.' She smiled. 'And I think you two are well able to take care of each other.'

She mounted swiftly and then was riding away, a slim figure in the moonlight.

'She'll be all right, she's a girl with the courage of a man! Arian Smale is going to do just fine in life,' Jamie said softly.

He put his arm around Fon's shoulder and began to lead her down the hill; then he paused for a moment and looked back at the farmhouse. Flames were shooting up into the darkness of the night sky, illuminating the unkempt land.

He stared down at Fon then, and she saw the glint of tears in his eyes. 'I don't know what I would do if I lost you.'

'You won't lose me,' Fon said. 'I live and breathe for you, Jamie, you know that.'

'I don't think I've ever told you, not properly,' Jamie said softly, 'I love you, colleen.'

'I know,' Fon said. 'There's a lot I haven't told you, too; but I will when the time is right.'

Fon's mouth curved into a smile. She put her hand contentedly on her still flat stomach and sighed softly; after the ordeal she'd been through in the last hours, childbirth would hold no fears for her. Contentedly, Fon nestled closer to Jamie as they walked across the fields towards their home.

Suddenly the moon slid from between the clouds, silvering the rooftops of the house. From one of the windows, a light gleamed, and Fon glanced up at her husband, so tall and strong at her side. Excitement filled her; soon there would be a new life, her baby and Jamie's, to join the little family who lived and worked on the sweet lands of Honey's Farm.

CHAPTER THIRTY-FIVE

The boarding house was spartan, to say the least, set on the outskirts of the town in a run-down area near the docklands. The rooms Eline occupied were small, sparsely furnished but clean, and she stared around her, her baby clutched in her arms, her small bag of possessions still not unpacked on the shelf.

She suppressed the flood of threatened tears, saddened in the knowledge that Calvin Temple had made up his mind to humiliate her as much as he could before the final humiliation of the divorce.

Not that she didn't deserve it; she had betrayed him, betrayed her marriage vows, and she could not blame her husband for being bitter.

Eline looked into the sleeping face of her child, Will's child, and love flowed through her; was she such a bad woman, really? All she had done in truth was to go to the bed of the man she really loved, had loved for so long that he seemed a part of her.

'Will . . .' she sighed softly. 'Oh, Will, why did I have to go and make so many mistakes?'

She was tired; the lonely hours had dragged. She put the baby carefully on the bed and lay down beside him. 'You have no father, now, *boy bach*,' she said softly. 'But I will make up for it. You are mine, my son, and we will survive, I promise you that.'

She looked around at the small room; this wasn't ever going to be her permanent home, both she and Calvin knew that. She had her own source of income and she could take on extra work; she and her baby would not live in poverty.

The tiny hand of her baby curled around her finger, and blue eyes looked up into hers. Eline sighed wearily, overcome with the riot of emotions that had almost made her lose all hope for the future. She closed her eyes, and soon she slept.

When she woke, the light had faded, but Eline's mind was suddenly clear. She rose from the bed and, pouring water from the jug on the table into the rose-painted bowl, splashed her face and hands. Refreshed, she sat in a shabby armchair near the window and looked out at the dingy streets outside.

Across the road was a public house, illuminated by a gas lamp, the name fading into the stone work, the windows badly needing attention. Alongside the public house was a grocer's shop, and behind the closed doorway stood sacks of corn and meal.

Why had she consented to come here? Eline thought angrily. She still had the gallery; she still had her skill as a designer. And, squaring her shoulders angrily, she told herself that she still had her self-respect. A sense of renewed hope surged through her. She must not lose her spirit; she must fight to give her son a good start in life, for there would be enough problems to face him when he grew to manhood.

There was a knock on the door, and the land-lady entered the room, a tray on her arm. 'I thought you might need a nice drop of hot tea and some scones.' She smiled amiably and Eline took the tray gratefully.

In one thing, at least, Calvin had slipped up; he had chosen as Eline's landlady not a dragon but a kindly, honest soul.

'Thank you, Mrs Jessop,' Eline said humbly. 'A cup of tea would be very nice.'

She noticed there were two cups on the tray, and the landlady nodded her head. 'Aye, I thought I'd join you, thought perhaps a bit of company would do you good.

You've been on your own too much, if you don't mind me saying so.'

'Please sit down. I'll pour, shall I?' Eline breathed in the fragrance of the tea as it poured into the spotlessly clean china cups. Mrs Jessop was a good, if thrifty, landlady and had a motherly air that made Eline warm to her.

'It's not my business,' Mrs Jessop said slowly, 'but you should think things out clearly now, Mrs . . . er . . . Lady . . . er . . .'

'Call me Eline.' Eline sipped her tea, feeling there was some sort of lecture coming but not knowing how to stop Mrs Jessop in her tracks; she obviously was well-intentioned.

'It's like this,' Mrs Jessop continued. 'Although your husband is about to divorce you and disown the child, you still have rights.

'The boy' – she nodded to the baby on the bed – 'was born in wedlock, that makes him Lord Calvin's responsibility, his heir, and . . . er . . . adultery, if you'll forgive me, is very difficult to prove.'

'You seem to know a great deal about it.' Eline was genuinely impressed. 'I believe you are very probably right; but I want nothing of Lord Temple's. I have my own business; I shall make my own way, without him.'

'I was in the same situation myself once, and it didn't turn out too badly.' Mrs Jessop smiled and gestured around her. 'I got the house out of it, even though my husband wasn't rich like Lord Temple, mind, and I want you to think very carefully before you give up anything you are entitled to.'

She rose and took up the tray. 'Supper will be ready soon, and if you want it in your room, just give me the word.'

Eline shook her head. 'No, I'll join the rest of the boarders; it will do me good to have company.'

At the door, Mrs Jessop paused. 'If ever you want me

438

to keep an eye on the baby, I'd be glad to' – she paused – 'at very reasonable terms.'

Eline smiled to herself as the door closed behind Mrs Jessop. She was kind but brisk, a good businesswoman, clearly; and she could be trusted, Eline felt that instinctively.

She was surprised by the way she settled into the routine of the boarding house and amazed at the ease with which she fitted in to the rules and regulations Mrs Jessop imposed. For the time being, she decided, she would remain where she was; it might be just as well to take Mrs Jessop up on her offer to look after the baby.

The baby – she would *have* to rename him now, Eline thought wistfully; she could hardly keep the names her husband had given the child. 'William.' She said the name softly, and it was tempting; but she hadn't the face to be so blatant about her son's paternity. Perhaps she should name him for herself; Emlyn was near enough to Emmeline.

'Emlyn,' she said softly. 'Yes, Emlyn would suit you very well, my son.'

Eline could not help but notice that she never received any money directly from Calvin; her board and lodging were paid for, it seemed, directly to Mrs Jessop. It didn't matter; soon she would tell Calvin not to bother at all. She would make her own way in life, pay her own bills. She didn't want to be beholden to anyone, not now, not ever.

What *did* irk Eline was that her life seemed to have lapsed into a rut of idleness, and afresh there rose the urge to go out into the world and to conquer it. As the days passed, the feeling became so strong, so irresistible, that Eline realized her days of sitting in her room, playing with her baby, were over; she must get back to work.

Mrs Jessop quickly came to an arrangement for the care of the baby, her practical nature making negotiations for her payment no embarrassment at all.

439

'I'll have him downstairs with me,' she said, and her words made sense. 'He can lie in the drawer of the dresser for now, but you should get him a carriage.' She smiled. 'Just send the bill to your husband; he won't object to such a modest request, I'm sure. You must be the most undemanding wife I've ever come across.'

'I told you,' Eline said, smiling to soften her words, 'I want nothing from Calvin, and once I get back into harness, I won't even need him to pay the rent for me.'

'Well, he should do that much, at least,' Mrs Jessop said dryly. 'He did have the joy of you as his wife and hostess, and anything else he chose to enjoy with you. Let him pay for it, I say.'

Eline didn't reply, but determination was growing within her to be free of Calvin, really free of him and of her role as his pampered wife. She was used to working; her life had never been easy, not until the last few years. She could and would work again, make a future for herself, find fulfilment not only as a mother but as a businesswoman.

It was a few days later when she made her way towards the terminus of the Mumbles train, her bag clutched in her hand, her nerves ragged. As she waited in the cold street, she felt apprehensive at the prospect of coming face to face with Calvin again at the gallery. She had not seen him since the day she had left his home, with the baby in the shawl – the fateful day when Calvin had found out the truth, the day she had seen Will and he had realized her child was his own flesh and blood.

Her thoughts veered away from Will. She could not, would not, drag him into the tangle that was now her life; he had enough problems without taking on hers.

She climbed aboard the train with a feeling of great thankfulness for the warmth of the crowded compartment. Her hands were chilled; she had found no gloves in the possessions Calvin had hurriedly flung together into a bag when he'd decided to throw her out of their home. Neither had he thought to pack any warm boots.

Eline smiled. At least that was something she could easily remedy; there would be leather aplenty in the workshop. She was determined to go there later, see how work was progressing, and ask one of the cobblers to make her some boots as quickly as possible.

She felt drowsy in the warmth of the train and, looking out, she saw that the sea was shrouded in mist. It was a cold, clammy day, and for an instant she thought with longing of the great drawing-room at Stormhill Manor and the huge fires that would be burning in the fireplaces.

Oystermouth came into view, and Eline looked out at the sands, where the women would be working on the perches, hands raw and stinging from the salt of the seawater and the cold bite of the wind.

She had worked on the perches only briefly, for she had been a failure at it, her hands, so deft at designing, lacking the skill for handling the oysters.

When the train stopped, Eline alighted almost reluctantly. Her footsteps dragging, she made her way along the road that edged the sea and led to the gallery.

The window, to her surprise, was empty of paintings. The door when she tried it was locked. With a sinking feeling, Eline realized that Calvin had closed the business down.

Anger swept through her then. How dare he do this without consulting her? He was only a partner in the gallery; that was all he had ever been. The business was hers, really, not his. She had founded it, built it up to what it had become; he had only taken over the running of it.

'Morning, Eline, you all right?' The voice of Nina Parks was like a hand reaching out from the past, Nina who had taken Eline's first husband from her and who had always been such a disruptive influence on her life. An enemy.

441

'Morning, Nina.' Eline felt as though she had been caught staring into the window of a pie shop with no money to buy the food.

'Closed then – the gallery, I mean,' Nina said. 'You come all the way down here to see it, then, have you?'

'No!' Eline could not help the note of sharpness that crept into her voice. 'I came down here for a breath of Oystermouth air.'

'Oh, Miss Sarcastic now, then, is it?' Nina crossed her arms. 'Pity you don't seem able to hold on to your husbands, isn't it, love?'

Eline turned and retraced her footsteps towards the train stop. If she remained with Nina Parks a moment longer, she would not be responsible for her actions.

On the return ride to Swansea, Eline's anger was mounting. Calvin had been high-handed; surely he should have consulted her before he closed the gallery? He had put little or no money into it; it was *her* enterprise, and it had not been for him to end it so precipitously.

A greater shock awaited her when she stood outside the premises she'd rented for a workshop. It, too, was boarded up, with no sign of occupation at all. Eline moved around to the rear of the building and, peering through the windows, saw that the rooms were bare of machinery and empty of workers.

She leant for a moment against the wall, feeling dizzy with bewilderment; what was Calvin up to, she wondered. Was all this closing down of her premises an extra punishment for her unfaithfulness?

Anger flowed through her then, like hot wine. She began to walk briskly in the direction of Stormhill Manor. She would confront Calvin; if he was not in the gallery then he must be at home. She would demand an explanation, ask him why he wanted to deprive her of her means of making a livelihood for herself and her child.

Eline clenched her hands into fists so tightly that her nails bit into the soft flesh of her palms. How could he do this to her? To take away the means for her to work was the cruellest blow he could have inflicted.

At first the servant she saw refused her admission to Stormhill Manor. It was only after creating a scene on the doorstep that Eline was allowed into the hallway. There she was kept waiting. It was a good twenty minutes later that Calvin deigned to appear.

He looked as immaculately dressed as always, his clothes neat and crisp, his boots gleaming.

'You have forced yourself into my house, why?' were his first words, spoken coldly.

'It's I who should be asking "why?",' she said icily. 'The gallery and the workshop, both have been closed; what was the reason for it, and by whose authority did you take such action?'

'My own, of course.' He sounded surprised. 'Why shouldn't I close the premises? I have no use for them.'

'But the gallery was *mine*,' Eline said forcefully. 'I bought the building; or have you forgotten that?'

'I have forgotten nothing,' he said. 'I sold the gallery because you needed the money.'

Eline was taken by surprise. 'I didn't want the gallery sold,' she said.

Her thoughts whirling, she looked up at him; this man, her husband, seemed like a stranger.

'I presume the proceeds will be at my disposal?' Eline asked, holding her breath, not knowing what to expect of the man who had shared her bed but suddenly become an enemy.

'In a manner of speaking, they have been at your disposal since you moved into rooms,' he said.

'What do you mean?' Eline asked. 'Have you put some money in an account for me?'

'I have not,' Calvin said flatly. 'But what, my dear woman, do you think you and your bastard child have been living on?'

'You mean the money, the proceeds from the gallery, is keeping me and the baby?' She was incredulous.

'Yes,' Calvin said. 'The bills have come in, and I have paid them out of what you call *your* capital.' He smiled thinly. 'Though, I warn you, the capital is rapidly diminishing; you will soon be penniless.'

Eline was struck into silence for a long time. His words rang round her mind as she wondered if what he had done was proper, morally or legally.

'But the pictures, the building – there must be quite a lot of money put by somewhere, surely?'

'Not really,' Calvin said. 'The paintings sold at very low prices, and so did the gallery itself.' He paused and smiled without humour. 'The building where you conducted your shoemaking business – at a loss, I might add – didn't seem a desirable property in anyone's book; it is virtually uninhabitable as it stands.'

Eline thought rapidly. She could live at the workshop premises with the baby, start up her shoemaking and designing there; everything was going to be all right after all.

'And so, to be kind to you, I bought the building myself.' Calvin dropped his bombshell.

Eline's heart sank. 'And I suppose you bought it at a knock-down price?' she said wearily.

'All the documents are with my solicitor,' Calvin said. 'If you wish to scrutinize them, then you may do so, of course; but you will find nothing untoward.'

'And so your revenge is complete,' Eline said. 'You are leaving me with nothing.'

'Let the father of your bastard take care of you,' Calvin said coldly. 'I have acted perfectly properly; I sold your assets to keep you and your child, and the proceeds, such as they were, are rapidly diminishing, just as I said.'

444

He looked directly at her. 'I will, of course, bear the cost of the divorce myself.'

Without another word, Eline walked out into the coldness of the driveway, uncaring of the curious looks of the servants. Before she had gone more than a few paces, the big door was closed, and the click of finality echoed in Eline's ears like a death knell.

It was only when she was returning to the boarding house that Eline realized just how bad her finances were. Soon enough the money to keep her and her son would all be used up; and then, kindly as she was, Mrs Jessop would be forced to ask her to leave.

But it must not come to that. Eline must find a job, anything to keep a roof over her head. It was no good turning to Emily Miller or even to Hari Grenfell; Calvin was one of them, one of the privileged set of Swansea. They met socially, at dinners and grand balls – a world where Eline had been admitted for a short time but was now firmly excluded.

When Mrs Jessop heard what had happened, she pursed her lips and frowned. 'I don't know how he could think up such a scheme,' she said, almost admiringly, 'but you have to admit, that husband of yours has got brains in his head, all right.'

'I'll have to find work,' Eline said. 'Perhaps I can get a position in some shoe emporium; I'll do anything to keep a roof over my son's head.' She felt near to tears.

'Look,' Mrs Jessop said, 'I know that someone is wanted in the public over the road. It's only a bit of cleaning, like – mopping up the floors, putting fresh sawdust down to hide the beer stains on the flags. It's hard work, but honest, and old Abe won't be funny with you, I can assure you of that.'

Eline was silent, thinking how Calvin would laugh at her when he knew she was a skivvy in some dingy inn.

'He'll want to know straightaway, mind,' Mrs Jessop said, 'and there's no point to waiting, is there?'

445

'I'll take it,' Eline said, 'and I'll pay you to look after Emlyn for me. Is that all right?'

'That's just fine,' Mrs Jessop said, 'and I know Abe will be willing for you to pop over from time to time to feed the boy. You'll be all right; don't you worry now.'

She shook her head. '*Duw*, it don't do to upset the gentry, mind.' She put a kindly hand on Eline's shoulder. 'It's a come-down for you, dear, but at least cleaning is honest and chaste, and you won't have men pawing you, not like the serving girls do.'

It seemed that, within the space of a few days, her whole life had been turned upside down. Eline could have easily given in to tears; but tears were weak and useless and solved nothing. But still it was with a feeling of trepidation that she crossed the road to the public, dressed ready for the job in a dark sensible skirt and a blouse with sleeves she could roll above her elbows.

'Good girl!' Abe was a wizened man with a sprinkling of grey curls covering his otherwise bald pate. He had few teeth, and his cheeks were sunken, but his eyes were lively and full of humour, and Eline liked him on sight.

'Now,' Abe said. 'Tuck your skirt up, girl, otherwise it will get wet and bedraggled – up into your bloomers, girl, have you no idea?'

He cackled. 'Don't worry about your legs. It's only me seeing them, and I'm well past any mischief these days.'

He went to the door and paused. 'For today only, I've lit the stove and boiled up water, but from now on that's all part of your duties. I'll treat you fair and honest, but I need a worker, not a shirker. If you agree with that, we'll get on just fine.'

Eline felt she had never seen such a messy floor in all her life; beer and tobacco stained the flags and, although she had brushed it furiously, a fine coating of sawdust lay in the cracks of the boards.

She sighed. This was what she must get used to now;

this was her life, and the sooner she came to terms with it, the better it would be for her and for her son.

Will handed the shoes to Mrs Jessop, and she examined them intently. 'Very good,' she said at last. 'I'll go and get you some money.'

Will was relieved by her praise; it was the first time she had come to him for cobbling, and he had known at once she would be a difficult customer to impress. But she would also be a loyal one.

Will's attention was drawn by a small cry from the other side of the room. Edging forward, he saw there was a baby in the open drawer of the dresser.

He knelt down, and, with an in-drawn, ragged breath, he realized he was looking into the face of his own son.

Mrs Jessop returned and smiled as she leant over Will's shoulder. 'Bonny, isn't he? Got no name, mind, bless him.'

Will straightened. 'Why is he here?' he asked.

Mrs Jessop smiled in assumed innocence. 'His mammy brought him – Eline Temple . . . I think you might know her.' There was a cunning smile in Mrs Jessop's eyes. 'She's boarding with me since her husband threw her out.'

'You know, don't you?' Will said. 'You know this boy is my son.'

Mrs Jessop had a coy look that sat strangely on her wrinkled face. 'I don't know what you're talking about,' she said, smiling. 'I just asked you to do some work for me, and you have. You can take things from there, if you like.'

'Where is she?' Will asked, looking round as if he expected Eline to appear from thin air.

'Eline, you mean?' Mrs Jessop said. 'She's working over the road, at the inn. Honest toil, it is, mind – scrubbing floors for old Abe, and her glad enough of the job.' She paused. 'I shouldn't be gossiping, but I'm sorry for the girl. Her husband sewed her up tight, took everything she owned; all legal, mind, and now the poor girl got to get down on her hands and knees and scrub floors.'

Will clasped Mrs Jessop in his arms and kissed her cheek. 'You're an angel,' he said, 'a bloody angel.'

'Go on with you, and there's no need to swear, mind.' Her words were reproving, but she was smiling.

Will left the house and stared for a moment across the road. He took a deep breath and began to walk towards the inn.

Eline's knees ached intolerably, and so did her arms. More, her blouse was slowly growing damp; the exertions had brought her milk in, and her heavy breasts told her it was time her son was fed.

A shadow fell across her, and Eline looked up at a tall sharp silhouette, dark against the light from the door. Hands helped her to her feet, and then she was looking into Will's face.

'Come on, my lovely,' he said. 'I'm taking you home.'

She leant wearily against him, her eyes closed. 'But, Will, I have nothing, I'm penniless,' she said softly.

'I haven't got much either,' he replied. 'But at least we'll be poor together – you, me and our son.'

As he led her outside, Eline felt relief flood her. Will was there; he would take care of her, they would be together for always. And suddenly it seemed that, on the cold winter day, the sun was shining.